Peter Watt has spent time as a soldier, articled clerk, prawn trawler deckhand, builder's labourer, pipe layer, real estate salesman, private investigator, police sergeant, surveyor's chainman and advisor to the Royal Papua New Guinea Constabulary. He speaks, reads and writes Vietnamese and Pidgin. He now lives at Maclean on the Clarence River in northern New South Wales. He has volunteered with the Volunteer Rescue Association, Queensland Ambulance Service and currently with the Rural Fire Service. Fishing and the vast open spaces of outback Queensland are his main interests in life.

Peter Watt can be contacted at www.peterwatt.com.

Author Photo: Shawn Peene

Also by Peter Watt

The Duffy/Macintosh Series
Cry of the Curlew
Shadow of the Osprey
Flight of the Eagle
To Chase the Storm
To Touch the Clouds
To Ride the Wind
Beyond the Horizon
War Clouds Gather
And Fire Falls
Beneath a Rising Sun
While the Moon Burns
From the Stars Above

The Papua Series
Papua
Eden
The Pacific

The Silent Frontier
The Stone Dragon
The Frozen Circle

The Colonial Series
The Queen's Colonial

Excerpts from emails sent to Peter Watt

'I have just finished reading your latest book *The Queen's Colonial.* It is without doubt the best book I have read in 2018. I found it absolutely riveting and could not put it down. I can't wait for the next book!'

'Just finished *The Queen's Colonial* and as usual it was superb. It never ceases to amaze me how you research the details in history and weave them into a fictional story which is so believable. I will be waiting anxiously for the next one.'

'Just finished *The Queen's Colonial.* Excellent detail . . . you haven't lost your touch! Another enthralling family saga.'

'I have just finished *The Queen's Colonial.* Truly excellent. I have now read all nineteen of your books. I thought the Duffy/McIntosh series was great, the Papua trilogy was fabulous (I have read those three twice) but I feel that the new book is possibly your best book yet. I am looking forward to the next instalment. Keep up the great writing.'

'Damn you, Peter Watt . . .!! Just finished *The Queen's Colonial* and can't wait to get the next one. Love your work.'

'A real page-turner. Your source for the Crimean War was inspired.'

'Just finished this wonderful book. You never cease to entertain me with your fantastic writing. Please keep writing. As always I'm waiting with bated breath for your next book . . .'

'Just finished *The Queen's Colonial.* Thoroughly enjoyed the book. The military history aspect is interesting to me and the storyline intriguing. What a family!'

'Thank you for taking the time to write the way you do. When I am reading one of your books I am in the scene with your characters.'

'I have just completed the Papua series. Your writing has been a constant companion and escape . . . It has been an absolute pleasure to immerse myself with the characters in a thoroughly entertaining blend of fiction and well-researched fact.'

'Another most enjoyable read. Having generally read factual military history most of my life it was pleasurable to read a fictitious work wherein I could not only enjoy the woven stories, but see and feel the characters. Well done!'

'Thank you so much for the years of storytelling, especially the Duffy/McIntosh saga . . . Your books will always take pride of place on our bookshelf to remind me of the many hours of enjoyment spent reading them. I think I will have to start over and re-read! Thank you again and please keep on writing.'

The Queen's TIGER

PETER WATT

MACMILLAN
Pan Macmillan Australia

First published 2019 in Macmillan by Pan Macmillan Australia Pty Ltd
1 Market Street, Sydney, New South Wales, Australia, 2000

Cataloguing-in-Publication entry is available
from the National Library of Australia
http://catalogue.nla.gov.au

Typeset in Bembo by Post Pre-press Group
Printed by McPherson's Printing Group

For my wonderful wife, Naomi.

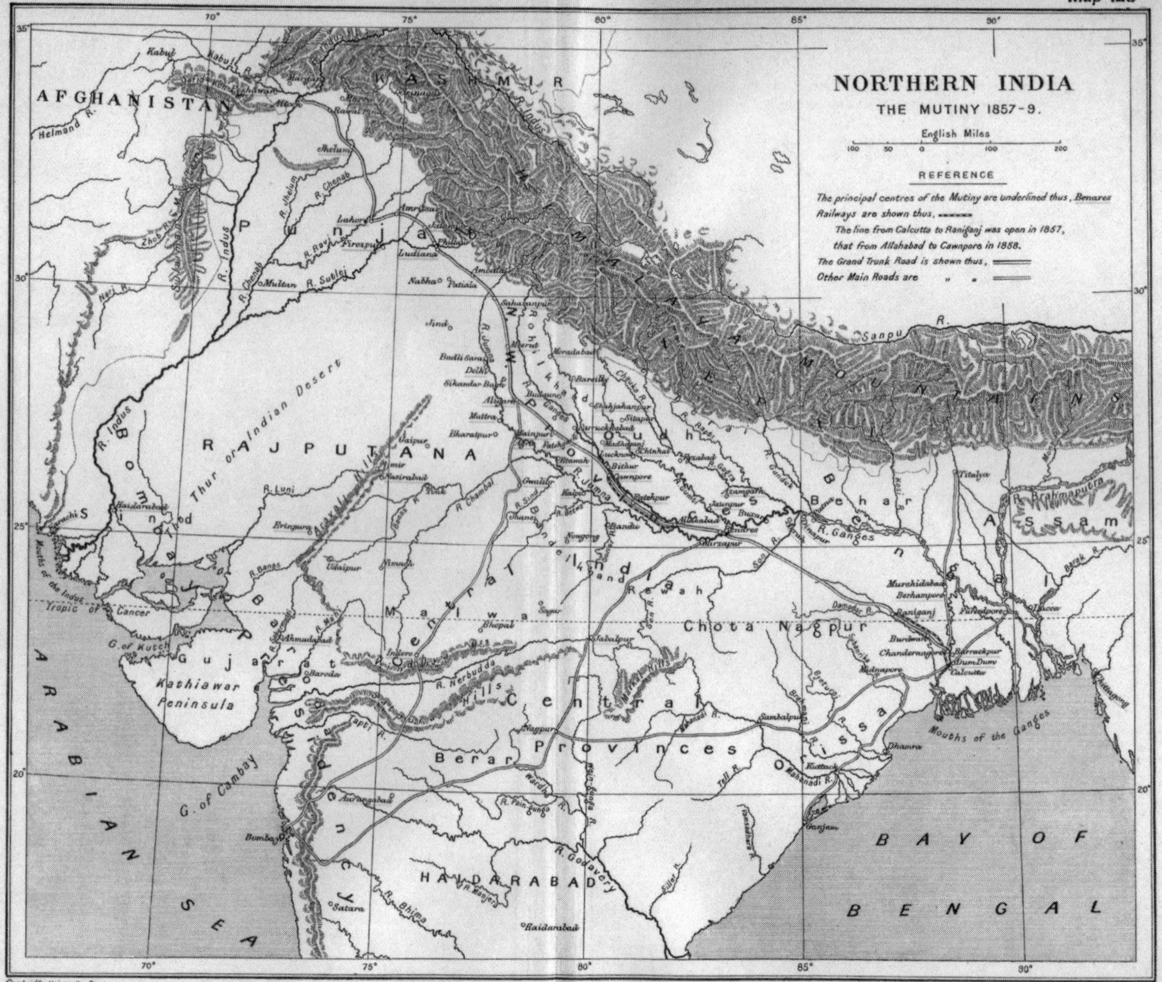

Map 123

NORTHERN INDIA

THE MUTINY 1857-9.

English Miles

100 50 0 100 200

REFERENCE

The principal centres of the Mutiny are underlined thus, Benares

Railways are shown thus,

The line from Calcutta to Raniganj was open in 1857,

that from Allahabad to Cawnpore in 1858.

The Grand Trunk Road is shown thus,

Other Main Roads are " "

Cambridge University Press

Stanford's Geogl. Estabt.

PROLOGUE

The Bengali Dry Season

India, 1857

Mrs Alice Campbell, née Forbes, the bride of Dr Peter Campbell, Canadian citizen and former surgeon to the British army in the Crimean War, marvelled at the exotic lands she and her husband had passed through on their journey to visit Peter's brother. They had arrived by ship in the Bay of Bengal and travelled up the River Ganges delta to Murshidabad in the Bengal Presidency of north-eastern India. Here Major Scott Campbell had a posting with British East India Company and, according to Peter, had become more British than Canadian.

The British here certainly knew how to hold a ball, thought Alice, looking around her. She and Peter had only arrived in Bengal this morning and already they had found themselves invited to a magnificent ball held for the expatriates of the region – senior civil servants and officers of the East India Company. Great fans moved the hot evening air around the candle-lit ballroom, which was alive with the colourful uniforms of the officers and the glittering jewellery of their ladies. Scattered around the room were Indian servants wearing smart uniforms, and on a dais a regimental band played dance music.

Peter wore a dinner suit and Alice an off-the-shoulder silk gown, although little in the way of jewellery. Major Scott Campbell was taller and more broad-shouldered than his surgeon brother and cut a dashing figure in his cavalry dress uniform. He strode towards them holding out two crystal coupes of champagne.

'Here, Mrs Campbell. Old chap,' he said, passing the champagne first to his sister-in-law and then to his brother. 'Welcome to India.'

Alice and Peter had met with him that morning when he had escorted them to quarters in his villa. The newlywed couple had been welcomed by a staff of Indian servants, both male and female, dressed in traditional clothing.

'So, my little brother saw action in the Crimea,' Scott said, taking a flute from a passing Indian servant circulating amongst the guests. 'You will have to tell me all about your experiences. Damned long time since we fought a war with a European nation. Not since Napoleon.'

'Not much to tell,' Peter said, sipping the chilled champagne. 'Just the usual – men dying in agony and calling out for their mothers as they did so.' It was obvious that Peter did not wish to remember the horrors he had encountered on his operating table, usually an improvised kitchen tabletop.

'I can see that you were able to marry the most beautiful woman in England,' Scott said with a glint in his eye and a broad smile that made Alice feel as if his compliment was almost a challenge to his younger brother. Peter was nearing thirty and clean-shaven with short hair, whilst his brother, a couple of years older, had a thick black beard and moustache. Scott was single, but Alice guessed he could have any single – or married – woman in the room if he chose.

'Thank you for the compliment, Major Campbell,' Alice replied.

'You must call me Scott – after all, we are family,' he said, clinking his glass against hers.

'Sir,' a young officer interrupted, 'I must apologise but the colonel wishes you to read this despatch from Berhampore barracks.'

Scott took the sheet of paper and read it with a frown. He passed the communiqué back to the young officer.

'You look concerned,' Peter said.

'It is nothing to be too worried about,' Scott replied. 'Just notice that our sepoys at the barracks have refused to attend musketry practice at the range there.'

'Why would they do that?' Alice asked.

'It is the new Enfield rifles,' Scott replied. 'The sepoys have to bite off the end of the paper cartridge case to load the powder into the barrel. There are wild rumours circulating that the paper is greased with pig fat, which is not acceptable to our Moslem soldiers, and Hindu soldiers have been told that the cartridges are covered in beef fat, and *that* is not acceptable to *them*. We suspect that the rumours are being circulated by nefarious types who would like to see a rebellion against us in order to seize power for themselves.'

'Well, it is their country,' Alice said, and both men looked at her as if she had suddenly used a profanity in the company of the Queen.

'I am afraid that the Indians are like squabbling children,' Scott said. 'They are not a united people. The Moslems and Hindus will kill each other at the drop of a hat, and the Sikhs are no better. They need us to keep them from slaughtering each other. At least my men are loyal to Her Majesty the Queen and not to some foolish idea of independence.'

'You might require the services of the British navy and army here,' Peter said cautiously.

'The East India Company has conquered and controlled this great subcontinent without any assistance from England,' Scott said. 'The matter at Berhampore will be rectified in due course and things will get back to normal. By the way,' he continued, changing the subject, 'some of us from the regiment are planning a tiger hunt in a few days and I would like to invite you and Alice as my guests. We shoot from elephants.'

'I would very much like to join the hunt,' Alice said. 'I think it would be thrilling to ride on the back of an elephant.'

'Good show,' Scott said without asking his brother's opinion.

The band struck up a waltz and Peter swept Alice onto the floor to join the swirl of sweating faces.

But beyond the extravagance of colonial India and the ballroom, a simmering volcano of nationalism was about to erupt and swamp the Indian subcontinent in a fire from hell.

Part One

Persia and India, 1857

ONE

It was a typical day in the life of a soldier in Queen Victoria's army.

The rain pelted down as Ian Steele, known to all as Captain Samuel Forbes, led his company of riflemen through the mud and sand of the desolate lands of the ancient terrain of Persia.

Ian bore a remarkable resemblance to the man whose identity he had assumed. In his early thirties, he was in fact more strongly built than the real Samuel Forbes – a legacy of his days as a blacksmith in the colony of New South Wales. The secret pact between English aristocrat, Forbes, and colonial blacksmith, Steele, had been forged for mutually beneficial reasons and had to be maintained for at least another seven years.

Leading the force Ian was part of, which comprised five thousand British troops and artillery guns, was the competent English lieutenant-general, James Outram.

The march had commenced in the filthy, disease-ridden Persian coastal town of Bushehr, captured the previous year by British forces. Their mission had been to attack the Persian army entrenched in its position forty-six miles from the ancient town of Bushehr, but the enemy had fled before the British artillery, rifled muskets and bayonets, leaving its military camp intact.

It had been one of Captain Steele's valued men, Corporal Owen Williams, who had discovered the small but valuable hoard of gold hidden under a carpet in a Persian commander's tent. Without any of his fellow soldiers observing, he had pocketed the coins which would later be divided equally between himself, his commanding officer and his best friend, Sergeant Conan Curry.

After a couple of days, everything else of worth from the captured Persian camp was packed for removal back to Bushehr, then enemy ammunition was destroyed in a massive explosion.

The night was dark and bleak as the British force marched. Sergeant Conan Curry strode easily beside Captain Samuel Forbes. A special bond had been forged between officer and non-commissioned soldiers on the bloody battlefields of Crimea only months earlier, but there was more to this relationship than that. Sergeant Curry knew the real identity of his commanding officer and it was a secret Curry had sworn he'd keep till the grave. Strangely, Conan Curry had once been Ian's best friend. They had grown up together in the shadow of the Blue Mountains outside Sydney, but their paths had separated when Conan had chosen an indolent life of easy money with a few of the bad apples of their village. They had come together again a world away, in England.

Ian had been able to have Conan attached to his company as acting sergeant major, whilst the third member of their trio, Corporal Owen Williams, remained with a platoon commanded by the brother of a close friend, Captain Miles Sinclair, who had been killed in the Crimean campaign. The young platoon commander, Lieutenant Henry Sinclair, was barely seventeen years of age and this was his first taste of war. Ian had asked Owen to keep an eye on the young officer and quietly guide him in his role.

'A bit bloody disappointing the Persians did not put up a reasonable fight,' Conan growled.

'They call themselves Iranians,' Ian said. 'Iran is the ancient name for this part of the Persian empire.'

Conan accepted this correction without question as he knew how knowledgeable Ian was about history. However, he was less interested in the name of their enemy than in the reason for their flight. The new Enfield rifled musket he carried was changing the nature of battle. The Enfield had great range and accuracy, whilst the old muskets their enemy carried required close-range volley fire to be effective. No doubt knowing they were outgunned had factored into the Persians' – Iranians' – decision to flee rather than fight.

'I don't suppose you know why we are in this godforsaken Musulman country,' Conan said as the rain drenched him to the bone.

'The old story, Sergeant,' Ian sighed. 'We are here to keep the Muscovites from extending their influence into India. For years the Tsar has been encouraging the Persians against us. Now we are taking a stand.'

Ian was about to give a short history to his acting sergeant major when shots interrupted him. The shots were coming out of the darkness at the rear of their column. The order to form a square was given and Ian ensured that his company fell in with the rest of the regiment. He was aware that two-thirds of his men were raw recruits out of the London barracks and hoped his veteran non-commissioned officers would steady them in the confusion of this unexpected event.

Ian took up a position in the front ranks of his soldiers. He knew the primary role of the British officer was to lead his men by personal example. Ian was armed with a rifle like his men, but also carried two loaded heavy-calibre revolvers in his waistband. He had found them far more effective than the sword at his waist, which denoted his rank as an officer of Queen Victoria.

Ian was crouched on one knee when he became aware that a man on a horse had just galloped past their front.

'That's the general!' Conan exclaimed. 'The silly bugger will get himself killed out there.'

Ian agreed and wondered why General Outram would do such a foolish thing as to detach himself from the defensive square in the dark.

'Mr Upton, you are to take command,' Ian yelled to a nearby officer.

He leapt to his feet and Conan followed him without question. They moved quickly in the direction the general had taken and eventually, somewhere ahead of them – Ian calculated it to be about a hundred yards away – they heard a horse whinny in pain.

Both men raised their rifles, surging forward to a small clearing amongst the desert scrub to see the vague shape of a horse down, its rider trapped beneath.

'I think it is the general,' Conan whispered. Both men could barely make out the downed horse with their night vision at its most acute.

'Over there!' Ian hissed. 'Figures moving around. They have to be Persians.'

Conan raised his rifle, not bothering to make an attempt to sight but firing blindly in the direction of the moving men. Ian removed his pistols and delivered a withering volley that seemed to scatter whoever was trying to encircle the downed horse and rider. The Persian soldiers quickly disappeared, probably unaware of the importance of the man they had attempted to kill or capture.

'Who is out there?' General Outram called as he brought his downed horse to its feet and remounted.

'Captain Forbes and Sergeant Curry, sir,' Ian called back. 'Are you injured?'

'Just my pride,' replied the English general, bringing his mount under control. 'I thank you, Captain Forbes and Sergeant Curry.' With that, he spurred his horse back to the British lines, leaving Ian and Conan to follow.

Ian resumed command of his men. They waited out the night and when the sun rose on another day of miserable, sleeting rain, they saw the Shah's Persian army formed into infantry squares to engage the Anglo-Indian force.

Ian glanced up and down the front rank of his men and could see little fear in the faces of his new recruits, both young and old, as they gripped their Enfield rifled muskets. Ian sensed that they had confidence in their training and their modern weapons. He had issued orders to his platoon commanders to ensure that the powder for the rifles was not damp and the soldiers had recharged with fresh powder. The Persians were wary and remaining a safe distance from the deadly accurate long-range fire of the British rifles.

'It's going to be the job of the cavalry to break the Persian square,' Conan said to Ian who was kneeling, using his rifle as a support.

'Very impressive, Sergeant Curry,' Ian grinned. 'We will make a soldier of you yet.'

Conan smiled. 'But not an officer.'

Even as they looked on they could hear the jangle of cavalry bridles, and Ian's men raised a hoorah from the ranks when they observed the Bombay Light Cavalry form their squadrons to charge the Persian square. The cavalrymen broke into a canter, then a full gallop, charging the Persians to Ian's company's front. It was a thrilling sight emphasised by the thundering hooves of the warhorses. The Indian unit smashed into the Persian ranks, wielding heavy sabres, slashing and stabbing with the fury of men possessed. Dust rose in swirling clouds, partially obscuring the desperate clash, but within minutes the Indian horse soldiers rode out of the melee with uniforms covered in the blood of the Persians. It was all over in mere minutes. Seven hundred of the enemy lay dead, and Outram's force was able to capture a hundred prisoners and two of the enemy's guns. Ian could hear the disappointed grumbles of his own company, as they'd had little to do with the victory at what would later be called the Battle of Khushab. Still, he knew it would not be the last bloody engagement in this campaign.

'The colonel wishes to see you, sir,' said a junior staff officer from regimental headquarters.

Ian followed the young officer back to the rear where he saw the man he most despised in the world, Colonel Clive Jenkins. His commanding officer had originally served as a lieutenant in Ian's company before being rapidly promoted thanks to his highly placed social contacts and family fortune. Ian had witnessed Jenkins' craven cowardice in the face of fire during the Crimean War and knew he was incompetent to lead soldiers. Jenkins hated Ian for this knowledge and had placed him in almost suicidal situations in Crimea.

Jenkins stood now with two of his senior officers, and when Ian arrived he reluctantly saluted.

'You wish to see me . . . sir,' Ian said. Despite their mutual hatred, Ian had had no choice but to swear his loyalty to the man he knew was a coward. Jenkins was of a similar age to Ian, but that was where the similarities ended. Jenkins was slim and had the patrician looks of an English gentleman; in contrast Ian was broad-shouldered and had a face that was not handsome but was nevertheless ruggedly appealing.

One of the officers present was a major and the other a captain. Both served on Jenkins' personal staff.

'I was informed that you left your post last night without permission,' Jenkins said in an accusing tone. 'You have a history of running your own show without respect for the established role of an officer and gentleman.'

'Sir, I had an urgent choice to make and did not have time to request your permission to temporarily hand over my command,' Ian said.

'Nothing can excuse your lack of obedience to your superiors, Captain Forbes. I will be –'

Jenkins did not get any further before a major from Lieutenant-General Outram's staff interrupted him. 'I am sorry to intrude, Colonel Jenkins, but I was informed Captain Forbes was at your headquarters. He is wanted by Sir James immediately.'

'Of course,' Jenkins replied, annoyed and confused as to why the legendary senior officer would want to speak with one of his company commanders. 'He is dismissed to accompany you.'

Ian did not bother saluting but turned on his heel and followed the major to a tent where James Outram sat at a small field desk scribbling notes. He was alone and looked up when his staff officer approached.

The major saluted. 'I have Captain Forbes, sir,' he said.

Ian stood to attention before an impressive man in his mid-fifties. Outram had a strong face, neatly cropped black beard and a receding hairline.

'You may relax, Captain Forbes,' the British general said with a smile. 'I summoned you here to express my personal thanks for your assistance last night. I suspect that if you and your sergeant had not found me, my head might have been stuck on the end of a spear for all to see when the sun rose. I did a stupid thing in riding out alone. I wished to ascertain the extent of the enemy opposing us, but I should have left that task to my staff. Your rescue cannot be mentioned in dispatches, although you deserve a mention. I pray that what happened will remain between you and I – and Sergeant Curry.'

'Yes, sir, I fully understand, and I can assure you that Sergeant Curry will be discreet,' Ian answered.

'I have been informed of your remarkable record of service in the Crimea,' Outram continued. 'And I am aware that there is some animosity between you and Colonel Jenkins.'

'Sir, despite my private opinions, he is my commanding officer and has my total loyalty.'

The general pushed himself from his desk and stood. 'An excellent answer, Captain Forbes.' He extended his hand to a startled Ian. 'If in the future I can be of assistance to you, do not hesitate to make contact with me. This is my way of thanking you for your service last night.' Ian accepted the handshake and felt the strength in the senior officer's grip.

'Oh, by the way, I have been informed that Colonel Jenkins had you summoned to remonstrate with you about your temporary absence from your post last night. Major Starke will inform your commanding officer that you were acting on secret instructions from my staff. I am sure Colonel Jenkins is wise enough not to question my authority.'

'Thank you, sir,' Ian replied, letting go of the general's hand.

'You may return to your men, Captain Forbes, and I hope that one day you may join my staff. I need competent officers around me.'

Ian saluted and marched away, knowing that this was a man he would follow through the gates of hell if asked.

Ian did not bother to report to his commanding officer, who he guessed was now being told in no uncertain terms that Ian had been acting on Outram's orders. Jenkins, for all his high-placed connections in England, would not dare question James Outram, a darling of the British government.

Ian was met at his tent by Conan, whose worried expression asked the question.

'Sir James asked me to thank you for our service to him last night but would rather it remain between the three of us,' Ian said.

Conan nodded. 'I was told by the boys that Colonel Jenkins wanted to see you. Whenever the bastard asks for you it only means trouble.'

'Ah, yes.' Ian smiled. 'Thankfully, a major from the general's staff rescued me from an accusation that I had deserted my post. I don't think Colonel Jenkins will raise the matter again.'

'That bastard Jenkins is out to get you killed,' Conan spat.

'It's not easy to kill us colonials,' Ian said with a grin, glowing in the knowledge that his and Conan's actions hours earlier had garnered the appreciation of the British force commander. He hoped that it would not be easy for Jenkins to cause him any further mischief in this campaign.

TWO

A man in his early thirties stood with his hands clasped behind his back by the great window of a three-storeyed house. He was gazing down on a vacant area of swamp and bushy scrubland lightly covered in snow. It was said that the vast vacant plot in the middle of the sprawling American city of New York, originally established by Dutch colonial pioneers, would be developed into a great park.

Samuel Forbes was deep in thought when another man entered the room.

'Samuel,' the man said, noticing the disturbed expression on his friend's face. 'Are you unwell?'

'No, James, but I have just received upsetting news from my dear friend Jonathan in London,' Samuel replied. 'It appears that Ian is in Persia fighting yet another campaign for the Queen.'

James placed his hands on Samuel's shoulders. 'Ian survived the worst of the Crimea and has proven to be a great soldier. You should not worry yourself about his welfare.'

Samuel detached himself from his friend, walking to the small polished teak table to retrieve the letter sitting next to a copy of *Uncle Tom's Cabin; or, Life Among the Lowly* by Harriet Beecher Stowe. The letter was from Jonathan, a former schoolmate of Samuel's. They had been in boarding school together and it was with Jonathan that Samuel had discovered a mutual attraction forbidden by the laws of England and the English Church. Jonathan had been able to remain close to Samuel's family – especially his sister, Alice – and regularly reported on events from the other side of the Atlantic.

'I do, though,' Samuel sighed. 'When we made our pact to exchange identities I did not give much thought to the fact that Ian would be constantly fighting in the British Empire's wars. He still has another seven years left of the ten-year period I was supposed to serve in my grandfather's regiment to be eligible for my inheritance. I feel that I was being absolutely selfish placing his life in jeopardy.'

'You know that Ian was more than willing to serve the Empire as a soldier of the Queen. It was as much his burning desire as it was your ambition to seek revenge against Sir Archibald, your supposed father. Captain Steele is where he always dreamed of being.'

'There is not a night that passes I do not have nightmares of Ian's body lying on some godforsaken battlefield,' Samuel said. 'I feel the need to return to England and speak with him. He may wish to renege on our agreement.'

Samuel, however, was not telling the entire truth. He did wish to return to England, but Ian was not foremost in his thoughts. Privately, he agreed with James that the man was more than likely content where he was. But how could Samuel tell his partner in life that he still dreamed of the precious moments he had spent with Jonathan in his youth, and of the deadly consumption that now racked his former lover's body? That he wished to see Jonathan – perhaps for the last time – and explore his feelings for his old friend?

'I doubt it,' James scoffed. 'From the little I learned of Mr Steele when we were in New South Wales, he was born to battle. His father fought at Waterloo and Ian expressed his overwhelming desire to follow the colours. If you return to London you might be recognised as the real Samuel Forbes, and that would incriminate Captain Steele as well. You have to consider that. You are by nature reckless and impulsive and I love you for that, but I fear your nature may one day get you into trouble you cannot escape.'

'I feel guilty that I am enjoying this privileged life while Ian takes all the risks in my name,' said Samuel.

'Are you sure you do not wish to return to London to see Jonathan?' James asked, his question tinged with a note of accusation.

'No, no,' Samuel quickly dismissed the idea. 'I will love you to the day I die, dear James. I have grown to love this country as you do. But I am not Ian Steele.'

James fell silent for a few moments. 'I will make a booking for us both to journey to London, then,' he said reluctantly. 'But you must promise me that you will not under any circumstances put yourself in a compromising situation with your family.' From what Samuel had told him about his brother, Charles, and his father, Sir Archibald, nothing good could come of encountering them.

'I promise,' Samuel said, embracing James with affection. 'Besides, my darling sister has married and is currently in India, so there is no reason for me to wish to contact my family. Although while we are in England I would like to visit the memorial to my late brother.'

James knew that Lieutenant Herbert Forbes had been killed fighting against the Russian army in the siege of Sevastopol, and understood why Samuel would wish to pay his respects. All that truly bothered James was that Samuel might renew his relationship with his old friend and lover, Jonathan. He reassured himself that it was his wealth that currently allowed Samuel's extravagant lifestyle and that his lover would not jeopardise this arrangement – at least until he was able to claim his inheritance from the vast Forbes fortune.

★

The London home of the Forbes family, situated in the most desirable suburb of the great city, still had an air of mourning about it. Servants moved quietly around their master. Sir Archibald had taken the death of his youngest son badly. He spent hours staring blankly at a black-framed sepia photograph hung on the wall of the library. It showed a handsome young man still in his teens wearing the dress uniform of an infantry officer, his hand on the hilt of his sword.

Charles Forbes secretly sneered at his father's grief. Sir Archibald was growing soft and sentimental. For himself, Charles was overjoyed that the family fortune need not be shared by his youngest brother. All the more for him. If only his sister, Alice, would also disappear – perhaps she would die of some exotic disease in India – that would leave only Samuel, and he would meet a painful end on the battlefield if Charles' plans with Clive Jenkins came to fruition. Then he would be the sole inheritor of the Forbes estates.

'A terrible tragedy,' Charles said to his father as they both gazed at the photograph.

'It should have been Samuel,' his father replied bitterly. 'Not Herbert.'

'Give the army time,' Charles replied. 'Officers on the Empire's frontiers usually have a short life span.'

*

Alice Campbell was never bored with the exotic culture she encountered daily in the Bengali city of Murshidabad. From the palace grounds of the rich and aristocratic Indians, peacocks screeched as they spread their colourful fan-like tails amongst an army of gardeners tending to the lavish gardens. The markets were filled with the aroma of a rich variety of unfamiliar food, spices and fruits. The mango quickly became her favourite delicacy. Each afternoon she would return to her brother-in-law's sumptuous villa with its beautifully manicured lawns and colourful shrubs and flowers, all surrounded by a high stone wall. Inside the villa high ceilings and marbled floors were a cool relief from the Indian sun. It was so different from the homes Alice knew in England. She felt herself being drawn into this exotic life in India.

However, there were plenty of reminders of the London life she had left behind. She and Peter would often attend tea parties at the homes of the British employees of the East India Company, where Alice found herself growing irritated at the patronising attitude towards the local Indian population. Not that she always disagreed with the British views, especially when she heard stories of wives sometimes being burned alive on their husbands' funeral pyres – a tradition being stamped out by British justice.

It was during the third week of their visit that Peter was

called upon by his brother to provide medical assistance to a British officer who had accidentally shot himself in the leg.

Peter packed his surgical bag and was escorted from the town by a section of four lancers from Scott's squadron. He was warned that it would be a week before he returned.

Alice was alone and bored when Scott visited on the second day of Peter's absence, reminding her of the tiger hunt that had finally been organised by a local Indian prince. Alice hesitated to go without Peter but Scott was persuasive, so very early the following day she was escorted by a tall Bengali trooper to a place outside of the town where ten elephants stood with baskets on their backs and handlers sitting forward on their necks. The sun was just above the horizon and Alice could see Indians milling around the elephants standing patiently in the dust. Scott was speaking with a richly dressed and rather handsome Indian with a jewelled turban and he broke into a broad smile when he saw her. Her brother-in-law was wearing his field uniform and carried a double-barrelled shotgun in one hand. He excused himself from the Indian and strolled over to her.

'Ah, Alice, your opportunity to get a taste of the real India,' he said. 'We will be going into the jungle in pursuit of the vile creature that attacks and eats humans. We are guests of the local ruler of these parts, and you and I will share a howdah. I am sure you will have a tale to tell my brother when he returns. Shall we mount our beast?'

A ladder was brought for Alice who wore a long flowing white dress and a broad straw hat with a scarf tied under her chin. Alice climbed the ladder and sat down in the basket. Scott settled down beside her, producing a second weapon, a wicked-looking double-barrelled pistol that resembled a shortened version of his four-bore percussion elephant gun. Its barrels were also loaded with great lead slugs. 'The pistol is just in case we need very close protection,' Scott said. 'Do you know how to fire it?'

'I suppose that I simply point it and pull the triggers,' Alice replied casually, causing a broad grin to break across Scott's face.

'That's my girl,' he said, and turned his attention to the mahout, speaking to him in Bengali. The man, wearing little more than a loincloth and holding a short rod with a metal spike, replied. Under the prodding of the Indian elephant controller the great beast lurched forward, as did the line of other elephants with their passengers, who comprised local royalty and a couple of Scott's fellow officers.

The convoy of elephants left the town behind and soon entered a thick green jungle of giant trees and shrubs. Alice felt as if she was back on the ship that had steamed to India weeks earlier as the elephant seemed to pitch and roll in its heavy gait. They were following a well-worn track to avoid the heavy foliage of the forest. Birds shrieked and monkeys howled in the treetops as the elephants plodded on. There was an alien strangeness to this land that was so different from the cold, wet country of her birth.

Alice leaned back against the edge of the basket and took in the aromatic and earthy scents of the jungle, both pungent and sweet. Despite the heat and the sweat now running in small rivulets down the inside of her dress, she started to doze. Suddenly a great cry rose from the men of the convoy. Alice immediately came fully awake and looked around to see what had caused the commotion.

'There!' Scott shouted, raising the heavy-calibre weapon to his shoulder. Alice saw the flash of yellow and black in the shadows of the jungle. A tiger!

The blast of the elephant gun almost deafened her, leaving her ears ringing. Scott fired the second barrel and other guns opened fire at the tiger that had disappeared into the heavy undergrowth.

Scott was quickly reloading. 'I think I got him,' he said as he poured black powder down the twin barrels and dropped the heavy leaf balls after it. The percussion caps followed and he leapt from the howdah to the ground below, leaving Alice alone as the elephant shifted nervously. It was obvious that Scott was going to hunt the tiger on foot but it had all happened so fast that Alice had had no time to react or protest. She saw Scott disappear into the jungle, followed by others from the hunting party, leaving her and the mahout alone.

For a while all she could hear were the shouts of men stalking the wounded animal, but gradually she became aware that the elephant she was sitting on was shuffling to one side of the track. The mahout was shouting and using his stick in an attempt to bring the great beast under control. Alice gripped the edge of the howdah with all her strength, and suddenly the elephant trumpeted its fear. Disbelievingly, Alice saw that the wounded tiger had doubled back and, in its rage, it leapt onto the hindquarters of her elephant. Alice swivelled to see the tiger clawing its way up the great pachyderm towards her, and she realised that the elephant was now preparing to launch into full flight to shake the beast off.

Alice could see the head of the tiger only a few feet away. She was both absolutely terrified and mesmerised by its beauty as it snarled in wounded anger. Alice was vaguely aware through her terror that she could smell its pungent breath. In the distance she could hear the concerned shouting of men crashing back through the heavy undergrowth, and realised to her horror that the mahout had deserted his animal in his own desperate fear.

The tiger fixed her with its smoky eyes and Alice knew that she was close to death. The muscles in the tiger's shoulders bunched as it prepared to make the last leap onto the back of the elephant, which now burst into full flight, smashing its way through small trees and heavy foliage.

Whether it was instinct or luck, Alice felt the butt of the pistol in her hand and she brought it up, almost touching the nose of the tiger. She pulled both triggers, and the tiger disappeared behind a cloud of gun smoke. The recoil of the pistol almost flung Alice from the basket. There was no time to pray, so she closed her eyes, awaiting the inevitable gory death the claws and teeth of the great cat would bring to her. There was not even time to think of Peter as she fell back in the basket, hitting her head.

Then all she remembered was a babble of voices in English and Bengali. The terrified elephant was standing still, trembling, as she lay on her back in the howdah.

'My dear Alice, have you been hurt?' Scott's worried voice drifted down to her as she opened her eyes to see his face above hers.

'No, I don't think so,' she replied, shaking her head to ensure she had not been dreaming the nightmare of seconds or minutes before. 'The tiger?' she asked.

'You bagged it,' Scott replied. 'We have never known a woman do that. What a story you will be able to tell my brother.'

Alice pulled herself into a sitting position in the howdah. Scott helped her climb down a ladder and she could see the bloody claw marks on the hindquarters of the elephant's thick hide. She could also see a few feet away the body of the tiger she had killed. Men were gathered around it, and when she stood unsteadily beside the elephant, a cheer rose up from all those present, from the loinclothed elephant handlers to the richly dressed Indian aristocrats. Alice could see admiration for her feat in their expressions. The turbaned and bejewelled figure Alice had noticed talking with Scott earlier that day stepped forward with a smile. She could see that he was in his mid-twenties and had a handsome, dark face. He sported a neatly clipped short beard and his brown eyes were full of sparkle.

'I think we should call you the daughter of Kali,' he said, taking Alice's hand and kissing it. She was surprised to hear him speak in fluent English, although she did not know who Kali was.

'Thank you,' she politely replied, her heart still beating hard in her breast. 'But I shot the tiger because I was terrified.'

'No matter why you did it, you faced the fearsome beast and triumphed.'

'Khan,' Scott said, addressing the aristocratic Indian, 'may I introduce you to my brother's bride, Mrs Alice Campbell.'

Alice thought that she detected a note of annoyance in Scott's introduction but dismissed her suspicion as she gazed into the face of the handsome young man.

'I must present you with a gift to celebrate your great victory today over the demon tiger,' the Khan said, taking a huge blue sapphire pendant on a gold chain from around his neck and pressing it into Alice's hand. Alice gasped at the beautiful piece of jewellery and began to protest the generosity, but the young Indian prince shook his head.

'I was educated in England and I know that it is your custom to present soldiers with medals for bravery. This is my medal of bravery for you.'

Alice was at a loss for words. When she gazed into the dead eyes of the tiger at her feet, she felt conflicted about what she had done. She had seen the beauty in those eyes before she killed the magnificent creature, but at the same time she realised that had she not killed the tiger, it would have killed her.

'I must return to my servants,' the Khan said with a polite nod of his head and he turned away, leaving Scott and Alice alone.

'Who is Kali?' Alice asked, and Scott frowned.

'These damned savages have so many gods, but Kali is of particular importance to them. She is their goddess of death, time and doomsday. But she is also associated with the mother earth figure and, dare I say it, sexuality and violence. The Khan is one of those jumped-up rulers we have to pander to in these parts. It seems that we will be ending our hunt and returning to the city. You have the honour of bagging the only tiger today.'

Alice held the precious pendant in her hand, her thoughts still reeling from the deadly encounter and the mystifying events that had followed. It was a day she knew she would always remember.

That night she returned to her brother-in-law's villa and went to her room to sleep. As she passed into the dark world of dreams she remembered a verse from a poem she had once read when she was young. William Blake's poem echoed in her dreams.

Tiger, tiger, burning bright
In the forests of the night,
What immortal hand or eye
Could frame thy beautiful symmetry?

Even as Alice tossed in her sleep, at the Barrackpore barracks, only miles from the scene of the hunt, a mutiny had just occurred and two British officers had been wounded. Already the opening events of the Indian mutiny were beginning to ripple out, and those ripples would become a tidal wave of death and destruction.

THREE

Captain Ian Steele spread the coins on a wooden table in his seconded quarters in Bushehr where he and his regiment awaited the order to move out against the Persian army. Corporal Owen Williams had divided the prize he'd discovered hidden in the tent of a Persian commander into three equal parts and handed Ian his share in a small leather bag. Under the flickering candlelight Ian could see that it was a tidy sum to add to the considerable fortune in jewels his company had taken from a Russian baggage train as the Muscovites fled from the battlefields of the Crimea. The fortune he'd always dreamed of as a soldier of the Queen was coming true.

Ian scooped the coins back into the leather pouch and secreted the pouch within his bundle of uniform kit. He leaned back in the rickety chair to stare at the mudbrick wall of his tiny room. His quarters were in what had once been the residence of a Persian businessman who had fled the city when the British army came.

'Sir,' a familiar voice called from the other side of the wooden door to Ian's room. 'The commanding officer wishes to speak with you.'

'Thank you, Mr Sinclair,' Ian replied. 'Inform the colonel I am coming immediately.'

Ian threw on his jacket and straightened his uniform. No doubt he was in trouble again. He walked through the evening shadows to the HQ building where he was met by the regiment's second-in-command, Major Dawkins.

'The colonel will see you now, Captain Forbes,' the major said in a tone that did not bode well.

Ian stepped inside the room being used as the office of the regiment. It contained little other than a map on the wall, a table and three chairs. Jenkins sat behind the table, which was strewn with papers. Ian saluted but Jenkins did not return the salute.

Jenkins rose and walked to the wall map, his hands clasped behind his back. 'General Outram has ordered that the regiment remain in this godforsaken place while he continues his advance against the Persian army upriver,' he said in an irritated voice. 'However, he has requested that I allow your company of rifles to join his expedition with Brigadier Havelock's brigade.'

Ian was thrilled at the opportunity for his men to join the mission to confront the enemy. Living in Bushehr was miserable, with the desert winds blowing dust so fine that it was able to penetrate into every crevice of the township. The regiment had been stood down but Ian still took every opportunity to take his company beyond the town's walls to conduct light manoeuvres and target practice. A few of the new recruits grumbled at the duties but the old hands explained it had always been the habit of the officer nicknamed 'the Colonial' for his long time in the British colony of New South Wales. There he appeared to have taken on some of the colonial's philosophy of equality amongst men, regardless of class. The old hands also knew of the company commander's courage, wise leadership and daring, and admired him for that. They were similarly aware of their colonel's poor record during the Crimean War, but they kept that to themselves as good soldiers should.

'Sir, I will lead my company with the knowledge that I must uphold the regiment's sterling reputation,' Ian replied tactfully. From the dark expression on Jenkins' face, he suspected that his commanding officer was angrier about this potential opportunity for Ian to bolster his already glorious reputation than he was about being left out of the coming battle – about which Jenkins, in his cowardice, was probably quite relieved.

'I cannot understand why General Outram would specifically request your services when we both know that you are not a true representative of the gentlemen officers I have in my command, Captain Forbes. I was sorely tempted to inform the general of your poor performance as a company commander.'

'Sir, it does not fall to humble soldiers to question a general's orders,' Ian said, and received a glare from the man he knew was using his self-purchased commission to further his prospects of a political career in England. It had been ever thus since the days of the Roman armies, Ian thought.

'You are dismissed, Captain Forbes. You are to join with General Outram's expedition within forty-eight hours.'

Ian came to attention and saluted Jenkins who, once again, did not return the salute. But Ian felt that nothing else mattered except to join the continuing war in this ancient biblical land.

His first stop was the quarters of his four junior officers to inform them of their new mission. They in turn summoned their sergeants and with them came acting company sergeant major, Sergeant Conan Curry.

'It's on,' Ian said, and a broad smile spread across Conan's face.

'Sir, is the regiment going with General Outram?' Conan asked.

'No, just our company,' Ian replied. 'The regiment remains at Bushehr.'

Conan grinned again. 'It pays to save the odd general from time to time.'

'Paddy, it certainly does,' Ian replied, using Conan's company nickname. 'I want you to assemble the company on our parade ground within the hour and I will announce the good news.'

'Sah!' Conan replied with a smart salute. 'The men will be happy to hear they will be earning the Queen's shilling.'

Conan hurried away, bawling to the men in their quarters to fall out with arms, whilst Ian glowed with a feeling of deep satisfaction. It was rumoured that the small war was near an end, and he wanted to see the last battle before they returned to their barracks in London. This was the life he had chosen. But as Ian packed his kit for the expedition, the same old fear nagged at him: would he prove to be the leader his men expected?

⋆

Dr Peter Campbell stared at the beautiful sapphire pendant his wife held in her hands.

'You must return it,' he said with a frown.

'It was a gift from the Khan in recognition of my killing the tiger,' Alice protested. 'It is not the monetary value of the gift that I care about but what it symbolises.'

Peter had barely returned to the gates of Murshidabad before he had been regaled by stories of how Alice had single-handedly shot a large tiger. Even now the tiger's magnificent pelt was being prepared by the Indian prince's staff to be presented to her.

The couple stood in the garden of Scott's villa. Beside them a fountain trickled water into a pond covered with colourful lilies.

'I trusted Scott to keep you safe whilst I was away,' Peter said bitterly, 'and what did he do? He took you into the jungle to hunt tigers and you were almost killed.'

'It was not Scott's fault,' Alice countered. 'I was missing you, and it was boring being left alone here. What occurred on the hunt is the most exciting thing that has ever happened in my life! For a moment when the tiger attacked I felt both desperate fear and absolute exhilaration. I think that I now know how you must have felt during those battles in the Crimea.'

'I never experienced exhilaration,' Peter said. 'Just fear – and helplessness when I could not save all the soldiers who came across my operating table. There is something unnatural in what you are saying.'

Alice strode away to slump on a divan. 'I have only ever known the mundane life of an Englishwoman and suddenly I find myself in a world of strange sights, sounds and smells. It is exciting and even wondrous to me. I am truly happy we came because when we return to London I will once again have to assume the stuffy and boring life of an English matron.'

Peter stood staring at his wife and felt a surge of love for her. She looked so vulnerable and yet had proved her steely courage under the direst of circumstances. He walked over to her, knelt down and took her hands in his own.

'I will tell our children when they are playing on your tiger-skin rug how their mother shot a ferocious man-eater in the wild jungles of India.' Peter kissed his wife's hands. In spite of his misgivings about the tiger hunt he was starting to realise that this woman was a diamond with many facets.

'Ah, how romantic,' Scott said, entering the garden in his uniform of red coat, tight white trousers and knee-length boots. A sword dangled from the belt around his waist.

Peter rose to greet his brother. 'You put my wife's life in danger,' he growled. 'I ought to give you a thrashing.'

Scott came to a stop paces away, a tight smile on his face. 'If I remember correctly, when we were younger I gave you the thrashing of your life. I would take you up on the offer, except I have been recalled to duty and do not have the time. Two of my colleagues at the Barrackpore barracks have been wounded by the sepoys there. This mess about the cartridges is getting out of hand, and it appears we will have to disband the native infantry unit until they execute the ringleaders of the mutiny.'

'Will you be in danger if you go?' Alice asked, rising from the divan.

Scott turned to her. 'My dear Alice, it is touching that a beautiful woman would be concerned for my welfare, but I can assure you that this is not the first time I have had to face down rebellious natives.'

Peter's anger was spent when he considered Alice's concern for his brother's safety. There had always been a fierce competition between the two brothers, but there was also a deep love. He would not wish his brother to be harmed in any way.

'Go safely,' Peter said gruffly and Scott grinned.

'I go knowing that Alice is safe in your care, little brother,' Scott said, and turned to walk away into the house. Peter suspected something facetious in his brother's departing remark and glanced at Alice, whose face reflected nothing but genuine concern for her brother-in-law.

'Do you find my brother attractive?' Peter blurted, startling Alice.

'Goodness, Peter, he is your brother,' she replied. 'It is you I find attractive, and he is almost your opposite. You are a good man, a healer of the sick and poor. I think your brother is what might be described as a cad. It is you who I love.'

'I am sorry, that was a stupid question,' Peter mumbled, and Alice placed her hand gently on his cheek.

'Do I sense a little jealousy?' she asked. 'If I do, then I can tell you that your thoughts are misguided. I am the proud and loving wife of Dr Peter Campbell.'

Even so, Peter could not shake off his distrust of his brother. He tried to banish from his mind the dark thought of an affair between the two people he most loved in the world.

★

Ian gazed at the riverbanks covered in thick groves of dates, beyond which was a desolate land of arid desert. The warship conveying them upriver flew colourful signal flags and the blue-coated Indian sailors worked quietly and efficiently. On the deck of the steamer stood Ian's company of around eighty men watching the shore drift by.

Now and then herds of cattle were seen on the shoreline, along with native herdsmen. The river was only about three hundred yards wide and Ian wondered nervously why the Persians had not chosen to set up ambushes on this narrow strip of water. A fusillade of fire could sweep the deck clean of his infantrymen.

Orders were issued before nightfall and Ian understood what he must do when they encountered the Persian river defences upstream. He tried to repress the bloody memories of hand-to-hand fighting in the Crimea, praying that the Enfield rifled muskets would do the job of defeating the enemy from a distance as they stormed ashore.

It was just on nightfall that the expedition observed the Persians throwing up earthen berms to provide cover for two artillery field guns. But an accompanying British ship commenced firing its guns at the Persian artillery, and the explosions indicated the devastating effect of the ship's fire. When the smoke cleared, the men could see the shattered bodies of the Persian gunners and others fleeing to safety.

Night fell without any further disturbance and a party of engineer officers used the dark to make a reconnaissance of the Persian defences. They were accompanied by a raft towed into the channel on the far side of a low, swampy island. On the rafts were two eight-inch mortars and two five-inch mortars.

Ian spent the early evening smoking his pipe and sharing his small stock of brandy with his junior officers. Sergeant Curry moved amongst the soldiers, sharing a quick nip of rum, joking and generally reassuring the men that the following day it would be Persians – and not Englishmen – who would die. The eve of a battle was a time for reflection on the meaning of what could be a short life with a violent end.

When his officers made their way back to their respective men, Ian lay down on the deck to stare at the star-filled night sky. The difference in the constellations of the northern hemisphere was something he was growing used to, but he missed the reassuring set of stars so well known in New South Wales as the Southern Cross. He dozed off with his rifled musket by his side and his two pistols. Through the darkness came the whispers of soldiers unable to sleep, and the sound of a mouth organ playing a mournful tune. Ian slipped into a deep sleep, although it was racked by nightmares of exploding Russian artillery shells and the screams of the dying.

Ian was jerked awake by the sound of an exploding mortar bomb as the first rays of the sun touched his face. He leapt to his feet, scooping up his pistols and rifle. When he looked to the shore he could see the smoke rising from the enemy fortifications. The battle had begun.

FOUR

'Fix bayonets!'

Ian roared out the order above the din of the exploding mortar bombs and the sound of the long deadly bayonet blades clicking as they were twisted into place at the end of the Enfields. Very soon they would be storming ashore, shouting defiance at the entrenched enemy, and Ian knew it was inevitable that many of his men would fall to the enemy's musket balls before they could get close enough to wreak havoc in hand-to-hand fighting.

For the moment the flotilla of British paddle-steamer warships continued to pound the formidable entrenched positions of the Persians. The Persian artillery batteries responded with a hail of solid cannonballs that ripped into the British warships.

As he stood on the deck of the troopship, his sword at his hip, his two revolvers tucked in leather holsters and his bayonet-tipped Enfield gripped in his hand, Ian noted vaguely that it was a clear and temperate day with a gentle breeze. It was too nice a day to die. When he looked up and down the river he could see the colourful flags flying from the masts of the warships and thought that it could have easily been a regatta day – except for the explosions threatening both Persian and English soldiers. The river was glittering under a rising sun and the smoke from the naval guns drifted gently in the air.

On the riverbank Ian saw colourfully dressed Persian horsemen riding between the groves of date palms. He heard the heavy thumps of trunks hitting the earth as the naval shells smashed into the trees. Ian's men were crouching on the deck with grim faces. No doubt each man was pondering the fate that awaited him when they finally went ashore to engage the Persian infantry hidden behind their carefully prepared earthen parapets. What was reassuring to Ian was that the naval bombardment was slowly reducing the defences. For three hours the cannonade continued. In that time Ian relaxed, drew on his pipe and puffed smoke that curled away in a lazy cloud. He was joined by Sergeant Conan Curry, who also took out his battered pipe and lit it.

'It reminds me a bit of the Redan,' Conan said.

'But this time we have the navy providing artillery support,' Ian replied. 'All we have to do is wait for the navy boys to do their job smashing holes in their defences. Make sure the men have a good supply of water in their canteens and drink as much as they can now before we disembark. It is going to be thirsty work.'

'Will do, sir,' Conan answered. 'I notice that the Persian guns are going a bit quiet.'

Ian could see that the fire from the shore had slackened off and that their ship was altering course to disembark them a few hundred yards north of the Persian artillery guns. The point of landing was relatively clear of date trees, although swampy and intersected by creeks that clearly filled at high tide. Scattered musket shots covered the landing point and Ian watched as the fierce Scottish Highlander infantry – accompanied by grenadiers – poured ashore.

'Riflemen! Time to go ashore!' Ian yelled to his men.

He felt the mud grip his boots as he clambered from the troopship, followed by Conan and the rest of the company. Very little musket fire met them as the enemy skirmishers fell back at the advance of the British troops while the company slogged its way through the mud, relatively safe from enemy fire for the moment.

The order came down from General Outram's HQ that the company was to form a defensive ring to protect the British artillery being offloaded to provide support to the infantry. By mid-afternoon this was completed and the rising tide was filling the muddy creeks of the landing place. It was time to move. Ian was pleased to be with his company in the advance on the main Persian camp beyond a date grove on the riverbank.

En route, the company was fired on, but the musketry fire proved ineffective. From time to time Ian ordered his men to engage an enemy target, and the result was a string of dead Persians off to their flank, having foolishly exposed themselves to the lethally accurate Enfield fire.

The order was passed down to Ian that the infantry were to halt at the edge of the date grove. General Outram rode past Ian's company and Ian saluted him. The general returned the salute, calling out, 'Damned fine work by your men, Captain Forbes,' before continuing his reconnoitre of the enemy camp now clearly visible to the advancing British and Indian troops. The general sent forward troopers of the Scinde Horse to get a closer look. His military secretary who had gone with the Indian unit reported back that there were two camps on either side of a village and the Persians had drawn up their army into a formidable force to resist the advance. Even as he reported, the men with Outram's expedition could still hear the navy guns firing in the distance at a few remaining Persian guns.

A rider came to Ian, who was smoking his pipe and leaning on his rifle.

'Captain Forbes, General Outram would request that your company be used as skirmishers in our advance on the enemy encampments.'

The young lieutenant delivering the message was breathless with fear and excitement and Ian suspected that this was his first action.

'Inform General Outram that my men will be in place within ten minutes.'

The young officer saluted, wheeled his horse around and galloped away.

Ian called in his officers and senior NCOs to instruct them on their role in the advance. It was a quick briefing and the orders then delivered to each and every soldier. Under command of the junior officers the riflemen deployed to the front of the line arranged for the attack. Each rifleman moved forward, selecting any cover he could find, always ready to pick off an enemy target.

Ian had placed himself just behind his line of skirmishers with Conan at his side. They could clearly see the Persian troops opposite them prepared for battle near the town of Mohammerah. British artillery had been sent to their flank to provide cover fire, and the assault forces was composed of a combination of British and Indian infantry.

General Outram had chosen to initially attack the encampment to the left rear of the village where his opposite, the Shah-zadeh, had the bulk of his artillery and cavalry. It was obvious that the British general knew he must knock out the Persian's most potent weapons before taking on their infantry in the second encampment about five hundred yards to the right, where groves of date trees provided some cover for the Persians.

Ian gazed at the distant target and felt a knot in his stomach. They were to advance across an open plain. This would be the time they were most vulnerable and it was possible many of his skirmishers might die.

Bugles and drums signalled the advance, and Ian stepped forward, his rifle across his chest as his own company moved well forward of the red squares of the vastly outnumbered advancing British troops.

'Tell Molly that I died well this day,' Conan mumbled as he and Ian trudged forward, acutely aware that they would probably be the first to die when the enemy commenced firing. Ian was very aware of the love that existed between the colonial Irishman and the pretty Welsh girl. Molly was the sister of Owen Williams; a bright, educated young woman who had invested her brother's money – as well as Conan's – into a very successful confectionary shop in London.

'You bloody well tell her yourself,' Ian replied, staring at the mass of waiting enemy still holding their fire. Range was all-important to the much shorter-range enemy muskets, and Ian was pleased to hear the occasional crack of one of his riflemen opportunistically firing at a target.

Before the advancing British formations, the Shah's army seemed to dissolve. They could see the Persians fleeing the front lines, throwing away their arms in their haste to make their retreat faster.

'Bloody hell!' Conan swore, hardly believing his eyes. 'The bastards are running away when they had the best opportunity to defeat us in our advance!'

A strange thought went through Ian's mind that it was, indeed, too nice a day to die.

'Conan, spread the word to the skirmishers to keep a lookout for landmines,' he said, aware that the Persians often buried casks of gunpowder with protruding metal tubes that when stood on fired a charge into the powder. He had witnessed the devastating effect of such hidden weapons in the Crimea.

Suddenly there was a massive explosion from within the Persian camp and the shock wave almost blew Ian off his feet. A thick column of smoke rose into the blue skies and he guessed that the fleeing Persians had detonated their reserves of ammunition. The British squares continued the advance until they were inside the rows of tents. The desert earth was strewn with muskets, small-arms ammunition, bedding, carpets, saddlery, band instruments and even half-eaten meals. Amongst the debris of war were a few unexploded British artillery shells. Very few Persian wounded remained and it appeared that most of the wounded had been carried away or had sought refuge in the nearby village.

General Outram would not rest until he had finally cornered the Persian army and brought them to the point of surrender. He ordered his units to continue the pursuit, leaving the Persian camp behind. Outram despatched his Scinde cavalry to track the path of retreat but they returned to report that the enemy were fleeing so fast that only cavalry reinforcements had any hope of catching them.

The order was given to camp for the night, which proved to be bitterly cold in the open. Neither soldier nor officer had tents, and after looking to the welfare of his junior officers and their men, Ian huddled by a small fire that Conan had been able to make. A tin pot boiled water for a much-anticipated cup of hot tea. They were joined by Corporal Owen Williams, who was offered a spare mug.

'We never had the chance to go through the Persian's camp for any loot,' Owen complained.

'No doubt the local villagers have done the job already,' Conan added, sipping his black tea and adding a good dose of sugar to sweeten it.

'You are both alive, that has to be a consolation,' Ian said, poking at the small fire as if attempting to extract more heat from it. 'This war is not over and we might run into a rear-guard defence by the Persians. They still outnumber us.'

'What I wouldn't give right now to be back in that pub near the barracks with an ale and a big meal of Yorkshire pudding by the log fire,' Conan sighed.

'You forgot to mention Molly on your lap,' Ian grinned, knowing that his friend had promised the pretty Welsh woman that he would marry her when his term of enlistment was up.

Conan glanced at Owen, a hint of self-consciousness visible on his face in the flickering shadows of the campfire. 'That, too,' he said quietly.

'You had better do the right thing by my sister, boyo,' Owen said good-naturedly.

Rank and class did not exist around this small campfire under the Persian night sky. These were three friends bound by blood and war.

'What do you think General Outram and Brigadier Havelock plan to do next?' Conan asked.

'If I were them, I would continue to pursue the Persians upriver until they sue for peace,' Ian replied. 'We have a formidable flotilla of warships, and from what I have gleaned the enemy has a well-fortified position on the river at Akwaz.'

Conan nodded, trusting Ian's knowledge of military tactics and strategy.

In the darkness a jackal yipped its call and the three men settled into the comfort of their companionship and small campfire.

*

When the sun rose over the desert the order was given to return to the town of Mohammerah and occupy the abandoned Persian camp. By day Ian's company took shelter under the shade of the date palms, but they moved camp to the desert at night to avoid the malarial waterways. They moved between diurnal swarms of annoying flies and nocturnal clouds of biting sandflies. Ian had to release many of his company to guard private property in the town, which at least garnered respect from the local inhabitants who had expected their homes to be looted and burned to the ground. Nonetheless, the British army had acquired great stores of grain, a good amount of ammunition and some cannons left behind by the retreating Persian army. However the stench of unburied Persian soldiers mixed with the other pungent smells around the town, so it was not a pleasant place to be.

Mohammerah was located at the junction of the Karoon and Euphrates rivers and was a filthy mud-bricked settlement with a large bazaar. Its only redeeming feature was the governor's house with its well-maintained gardens. The town was surrounded by a patchwork of swamp and cultivated farmland. Beyond the village was an endless horizon of flat desert. The river was the lifeblood of the people, who lived as they had for thousands of years. Throughout the day the British and Indian troops heard the routine call to prayer from the tall minarets of the mosques.

Ian had a chance to tour the town and was impressed by the variety of fruit trees in the governor's garden. He saw apple, mulberry, plantain and pomegranate trees side by side and noticed a small boy selling the fruit by the road. Ian guessed the boy had used the confusion of the fighting to raid the orchards, and admired his enterprise. Ian purchased a basket of mixed fruits for distribution amongst his troops and determined to send back a party of his men with money to purchase more so that each man would have at least one piece of fruit.

Ian had been tasked with carrying out a review of the Persian defences, accompanied by a villager who had a good grasp of English. The old man had once worked in the lucrative local trading houses when goods from India had poured into the town. Conan also went with Ian, as well as a platoon under the command of Lieutenant Sinclair. They crossed to the right bank to examine the earthen ramparts the Persians had erected and came across three dead horses still harnessed to a capsized gun carriage. The bodies were bloated and decomposing, covered in clouds of evil-looking flies. Beside the carnage lay four human bodies with massive injuries, and it was apparent that an English naval shell had found its mark, taking out the gun crew. Ian recognised the rank of captain on one of the corpses and knelt down to search his stretched uniform, maggots falling onto the sandy desert as he did so. He slipped a letter out of one of the pockets and passed it to his interpreter.

'What does it say?' Ian asked as his men stood upwind of the foul stench of death.

The interpreter scanned the letter. 'The man writes that

he might die in the great battle to come, and wishes that his brother in Tehran look after his wife and children if that happens.' He passed the letter back to Ian, pointing out a forwarding address.

'Sergeant, see that this letter is passed on to brigade HQ for posting,' Ian ordered.

Conan frowned. 'Yes, sah. It will be done.'

The party spent the rest of the day moving amongst the shattered bodies of their enemy. Arms, legs, decapitated heads and entrails lay scattered around them as they continued the review of the defences on the riverbanks. It was not a day Ian wanted to repeat, and that night he prayed that the advance would continue and put some distance between them and this obscene place of death. He had made the same prayer when he was in the Crimea.

Over the next couple of days, the expeditionary force of British and Indian troops went about the business of landing more stores, including tents. The work kept the men of Ian's company busy whilst General Outram planned his next move. As Ian had predicted, the fortified town of Akwaz, on the river upstream, was his objective.

Ian's company was to board the steam warships allocated the task of taking the town by force of arms. This time it appeared the enemy was going to make a determined stand and Ian knew that his company's bayonets would be stained red in the battle to come. He also knew that many would likely be killed and wounded, and the faces of his soldiers boarding the Indian navy ships showed that they knew it too.

Ian had little interest in the politics of campaigning. All he knew of their reason for being in Persia was that an emir in the Afghan province of Herat had rebelled against the occupying Persians and, with the support of the Kabul emirate, had appealed to the British in India for support. He knew, too, that the reasons for war were complex and varied. What really mattered to Ian was that God was on their side – and the Enfield rifled musket.

FIVE

There had been an air of unspoken tension between Alice and her husband since his return. It annoyed Alice as she knew she had nothing to feel guilty about. She had remained loyal to Peter, although she had to admit that Scott flirted with her whenever he had the opportunity.

The endless round of tea parties, visits to the homes of influential families of the East India Company and afternoons spent under the shady trees of the villa garden were becoming boring. It was as if she was still in England, albeit with an unfamiliar world beyond the gates.

One way to break the boredom was to visit the local markets where the colourful mix of people and cultures never failed to fascinate Alice. Whenever she took a trip to the markets Scott had insisted that one of his troopers accompany her to keep away the riffraff that loitered to pick pockets or even rob the wealthy – Indian mostly,

English rarely through fear of the severe reprisals that might follow.

Alice had planned such a trip today and was waiting impatiently at the spacious residence for her escort, who had failed to arrive at the designated time. Peter was away treating some of the poorer residents of the Bengali town, so apart from the servants going about their daily chores, the house was deserted. Alice impulsively decided to go to the markets on her own. After all, she had looked into the eyes of a tiger and defeated the great and magnificent beast.

Parasol aloft, Alice made her way out of her relatively safe neighbourhood dominated by European homes. After several wrong turns she eventually found herself in the marketplace crowded with vendors selling everything from local produce to imported silks. A man sat cross-legged playing a musical instrument Alice did not recognise whilst a deadly cobra appeared to sway to the rhythm of the music. Alice stopped for a moment to watch in fascination at the seeming bravado of the turbaned man in the loincloth and dropped a couple of coins at his feet, carefully keeping her distance from the hooded snake. She approached a stall festooned with colourful silks and began looking through them. Gradually she became aware that the mood of the people around her seemed unusually sullen. A man bumped into her roughly and growled something in a language she did not understand. Others in the marketplace cast angry looks at her. Something had changed since her last visit and she experienced a twinge of unease.

'This might not be a good time for an Englishwoman to be alone in the markets,' a familiar voice said behind her, and Alice turned to see the Khan. He was not dressed in his finery but wore a loose-fitting long shirt over a skirt-like cloth wrapped around his waist. He was accompanied by a bodyguard of four bearded men wearing turbans and armed with curved swords. The silk vendor bowed his head, obviously recognising the importance of the man speaking with the Englishwoman.

'Prince, it is good to make your acquaintance again,' Alice said, relieved to have his immediate protection. 'It appears that the people here resent my presence.'

'It is understandable when one knows of the hanging of a mutineer leader, Pandey, at the Barrackpore barracks,' Khan said. 'His stand against the Queen's Empire made him a hero to the common people, and now he is a martyr to them. You are in the wrong place at the wrong time, and I would strongly suggest that you allow me to escort you safely from the markets. My palace is only a short distance from here, and I am sure you would like to see how the other half live.' There was something facetious in his last words, and they were accompanied by the hint of a smile.

Alice had to admit to herself that she was fascinated by the Indian prince, who was handsome, charming, very intelligent and had a wry sense of humour.

The crowd made a pathway for the prince and his bodyguards as they escorted the Englishwoman away, closing behind them with shouts of anger. It seemed the prince had arrived just in the nick of time. Soon Alice was free of the stifling mob and on a wide avenue lined with shade trees. They walked for a distance until the pungent smell of the markets was behind them. Eventually they came to a whitewashed wall surrounding a magnificent building rising three storeys above the street.

A great wooden gate ornately adorned with Arabic script swung open and the party of six entered a beautiful garden with manicured lawns and flowing stone fountains. Servants in loincloths tended the garden and well-dressed male and female servants greeted them at the top of the broad stone stairs leading into the palace.

'So this is how the other half live,' Alice said with a grin, feeling secure and comfortable in the company of the young man who wielded such power.

'Perhaps you might enjoy a cool sherbet before you are escorted back to your husband,' the Khan said politely. 'I am sure that my wife would love to meet with the daughter of Kali.'

Alice was fascinated with this introduction to the palace of one of the ruling elites of the Bengal region. From what she had learned from Scott, these princes owed their positions to their alliance with the East India Company.

'I would be honoured to meet your wife,' Alice said as the prince escorted her to a room with marble floors and sumptuous divans. Two servants hovered nearby and the Khan issued instructions. They disappeared and moments later a beautiful dark-eyed young woman wearing a long silken dress embroidered with pearls entered the room with a young boy Alice guessed to be around five years old. He was dressed in the rich traditional clothing of an adult, with a turban, like a miniature version of the Khan on the tiger hunt.

'This is my wife, Sari, and my firstborn son, Ali,' the Khan said. 'Neither speaks English but I will be sending my son to England to be educated next year.' The boy standing by his mother stared intently at Alice, and the prince noticed.

'My son has never seen a beautiful Englishwoman with hair the colour of gold,' he smiled. 'I think he would like to touch your hair.'

'If he wishes,' Alice replied, and the Khan summoned his son forward. Very gently the boy reached up to touch the hair piled on Alice's head. He looked into her eyes and smiled shyly, before running back to his mother, who smiled with the same shyness. The Khan spoke some more words and Alice could see a sudden look of interest in Sari's dark eyes.

'I told her how you single-handedly killed the tiger,' he said. 'My wife is impressed. You may be the daughter of Kali to my Hindu subjects, but I suspect that you are our Queen's tiger to your own people. But now I should extend our hospitality.'

As if on cue the two servants returned with silver trays upon which were crystal glasses filled with sherbet and ice. They were set down on a low polished teak table and soft cushions were brought for the Khan and Alice. Alice realised that the prince's wife and son had disappeared from the room. She suspected it was not quite proper for her to be alone with the Indian prince, but to say so would only cause offence; besides, she was intrigued. She took a cushion opposite the Khan and accepted the glass he passed her. The thick, cold drink was delicious.

'Why do the people resent us?' Alice asked without the polite niceties of genteel conversation.

The prince raised his eyebrows at her bluntness. 'I am sure that Major Campbell has told you about the issue of the cartridge cases,' he said, sipping his own drink. 'But there is the underlying issue of being free from the yoke of the British or, in our case in Bengal, the East India Company.'

'But my brother-in-law has informed me that you hold your position because of the East India Company's administration of this region of India.'

'Before you English came, my father and his father before him ruled an area ten times larger than I do now,' the Khan said, and Alice noticed that he was frowning. 'The Company cunningly took our lands for their own purposes and promised that they would protect my rule. But now they have disobedience in the ranks of the army and I fear this will become a full-scale rebellion by the people of India bent on throwing out all Europeans.'

'If that eventuates, how would it affect your family?' Alice asked.

For a moment the Indian prince did not answer. 'I would have to see which way the winds of war blew,' he said in a quiet voice. 'My priority is the survival of my family and my regime. But I do know that it is very much in the Company's interests to ensure my safety.'

His answer sent a chill up Alice's spine, and for the first time she had a sense that she and Peter ought to cut short their stay in India, despite Scott's reassurances that the mutinous acts of the East India troops were being squashed. How could such a tiny number of Company soldiers and administrators guarantee control over a land of such huge geographic size and vast multitudes of people?

'I have arranged to have my carriage take you back to Major Campbell's residence,' the Khan said, as if displeased with the conversation Alice had initiated. 'It has been a pleasure having you under my roof for this very brief time. My servants have almost finished preparing the pelt of the tiger. I will have it sent around when it is ready.' He rose, extending his hand to assist Alice from her cushion. She accepted and felt his firm grip linger even when she was on her feet.

'You are a beautiful woman in any culture,' he said softly. 'Dr Campbell is a fortunate man to have you in his bed.'

'And you are similarly fortunate to have such a beautiful wife and son,' Alice stammered, embarrassed by his choice of words. She slipped her hand from his and bade him farewell.

Alice was escorted to the carriage and delivered to her residence. She was met by Peter, who was standing in the gateway as she alighted from the coach. She could immediately see the dark expression on his face.

'I was informed that you left for the markets without a bodyguard,' he said by way of a greeting. 'If I am not mistaken, that is the local prince's coach.'

'I chose to go to the markets alone as the trooper Scott assigned me did not keep his appointment. I have been before without mishap but, I must confess, the crowd in the markets was not very hospitable and I was fortunate the Khan happened to be in the area and could provide me with a safe escort home. He has proved to be a good and honourable man.'

Peter frowned and without a word turned and strode back to the bungalow. Alice hurried after him.

'Peter, what is wrong?' she asked, and Peter suddenly stopped.

'Do you know how this looks to the people who live here?' he said with a pained expression on his face. 'Every time I go out on my medical rounds you seem to find entertainment in the company of my brother – and now that has extended to the local royalty. Do you know that the Khan has four wives?'

'I did not know that,' Alice answered. 'I only met one of his wives, and her son.'

'That is the low morality of these people,' Peter said. 'Bloody harems and forced marriages. Is that the type of person you would rather socialise with than your husband?'

'That is not true, and nor is it fair,' Alice exploded. 'I love you, and I have no romantic interest in any other man. Surely you know that.'

'All I know is that you get presents from a bloody native

prince and my own brother takes to you as if you were more than his sister-in-law. All my childhood Scott was the favoured son and would make a point of taking anything that I valued. Now I think he wants you.'

Alice was disturbed by Peter's revelation of his insecurity. It had never occurred to her that this gentle and courageous man who lived to make other people's lives better could doubt her love for him.

'I think we should consider returning to England,' Alice said.

'Would that change anything?' Peter retorted. 'Or would you find comfort in the arms of another man there?'

Shocked, Alice stumbled in tears to their room, leaving Peter standing alone.

He cursed himself and shook his head. What was wrong with him? He walked slowly to the garden, grabbing a bottle of unopened Scotch whisky on the way. He did not need a glass. He would drink from the bottle.

Peter sat down on a stone bench. It was mid-afternoon and the hot sunlight blazed down, filtered through the leaves of the shady trees. If only Samuel were here to talk with, Peter thought, and not off somewhere in the biblical lands of Mesopotamia fighting another war for the Queen. Alice's brother was Peter's closest friend. The soldier and the surgeon had shared so much on the battlefields of the Crimea only months before. No doubt Samuel would tell him that he was acting as an insanely jealous man and that he should put more trust in Alice.

Peter opened the bottle and took a long swig. Meanwhile Alice lay on the big bed, sobbing tears of frustration for her husband's lack of trust. She only wished that her brother Samuel could be here to talk sense into the man.

*

Captain Ian Steele watched as his men boarded one of the three steamers conveying troops up the river to engage the Persian army. He was pleased to see the look of confidence in their faces as they passed, and many gave him a nod of respect.

Ian had attended the briefings at brigade HQ and knew that what lay ahead would take lives, but he reminded himself that this was the lot of professional soldiers. He was reassured to learn that the naval commander of their small fleet was a man with a considerable reputation in similar campaigns in Burma and China.

A company of Highland infantry had boarded the steamer lying alongside their own, and a cheerful banter was exchanged between the English and Scottish troops. Ian could see that morale was high amongst his men.

At ten o'clock in the morning the steamers pulled out of Mohammerah. The steamship the *Comet* led the flotilla, towing the slower *Assyria*, whilst the *Planet* brought up the rear. Each steamer also towed a gunboat armed with two twenty-four-pounder howitzers, artillery guns capable of firing at a high angle to drop explosive shells behind fortified constructions. Ian passed the order for the men of his company to prepare the tea that the British army marched on.

'At least we don't have to march to the next battle,' Conan said beside Ian. 'And this is not as bad as the bloody troopship that brought us to Persia. At least it is hard to get seasick on the river.'

'Very true, Sergeant Curry,' Ian said. 'I'd consider transferring to the navy if all wars were fought on rivers. No marching through sleet and cold, or living in the open in drifts of snow, wondering if rations will be delivered to fill my empty stomach.'

'But it is the seasickness,' Conan said, knowing that his company commander had suffered badly on the sea voyage to Persia.

'Yes, the bloody seasickness,' Ian replied with a twisted grin. 'How about you fetch us a mug of tea as sweet as you can make it, Sergeant?'

Conan nodded and went in search of tea. Ian gazed across the water at the right bank of the waterway fringed with palm and date trees intermingled with shepherd boys grazing their herds of goats. How far he had come from the riverbanks of his favourite swimming hole in the shadow of the Blue Mountains that hemmed in Sydney Town. The real Ian Steele was long dead now, and he was Samuel Forbes.

SIX

Great flocks of duck and teal scattered before the bow wakes of the war steamers pushing up the river. On the banks dwarf poplar and thick willow trees flanked the flotilla, beyond which the desert dominated, with the occasional tufts of coarse, dry grass. No longer were there orchards of date palms or any other signs of human habitation.

This was what the real Garden of Eden must have looked like, Ian thought as he stood gazing out at the riverbanks.

It was just after sunset when the flotilla anchored below the ruined Arab fort of Kootul-el-abd. Ian landed with a party of officers and found the fireplaces of the enemy's bivouac within fifty yards of the river. They also found the wheel marks of artillery guns and Ian knew they were closing on the retreating army as the impressions were relatively fresh.

The following morning the flotilla set off again, and by mid-afternoon the ruined mosque of Imaum was spotted.

Again, a party of officers landed and found evidence that the combined Anglo-Indian expeditionary force was yet closer to their objective. They found freshly dug graves and a ruined mud house that appeared to have been the temporary shelter for the Shah-zadeh himself. One thing Ian commented on to his fellow officers was the absence of the usual scraps of food around the enemy campsite. They agreed that the Persian force must be low on provisions. It was hoped that they might reach the vanguard of the retreating enemy before it could reach the prepared fortifications. However, the next day the flotilla ran into a series of narrow bends in the river where the water was channelled into a strong current that slowed them down.

On the third night the Anglo-Indian steamers came opposite the Arab village of Ismaini where information was gleaned that the Persians had passed by the previous day with seven regiments and two thousand cavalry. It was still a formidable force. A straggler from the enemy army had been captured. He was almost dead from hunger and informed his captors that a couple of the Persian commanders had died from their wounds and had been buried back at Imaum-Subbeh. More graves were discovered, and even the footprint of a desert lion.

Eventually the Arab encampment of Omeira was reached and the unwelcome news imparted that the previous day the Persians had arrived at their fortified base at the town of Akwaz, fourteen miles north of their current position.

The fleet was secured for the night against a surprise attack and a reconnaissance organised for the following day. Ian knew his men would see action tomorrow against a large dug-in enemy force. He gathered his company on the deck of their steamer and addressed them as to the forthcoming fight. He spoke calmly and reminded the red-coated soldiers that they were the finest light infantry in the British army and would make the regiment proud. His quiet and calming talk brought about a cheer from the men. Ian dismissed them and was joined by Conan.

'So, this is finally it,' Conan said, plugging his pipe and gazing at the star-filled sky rocking gently above.

'Let us hope that the Persians repeat their efforts of the last time we met them,' Ian said, also looking at the night sky, wondering if the people of the Bible had done the same thing in the times described in the Old Testament. 'I have noticed that Molly has been writing to you,' he commented.

'She is a grand lady,' Conan sighed. 'I don't know what she sees in me.'

'Neither do I,' Ian grinned. 'But she *is* a grand lady.'

'What about you, sir?' Conan asked. 'Is there someone waiting for you when we return to London?'

'I don't think there is anyone waiting for me,' Ian replied, but an image of the beautiful young Ella Solomon, waving goodbye to his ship steaming from the London port, flashed before him. He tried to dismiss the memory of her sad smile. There was no future for a soldier of the Queen and the daughter of Ikey Solomon, one of London's most ruthless men. After all, her Jewish religion put them in different worlds. Although Ian had been baptised a Catholic, he had never really been a religious man. His mother had been a Presbyterian who had despaired of her only child ever practising any Christian faith.

As well as Ella, there was Ian's first true love, Jane Wilberforce, who had mysteriously disappeared when she was pregnant with his child. Ian had not given up his search for her, even though it seemed very likely she was dead, probably at the hands of Charles Forbes. Jane's identical twin, Rebecca, certainly thought so. Rebecca had been adopted as a baby and raised by the rich and powerful Lord Montegue and his wife. The sisters had been reunited in secret only months before Jane's disappearance.

The bell on the steamer tolled the time, as was the naval tradition.

'Funny how you think about those you love just before a battle,' Conan reflected as he puffed on his pipe. 'I suppose it is somewhat selfish to do what we do. If we fall, we leave the living to continue without us.'

'From what I have heard of Molly's business she will not be destitute,' Ian consoled. 'But we aren't going to fall in battle tomorrow. It will be the other bugger.' He sighed. 'Right, it's probably time to get some sleep.'

Both men tapped their pipes on the boat's railing, watching the sparks of dying tobacco fall into the dark waters of the river.

Neither slept well that night on the deck under the Persian stars. Ian could hear the worried, whispered conversations of his company around him, and he understood their fears. Eventually, sleep came, but with it the endless nightmares of the Crimea as men were blown into scraps of bloody meat by the Russian artillery and bodies shattered by the hail of musket balls.

*

It was early dawn and the British flotilla steamed to within three thousand yards of the Persian defences, partly screened by a low range of sandhills. Three enemy artillery guns were seen positioned near a small mosque. Persian cavalry galloped along the bank, observing the flotilla.

Some Arabs hailed the war steamers from the bank and they were taken aboard. It was well known that the Arabs had no love for their Persian occupiers. They informed the

British high command that the force opposing them only consisted of around five hundred infantry and thirty cavalry, tasked with the protection of Persian army stores. It came as a pleasant surprise to the British force but also a caution that the enemy's main strength was somewhere ahead of the advance. It was decided that the town on the opposite bank should be taken as soon as possible as this would ensure the landing force was out of range of the deadly Persian artillery. As such, one of the gunboats was tasked to engage the enemy guns.

Again, Ian gave the order to fix bayonets, and his company was landed midmorning. The order came down that his best men were to be deployed as skirmishers, leading the files of Scottish Highlanders into the town. The order to the troops was to destroy any enemy supplies they encountered. In the distance Ian could hear the explosions of the artillery duel between gunboat and on-shore Persian artillery.

Ian, with the bulk of his company, followed his skirmishers, ever alert to any possible resistance from enemy snipers. They did not see any civilians on the streets and alleyways, which were bordered by miserable stone and mud hovels, and Ian guessed they had wisely remained indoors. But it appeared after some time that the town was undefended.

'Sir! Sir!' A young officer from Brigadier Havelock's brigade staff hurried towards Ian, his face flushed with excitement. 'Compliments of the brigadier. He wishes all his officers to know that the Persian commander has surrendered.'

'Why in bloody hell would they cede to us when they have the advantage of numbers and arms?' Ian frowned. 'Is it some kind of trick?'

'From what I have heard, the sheik has bad memories

of our bombardment back at Mohammerah, and is under the impression that our expeditionary force is merely the vanguard of a much larger force,' the young officer replied with a smile. 'It appears that his army has chosen to retreat another hundred miles to Shuster. The brigadier has also issued an order that none of the private homes in the town are to be looted.'

Ian passed on the order to his company and retired to the riverbank as the Scots continued guarding the town and searching for supplies. He and his men watched the vast Persian army marching away. They had no provisions and had chosen starvation over confronting the numerically smaller Anglo-Indian force.

The Persian cavalrymen numbered around two thousand and wore the distinctive black lamb-skin cap. They wore long blue robes, lighter coloured trousers and a white belt. Each cavalryman carried a sabre, with a matchlock musket slung across his back. They appeared to Ian to be a formidable enemy and he shook his head in disbelief at their retreat.

Suddenly a musket shot broke the silence and Ian saw that one of the cavalrymen had concealed himself as his unit retreated. The shot was wild and fired towards the town before he leapt on his mount and galloped away to join his squadron.

'At least one of the buggers made a stand,' Conan chuckled. 'I think the boys are pleased that they did not bloody their bayonets.'

'So am I,' Ian said. 'The best kind of war is one where no one gets killed – except for the foe. But you can bet we will get back on the boats and steam after them. Sooner or later it will have to come down to a bloody confrontation.'

However, orders were issued to regain law and order in the town as the Arab occupants fought each other for the

Persian stores that had not been destroyed by the British troops. Conan grumbled that they were not acting as fighting troops but as policemen.

Ian and his company of men camped outside the town, awaiting further orders. From here they could see the snow-topped Bakhtiari Mountains a hundred miles away rising above the arid desert lands.

A day later Ian and his company boarded the warships and steamed back downstream to Mohammerah, where a fully functioning city of army tents awaited them a mile from the town on the vast plain. The returning men were also provided with the welcome news that a peace treaty had been signed in Paris, bringing to an end the small but decisive war with the Persian empire. Ian's company was to re-join the regiment and return to England.

A translated copy of the *Tehran Gazette* provided some amusement to the soldiers before they departed. The version published for the local population proclaimed that the British army had suffered terrible casualties in their encounters with the Persian forces along the river; in fact the British had been soundly defeated.

Conan found a copy of the newspaper, tore it up and wandered off in search of privacy to put the paper to good use.

★

In the sumptuous villa of Major Scott Campbell, the tension grew between Alice and Peter. Very few words passed between them but their schism continued in relative privacy as Scott was often away dealing with the ongoing unrest amongst the sepoy troops.

Peter spent the days tending to the local people. He had set up a clinic to treat the many exotic diseases and injuries presented by the people who waited for him in long lines.

His reputation as a healer spread, and he received the gratitude of the poverty-stricken populace.

One evening in April Scott returned home to inform Alice and Peter that he was being posted west to a Bengali regiment at a place called Meerut near the city of Delhi.

'I think you should both travel with my squadron,' Scott said, pouring himself a large whisky from a crystal decanter. 'After all, you have seen so little of the country.'

Alice frowned. She would prefer to depart India and return to England. She could sense the hostile glares of the people on the streets whenever she travelled to and from Scott's residence to the houses of other Europeans. She felt that she was living on the slopes of a dormant volcano rumbling its warning of an imminent eruption.

'Alice and I intend to return to the coast and take a steamer back to England,' Peter said, and Alice glanced at her husband, pleased to hear him express her wishes.

'I have an ulterior motive, old chap,' Scott said. 'We could do with a battle-experienced surgeon to accompany us to Meerut. I feel there may be some unrest amongst the natives and I know that you will be safer with me rather than risking a journey to the coast by yourselves. It will only be until we settle this matter with our sepoys, then things will get back to normal and it will be safe to travel again.'

'Is it that bad?' Alice asked quietly.

Scott turned to her. 'I do not wish to alarm you, but we need time to get the situation under control. In the past a few rabble-rousers have attempted to stir up trouble and the East India Company has quelled it.'

Peter turned to his wife. 'What do you think?' he asked gently, and Alice felt a surge of love for the man who had in recent weeks avoided her.

'I will let you decide, Peter,' she replied.

For a long moment Peter pondered his decision. 'I accept the opportunity Scott has offered us to see more of India. It is not worth the risk of returning to the coast until the Company has ended the unrest.'

Scott swallowed the last of the whisky and held out his hand to Peter. 'Good show, old chap. I promise our journey will reveal to you both the real India, the one so many in England only read about. It will be an adventure, and you will always be safe around my men and I.'

Alice gave a wan smile, and Peter reached for the decanter of whisky to pour himself a stiff drink.

'I have to return to the barracks but will inform the commander and have extra provisions made for you both. I must apologise that we will not be able to take a carriage but we will provide good horses for your journey. We leave within forty-eight hours.'

When Scott had departed, Alice went to Peter. 'You were gracious enough to ask my opinion on whether to leave now or later,' she said. 'You must know that I am your wife and love you more than any other man in the world. No matter your decision I would have happily agreed.'

Peter did not reply but took a long sip of the fiery liquid as Alice walked to their bedroom, which she had not shared with her husband for some time.

He watched her leave and pondered her words and actions. He placed the stopper back in the decanter, leaving his almost full glass, and followed her. It was time to swallow his self-righteous pride and ask forgiveness for his unfounded jealousy.

SEVEN

Back in Bushehr Ian delivered his report of the river campaign to regimental HQ where it was read by his commanding officer, Colonel Jenkins.

Ian stood at attention while Jenkins finished reading the report.

'So, you brought no glory to the regiment,' Jenkins scowled.

'We gained a lot of experience for the regiment,' Ian replied. 'Of more importance is that we did not lose any men to enemy action.'

'We have been ordered to return to England,' Jenkins said. 'According to regimental records you are due a month's leave, and tomorrow you are to report to General Outram's HQ before we depart. God knows why when you have done nothing of any significance with Havelock's brigade.'

Ian guessed that the general was simply going to thank him for his command of the rifle company on the river expedition. When he looked into the face of his commanding officer he saw the bitterness of being left out. After all, unlike the earlier clashes of the Anglo-Indian forces who first arrived in this war and saw bloody action, this expedition had proved relatively safe, and Ian knew from past experience that this would have suited Jenkins well. A chance for glory without the danger.

'You may go, Captain Forbes,' Jenkins growled, and Ian stepped back, saluted and left the regimental commander stewing in his anger and resentment.

The next day Ian reported to General Outram's HQ, one of the better buildings in Bushehr.

'Captain Forbes, please be at ease and take a seat,' the general said kindly. 'I wanted you to know that your service with my expeditionary force and the way you led your company were exemplary. I must admit that I am bitterly disappointed the Persians did not stand and fight. I would have liked to have shown them the truth worth of British arms.'

'By simply being on the battlefield we succeeded in winning the war, sir. And that, I believe, is the prime reason for our existence,' Ian said.

The general smiled. 'You sound more like a damned politician than a soldier, Captain Forbes. But I have another reason for summoning you here. This correspondence has been sent to me from London concerning one of your men, a Sergeant Curry.' Ian took the sheet of paper with the royal coat of arms embossed on it and read the few words written there. Ian's eyes widened and he let out a small gasp.

'Do you concur with the elements of the letter, Captain Forbes?' the general asked.

'I most certainly do, sir,' Ian replied, passing back the sheet of paper.

'Then as Sergeant Curry is currently still under my command, it is done, and I think I do not have to tell you that the contents of the letter remain a secret between us until the appropriate time.'

A faint smile passed across Ian's face. 'Sir, I completely agree, and thank you.'

'Sergeant Curry should be thanking you, Captain Forbes, as it was you who submitted the original report.'

'Sergeant Curry is a fine soldier and deserves what he has won,' Ian said.

'Before you return to your regiment I want you to know that my offer of a place on my staff will always stand. I am returning to India after this rather unsatisfactory campaign and expect to see some real soldiering there.'

'Thank you, sir,' Ian said respectfully. 'I am honoured that you would want me on your staff.'

'You are free to leave now,' General Outram said, and Ian stepped back, snapped the best salute he could muster, and marched out of the office with the words of the report swirling in his head. He knew that what was to occur in England would change Conan Curry's life forever.

⋆

It had taken just over two weeks to journey across the Atlantic Ocean by steamship from New York in the United States of America to Liverpool on the west coast of England. The real Samuel Forbes and his friend, James Thorpe, had travelled in style as befitted their wealth – or rather, James' wealth. After disembarkation they travelled by coach and steam train to London, where Samuel travelled under the assumed guise of Ian Steele, English traveller and man of means.

At the end of their long trip a coach brought them to a respectable gentlemen's club on London's Pall Mall.

'I feel that you have made a bad choice in returning to London,' James said fretfully as a porter unloaded their luggage. 'What if you are recognised?'

'Do not worry, my dear James, it has been so long since I was last in England that I cannot think of anyone who would recognise the callow youth who left these shores so long ago. I doubt anyone would ever remember me from my time in England.'

'According to your friend Jonathan, Captain Forbes is campaigning in Persia,' James said as they followed the porter into the expensive club. James had telegraphed ahead from New York to make reservations, and when they entered he was impressed by the elegance of the interior. 'But from what is printed in *The Times* it appears he will be returning soon as a treaty has been signed over the issue of Persian territorial claims in Afghanistan. I still think it is extremely risky for you two to meet in person.'

'I doubt that we look very much alike now, dear boy,' Samuel said. 'The risk is minimal.'

James was not reassured and had an uneasy feeling as they were ushered to separate rooms, elegantly laid out for visiting men of substance. They met later in the dining room where they were surrounded by many of London's most notable and wealthy merchants vying for a way into the ranks of the English aristocracy. James was further impressed by the decor and the dining room. They were shown to a table laid out with a white linen cloth and fine cutlery.

James perused the menu carefully. 'The meals here seem to reflect a certain amount of good taste,' he said, looking around. He shifted uncomfortably in his seat, glancing over Samuel's shoulder. 'I don't know if you are aware but a gentleman at the other end of the room seems to be watching us with more than the usual amount of interest. As a matter of fact, he is leaving his table to approach us.'

Samuel blanched. Who could ever recognise him after all this time? He'd been so sure he would go unnoticed.

'Mr Forbes, it has been a long time since we both served in New Zealand with the regiment,' said the tall man in his early forties, extending his hand.

Samuel recognised the man immediately. Captain Brooke was one of the commanders he had served under when his regiment had been garrisoned in New South Wales, before its deployment to New Zealand to face the fierce Maori warriors.

'I must have a rather unusually similar appearance to this Mr Forbes you mention,' Samuel said, standing and accepting the handshake. 'But, alas, I fear you have the wrong man. My name is Mr Ian Steele, of New York, sir.'

The tall man frowned. 'I must say that you bear an uncanny resemblance to an officer I once served with,' he said. 'I would dare to say you could pass as his twin. You even sound like him. I apologise for my interruption and will recommend the lamb cutlets if you are new to the club. The lamb comes from Wales.'

The man returned to his table shaking his head, and as Samuel sat down he realised that his hands were trembling.

'That was damned close,' James hissed, leaning across the table. 'I warned you that returning to London was a grave mistake.'

'I am sure that I was able to convince Captain Brooke I am not the man he thought I was,' Samuel replied, but James was not convinced. Already he could see another man joining Captain Brooke at his table and Brooke speaking and looking across at them. It was obvious what the subject of their talk was. Samuel had suddenly lost his appetite but knew he could not leave the dining room without first eating as that might raise further suspicion.

The lamb cutlets arrived and they were as good as Captain Brooke had promised. Both Samuel and James ate in relative silence and when the waiter arrived at their table they waved off any further courses. The journey had started on a sour note and Samuel was beginning to think that maybe he should have taken James' advice and stayed in New York.

*

A military band on the wharf met the troopship as it sailed in from Persia. Rain sleeted down from the grey spring skies of London. The regiment disembarked and the only people waiting to greet the returning soldiers were a few women and children – families of the soldiers. Unlike the farewell for the Crimea, the action in Persia had not attracted the attention of the English public who were used to troopships returning from the minor wars that glued the Empire together.

Amongst the people waiting on the wharf was Molly Williams, the love of Conan's life. She was waving with a small handkerchief and looked as if she was almost bursting out of her skin.

'You have a duty to your Welsh lass, Sergeant Curry,' Ian grinned.

'Yes, sah!' Conan replied, a smile so wide it seemed his whiskered face might split. He saluted smartly and hurried down the gangplank. He held out his arms and the slight, pretty young woman ran into them, embracing Conan tightly.

Ian felt good that the man who had come to be as close as a brother to him had found so much happiness. He knew it was stupid but he gazed around the crowd of civilians milling on the wharf for one particular face. Although he had not encouraged Ella's attraction to him, he admitted to himself that he would have given anything to see her upon his return. But the beautiful young Jewish woman was nowhere to be seen.

The regiment would soon fall into ranks and march with the band to their barracks, where many would be granted overdue leave. The pubs near the barracks would do well in the next few hours, and Ian arranged to have his kit taken to his club where he intended to have the most expensive meal on offer, followed by a couple of bottles of their best wine.

'Are we ready to fall in, sir?' Lieutenant Sinclair asked.

'Yes, Mr Sinclair, inform Sergeant Curry he is to parade the company and join the regiment.'

'Very well, sir,' the young officer replied, saluting and marching towards the gangplank.

Ian sighed. The young officer was so much like his brother, he thought. But Captain Miles Sinclair lay buried on the Crimean Peninsula – as did so many other fine British soldiers and officers.

*

Once he had been granted leave from the regiment and spent a luxurious night at his club, Ian made his way to Soho, to visit Ikey Solomon. He was met warmly by the big, bearded man with a handshake that almost crushed his hand.

Ian had hired the services of the shady but very wealthy Jewish entrepreneur to investigate the mysterious disappearance of his lover, Jane Wilberforce. Ikey had not been successful, but during their dealings Ian had met his beloved daughter, Ella, who had become smitten with him. Sadly their love was both dangerous and forbidden. Ian was a Catholic and she was of the Jewish faith. Such a match was frowned upon by both religions.

However, Ian had not been able to dismiss Ella from his mind and had decided he needed to see her again, despite all the obstacles facing them.

'So, my friend, you have returned from Persia,' Ikey said. 'I think your victory over the unbelievers requires a toast.'

Ikey produced a bottle of gin and poured two tumblers. One he handed to Ian.

'To the glory of the Queen's Empire,' he said, handing a tumbler to Ian. 'May the sun never set upon her.'

Ian responded, taking a swig then setting down his glass on Ikey's desk and taking a seat.

'What can I do for you?' Ikey asked, wiping his beard with the back of his big hand.

'I was hoping that you might have had some news on the whereabouts of the lady I sought before leaving for Persia,' Ian said.

A dark cloud spread across Ikey's face. 'I am afraid, my friend, that there has been nothing, and I can assure you that if Miss Wilberforce was in London I would know by now. My thoughts are that she may be dead.'

Ian took another sip of the clear, fiery liquid. 'I am afraid you might be right,' Ian said quietly. 'Now I need to know why – and who is responsible.'

'That is a matter for the police,' Ikey said.

'I doubt they would be interested in investigating the disappearance of a country girl from a Kentish village,' Ian replied. 'But I would put my trust in your people to keep an ear out for any rumours on the streets. I am prepared to pay.'

'There is no reason to pay me any more,' Ikey said. 'You were more than generous the first time. If I hear anything I will inform you immediately. You were very kind to my princess and I know that she speaks fondly of you.'

Ian felt a twinge of guilt as he knew Ella's feelings were more than fondness, and he remembered her passionate kisses when they had stolen time together.

'How is Ella?' Ian asked, trying to sound nonchalant, and noticed a touch of anger in Ikey's expression.

'The foolish girl has gone to America to study medicine. She has aspirations to become a surgeon – which is impossible, of course. Medicine is a man's profession. Unfortunately, she fell under the spell of Dr Elizabeth Blackwell. This Blackwell woman was able to receive her medical practitioner's certification after attending the Geneva Medical College in New York, and Ella has gone to America to attempt to enrol in that same college. I have foolishly provided financial support to her endeavour, but suspect she will return when they reject her admission.'

Ian remembered how Ella had said she wished to be a doctor, but even Dr Peter Campbell, more liberal-minded than most, had scoffed at her dreams to become a surgeon. Ian was disappointed to learn that Ella was on the other side of the Atlantic Ocean. But for now, while he had leave from the regiment, he had a mission. He would return to the Forbes manor in Kent and begin his own investigation into Jane's disappearance.

EIGHT

Samuel stood before the entrance door to the elegant tenement house in a salubrious part of London. He was trembling and he felt racked with guilt. He had told James he was going shopping for a new hat. When James had said that he would join him, Samuel had replied that he would prefer to go alone, leaving James hurt and disappointed.

The front door opened and a severe-looking middle-aged woman fronted Samuel.

'I am here to visit Master Jonathan,' Samuel said, passing her his calling card. 'I am sure he will accept me.'

Without a word the woman closed the door and Samuel continued to wait nervously. Within a couple of minutes the woman returned, ushering Samuel inside. She led him through a hallway adorned with paintings to a bedroom where an emaciated man lay back against heaped pillows.

Samuel was shocked when he looked upon his first love.

Jonathan lay pale, gaunt and sweating in the bed. Samuel smiled weakly at the face he had not seen since it belonged to a healthy young officer of the London barracks many years earlier.

'Ah, dear boy,' Jonathan said faintly and fell into a coughing spasm, spitting up blood into a handkerchief. 'You should not have come all the way across the ocean to see me in my present state.'

Samuel recognised the dreaded signs of consumption and knew that Jonathan was in the final stages of the insidious disease. 'When you wrote about your condition you did not say how bad it was,' Samuel said, moving across the room to the big double bed and standing over Jonathan. 'I would have come earlier if I had known.'

Jonathan reached out a hand and Samuel gently took it in his own. 'I am glad that I have the opportunity to see you one last time. I find comfort remembering when you and I were boys and discovered our love beneath the branches of the willow trees on your family estate. It was so beautiful by that stream watching the waters flow gently past,' Jonathan sighed.

'I often remember those times,' Samuel said softly, forcing back the tears.

'You have written of your friendship with an American,' Jonathan said. 'I do not blame you, dear boy. I know that your service for the Queen in the far-off colonies forced us apart. Possibly I could have followed you, but I selfishly chose to study at Cambridge. I confess that I too found a new lover. So do not grieve for what was lost between you and I. Time moves on and life must keep pace with it.'

'Is there someone in your life now?' Samuel asked.

'There was, but he is now with the Church and a rising force. He chose religion over me,' Jonathan said, a slight note of bitterness in his tone. 'But you are here in my last days on this earth,' he said, squeezing Samuel's hand. 'It is good to see you, though we both know that your being in London is putting your venture with Captain Steele in dire jeopardy.'

'I had to see you again,' Samuel said, tears now trickling down his cheeks. 'Nothing on earth was going to stop me.'

'You should return to New York immediately,' Jonathan gasped, a coughing spasm once again racking his frail body. When it was over he removed his hand from Samuel's and stared at the ceiling of his bedroom. Jonathan smiled. 'If only time and circumstances had been our friends . . . but you have always been an impulsive soul.' His voice tapered away.

The stern woman came back into the room. 'I think Master Jonathan should rest now,' she said, assessing her patient's condition. 'I am sure that you understand, Mr Steele.'

Samuel glanced down at the illness-ravaged face of his first love and realised that the nurse was correct. Jonathan was on the verge of drifting off after the emotional exertion their meeting had caused them both.

Jonathan's family was as wealthy as Samuel's, but his parents had distanced themselves from him when it had been revealed that his attraction was to those of his own sex. They had exiled him to this London property with a generous allowance, and even when he contracted consumption they did not visit him for the shame he had brought upon their family name. Instead they had appointed a full-time nurse as a way of compensating for the alienation.

Samuel leaned over his dear friend and former lover to brush aside the long, lank hair falling over Jonathan's eyes. He bent down and kissed Jonathan on the forehead and turned to walk away. Samuel could not bring himself to say goodbye; the word had a terrible finality to it.

He stumbled out onto the street and hailed a hansom cab.

As the horses clattered through the streets of London Samuel reflected on the emotions that had coursed through him upon seeing Jonathan after such a long time. He felt guilt that his passion of the past had not come rushing back to him, but at the same time he knew there were still remnants of his first love deep within his being.

Once back at the club, James immediately sensed that Samuel was extremely upset but wisely did not ask why.

Samuel turned to James with tears streaking his face. 'I love you, James. I always will.'

James felt the conviction in Samuel's words and was satisfied with that. Maybe now, he thought, they could get out of London and return to New York.

*

Ian took a carriage to the Forbes manor in Kent, and when he arrived he strode up to the grand entrance of the impressive stone building. He was met by the head servant, a man who had been informed that Master Samuel Forbes was barred from the house.

'I'm sorry, sir,' the man said, standing in the doorway, 'but I must ask Sir Archibald for permission for you to enter.'

'Do that,' Ian said and the man disappeared, closing the door behind him. After a while he returned and said that Sir Archibald would see him. Ian followed the servant inside and was met by the man who was supposed to be his father, although both men knew that he was not. The real Samuel Forbes had been fathered by Sir Archibald's brother, George, now living in the British colony of New South Wales as a successful farmer raising sheep for the lucrative wool trade.

'What are you doing here?' Sir Archibald asked in an angry voice. He was attired in a dressing gown and slippers. Ian thought that he had aged since the last time he had spoken with him. His hair was grey and thinning and he had lost weight. 'You know that I issued an order for you to be barred from my home.'

'I thought you might welcome home the man who is bringing glory to the Forbes name,' Ian said sarcastically. He knew this meant little to the English aristocrat; Sir Archibald was more interested in the profits the colonial wars brought to the Forbes fortune, supplying provisions to the army and navy.

'You still have not answered my question, Samuel,' Sir Archibald reiterated.

'I have leave from the regiment and thought that I might receive temporary accommodation in our house. After all, after ten years of service with my grandfather's regiment I will be entitled to a share. I promise I will not overstay my welcome.'

'I expect Charles to arrive tomorrow, and your presence here will not be welcomed by him.'

'I am sure that we can stay out of each other's way,' Ian said smoothly.

For a moment Sir Archibald appeared to consider the request.

'You may stay, but only in the guest cottage,' he relented. 'I will have the stableboy assist you with any luggage.' Sir Archibald issued an order for this to be done, then turned and walked away.

The stableboy arrived at the front entrance. 'Is there anything I can carry for you, Captain Forbes?' he asked, clearly in awe of the man whose reputation preceded him. He was a gangling youth in his late teens and awkward around this heroic figure.

'Just help me get my luggage inside the guest cottage,' Ian said. 'You must be Harold,' he added, and the boy puffed up with pleasure that Captain Forbes would remember his name.

'Yes, sir,' he replied. 'Most people just call me Harry.'

'Well, Harry, it is good to see that you are still in employment here.'

Ian was guided to the cottage, which was built of stone and comfortable enough. Harry placed the luggage inside the room and began to help unpack. His eyes widened when he saw two revolvers inside one of the captain's bags.

'Did you use those against the Persians, sir?' he asked.

'We did not get much of a chance to do any real fighting,' Ian replied, placing the pistols on a table for future cleaning. 'But they came in handy in the Crimea.'

Harry would have given anything to handle the big six-shot cap and ball pistols but he dared not ask.

'Have you ever held a pistol?' Ian asked, noticing the fascination on the boy's face.

'No, sir,' he answered.

Ian passed an unloaded pistol to him and Harry almost fell over in surprise. He took it gingerly in his hand.

'It's heavy,' he said, then blurted, 'I want to join up and go away to fight the Queen's enemies.'

Ian smiled, taking back the pistol. 'Soldiering is not an easy life, and there is always the chance you could be killed – or maimed,' he said gently. 'Life on the manor is much safer, and you don't have to sleep in the rain or march under the desert sun. I would think twice about joining the army if I were you.'

'Yes, sir,' the boy replied, disappointed that Ian had not encouraged his aspirations to become a soldier. 'But you get to go to places I have heard are strange and exotic.'

'That you do,' Ian said. 'But for now you have the estate's horses to tend to, and if you did ever enlist you might find the cavalry to your liking. They have fine uniforms and don't have to trudge the paths we do in the infantry.'

Harry departed to go to his duties, his head suddenly full of ideas of enlisting. Maybe he would consider the cavalry, but his real ambition was to be a member of Captain Forbes' company.

Ian organised for a horse to be saddled, and in the clear crisp spring air he rode to the village and secured his mount outside the pub. His arrival drew curious glances from a few of the locals hunched over tankards of ale and smoking pipes. Ian walked to the bar where a surly innkeeper wiped the suds of spilt ale from the counter.

Ian withdrew five gold coins from his jacket and placed them on the bar. The publican's eyes widened at the sight of the small fortune.

'Tell all your customers and anyone else in the village that whoever brings me information on the whereabouts of a former resident, Miss Jane Wilberforce, will have claim to this money.'

'The witch,' Ian heard one of the customers mutter.

Ian scooped up the coins and left, leaving a loud murmur of voices behind him. He had hardly stepped onto the street when he noticed young Harry standing by a small cart and horse. Ian recalled that Harry had mentioned he was to go into the village to pick up supplies. The boy was surrounded by three lumpish-looking lads and Ian could see that they were menacing him.

Ian strode over. 'Lads, you are preventing Harry from going about his duties for me,' he said, and the three older boys turned to face him.

'Who are you, mister?' the eldest asked with a sneer.

'Captain Samuel Forbes,' Ian replied. 'And killing is my profession.'

The latter statement was delivered with an icy edge that caused uncertainty to cross the faces of the three youths. They shuffled away with their hands in their pockets, unsure if the tough-looking but well-dressed gentleman was bluffing.

'What was that about?' Ian asked Harry when the three young thugs had disappeared.

'Ron Berwick says I have been too nice to his girlfriend, Emilia,' Harry said. 'He and his pals were going to teach me a lesson, but you stopped them. Thank you, sir.'

'I have no doubt that you could have taught Ron a lesson had he been alone. Have you been too nice to this Miss Emilia?'

'I like Emilia a lot, but I am poor, and she will step out with someone who has money, not me,' Harry sighed. 'If I had money, she might think about going for a walk with me to the river on Sunday when Sir Archibald allows us to attend church.'

'It sounds like Miss Emilia is another good reason for not joining the army,' Ian said. 'I don't think those three ruffians will bother you again today.'

He walked back to his horse, mounted it and rode out of the village past the ancient tree-topped hill where the small circle of Druid stones was located. It had become almost a shrine for Ian to the memory of Jane.

When he returned to the cottage a meal and bottle of wine was brought to him by one of the servants, and Ian was thankful for both. He had laid the bait and hoped the idea of owning the gold coins might prompt a response. Someone had to know something about Jane's disappearance.

*

News of the reward spread through the village faster than a bushfire in the colony of New South Wales.

Harry was loading the cart when the shopkeeper told him about Captain Forbes' announcement at the tavern. So that was why the captain had returned to the Forbes manor, Harry thought. He had heard gossip from the other servants that Charles Forbes had been known to visit the local witch, and from time to time Harry had glimpsed the beautiful young woman when he visited the village. He had trouble imagining Jane Wilberforce as a witch because all the stories he knew about witches described ugly old crones with warts on their faces. He was not sure why Captain Forbes would be interested in the woman's whereabouts, but he wished he had some information to give in exchange for the reward. If he had that much money, surely Miss Emilia, the daughter of the shopkeeper, would take him seriously and step out walking with him. He could buy a new suit of clothes and a beaver-skin hat.

As Harry journeyed home to the manor with the supplies that evening, a thought came to him. A while ago, and he thought it might have been around the time Jane Wilberforce disappeared, he had woken in the night when he'd heard Master Charles returning late on his horse. Harry had stumbled from his bed, but Master Charles had already gone up to the big house. Harry was still waiting in the stables some time later, wondering whether he was needed, when Master Charles hurried back in and saw him.

'I heard you return a while ago, Master Forbes, and thought that you might need my help putting away your horse,' Harry said nervously. He had always been somewhat afraid of Master Charles.

But the master had dismissed him curtly, and Harry had swiftly departed.

He hadn't been able to sleep, though, worried that the master's horse would need brushing down and feeding and watering, so Harry had crept back to the stables. There, as he tended to the horse, he'd found something under the hay.

Harry had recoiled when he smelled the blood. Nonetheless he picked up the item and saw that it was a frock coat soaked with blood. He recognised it at once as belonging to Master Charles. Had the master had an accident? he wondered, although the man had not appeared to be injured. Harry had suddenly grown frightened. He'd wrapped the jacket in a hessian cloth bag and hidden it behind a loose plank in a space between the walls where, he presumed, it still was.

Harry had dismissed the distressing memory – until now.

He knew that it was the downstairs kitchen staff who had all the gossip about the family. Bridie, the seventeen-year-old kitchen hand, always seemed to know the latest snippet of news.

Harry delivered the provisions to the kitchen, where Bridie was cutting carrots.

Harry did not know that Bridie had a crush on Master Charles, and that the skinny young girl with the lank hair daydreamed of being his wife. It was an impossible dream, but the young woman didn't care.

Oblivious to this, Harry sat down at the table where Bridie was working and decided to confide in the girl.

'Did you hear about the reward Captain Forbes has offered for any information about the disappearance of the witch who used to live in the village?' he asked.

'Everyone knows about the reward,' Bridie sniffed. 'A traveller told us this afternoon.'

'What do you think happened to her?' Harry asked.

'She was a witch, so it is possible she used her magic to disappear and is with the fairy people,' Bridie said, reaching for sticks of celery.

'Do you think that Master Charles might have done her some harm?' Harry asked cautiously.

Bridie paused, her hand hovering over the celery. 'Master Charles is a good man, he would do no one harm,' she answered defensively.

'What if I said I have something that might prove otherwise?' Harry said, and Bridie paled.

'You are a fibber, Harry, what could you possibly have that would show Master Charles harmed the woman?' she asked.

'I have a coat he was wearing one night and it is covered in blood. Maybe I should take it to Captain Forbes and see what he thinks.'

'Where is this coat then?' Bridie asked, trying to sound nonchalant.

'I hid it between some loose planks in the stables,' Harry said, pinching a piece of carrot and getting a slap on the hand from Bridie for his trouble.

Bridie seemed to contemplate this. 'Well, I don't think it is our business to meddle in our betters' affairs,' she said eventually. 'I think you should forget about the coat.'

Rather disappointed by this reaction, Harry left the kitchen to return to the stables, where he began to brush down the horses in his care. As he began rubbing down one of the stallions he decided that, despite what Bridie thought, he would take the frock coat to the guest cottage and give it to Captain Forbes. Maybe the coat was important and he would receive the reward, and with it Miss Emilia's respect. He was unaware that Bridie had already passed on his news to Master Charles, who reacted by telling the smitten young girl that she was to tell no one else under threat of dire punishment. Frightened by this reaction, the girl agreed.

The horse he was brushing snorted and shifted slightly. Harry realised he was no longer alone in the stables. Under the dim light of the lantern he turned to see who had entered and saw a shadowy figure approaching. Harry peered into the gloom and saw that it was Master Charles, a pitchfork in his hand. Before Harry could cry out, he felt searing pain in his chest.

He tried to scream but instead slumped to the ground, gasping out his last breath.

Charles withdrew the pitchfork prongs from Harry's chest and knelt to look into the eyes staring blankly at the roof of the wooden building. If what a breathless and excited Bridie had told him minutes ago was true, Charles was safer with this young miscreant out of the way.

Charles quickly went from one stall to the next, ripping away the old loose planks. Finally his terrible secret was revealed. He did not touch the mouldy item of clothing still stiff with the blood of Jane Wilberforce, but instead found a drum of kerosene which he tipped over, letting the liquid run along the stable floor. He went around and opened all the doors to the stalls, where the prized Forbes horses were stabled. Next he took a lantern, flinging it at the trail of kerosene, which burst into flame, enveloping the stableboy's body and licking at the dry hay all around. The fire ran up the old wooden walls, engulfing the stables in an inferno. The terrified horses bolted past Charles to safety.

Satisfied the fire as well alight, Charles retreated, leaving the evidence and potential witness to be consumed by the roaring flames.

He was already back in the manor when the alarm was raised. Charles raced outside in the dark with the servants, pleased to see that the building was beyond hope of saving. He shuddered when he saw Ian standing alone, watching the fire. It was too bad, Charles thought, that the man he most despised in this world had not also been in the burning building.

NINE

'He was a brave young lad,' Charles reflected as he, Sir Archibald and Ian stood at first light gazing at the smouldering ruins of the stables. Servants milled around sniffling back tears and, in a couple of cases, sobbing. Bridie stood to one side, pale-faced and silent. 'He must have released the horses when he realised that he had accidentally started the fire,' Charles continued.

Ian said nothing but began to poke amongst the ruins.

He found the barely recognisable charred corpse of Harry lying on his back, hands curled inwards like a boxer's. Ian was used to death, so he leaned over to examine the remains of the naïve and gentle lad. What struck him were the two almost bayonet-like wounds to his chest. They could hardly be seen by the untrained eye but they were clear to Ian from his experience of seeing charred bodies on the battlefields of the Crimea. Nearby he saw the head of a pitchfork used to toss hay, and he noticed that the spacing of the wounds was approximately the same as the distance between two of the prongs of the pitchfork.

'We will arrange a decent Christian burial for the boy,' Sir Archibald said. 'He deserves at least that much for saving the horses.'

Ian stepped back from the corpse and walked across to Charles.

'Where were you when the fire started?' he asked in an icy voice.

Charles looked startled, stepping back a pace. 'I am not sure what you are suggesting but I resent your insinuation. As a matter of fact I was in the house, and in any case, why on earth would I want to cause any injury to young Harold? What has happened here is a terrible accident.'

Ian knew he could not prove Charles had been involved in Harry's death, even if he could persuade the police to investigate, which was unlikely given the Forbes' influence. He stared hard into Charles' face, which still bore the faint scars of the time Ian had attacked him before steaming to the Crimea. Charles blanched, and Ian took some satisfaction in that, then shook his head and walked away.

Later that morning he took a coach back to London. His regiment had informed him by letter that a dinner was to be held for officers and his attendance was required. Under military protocol, the request could not be ignored.

He signed into his club and was handed an envelope by one of the staff.

He read the contents and almost fainted when he saw the signature at the bottom – Mr Ian Steele!

*

Ian followed the directions to London's Hyde Park. Despite being early spring, the weather had a chilly bite and he wore a heavy overcoat. He walked towards a park bench and immediately recognised Samuel sitting with the American, James Thorpe.

'Ian,' Samuel said, standing to shake hands. 'It is good to see that you are safe and well.'

'Samuel, what the devil are you doing in London?' Ian greeted him with a frown.

'My sentiments precisely, Captain Steele,' James said. 'But it is good to make your acquaintance again.'

'I have been haunted by our pact,' Samuel said. 'I fear that you may not survive the ten-year contract we made.'

'It is not the Queen's enemies I fear, but your father and brother,' Ian answered with a hint of a smile. 'At least on the battlefield my enemies are generally in front of me, not trying to stick a knife into my back. They really hate you. Are you not afraid that someone in London will recognise you?'

'Too late for that,' James said pointedly. 'Samuel has already been recognised and we have had to change our accommodation as a result.'

'Damn!' Ian swore. 'Your presence here could make life difficult for me – and for you, of course.'

'I am sorry,' Samuel apologised. 'But I had other reasons for returning, not least to visit Herbert's memorial.'

'He was a fine young man,' Ian said sadly. 'I was with him when he was killed at the Redan.'

Samuel lowered his head, and Ian could see tears in his eyes. 'He died bravely,' he added awkwardly. 'He was as close to me as a brother. I understand your need to travel to Kent, but I feel it is too dangerous.'

'We shall go in disguise,' Samuel said. 'I will dress as a woman.'

Ian shook his head, suppressing his alarm. 'Something could go wrong and then both you and I will be exposed.'

'I promise that James and I will return to New York as soon as I have visited my brother's memorial,' Samuel said.

Ian sighed. 'It is not wise for us to meet again. However I wish to reassure you about our pact. Despite the horrors of war, I am doing very well and wish to continue as Captain Samuel Forbes.'

'Thank you, Ian,' Samuel said with absolute gratitude in his voice and face. 'You have put to rest the guilt I have felt since we last met.'

James rose from the bench and extended his hand. 'I, too, thank you . . . Captain Forbes,' he said. 'May you remain safe and well.'

The two men walked away, leaving Ian worried. Although London was a populous and busy city, at least one person had recognised Samuel. How could the man be so foolish as to stay?

*

Charles Forbes was a member of many gentlemen's clubs, but his favourite was the oldest established club in London, situated on St James Street in Westminster. At the White Club for aristocratic gentlemen the stakes at the card tables were high, and Charles had had to draw on the Forbes fortune in order to indulge in his favourite vice.

His wife, Louise, was almost permanently away, living in Italy, in a Tuscan chateau.

While she remained out of England, Charles was able to indulge in his second-favourite vice as well, which was seducing young ladies. Now he was considering adding murder to his list of favourite pastimes. The power he experienced from taking a life and getting away with it was thrilling. He felt like God with this new authority over life and death.

Charles was feeling lucky and the club offered him the opportunity to prove it.

He sat down at a table opposite a man he vaguely knew, a Captain Brooke. Charles remembered his name from the time Samuel had served with him in New South Wales. The cards were dealt, brandy served and cigars produced for the game.

'I think I ran into your brother at my club,' Captain Brooke said, puffing on his cigar as he dealt the cards.

'You probably did,' Charles said, taking the cards in his hand and fanning them out. 'His regiment has returned from the Persian campaign.'

'The odd thing was that the fellow denied he was Samuel Forbes. He said his name was Ian Steele,' Brooke said, taking a sip from his brandy.

'Very odd,' Charles commented, gazing down at his hand of cards.

'I served with Samuel for three years and I am sure that the man I met was he.'

'When did you meet this Mr Steele?' Charles asked. When the army officer gave the date of the incident, he replied, 'Ah. That could not have been Samuel as he was at our manor in Kent at that time.'

'Are you sure?' Brooke countered, and for a moment Charles stared at his cards without seeing them.

His mind started whirring. When Samuel had first returned from the colonies, Charles had doubted his authenticity. The boy who he had once bullied mercilessly had transformed into a tough and confident man. Charles had been persuaded by his father that he was Samuel returned to them, but there was something that did not ring true about this new, powerful version of his brother.

'How did this man look?' Charles asked.

'He looked just as I remember your brother,' Brooke said. 'Still the callow youth who stood with us against the Maori in New Zealand. He has not changed.'

Charles played badly that evening, his mind going over and over what he had learned. Was the meeting simply a case of mistaken identity? Yet Brooke was so adamant he was right. Surely he would know, as he and Samuel had served at least three years together. But if Brooke was right, why would Samuel claim to be someone else? So many questions without answers. Charles decided that it was vital he find this Mr Steele and ascertain for himself whether he was in fact his brother, Samuel Forbes. After all, the Samuel Charles remembered was a shy and introverted young man. The man who had returned in his place was the opposite. Surely a man's character could not change so dramatically?

*

Dr Peter Campbell stood alongside his brother at the edge of the Meerut barracks' parade ground. The sun beat down on the ranks of Indian cavalrymen standing to attention as the eighty-five prisoners were brought out to parade before their comrades.

'They are lucky devils,' Scott said. 'The original sentence for refusing to use the cartridges, a crime of mutiny, was ten years' imprisonment, but General Hewett has commuted the sentence to five years.'

Blacksmiths stepped forward with their tools of trade and native soldiers watched with sullen faces as ankle irons were hammered into place. The prisoners cried out for help from the men on parade, as well as cursing the British Empire.

'The men on parade don't look happy about British justice,' Peter said. 'They appear to be on the verge of attempting to rescue their fellow troopers.'

'They will not,' Scott replied. 'We have the artillery gunners standing by, as well as the Dragoon Guards. It would be suicide for them to try.'

The process continued for an hour, and all the time Peter noted uneasily the barely restrained hatred in the faces of the sepoys forced to hear the sentences read out and enacted. Eventually the prisoners were marched to the barracks' cells by a guard of sepoy troops and the men were dismissed from the parade ground.

Peter and his brother returned to Scott's temporary accommodation. He had been billeted in a small but comfortable and well-kept bungalow in a neat, well-maintained compound. It had been designed to cater to the tastes and needs of the British families accompanying their East India Company men in military service and civil administration.

They were met by Alice, who gave Peter a peck on the cheek.

'I have asked the house girl to prepare drinks,' she said.

Scott and Peter followed Alice out to a veranda overlooking a stand of tall tropical trees filled with raucous birds. Soon the sun would set and Alice had requested a native meal of spiced lentils and other local delicacies for them to dine on in the evening breeze.

'So, what do you think about this part of India?' Scott asked, taking off his sword and hanging it on the back of a chair. 'Are you pleased that you chose to travel with us to Meerut?'

'It was certainly an adventure to travel here,' Alice said, remembering the weeks-long journey on horseback through small villages, along winding roads that took them through primeval forests filled with wildlife. They had often camped under the stars and occasionally experienced heavy downfalls of rain, but it had been a thrilling experience for Alice.

The servant girl, wearing a long flowing colourful dress and headscarf, brought a tray of alcoholic drinks to them. Gin and tonic was the preferred choice, and she poured the gin with a dash of bitter tonic water.

Scott raised his tumbler. 'Chin, chin,' he said, taking a sip.

'You are not worried about your troops causing trouble after what happened today?' Peter asked.

'Not at all,' Scott replied. 'The purpose of the display was to ensure the rest of the rabble knew what was in store for them should they disobey orders. It will all settle down now and we can get on with the job of administering the territory.'

'Do you have concerns, Peter?' Alice asked, noticing her husband's expression.

'I watched the faces of the men on the parade. I saw hatred there, and fury at their powerlessness.'

'Your concerns are unfounded,' his brother scoffed. 'This is India and the natives know their place.'

Peter was not reassured. It was eerily quiet when he and Alice retired that evening and he lay on his back under the mosquito net, staring into the dark. He had a bad feeling and wished that he had chosen to leave India before the journey to Meerut. But it had been an opportunity to share something exotic with Alice before they returned to the grey shores of England.

Alice also found it hard to sleep and thought about the news she still held secret. Maybe she could share it with her husband when his disquiet about today's events was lessened. She resolved that she would tell him after church the following day, when the sun was setting and they were alone on the veranda. Hopefully then they could share what she imagined would be a peaceful and precious moment together.

Part Two

Mutiny!

TEN

Major Scott Campbell settled back on the veranda in a comfortable cane chair to read *Dombey and Son*, a novel by his favourite author, Charles Dickens. He had cheerfully seen off his brother and Alice as they left in a covered light-sprung one-horse coach to drive to the chapel for a service on this pleasant Sunday evening.

Scott was not a religious man and the choice between God and Charles Dickens was an easy one. He reached for the gin and tonic at his elbow and flipped open the pages of the book. All had gone well today. The sepoys had learned their lesson and things were calm at the regimental barracks.

The sound of voices drifting on the gentle evening breeze was faint, but Scott set down the book, listening with a frown on his face. He swore that he could hear the word *maro* being repeated. He knew that was an Indian word for *kill*.

Then it grew louder, *Maro! Maro!*

Scott leapt to his feet just as one of his Indian troopers rushed in shouting, '*Hulla goolla!*' Riot! The young soldier was in uniform and flushed with fear and excitement.

Scott was aware of key phrases in the local language and asked his soldier what was happening. The soldier breathlessly explained that the native regiments had gone on a rampage, with weapons seized from the regimental armoury. At first Scott tried to convince himself this was simply a small-scale mutiny by a few disenchanted sepoys protesting the treatment of their comrades. The young trooper was surely carried away by excitement and had exaggerated the situation.

Scott quickly dressed in his field uniform, strapping on his sword and holstering a loaded revolver. He mounted his horse, leaving orders to the trooper to remain in the bungalow in the event Peter and Alice returned. He galloped from the gates of the compound towards the regimental barracks, where Scott could see a cloud of dust being raised by a mob swarming towards him. A few of the men running ahead of the mob reached Scott on his horse, and an infantry sepoy slashed at him with a sword, cutting Scott's right shoulder lanyard. Scott had no time to draw his own sabre as the horse lunged forward, knocking down the sepoy infantryman.

Scott wheeled his steed around, sword in hand, ready to engage the soldier on the ground, but the sepoy was not prepared to engage a mounted cavalryman and wisely fled over a low wall to safety.

Scott pulled his horse around again to see a small column of his cavalry troopers galloping towards him from the regimental lines. For a moment he felt a sense of relief and ordered them to halt. They did, but immediately encircled Scott, and he knew that they were not friendly but hostile. Their sabres were drawn and they attacked immediately. Scott was hopelessly outnumbered but he parried the many slashing blades aimed at taking his life. He was an expert with the cavalry sword, and it was only his many hours of practice that kept him alive. From the corner of his eye he could see one of his mounted junior officers galloping towards the melee, cutting down one of the Indian cavalrymen threatening Scott. The sudden intervention of a second British officer was enough for the small enemy detachment to scatter and gallop towards the compound bungalows a few hundred yards away.

'God, sir!' the young officer gasped. 'The rascals are heading towards our unarmed loved ones attending church.'

'I can see that, Mr Craigie,' Scott said, observing that the detachment that had attacked him had already disappeared into the compound. His first thought was to gallop after them and save his brother and Alice, but he knew he was probably too late. All he could hope for was that they had found some kind of safety, but for now he, as a senior officer, had to address the main problem of the mutineers. It was an agonising decision to make – rescue those he loved or attack the main problem in the regimental lines.

'Follow me, Mr Craigie, we must reach the lines!'

Scott and the young British officer galloped into the lines and entered a confused melee of Indian troops and British officers milling around the great parade ground. Scott's hopes fell when he saw many of his men already mounted, brandishing swords, firing off pistols and carbines in the air. Others were saddling their mounts whilst horses careened wildly around the parade ground. It was a scene of absolute chaos. Scott could see his fellow British officers attempting to bring the mutinous soldiers to their senses, sometimes pleading with them, other times threatening them, but nothing was working to quell the mutiny.

Scott was pleased to notice that the mutineers at the barracks were not attempting to attack the small number of European officers but yelling at them to be off and that the days of the British Raj were over. It was then that Scott sensed this was no longer a mutiny but the beginning of a full-scale rebellion by the people against Queen Victoria's Empire in India.

The young officer accompanying Scott was a fluent speaker of the local language and had been able to persuade around forty of the would-be mutineers to avoid joining their comrades.

The sun was beginning to set and the dust was like a ghostly haze.

'Sir! Sir!' The frantic words came from another one of Scott's young officers galloping towards him. 'The mutineers are attacking the gaol and releasing the prisoners.'

As the loyal Indian troops and the British officers galloped towards the gaol, they passed crowds of Indian civilians along the road cheering them on.

'They think we are mutineers,' Lieutenant Craigie yelled to Scott. 'It does not bode well.'

Scott could see the clouds of smoke boiling up from burning houses near the prison and suddenly he felt something hit him in the chest, flinging him from his horse. He hit the ground, stunned for a moment. When he regained his focus and sat up he saw Lieutenant Craigie reaching down to him.

'They have cut the telegraph lines,' he said. 'You had the misfortune of being caught up in one.'

Scott scrambled back into the saddle of his horse and to his horror saw a driverless hooded carriage slowly making its way along the road. A mutineer cavalryman was riding alongside, plunging his sabre into the carriage. The two junior officers wheeled about to attack the mutineer and he was killed by Lieutenant Craigie with a slashing blow to his neck. Scott rode up and when he looked inside he could see the blood-soaked body of a European woman slumped across the seat.

Nearby another mob of around twenty mutinous cavalrymen saw their comrade killed, and in their rage commenced screaming, '*Maro! Maro!*' but dared not attack the determined body of troopers accompanying Scott and his officers.

Scott and his party of loyal sepoys reached the gaol but the prisoners had already been freed. A few scattered ineffectual shots were aimed in their direction.

'What do we do now, sir?' Lieutenant Craigie asked.

'There is nothing we can do here,' Scott answered wearily. The sun was just disappearing beyond the horizon. 'I think we should ride back to our bungalows and ascertain the situation there.'

The British officer nodded agreement and Scott led his troop back to the European residences. As he rode he tried not to think about the bloody state of the dead woman he had seen in the carriage. Would he find Peter and Alice in a similar state? When they wheeled about, the full horror confronted Scott. Flames rose above the rows of bungalows and it did not seem that any had been spared. He broke into a hard gallop and his men followed.

★

Scott's residence was fully aflame, but Lieutenant Craigie's large, double-storeyed bungalow, surrounded by a mud wall, had been untouched by the mutineers.

'Sir, I will see if my wife is safe,' Craigie said, leaping from his mount. Scott continued staring at his burning house but could see no sign of his brother and sister-in-law. If they had been fortunate enough to return at the first outbreak of the violence, then their fate had been sealed when the house was ransacked and set alight.

'Sir! Your brother and his wife are safe in my house,' Lieutenant Craigie called to him, and Scott felt a surge of elation. They were safe! He dismounted and rushed into the house where he saw Peter holding Alice in his arms. Peter broke the embrace, taking strides towards him.

'You are safe,' Peter said, grasping his brother by the shoulders. 'God help me, I thought you might be dead.'

'How the devil did you dodge the murderous mob?' Scott asked.

'We were in our carriage driving through the village when a soldier burst from a side alley. He was being pursued by a mob of villagers. He was shouting for help so Alice and I pulled him in and drove as fast as we could back to your bungalow. The mob were on foot and we soon outdistanced them. But when we got back we could see that they had already got to the compound and had pillaged the houses and set them afire – except for Lieutenant Craigie's residence. We climbed over the wall and found Mrs Craigie, who immediately provided us with shelter. I was told by the brave woman that her husband had weapons in the house, and I secured them. Our arms consist of three shotguns, with an ample supply of powder and shot. We were prepared to make a stand here.'

'You do the Campbell clan proud,' Scott beamed through his fatigue. 'Is Alice in any way harmed?'

'No, but she is in shock – as is the soldier we brought back, and Mrs Craigie. I think seeing her husband safe is helping her state of mind. What is happening?'

'I think the mutiny is more like a rebellion,' Scott said,

exhausted. 'In that case, we are on our own until word gets to our general HQ that we need reinforcements. God knows when that will happen, so we have to take all measures to protect our women and children. I have a troop of loyal men outside but I cannot vouch they will remain loyal as this rebellion gathers force.'

'I think I have an idea, sir,' Lieutenant Craigie butted into the conversation between brothers. 'I have a fair understanding of the local Indians. I will go outside and talk to the men.'

'I have faith in your knowledge of these people, Mr Craigie. Do what you can.'

The young officer stepped outside and those in the residence could hear his voice ring out fluently in the local language.

'I wish I knew what he was saying,' Alice said, joining Scott and Peter.

Craigie ceased talking and returned. 'I need to escort your wife, Dr Campbell, and my wife outside to meet our men,' he said.

'Why?' Peter protested. 'They are safe in here.'

'Dr Campbell, without those men's loyalty I dare say we will all be dead by first light. Please trust me.'

'Mr Craigie knows what he is doing, Peter,' Scott said, laying his hand on Peter's arm.

'I am not afraid to go outside,' Alice said. 'It cannot be as frightening as facing a tiger eye to eye.'

Alice accompanied Lieutenant Craigie and his wife to the Indian cavalrymen lined up in disciplined ranks on the horses as if they were still back on parade.

Peter and Scott watched with some trepidation as the young British officer made another address to the troops, who suddenly flung themselves from their horses. Peter raised the shotgun ready to fire at the unexpected movement. But the men were prostrating themselves on the ground, sobbing and reaching out to grab the feet of the two ladies, laying their foreheads on them.

'They are promising to protect the ladies with their very lives,' Craigie shouted back to Scott and Peter. 'I know they will remain loyal to us.'

Both women re-entered the house, a little overwhelmed by the touching display of sworn promises to die for them. Meanwhile, Scott ordered his small troop to remount and patrol the large gardens of the bungalow.

'I think we should retire upstairs,' Peter suggested. It seemed best to defend the house from high ground. He had enough military experience from the Crimean campaign to understand such tactics, despite the fact he had been an army surgeon.

Through the windows the light of the numerous fires lit up the rooms. The smell of the burning timber drifted to them. They could hear the shouts of the mobs rampaging through the compound, accompanied by occasional small-arms fire. Peter looked to his wife, fearing she would be terrified, but instead she was calmly loading one of the shotguns. When he glanced at Lieutenant Craigie's wife he saw that she was also composed. They gave Peter confidence and he wondered not for the first time why it was thought by society that women were incapable of remaining calm under such conditions.

Lieutenant Craigie spoke quietly to Scott. 'I think I should take an escort of some of our men back to the barracks to see if I can convince the others who are undecided that they should side with us,' he said.

'It's a damned dangerous thing to do,' Scott said. 'You will have to fight your way through the mob, but I agree that our only hope of survival is to gather a stronger force until we receive help to quell this rebellion.'

Scott watched the young officer walk over to kiss his wife, before organising an escort party. It was the kind of courage displayed by Mr Craigie that would surely overcome the rebellion, Scott thought. He stepped out onto the upstairs veranda with a shotgun and was spotted by the mob on the opposite side of the street setting light to a house. They cried out and ran at the wall of the compound with fire brands, but Scott levelled the shotgun at them and they retreated. Scott knew that it was only a matter of time before they succeeded in burning the house, given their sheer weight of numbers.

Peter joined him on the veranda. 'There is a small Hindu shrine not far from here,' he said. 'Alice and I visited it a couple of days ago. It has thick walls of stone and is set on high ground with only one entrance. It is like a small fortress, and I suspect impervious even to artillery fire and arson.'

'I know the place you mean and it is a good plan. We will need to get our guns and ammunition across open ground to reach it,' Scott said. 'We will wait an hour to ensure that Lieutenant Craigie knows where we are.'

The two men remained on the veranda, using it as an observation post. Craigie's loyal troops continued their patrols, discouraging the looters from getting too close, but they reported the mobs were growing larger in numbers and better armed, having captured weapons from the regimental armouries.

Lieutenant Craigie returned and he had in his possession the regimental colours discarded by the mutineers. 'We had no luck convincing the remainder at the barracks to join us,' he said. 'And we had to fight our way back. The situation appears to be growing grimmer by the minute.'

Scott told him of their plan, and he agreed it was their only hope to hold out until reinforcements arrived.

Scott stared down at the tattered colours lying on the floor of the house, thinking bitterly that the mutiny had forever disgraced them. However, his main focus now was on reaching the Hindu shrine. He would order his troopers to continue patrolling while the European civilians in his charge took shelter inside the shrine. Scott gathered together his charges and briefed them on the plan. They nodded grimly and all available weapons and ammunition were gathered.

While Scott's troopers held back the rioters, he and the others made a dash for the shrine. The women carried bundles of essential supplies, whilst the men carried the guns. Under cover of darkness and away from the light of the fires they made their way to the relative safety of the shrine, climbing its stone stairway to the interior. Scott was pleased to see that the massive stone walls had slits through which they could fire on any Indian rebels attempting to assault the building. It was dark in the small room but its stoutness made them feel safe for the moment.

Peter took up a position in a corner with a loaded shotgun, as did Alice at another. They could still hear the frenzied and chilling cries of the mob swirling through the European compound.

One of the patrolling sepoys reported to Scott, telling him of the atrocities they had observed. He held a bloody cloth found on the body of the pregnant wife of an officer hacked to death in one of the houses which was now well alight. He said he had observed similar mutilated bodies of European men and women throughout the compound – one, a little girl whose head had been cleaved with a sword. The roll of horror continued.

'The soldiers are leaving Meerut and advancing towards the city of Delhi,' the Indian cavalryman said. 'But the mob remains, still searching for Europeans to kill. However I do not think they have the stomach to attempt an attack on the sacred place.'

Scott was reassured by this news but shocked by the extent of the rapidly spreading massacre of the European civilians in Meerut. He strained to hear the sound of rescuers arriving, but there was no sound except the roar of fires and the blood-curdling shouts of the rampaging mobs.

'That poor woman,' Alice said. In such a small space it had been impossible not to overhear the sepoy's report. 'Murdered with her baby still inside her.'

'We are still alive,' Peter said. 'And help is sure to come.'

'There is something I was going to tell you this evening, but matters changed all that,' Alice whispered, looking up into Peter's face. 'I think I am with child.'

Peter's first thought was that in the midst of death came life. He was both overjoyed and deeply fearful of their fate.

ELEVEN

He was a portly middle-aged man with watery eyes, clean-shaven save for a neat moustache. Charles Forbes sat in the modest office in London and wondered if this man, the subject of a short essay by Charles Dickens titled, *On Duty with Inspector Field*, was as good as many said. The retired head of detectives from the Metropolitan Police was now a private investigator and, it was said, not much liked by his former employer.

'Inspector, I have a case for you,' Charles said, and the man on the other side of the desk lifted his corpulent forefinger.

'Mr Forbes, I am no longer an inspector. You can call me Mr Field,' Charles Field replied in a gravelly voice.

'Mr Field, I am prepared to pay generously for your services in tracking down a man who goes by the name of Ian Steele,' Charles said.

'Does this man owe you money, Mr Forbes?' asked the famed former police detective.

'No, but I think he is involved in some kind of fraud against my family. I am not sure of the details, but I feel that if you are able to locate him, all will be revealed. As far as I can ascertain, this Mr Steele was staying at a private gentlemen's club on Pall Mall and has since disappeared. My informant told me he was in company with another man of his age who has an American accent. The two seem to be travelling together.'

'Do you have a description of this Mr Steele?' Field asked.

Charles reached into his pocket and produced a photograph of Samuel and Herbert standing side by side in their best dress regimental uniforms, hands resting on sword hilts. It had been taken in a studio at Alice's insistence. Charles had taken the photograph of the two grim-faced men from its frame and now he handed it to the private investigator.

'Which one is Mr Steele?' Field asked, staring at the photo.

'This is the queer bit,' Charles said. 'The man on the right is supposed to be my brother, Captain Samuel Forbes, but he is identical to the man purporting to be Mr Steele.'

Field looked sharply at Charles as he leaned back in his chair. 'Do you think this man in the photo may be an imposter?'

'Mr Field, I cannot be certain, but there is a strong possibility. If so, it has grave implications for the Forbes name. I trust that my generous fee for your services will also buy complete confidentiality.'

'I am aware of your family's social position, Mr Forbes. This is a delicate matter, not least because your father has a seat in the House of Lords. Who is the younger man in the photograph?'

'He was my youngest brother, Herbert, who was tragically killed in the battle for Sebastopol.'

'I am sorry to hear that, Mr Forbes. He looks like a fine young gentleman.'

Charles nodded and pretended to look sorrowful for his brother's death.

'How will you track down this Ian Steele?' Charles asked.

'I have an assistant, Mr Ignatius Pollacky, known to most in the business as Paddington Pollacky. Between us we will find this Mr Steele. I will require a gesture of good faith from you before we commence our investigation, Mr Forbes.'

'Certainly,' Charles said, and placed a small pile of paper currency on the private investigator's desk.

'Very generous,' Field said, counting the notes. 'I can assure you your money has been wisely invested.'

*

Charles Field had once aspired to be an actor on the stage, and as such used acting skills and disguises to pursue his role as a private inspector. The doorman at the gentlemen's club nominated by Charles Forbes did not question the portly well-dressed man with the expensive top hat and cane.

'I am seeking the whereabouts of a dear friend, a Mr Steele, who informed me that he was staying here,' Field said.

'I am afraid Mr Steele and his American friend booked out of the club some days ago,' the doorman replied.

'Damn!' Field said. 'I was to pass on an amount of cash for him for his stay in London.' Field reached into his pocket, producing a pound note. 'It is important that I locate Mr Steele as he may find himself short on funds.' Field passed the pound note to the doorman, whose face lit up with surprise and greed. He took the note and quickly pocketed it.

'I am afraid that Mr Steele did not leave a forwarding address, but I do know that he will return to pick up his mail very soon.'

'How soon?' Field asked.

'I am unable to say,' the doorman said. 'Could I contact you once he returns?'

Field frowned. He knew that he could stake out the club, but that would require him and Pollacky doing long shifts. 'Are you able to send someone to inform me the moment Mr Steele arrives and possibly find an excuse to keep him here?' Field asked, peeling off another pound note.

'I can do that, sir,' the doorman said.

Field presented him with a card inscribed with his office address. He was not mistaken in the look of avarice in the doorman's eyes and he knew the man would comply with his request. Mr Steele was as good as found.

*

It was just after midnight and a relief force had still not arrived. Scott consulted with Lieutenant Craigie and it was decided that they would have to get the women out of this dire situation. A mob of mutineers and their civilian supporters were gathering outside the shrine. Being besieged was not an option for the Canadian officer of the East India Company, and already a handful of the supposed faithful troopers had deserted.

Earlier, Scott had noticed a carriage nearby that was still intact, its horse in harness. That was their best hope.

'We need to get as far from here as possible and head north towards our outlying picquet lines,' Scott said. 'Peter will go in the carriage with you two ladies, and he will be armed. Mr Craigie and I will ride escort beside the carriage.'

None disagreed with the desperate plan as they all realised that if they did not escape under the cover of darkness, they would likely not escape at all.

When the carriage was secured Alice and Mrs Craigie stepped into it, Alice carrying one loaded shotgun whilst Peter held another. They could smell the acrid smoke and hear the crackling of the burning buildings. The few remaining loyal troopers formed a column of ten men behind the carriage and Scott and Lieutenant Craigie took up positions either side of it, their swords drawn.

They were ready to move when a large group of civilians surged out of the darkness, brandishing clubs and ancient curved swords. They were accompanied by a handful of mutinous cavalrymen. Scott could see the mob hesitate when they saw that the Europeans were defended by a column of troopers.

'Charge!' Scott yelled, and the native soldier assigned as carriage driver whipped the horse into a fast trot as the loyal troopers screamed war cries. The mob scattered as the carriage came on at full speed, and the cavalrymen slashing with their sabres swept through those members of the mob who had been slow to retreat.

Scott led his party out of the gates of the European compound until they came to an open plain, which to their relief was deserted. The carriage slowed, as did the horsemen accompanying it.

'A port fire!' Mr Craigie said when a faint light was seen in the distance. Both officers recognised it as the signal light used by the British army to indicate a small bridge over a gully.

'We will need to be very careful,' Scott said. 'If it is our men, they will be suspicious of our approach. You and I will go first.'

The two men kicked their mounts into a gallop and screamed at the top of their voices, 'Friend! Friend!'

They came to a stop before the bridge and could see an artillery cannon covering the route they had come from. Beside the artillery piece was a subaltern who recognised the two riders.

'Thank God you identified yourselves,' he said as Scott dismounted. 'I was on the verge of giving the order to fire at your party.'

'I am glad you kept your head, then,' Scott said. 'I will have my party join you. We have women and a few sepoys who have remained loyal.' He looked around and even in the dark could see the faces of British troops. Scott knew that for the moment they would be safe in the British lines north of Meerut. The sun was yet to rise and what lay ahead was an unknown.

Peter helped Alice and Mrs Craigie from the carriage and they were ushered to a small hut not far from the bridge where the women could sleep overnight.

'I have not had the opportunity to say how happy I am at your news,' Peter said, holding Alice's hand. 'Now I have two people to protect.' He would have loved to hold his wife in his arms, but public demonstrations of affection were not the done thing. Instead, he gave her a peck on the cheek before she entered the hut.

Peter left Alice and joined his brother in animated conversation with an officer of Scott's own rank.

'Why the devil did we not pursue the mutineers on their way to Delhi?' Scott was demanding. 'We have the men and guns to teach them a lesson before they get themselves organised.'

'I am of the same opinion,' the other officer said. 'But the general's orders are to remain here and gather our forces.'

Peter could see that Scott was fuming. His once clean uniform was covered in black soot and partly torn at the shoulder. Scott shook his head and the other major walked away.

'Not good news,' Peter said.

'Not good news,' Scott sighed. 'We have also learned that many from our compound fled before the mutineers marching to Delhi. In my opinion it is our duty to mount a rescue of any British survivors. If I am able to get permission, I would value your service with us, although it will mean leaving Alice.'

'Of course, brother, I would gladly be of service,' Peter said. 'I am sure that Alice will be safe here, and I will explain the situation in the morning.'

'Please be careful,' Alice pleaded with him the next day, touching his unshaven face with her hand. 'Remember, you have two of us to return to.'

When Peter looked at his wife he was almost overwhelmed with love for her. He understood now that she and the baby growing inside her were the centre of his universe. Yet he knew that he had a duty to others with his skills as a healer.

Peter swung himself onto the mount that had been prepared for him. A rudimentary medical kit had been put together from scrounged instruments, whilst his shotgun had been slipped into a carbine case attached to the saddle. Scott's force numbered around fifty mixed British and Indian troopers and included Lieutenant Craigie. They prepared to ride south towards Delhi in a possible rescue mission.

Alice waved to Peter as he rode away and he wondered with a heavy heart whether this would be the last time he saw the angelic face of his beloved wife.

On the first day they passed through several villages, and each time they received a sullen reception from the locals. At the second village one of the less hostile inhabitants quietly sidled up to Scott, informing him that a large party of Europeans had fled south through their village. There were both men and women who had escaped the massacre at the compound. There were also some men in military uniform who had acted as protection to the party of escapees.

On the eve of the second day the rescue party reached a mud-walled town with a big wooden gate barred to them. Scott knew he and his men were wearing the same grey uniforms as the mutineers, and he suspected the villagers feared they were the deserting East India troops wishing to enter in order to loot, rape and kill.

Scott, Peter and Lieutenant Craigie rode up to the gate. When the faces observing them from a parapet registered that they were European, their expressions changed from fear to relief. The gate was swung open and the trio were led to a mud-brick house that was the home of the town headman.

An old bearded man sat in a chair out the front of the house, an ancient firelock musket across his lap. Lieutenant Craigie addressed him in the dialect of the region, and he responded.

'What did he say?' Scott asked.

'He bids us welcome and says that amongst his people, he has hidden those who escaped from Meerut. He has sent someone to fetch them and reassure them that help has come.'

In minutes bedraggled men and women appeared from the various houses, cheering at the sight of the three rescuers. Amongst them were the wives of officers, some of whom had been killed during the initial stages of the mutiny. Scott also recognised a couple of fellow officers, and even a colonel.

Oxcarts were organised for transport of the civilians back to the British lines north of Meerut, and Scott ensured that the town's headman was paid for supplying the carts and oxen, as well as food for the travellers and grain for the oxen. Just after dark, they moved out of the town, the cavalrymen riding on the flanks and in front to prevent any attack. By the next evening they arrived and were directed back to Meerut, which had been recaptured, and temporary accommodation erected to house the survivors.

Peter flung himself off his horse, searching for Alice to tell her that he had returned, safe and well. He was directed to a semi-burned house in the compound where an Indian servant girl with a worried face greeted him. She spoke some English and as Peter was about to step inside, she stopped him.

'I sorry, Doctor,' she said with tears welling in her eyes. 'The mistress sick. She lose baby.'

With a feeling of dread Peter stepped inside to find Alice lying on a small bed, deathly pale, her skin clammy.

'Oh, Peter, I am so sorry,' she said, breaking into a sob. 'Our darling baby is gone.'

Peter fell to his knees beside the bed, gripping his wife's hand. He looked closely at Alice's face and his grief for their loss was worsened when he saw something else in her face. As a medical practitioner he had seen it many times before.

Alice was in the deadly grip of cholera.

TWELVE

It was the last month of springtime in London and the weather was warming. Ian spent most of his time at the regimental barracks overseeing the training of his company, although he knew the tradition of allowing the senior non-commissioned officers to look to the routine of managing the troops. His company, however, had come to learn he was an officer who took seriously his role as their leader, and although his training was rigorous, they also knew he cared for them. That endeared the Colonial to them.

It was the end of the day at the barracks and Ian prepared himself to return to his club for the evening. He was in his dress uniform when he took the salute at the gates of the regiment and walked onto the busy street outside.

Ian had hardly taken a step beyond the gates when he felt his heart skip a beat.

Ella!

The beautiful young woman stood smiling uncertainly at him as she held a parasol above her head. Behind her was an expensive covered coach drawn by two fine horses, a well-dressed driver on the seat.

'Hello, Samuel,' she said.

'I was told by your father that you were in America,' Ian said, hardly believing his eyes or trusting his feelings. 'How is it that you are here?'

'I was rejected by the medical schools in New York,' Ella replied, 'so I have returned home to London.'

'It is good to see you, but you have my sympathy for your failure to obtain a place in medicine. I know how much it meant to you. I am truly sorry,' Ian said. 'How did you know to meet me here?'

'It was not hard,' Ella said with a laugh, and Ian thought he was hearing the sound of an angel. 'People have said that you are an officer who spends his time with his men. So I am here, Captain Forbes . . . Samuel.'

'I am at a loss for words,' Ian said gently, fighting off an almost overwhelming desire to take her in his arms.

'I thought we might take tea at that little shop where we used to meet,' Ella said. 'My carriage can take us there.'

'You can tell me all about your adventures in New York,' Ian said, taking her arm.

He assisted her into the carriage and took a seat beside her. The simple fact that he could smell her perfume and knew that mere cloth separated their bodies caused him rich and complex feelings. He felt like a young man again, full of hope and possibility.

Both remained silent during the short trip to the fashionable street of coffee shops and milliners. It was as if they were happy simply to be in each other's company.

The tea shop was almost empty. Ian ordered tea for two

and sat down opposite Ella. She reached across the linen-covered table and took his hands in her own. Ian knew that this was the time to explain that as delighted as he was to see her, there could be no future for them. But her large eyes were gazing into his own and he suddenly forgot all logical reasons for restraining his feelings for her. He knew he could easily fall in love with this woman almost a decade younger than he.

'I could never forget you, Samuel,' Ella said. 'Even in New York I would think about you day and night. I would dream that I was in your arms and that we were planning a life together.'

Ian frowned. 'I must confess that you have always been in my thoughts too,' he said. 'I would be under the stars in the silence of the Mesopotamian desert and I would see you there. Before we went into battle you were always my last thought. But I also know that your father could never accept me. I am not of your faith.'

'Is that all you fear?' Ella asked as the china cups and teapot were placed on the table by a young woman in a spotless dress. 'We could leave England and go to one of the colonies to start a life together. I know you spent some time in the Australian colonies; we could go there where no one would care where we came from. My mother left me a substantial inheritance and I am independent of my father's money.'

'It is a wonderful dream, but I am a soldier.'

'You could sell your commission,' Ella said. 'You are an intelligent man and I know you would be capable of finding other work.'

'I cannot tell you why – and please don't ask me the reason – but I must serve seven years more as an officer with the regiment,' Ian said. 'There are just too many reasons against us being together.'

'Do you love me?' Ella asked tearfully, trapping Ian in a position from which he could neither retreat nor advance.

'My feelings for you are not the issue,' he said gently. 'You are a beautiful and intelligent young woman and any good man would wish to spend his life with you. In another seven years I will be in a position to resign my commission, but until then I am not the master of my own destiny.'

'I cannot believe that,' Ella replied, wiping away her tears with a delicate lace handkerchief. 'You do not love me.'

Ian desperately wanted to tell her that this was not true, but he could not reveal the truth to her. All he could do was reach out and hold her hand. He felt awkward and uncertain. Facing the Russians had been easier.

'I think you should return home,' Ian said, and Ella withdrew her hand angrily.

'I do not understand you.' She flared. 'I can see the desire in your eyes and yet you push me away. I never wish to see you again, Captain Forbes.'

Ella rose from the table and hurried outside to her carriage, leaving Ian caught up in a storm of emotions. It was obvious that she loved him, and he knew he loved her, but circumstances had conspired to separate them. Beyond the cosy tea house, the drums and bugles were even now calling him to yet another bloody campaign in a far-off country.

*

Dr Peter Campbell wrung out the wet cloth and applied it to his wife's fevered brow. Alice was drifting in and out of consciousness and Peter fought back the tears as he desperately sifted through all the medical knowledge he possessed for something that might save her life. So many times he had watched patients with cholera die – and yet he had seen others miraculously live.

He remembered how the Khan had called his wife the daughter of the goddess, Kali, the ultimate warrior. Alice had to fight like Kali, and he whispered in her ear, 'Daughter of Kali, I need you. Fight this thing with every breath you have.'

It was hardly logical, but Peter was desperate. Suddenly, Alice reached out to grip his hand and squeeze it. His hopes soared. She was alert enough to hear his voice.

'Fetch boiled water laced with sugar,' Peter ordered the Indian servant girl hovering in the room. 'Bring more clean cloths.'

When the servant girl reappeared with the water she was accompanied by Scott.

'How is Alice faring?' he asked in a concerned voice.

'I pray that she is fighting this insidious disease with all that she has,' Peter replied, looking up at his brother dressed in his dusty field uniform. Scott took a chair a short distance from the bed that Alice occupied.

'The word is filtering through that the mutiny has broken out across all of India. Unit after unit is deserting to form a rebellion in an attempt to declare independence from the East India Company. We are going to need reinforcements from England,' Scott said wearily. 'Your services here as a surgeon will be badly needed in the days ahead.'

'As soon as Alice recovers and is well enough to travel, I intend to get her out of India and home to England,' Peter said. 'There are other surgeons in the Company.'

'Not as good as you, little brother,' Scott said gently, and Peter was surprised to hear Scott finally praise him for his medical expertise. It caught him off-guard.

'Think about it,' Scott said. 'When Alice recovers, we can endeavour to have her return to England, but I know that she would want you to remain to minister to the sick and wounded here.'

Peter considered that the loss of their baby was bound to haunt his wife and it was his duty to be by her side to provide comfort. But he was also a surgeon and many lives might be saved in his hands. It was a dilemma, but his wife's welfare was his priority.

'I will think on your proposition,' Peter said, deciding to keep his options open and returning his attention to Alice, who still lay in a fevered state. Peter knew that the next few hours were critical and also that the odds were against her surviving the deadly disease. He had been a witness to this terrible death countless times. Tears streamed down his face as he held Alice's hand, feeling utterly helpless.

*

The doorman at the Pall Mall gentlemen's club had his plan in place. He had paid a couple of street urchins to hang around the entrance, ready to deliver a message to Mr Field. Early one morning, a man arrived and requested any mail addressed to a Mr Ian Steele. The doorman recognised the man as Steele's travelling companion.

The doorman passed a small pile of letters to James, who thanked him and quickly departed, leaving no time to detain him. The doorman quickly summoned one of the boys, instructing him to follow the man and report back where he went, whilst the second boy was to run to Mr Field's office and fetch him.

It did not take long for Field to arrive in a hansom cab. Both men waited and finally the breathless young lad returned, delivering his news. He had followed the man to an expensive boarding house only three blocks away. Field tipped the boy a few pennies and asked him to take him to the residence, which he duly did.

''E's in there, mister,' the boy said, pointing at the building. 'Saw 'im go in with me own eyes.'

Field dismissed the boy, who ambled away, gripping his precious pennies.

Field noted the address and mulled over whether he should enter to confirm that Mr Steele was inside. He decided against this in case the man turned violent. No, he would return with his partner, Paddington Pollacky, and armed with coshes, they would enter the building together.

⋆

'Water.'

The croaky voice brought Peter out of his dozing slumber beside Alice's bed. He sat upright in the chair then rose to lean over his wife.

'Alice, my darling, did you ask for water?'

'Yes,' she replied in a weak voice, and Peter observed that the fever appeared to have broken, although Alice lay still against the sweat-drenched pillows.

Peter bade the servant girl fetch clean, boiled water laced with sugar. When the water arrived he helped Alice sit up and sip the drink. She slept again and when she woke seemed brighter and stronger.

'As soon as you are well enough to travel, we will leave for England,' Peter said. 'My brother has asked me to remain as surgeon to the Company, but I will be informing him that getting you home comes before anything else.'

'Peter, my love,' Alice said, her voice sounding faint and shaky, 'Scott is right. You must stay to be of help to so many who will need your skills. I wish to remain at your side until this terrible situation is resolved.'

Peter frowned. His love for this truly marvellous woman grew by the day. 'It is too dangerous for you to be here,' he protested. ‘I could never live a day if anything were to happen to you.’

‘It already has, and I am still here,’ Alice replied with a wan smile, reaching out for her husband’s hand. ‘I am so sorry that I lost our child,’ she continued in a sorrowful voice.

‘It was not your fault,’ Peter said, gripping her hand. ‘Such things are in the hands of God, my love. Do not blame yourself.’

Peter was about to assist Alice from the bed, intending that she be helped to wash by the servant girl, when Scott arrived. His face broke into a beaming smile when he saw that Alice had begun her recovery.

‘Your brother has agreed that we should help in any way we can,’ Alice said, and Peter looked at her in sharp surprise.

‘Good,’ Scott said. ‘Because very soon we will be marching on the mutineers to give them a taste of cold British steel and lead.’

THIRTEEN

The knocking on the door of James and Samuel's rooms in the London boarding house was loud and urgent.

The men glanced at each other and James went to the door and opened it a fraction. He peered through the small gap and was taken aback to see the rough bearded face of a very large man.

'Who are you?' James asked, just a little fearful of the ferocious-looking man.

'Captain Forbes asked my boss to keep an eye out for you,' the man answered. 'I need to tell you that you have been recognised and that you have to leave London.'

James was slightly confused.

'Let the gentleman in,' Samuel called, and James opened the door.

When the man entered the room, it was his turn to be shocked by what he saw: a man dressed in women's clothing!

For a moment he stood blinking in silence. Egbert Johnson was an enforcer for Ikey Solomon, and his face reflected the scars of his work collecting debts from other hard men.

'Cor blimey!' he uttered. 'What is going on?'

'You mentioned Captain Forbes,' Samuel said, ignoring the question. 'You said he has hired your boss to look out for us.'

Egbert recovered his composure, staring at the man in women's clothing. 'My employer is Mr Solomon, and he had me keep an eye out for you two. I was watching this place when Field turned up and gave it the once-over.'

'Who is this Field chap?' Samuel asked.

'He's a private investigator, and a good one. I can only think that he was looking for you two. No other reason he would show any interest in this place. Which one of you is Mr Steele?'

Samuel identified himself and introduced James.

'You ain't got much time to get your stuff together and get out of here,' Egbert said. 'Matter of fact, that dress you are wearing might be a good idea when we get out on the street. Less chance of you being recognised.'

Samuel and James had to accept that the man was working in their interests so they quickly packed their possessions. They had been preparing to travel to Kent, to Herbert's memorial – hence Samuel's disguise – but their plans would have to change.

'What do we do now?' Samuel asked when they were ready to depart.

'I go downstairs and hire a hansom cab to take you to a place Mr Solomon has near the docks. You should be safe there for a while.'

Egbert departed, leaving the two men alone.

'Who is responsible for finding us?' James asked.

Samuel slumped on the bed. 'Don't ask me how I know, but I suspect my brother Charles has a hand in this. Somehow my visit to London has got back to him, which can only mean Charles suspects Ian is an imposter.'

'If your theory is correct, we need to get away from London and return to New York,' James said, pacing the small room. 'To remain will only put Ian's freedom in jeopardy. Your contract with him will have little bearing on his defence if he is arrested.'

Suddenly they heard the heavy thump of boots on the stairway. The door opened and both men were relieved to see Egbert appear.

'The good news is that I got you a cab downstairs and the driver has instructions to take you to the address at the docks. The bad news is that I just saw Field and another man turn up at the end of the street and they're coming this way.'

Samuel and James followed Egbert downstairs to where a hansom cab awaited. Samuel cast a quick look at the two men approaching and recognised his brother, Charles.

'Get in!' Egbert hissed as Field and Charles were a mere fifty paces away, hurrying towards them.

Charles Forbes glanced at the man and woman boarding the hansom cab but returned his attention to the entrance of the boarding house.

The hansom cab moved away, leaving Egbert on the footpath. He saw Field and the stranger enter the boarding house and grinned through his thick black beard. It was obvious that fortune had been on his side today. Mr Steele – or whoever he was – had been made up so well as a woman that under other circumstances he might have been propositioned by the men in search of carnal pleasure. Egbert shook his head in disbelief and continued back to his employer's office.

★

It was a glittering night of pomp and ceremony. Ian sat in the centre of the long table whilst Colonel Jenkins sat at the head. Candles threw their flickering light over the colourful uniforms of the officers, and the food and wine flowed. Ian noticed that there were a few new officers posted to the regiment, and they stared enviously at those more senior officers sporting the medals of their campaigns.

Beside him sat a young newly commissioned lieutenant.

'Sir, I believe that your company was involved with General Outram's river expedition in Persia,' said the lieutenant. 'You were most fortunate as the rest of the regiment was left out.'

'The regiment was required to remain at our depot and guard against a possible Persian counterattack at Bushehr,' Ian defended.

'Oh, I am hoping that we see some action in the near future,' the young officer sighed.

'I think you will,' Ian replied, suspecting what would be announced tonight.

When the president of the mess committee banged the gavel on the table, all fell silent. On cue, Colonel Jenkins rose to his feet.

'Gentlemen, no doubt you have been following the tragic events in India in *The Times*. It is with great pleasure – and honour – that I announce our regiment has been ordered to India to assist the East India Company in putting down the mutiny.'

Before he could continue, a roar of approval went up around the room as the officers banged the table with their fists and forks. Jenkins smiled, waiting for the outpouring to die down, then raised his hand to quell the boisterous cacophany.

'We are to ready ourselves and will be departing these

shores late June,' he continued. 'Gentlemen, a toast to our Queen.'

All officers rose to their feet, lifting their goblets of port wine. 'The Queen!' they chorused, and those of major rank and above added, 'God bless her.'

The royal toast over, the men resumed their seats and an excited chatter broke out amongst them.

'Sir, what exciting news!' the young officer sitting next to Ian exclaimed. 'A chance to prove oneself.'

Ian could see the radiant expression on the young man's face and was momentarily reminded of Herbert. Would this young man share the same fate as Herbert, dying before his life had even begun? Ian well knew that luck was about the only real decider on the battlefield. Maybe this time his own luck would run out.

⋆

The Indian soldier tried to resist the agonising pain from his knee, shattered by a lead ball from a mutineer's musket. Beside him an ashen-faced British cavalry officer slouched in a chair, clutching his chest.

Dr Peter Campbell had converted a room in the Meerut house he had been allocated and set it up as a makeshift surgery, and it was to this that Scott had had the two wounded men transported.

'We clashed with a rather large party of mutineers about three miles away,' Scott said. 'Captain Lockyer was shot in the chest.'

The wounded sepoy lay on the floor bleeding, but Peter knew the officer would have to be examined first. He carefully removed the captain's jacket until his bare chest was exposed and he could see the entry wound of the musket ball on the man's lower right-hand side. There was little bleeding and when he ran his hand around to the man's back he found what he was looking for. An exit wound.

'The captain is fortunate,' Peter said, looking up at his brother. 'The projectile has entered his chest just under the skin, travelled along his ribs then exited. It has not hit any internal organs, so the task now is to ensure he does not get an infection.'

A look of relief swept Scott's face. 'Thank God,' he uttered. 'Captain Lockyer, you will be back in the saddle before you know it.'

Captain Lockyer groaned but flashed a weak smile, and Scott summoned a couple of sepoys to assist him next-door to a room that was to be used as a makeshift ward.

Peter turned his attention to the badly wounded sepoy.

'Help me get him onto the table,' he said to Scott, and both men lifted the soldier onto a stout wooden table Peter had procured. The two sepoys returned and looked uneasy at the sight of their comrade lying on his back on the table, moaning in pain.

Peter rustled through the bag of medical supplies he had been able to scrounge and noted that they were from the Napoleonic wars. Still, he had the basic tools. He retrieved a canvas ligature with a screw-like apparatus on top and applied it above the shattered knee, using the screw lever to apply pressure, cutting off the blood flow to the lower leg. He had been unable to find any form of anaesthetic, so he knew that the operation would have to be carried out without pain relief.

'Get your men to hold the soldier down,' he instructed as he retrieved a crescent-shaped blade from the medical kit. The men obeyed Scott's instruction and grasped the patient. Peter was about to commence cutting when Alice appeared in the small room.

'Alice, this is no place for you,' Scott said, spotting her first.

Peter turned to his wife. 'You should be resting,' he said. 'Scott is right. This is no place for a lady.'

'Why not?' Alice retorted defiantly. 'After all, it was you who praised the nurses in the Crimea, and I am sure they were witness to such sights. I am the wife of a surgeon and it is my place to assist my husband in any way I can.'

Scott and Peter looked at each other, and Scott shrugged his shoulders. It was hard to counter her argument.

'I warn you,' Peter said, 'what you are about to assist me with is very unpleasant, and if at any stage you find it overwhelming, promise me you will leave the room. You will be no use to me in a dead faint on the floor.'

Alice nodded and Peter could see how she paled at the sight of the wicked-looking blade in his hand.

'What should I do?' she asked, and Peter instructed her to assist the two sepoys, one holding the legs of their wounded comrade, the other his upper body. Scott also stepped in, although Peter could see that he did so somewhat reluctantly.

'This is the glory you soldiers inflict on one another on the battlefield,' Peter said. 'Alice, make sure that the leg is held firmly.'

Peter bent down, placing the curved blade under the leg, and with a deft movement cut a neat circle around the leg above the knee, opening up the skin. The wounded soldier arched and screamed, unnerving his comrades. Peter did not hesitate but grabbed a tenon saw, pushing down hard on the bone, and began sawing with less pressure on the forward stroke. He glanced at Alice. She had gone deathly white but remained holding the leg firmly against the patient's desperate kicks. Blood sprayed all around and Alice's white dress was splattered with red.

The saw did its job and the leg came away in Alice's arms, causing her to stagger backwards under the unexpected weight of the limb.

'Just drop it on the floor,' Peter said as he continued his post-operational procedures to seal the wound before releasing the ligature clamp. The sepoy had mercifully fainted under the pain of the amputation and lay still on the blood-covered table.

'Get him to a bed,' Peter ordered. 'If he does not get an infection within the next twenty-four hours he may live.' Peter wiped his bloody hands on the apron he was wearing and tossed the tenon saw in a washbasin of water.

Alice stood in the room, the colour returning to her face. Peter went to her and placed his hands on her shoulders whilst Scott supervised the removal of the patient from the makeshift operating theatre.

'Are you unwell?' Peter asked gently and Alice shook her head, though he could see that the amputation had been a shock to her.

'You were so skilled in the way you carried out the removal of the poor man's leg,' she said. 'I know that I can assist you in such future operations.'

Peter knew now that his wife was a lot tougher than most men would ever credit. He would need her by his side as his surgical assistant, despite the protests of his European colleagues that medicine – especially surgery – was beyond the capabilities of the weaker sex. The Indian mutiny was growing worse by the day, and their lives were in real danger if British forces did not arrive soon from England. Many more men would pass through this ill-equipped surgery before then, and Peter would need Alice's help if he had any hope of ministering to them all.

FOURTEEN

It was a truly impressive gathering in London's Hyde Park. One hundred thousand civilian spectators watched as a huge military guard of honour wearing red uniforms formed up on foot and on horseback.

Ian stood beside Molly Williams, who was holding her dainty parasol against the morning sun of the London summer. Only a few scattered high-flying clouds broke the brilliant blue of the sky.

At the centre of this great formation sat the Queen on a magnificent horse. Ian had a clear view of her and thought how short she was but still attractive. Standing beside the mount was the tall and handsome Prince Consort, husband of the Queen.

'I can't see him,' Molly said anxiously.

'You will,' Ian reassured.

On a dais draped in a red cloth, attendants to the Queen

held platters laid out with the newly issued medals the monarch had instituted and named in her honour. Then the line of recipients marched forward, and each of the sixty-two medals was pinned on a soldier or officer's chest as the Queen leaned down from her horse.

'Sergeant Curry!' Conan's name was called and Molly raised up on her toes to witness this historic moment. She could not hear Queen Victoria utter the words as Conan halted smartly, saluted, standing rigidly at attention.

The spectators politely clapped their appreciation, and Conan saluted one more time before turning and marching back to the ranks of the regiment. Ian noticed how the Prince Consort bowed to each of the men receiving the new medal of the Victoria Cross, a medal cut out of the barrel of a Russian artillery gun captured at the fall of Sevastopol. Ian's recommendation for Conan to be awarded a medal for bravery had been countersigned by General Outram whilst in Persia.

When the ceremony was completed, the gathered military units presented their salute to the Queen as she rode off the temporary parade ground. Military bands struck up tunes to entertain those civilians remaining to enjoy the beautiful summer's day.

Eventually Conan and Corporal Owen Williams made their way through the crowd to join Ian and Molly.

Molly ignored all social protocols and flung herself into Conan's arms, kissing him.

'Congratulations, Conan, but I should parade you for being out of uniform,' Ian grinned.

'Sir?' Conan queried with a confused frown.

'You should be wearing the rank of sergeant major now, not sergeant. Your promotion has been approved. I should also have you charged, Corporal Williams. You can use

Conan's sergeant chevrons as he will no longer be needing them. Congratulations, Sergeant Williams.'

It took a few seconds for Ian's words to sink in, and then both soldiers broke into grateful smiles. Promotion meant better wages.

'Thank you, sir,' Owen replied, and Ian shook both soldiers' hands. 'No doubt the three of you will be off to celebrate. I know Colour Sergeant Leslie is lining up ales at the pub near our barracks, and he told me that you will be paying.'

'Thank you, sir,' Conan said. 'I am not sure even our promotion will afford us the payment for so many ales.'

'I know you both have a little gold stashed away, and I am sure it could be put to good use this day,' Ian said. 'Molly, I am commissioning you to ensure your brother and Sergeant Major Curry behave themselves.'

Molly leaned forward and kissed Ian on the cheek. 'Thank you, sir, for all that you have done for my Conan and my Owen. You have made good men out of them.'

Ian shook his head. 'They did that themselves,' he replied gently. 'Go now and enjoy this very special day.'

Ian stepped back and saluted Conan. 'New rule in the army,' he explained. 'Even an officer must salute an enlisted man if he is wearing the Victoria Cross.'

Conan returned the salute. 'It is you who should have been awarded the medal for all that you did for us in the Crimea. But I know while our colonel is in command he will never recognise your courage.'

Ian did not comment but he knew Jenkins hated him and, he suspected, wished to see him dead.

'Go off with you,' Ian said and the three disappeared into the crowd to make their way to the pub.

Ian stood for a moment amongst the dispersing crowd of

ladies in long white summer dresses and gentlemen in tall top hats and suits.

'Congratulations, Captain Steele,' a familiar female voice said behind him.

He turned to see the beautiful face of Lady Rebecca Montegue. She was standing a few paces away, wearing an elegant summer dress and holding a parasol. Rebecca was the living image of her twin sister, Jane. The two girls had been separated just after they were born and Rebecca had been adopted by the wealthy Montegue family, inheriting the titles and estates of the now deceased Lord Montegue. It was Jane who had revealed Ian's secret to her sister.

'Oh, have no fear, Captain Steele, I have never broken my promise to keep secret your identity,' Rebecca said with a sweet smile. 'I am only here to congratulate you on your recommendation for Sergeant Curry's medal. I know Clive attempted to have your report quashed but was overruled by General Outram.'

'Thank you, Lady Montegue,' Ian replied.

'There is no need for such formalities between us, Ian,' Rebecca said. 'After all, under other circumstances you might have been my brother-in-law. Have you learned anything concerning my sister's disappearance?'

'Nothing,' Ian said. 'I am forced to confront the idea that someone may have murdered Jane.'

'I suspect that you are correct,' Rebecca said sadly. 'I have terrible dreams of a ring of small stones on a hilltop near my sister's village. The place we first met, when you thought at first I was Jane. I suppose that is because Jane had a spiritual connection to that old Druid place of worship.'

'Strange,' Ian frowned. 'I have a similar dream that troubles my sleep,' he said. 'It is as if Jane haunts that desolate place.'

'I suspect, though, that you do not believe in ghosts, given you have demonstrated what a practical soldier you are,' Rebecca said. 'I do not believe that those we love come back to haunt us either, but I have faith that you will discover who is responsible for my sister's disappearance.'

'I have no real leads, although I suspect Charles Forbes,' Ian said.

'If Charles knew that my sister carried your child, that may have been enough reason to kill her,' Rebecca agreed.

'I have considered that,' Ian said. 'But I cannot exact revenge without evidence. If I do prove Charles is her murderer, I will ensure he is slain.'

'You will be my angel of vengeance,' Rebecca replied, then changed the subject. 'There is to be a ball at my estate the week before Clive's regiment steams for India. Your name will be on the invitation list, and also that of the charming young girl you escorted to my last ball.'

'I am afraid Miss Solomon and I are not on speaking terms,' Ian said gloomily.

'That's a shame, I thought you made a very handsome couple,' Rebecca said.

Ian did not wish to discuss his relationship with Ella. 'It is well known that you have often been seen in the company of Colonel Jenkins. Do you intend to wed him?'

'It is presumptuous of you to ask me such a personal question,' Rebecca replied. 'But as you occupy a rather unique place in my life, I will tell you that I do intend to accept Clive's offer of marriage when he asks.'

'Why?' Ian asked.

'Because he is a man I will one day guide to becoming the prime minister of England. We both know Clive does not have what it takes to lead men in battle, but he does have the acumen to become a politician of renown, particularly if his family fortune is married to mine. Ah, I see that Clive is just over there.' Rebecca and Ian turned to see Jenkins standing with a group of senior officers some yards away. 'I will bid you a good morning, Captain Forbes. Do not forget my invitation. I look forward to seeing you again.'

Rebecca strolled away, leaving Ian alone to ponder their meeting. He understood that his real identity was known to a woman who could easily expose him, and yet she chose to protect him, despite her alliance with one of his most hated enemies. It was apparent Rebecca Montegue liked to play games, but Ian was perplexed by her attraction to Clive Jenkins, if indeed that was what it was. He knew one thing, and that was that the invitation to her ball was more an order than a request. Ian groaned. He had never liked the pomp and ceremony of the English aristocrats; he was more at home in the field with his infantry company. He watched as Rebecca laughed with the high-ranking officers and placed her gloved hand on Clive Jenkins' arm. He could not understand how twins could be so similar in appearance and yet so different in character.

⋆

Sergeant Major Conan Curry lay on the double bed in Molly's room above her shop. Colour Sergeant Paddy Leslie had organised a huge celebration at their favourite pub – at no small cost to Conan and Owen. The ale had flowed and tankards were repeatedly raised in toasts. Predictably, it had ended in a brawl when a group of engineers entered the establishment, but no one could remember why the fight had started. The regimental men were able to extract themselves before the constabulary arrived, and now Conan lay beside Molly.

'You were a disgrace, Conan Curry,' she said, but without

venom. 'Captain Forbes would have been ashamed of you and Owen if he had been present. The captain has been very good to you both.'

Conan groaned. One of the engineers had been a big, powerful soldier who had connected a heavy blow to Conan's jaw and he had lost a couple of teeth. Or perhaps the drunkenness was turning now into a hangover. 'Captain Forbes and I go a long way back,' he slurred. 'All the way to New South Wales when he was the village blacksmith, and me and my brothers did a bit of bushranging.'

'What are you babbling about?' Molly scoffed. 'How could you know Captain Forbes before you enlisted?'

Conan paused. The ale had loosened his tongue. On reflection he felt that in the privacy of the bedroom nothing he said could do any harm. And this was Molly, the woman he loved, and someone who could be relied upon to keep the captain's secret. 'He is not Captain Forbes,' he admitted. 'His real name is Ian Steele and he has fooled the Forbes family into believing that he is one of them.'

Shocked, Molly hardly believed Conan's confession. Were these simply drunken ramblings?

'Are you saying that Captain Forbes is an imposter?' Molly asked.

'Ian Steele is the best man I have ever known, and the boys would follow him into hell if he asked,' Conan said, gripping his head in both hands. 'You cannot tell anyone what I have just told you.'

'You know that I love you, and anything you tell me within these walls remains a secret between us.'

'You swear?' Conan demanded, realising that he had said more than he should.

'I swear on my love for you,' Molly replied. She was mesmerised as her lover went on to tell her about the history of the real Ian Steele. Conan even confessed to his role in the robbery that had resulted in the death of Ian's mother. Molly did not speak a word as the tale of the contract between English aristocrat and colonial blacksmith unravelled.

'So there it is,' Conan concluded. 'Now I need to get some sleep because it will be my duty to parade the company for inspection in the morning.'

Molly rested Conan's head in her lap as he fell into a fitful sleep. She was secretly pleased to learn that Ian was not the brother of Charles Forbes, who had once attempted to rape her when she worked for the Forbes family at their manor in Kent. Conan had told her that the men in the regiment had given Ian the nickname of 'the Colonial' and she thought, *If only they knew.*

The fact that Conan had confided the secret to her only made her love the big Irishman even more. They had all come a long way from the slum tenements of the inner city since the day Conan and Owen were on the run from the law and had to enlist in the British army to avoid arrest by the London police. War in the Crimea had financed her business enterprise with Russian loot, and after this last campaign, Owen had produced a small fortune in gold coins. Whoever Captain Ian Steele was, it only mattered to her that his deception had brought them good fortune.

His secret would always be safe with her.

⋆

The cross-Channel steamer to Calais had been part of the ruse to ensure that Samuel and James were not spotted leaving on a clipper sailing for the Americas. Ikey Solomon had been sure that private investigator Charles Field would be keeping a close eye on all the New York–bound vessels with the hope of intercepting his target. New passports in new names had been procured for the two men, so from France they would be able to book a passage home. As they waited to embark, they would have the chance to take in the sights and pleasures of Paris. This they did before eventually taking berth on a ship to the United States two weeks later.

However, the clipper had hardly left Calais to sail south when it was hit by a furious Atlantic-born gale, forcing it to seek shelter at the English port of Dover and remain there whilst substantial repairs were made to its sails and rigging.

James and Samuel shared a small but clean first-class cabin, and though a little perturbed, James was not overly concerned that they were once again in British waters. After all, the odds were low that any of Charles' paid informants would suspect a ship leaving from a French port could be their means of escape. If anything, they would be still watching ships *departing* English ports. They simply had to lie low and wait it out.

James poured gin for himself and Samuel into tumblers.

'Well, I did not expect to be back in England so soon, and I must say that I already miss the beauty of Paris.' James noticed Samuel gazing through a porthole at the wharves and docks of Dover. The gale had abated and the sun was shining in the early morning.

'Do you know, we are only a short carriage ride from our manor's chapel,' Samuel said, accepting the glass of gin.

'You aren't thinking of going ashore,' James groaned, aghast. 'We were damned lucky to get out of London.'

Samuel turned away from the porthole. 'We are safe, dear James,' he said. 'I could easily visit my brother's memorial and be back before the ship sails again.'

James pulled a face that displayed his frustration. 'I beseech you to reconsider yet another of your lunatic aspirations. We will not be safe until we are on our way back to New York.'

'I am sorry, James, but the opportunity is too good to ignore. It is as if this unforeseen deliverance to Dover has been granted me by God. Nobody would suspect we are here. You know how important it is for me to honour my little brother's death.'

'I doubt that you believe there is a God,' James scoffed. 'But your goddamned stubbornness will bring us undone.'

'I do not request you to accompany me,' Samuel said, taking a long swig of the gin. 'I would never put you at risk.'

James stepped forward, placing his hands on Samuel's shoulders. 'Despite your insanity, you know I would never allow you to face danger alone. If you insist on a visit to your brother's memorial, I will be going with you.'

Samuel had hoped that James would insist on accompanying him. He did not want to be parted from him. Since Jonathan, he had recognised that James was the only other man he would ever love in his life.

'Thank you, dear James,' Samuel said, tears welling in his eyes. 'We will arrange to leave immediately and be back before the ship sails.'

When Samuel turned to pack a few items, James shook his head, hoping that his lover was making the right judgement. Somehow he had his doubts.

*

Ian was announced on arrival in the magnificent ballroom at Lady Rebecca Montegue's manor just outside London. It was a dazzling affair of colourful military uniforms, glittering gowns and jewellery and a multitude of candles flickering soft shadows on the guests both military and civilian. Ian noted that all the officers of his regiment were in attendance, which was not surprising as the invitation had described the event as the farewell ball for the regiment before it steamed to India. He wore his own dress uniform and blended in with his military colleagues.

Ian took a coupe of champagne offered him by a servant wearing an old Georgian wig and equally ornate dress uniform.

'Here, sir, your dance card,' the servant said, passing Ian a slip of paper.

Ian hardly looked at the card, slipping it inside his dress jacket. He took a sip of champagne and glanced around at the guests already on the polished timbered floor for a quadrille. The regimental band struck up and Ian expected they would play until midnight when the guests broke for supper. He knew he would be bored by then as he had come alone, as prescribed by the invitation.

He saw Rebecca enter the dance floor on the arm of Jenkins, and he swallowed the last of his drink, looking around for a servant to replenish his empty glass.

As he did so, his eyes fell on a sight that almost caused him to drop the crystal coupe. 'God almighty!'

It was Ella, standing alone on the other side of the dance floor. She was holding a small fan and wearing a voluminous silk dress drawn in tightly at the waist, her shoulders bare. She appeared a little bemused and when she turned her head and caught sight of Ian, her expression mirrored his amazement.

Ian made his way around the tables to her.

'Ella! What are you doing here?' he asked.

'I would ask the same of you,' she replied. 'I was assured by Lady Montegue that you would not be attending tonight. That is the only reason I accepted her unexpected invitation.'

'Did your invitation specify that it was for you alone?' Ian asked, a suspicion forming in his mind.

'Yes, it did,' Ella replied, and Ian broke into a crooked grin.

'That is no accident,' he said, and remembered the dance card in his jacket. He retrieved it and saw his and Ella's names inscribed for a waltz following the quadrille. The quadrille had now finished and when the floor was clear, the bandmaster announced the next dance was a waltz.

'I believe this is our dance,' Ian said, taking Ella's elbow to escort her onto the floor.

He placed his arm around her waist and they stepped off in time to the rhythm of the music.

'I said that I would never see you again,' Ella said. 'Has fate brought us together tonight?'

'No, not fate but the scheming of Lady Montegue,' Ian replied. 'But I cannot think of a more beautiful woman to be in my arms right now.'

Ella blushed, tightening her hand on Ian's. It was said that the waltz was a licentious dance, leading to fornication, and for a moment Ian hoped that was true. With this beautiful young woman in his arms, floating across the polished floor together, his attempt to distance himself from her was forgotten.

'*I wonder, by my troth, what thou and I Did, till we loved?*' Ian said softly.

'*Were we not weaned till then?*' Ella said, looking into Ian's eyes. 'You are certainly a man of many surprises, Samuel Forbes. John Donne, "The Good Morrow". I would not expect a man whose life is devoted to soldiering to understand the pure romanticism of such a poem. I think we both understand its meaning, do we not?'

Just then the music stopped and the dancers left the floor. Ian was about to say something when he saw Rebecca gesturing to him. He escorted Ella to a table where some of the younger officers of the regiment were engaged in sipping claret and smoking cigars.

'Look after this lady, gentlemen,' he commanded as he pulled out her chair. 'I will be returning.'

The young officers said they would be delighted, and as Ian walked away he wondered if leaving Ella alone with those handsome and eligible men was such a good idea.

'I am pleased to see that you have been following your dance card,' Rebecca said with a smile.

'You planned this,' Ian said without any rancour. 'Why?'

'Let us just say that I learned that you have dealings with Miss Solomon's father and that he is a man with a formidable reputation for getting things done. I also remember that you escorted his daughter to her debut ball and he was very grateful. I gather that you have been seen many times in her company since, and when I look at the young lady, I can see why any man would risk the ire of Ikey Solomon. But he would have to be a very brave – or foolish – man to do that, and I know you are not foolish. You must have strong feelings for Miss Solomon. I ask that you escort her home after the ball. I promised Mr Solomon you would do that for him.'

'Good Lord!' Ian said. 'Jane was never this conniving.'

'It is because of my sister's memory that I have courted favour with Mr Solomon,' Rebecca replied. 'When the time comes for justice to be dispensed, I know he will be able to assist. Besides, if Clive does one day become prime minister, it will not hurt to have Mr Solomon as a discreet friend.'

Ian stared at Rebecca. 'I do hope I never get on the wrong side of you, Lady Montegue.'

She smiled warmly. 'I should also mention that when you escort Miss Solomon home, it will be in her carriage. Mr Solomon has arranged this with his man, Egbert.'

Egbert. Ian knew the employee as a tough and dangerous thug. Thoughts of the remainder of John Donne's poem melted away. Egbert was more than capable of breaking bones with his bare hands. He was almost as dangerous as Rebecca Montegue. She was one of the most manipulative people he had encountered but he respected her strategic mind. Ian almost felt sorry for Colonel Clive Jenkins in the hands of his future wife.

'You know,' Ian said, shaking his head, 'you would be a far more suitable commanding officer of our regiment than Colonel Jenkins. You have a fine head for tactics.'

'Ah, but it is well accepted that we ladies are simple, weak and frivolous creatures. It is not in us to be leaders, but simply the bearers of children and keepers of the house.' She gazed guilelessly at him.

Ian smiled broadly. He was not fooled for a moment.

FIFTEEN

The hulking man in the driver's seat of the carriage watched Ian like a hawk.

Ian helped Ella onto the carriage seat and sat opposite her for the journey to a small but comfortable cottage Ikey owned as his country retreat, away from the smog and slums of London. Ian ached with the desire to hold Ella and lie with her naked in a big comfortable bed and remain there forever in her arms. He knew by Ella's response to Donne's poem that she, too, wished to be with him. Of course, Egbert's presence ensured that would not happen. Ian did not doubt that if he had acted in an inappropriate manner towards Ikey Solomon's chaste daughter, he would likely not make it back to London alive.

Not even a kiss passed between them as Ian walked her to the door. The subtle, hidden touch of their hands was their only physical contact under the watch of eagle-eyed

Egbert. The touch was like an electric shock to Ian, who had experienced such a thing as a young man at a travelling show where a man demonstrated this new thing called electricity. Now he felt it again and knew the most important thing in his life was to be with Ella, regardless of the consequences. After all, within days he would be steaming to India and there his life might come to a brutal end at any moment.

'Excuse me for a moment, my love,' Ian said, and returned to Egbert in the carriage.

'Bert, I need a couple of hours alone with Miss Solomon,' Ian said, reaching into his trouser pocket.

'I have my orders from Ikey,' Egbert growled. 'You are to return with me now.'

Ian opened his hand, revealing a sparkling diamond he had retrieved when his company had looted a Russian baggage train in the Crimea. He always carried the precious gem for luck and considered it might prove to be so now.

'I appreciate your loyalty to Ikey but I am leaving for India very soon and would like to have a couple of hours in the company of Miss Solomon. She is agreeable to this, I assure you. This diamond is worth more than a working man's lifetime of wages and I think that you deserve it.'

Ian could see Egbert eyeing the glittering stone with intense avarice and awe. Loyalty to Solomon and greed seemed to battle inside him.

'As you are steaming for India, Captain Forbes,' Egbert eventually said, 'I can understand that you might wish to speak with Miss Solomon, but Ikey must never know about it.'

'That goes without saying,' Ian said, passing the diamond to Ikey's henchman.

'Two hours and I will be back, Captain Forbes,' he said, and flicked the reins to urge the horse forward. When he was out of sight, Ian returned to Ella.

'Do you want this?' he asked, and she nodded.

Hand in hand they walked through the cottage door.

What followed in the next couple of hours was worth all the diamonds Ian had ever possessed. He had almost forgotten how love could be expressed in such a physical way, with such joyful passion. All too quickly, however, their time together was over.

'It is time for me to leave,' Ian said reluctantly, rising from the bed and beginning to dress himself.

Tears began to stream down Ella's face. 'I can never love any man as I love you,' she said. 'Please come back to me safely and then we will be together always.'

Ian did not reply. He was acutely aware that war gave no guarantees.

He kissed Ella tenderly and then walked out into the darkness. Egbert was waiting for him, and Ian climbed aboard the carriage to return to London.

*

The regiment marched down to the wharf in the early evening. Their departure did not attract as much attention as when they had sailed to confront the Tsar's army in the Crimea. This time a scattered crowd of civilians lined the streets and urchins fell in behind the columns of soldiers marching to the beat of drums and the sound of trumpets.

Ian led his company and glanced from the corner of his eye to see if he recognised anyone amongst the gaggle of spectators. He hoped to see Ella, but by the time they arrived at the ships he hadn't sighted her. He spotted Molly, here to see Conan and Owen embark on the troopship.

When Ian had overseen his company boarding the ship, he clambered up the gangway to stand at the railings beside Conan and Owen. They had become a recognised trio in the company and many speculated about this. The old hands who had served in the Crimea and Persia with Ian's company soon set the newcomers straight. The trinity of the three men – two senior non-commissioned officers and a commissioned officer – brought the company luck.

Below them they could see Molly looking up at them with a tear-streaked face. She was waving a handkerchief and mouthing words drowned by the din of the wharf and the music of the regimental band playing the Scottish tune of 'Auld Lang Syne'. Soldiers on the ships and those waving farewell on the wharf joined in the singing.

Then Ian saw Ella.

She was not singing but staring up at him with a sad face. He saw her mouth some words and did not have to be a lip-reader to understand that she had said she loved him. He felt a lump in his throat and waved to her just as the ships slipped their ropes, taking advantage of the tide. It was like a recurring dream, Ian thought, as Ella became a small figure amongst all the wives, mothers, lovers, sisters and children saying goodbye to their soldier husbands, sons, lovers and brothers.

Ian made a vow there and then: if he returned from this campaign he would confront Ikey Solomon and declare his love for the formidable man's only daughter. He knew that could prove more dangerous than facing a battleline of well-armed enemy sepoys.

⋆

Major Scott Campbell sat astride his horse, gazing at the camp of white tents before the formidable walls of the Indian city of Delhi. Their own camp looked so insignificant compared to the expanse of the walled city. Forces composed of sepoys loyal to the Queen and British soldiers of the East India Company were here to take Delhi back from the Indian rebellion. Scott knew that his brother and sister-in-law had taken up residence in the British lines and he worried for their safety. As such, he had chosen to ride out to reconnoitre a position to the right rear of the British lines where their forces were thin on the ground.

Scott rode a mile and brought his horse to a halt. Observing a dust cloud rising on the horizon, he retrieved a small telescope from his pack. In the view he could see a tiny figure on a horse galloping at full speed towards him, and beyond the horseman Scott could see the tiny figures of enemy cavalry that had somehow got behind the British lines.

Scott pulled his horse around and set off at a gallop to return as fast as he could to the camp. He rode hard, his mount in a lather when he reached the lines. 'Saddle, boots and mount up!' he yelled. 'The enemy is upon us!'

Immediately cavalrymen tumbled from tents, throwing saddles on their horses and snatching weapons. Scott waited only a short time until a small force was ready for action, and suddenly realised that Peter was at his stirrup.

'What is happening?' Peter called up to his brother.

'The devils must have filed across the causeway behind us and formed up. They are coming in force.'

'I am coming with you,' Peter said, brandishing his big six-shot revolver.

'You need to stay and protect Alice,' Scott shouted down at Peter.

'If we don't stop them before they reach the camp we will all be finished,' Peter replied, comprehending the gravity of the sudden attack.

'Grab a horse and hurry then,' Scott said. Peter rushed to the horse lines, threw a saddle on a mount and quickly joined his brother. As soon as he did, Scott ordered the advance and the defending force set off to meet the attack.

They rode for a half-mile with outlying cavalrymen acting as picquets. When Scott spotted the dust cloud and the mutineer cavalry formation that had caused it, his heart sank. He guessed that his own meagre force was outnumbered at least four to one. He withdrew his curved sabre, held it aloft and roared, 'At a gallop, charge!'

The line of mutineer cavalry was taken aback by the absolute madness of such a small force galloping towards them, screaming their war cries, and the line halted before turning to fall back.

Scott had expected they would crash into the attacking force and be annihilated, but his bold move had unsettled the attacking enemy. Each of the British and loyal Indian cavalrymen knew his business and singled out their foe for combat as the enemy retreated. The British sabres descended, inflicting terrible wounds as the razor-sharp blades sliced through arms, shoulders and heads.

Peter kept close to his brother, who was locked in battle with a mutineer, slashing and parrying his opponent's desperate attempts to defend himself. The horses crashed together and whinnied their confusion. Peter suddenly noticed that the Indian cavalryman had taken advantage of an opening in his brother's defence and was on the verge of delivering a death blow. Peter was only feet away, fighting to control his panicked mount. He brought up his heavy revolver, firing at almost point-blank range at the head of the man about to kill his brother. The shot was true and the mutineer slumped from his horse, slamming into the hard and dusty ground below.

Scott swung around to see the smoking revolver in Peter's hand, realising that his brother had just saved his life.

He nodded his appreciation and spurred his mount towards a group of fleeing enemy. Peter followed and they went in pursuit of the larger force now attempting to retreat to a causeway. In their panic the enemy had milled into a confused mass, all attempting to cross the narrow causeway at once. The smaller British force took advantage of their disorganisation, and the slaughter continued at the entrance to the causeway in close-quarter killing.

The frenzy of battle had overtaken Peter's senses and he picked out an enemy lancer who wheeled around to confront him. Peter raised his pistol, firing two shots which missed, and suddenly the enemy horseman was on him. Peter felt the lance pierce his side, dragging him from his mount, and he crashed onto the earth, winded. He could taste dirt in his mouth and felt the lance being withdrawn from his body. Peter screamed his pain and realised that he had lost his pistol in the fall. He looked up to see the mutineer cavalry lancer rearranging his blood-tipped lance for a second strike.

Knowing he was about to be skewered, Peter experienced more regret than fear. His last image was of Alice's face. The look of triumph on the enemy lancer's face suddenly evaporated as it was smashed by a bullet. From the corner of his eye, Peter could see his brother's arm holding his own revolver, smoke drifting from the end of the barrel.

The lancer toppled from his horse, and Scott reached down from his own mount to grip Peter's outstretched hand.

'Get on your horse, old boy,' he yelled above the terrible din of men screaming, horses neighing and the metal clash of swords and sabres.

Despite the pain, Peter dragged himself into the saddle and scooped up the reins. The exhausted British force fell back into a disciplined formation as the remainder of the enemy cavalrymen retreated across the causeway, galloping back to the protection of the great walls of Delhi.

Peter realised how thirsty he was as the dust choked his throat and the adrenaline of battle began to seep away. Even Peter could see there was no sense in pursuing the survivors of the fierce battle. The retreating force still outnumbered them; if they attempted to finish the mission, they would have to file across the causeway, and the enemy might suddenly find the courage to fall into a formation to counter them.

'How bad is your wound?' Scott asked, seeing the wet, dark patch on his brother's left side.

'I will have to make my examination when we return to our lines,' Peter grimaced.

Scott gave the order to withdraw, and the weary column fell into a march after reclaiming their own wounded from the battlefield. Within the hour, Peter sat in his tent with his blood-soaked jacket on a chair beside him. Alice was fighting back her tears while chiding her husband at the same time.

'It is not your role to fight like your brother,' she said, washing the two-sided jagged wound from which blood still oozed. 'What insanity persuaded you to go with him?'

'I could see that our plight was desperate, and Scott needed every man he could muster to ward off the attack on the camp. I knew we must stop them from getting to our lines. It was our only hope.'

'But you are not a soldier. You are a surgeon,' Alice countered.

'I wear the uniform of a British officer, albeit without any commissioned rank. I am both soldier and surgeon,' Peter replied.

Alice reached for a glass bottle of antiseptic and with

it swabbed the open wound. The liquid burned and Peter groaned in pain.

'What do I do now?' Alice asked, wiping her bloody hands on an apron around her waist.

'You will have to sew it up,' Peter answered through gritted teeth. 'I know that you used to sew when we were in London, so I will leave the choice of stitch to you.'

'We have no anaesthetic,' Alice protested.

'Never mind. Just sew.'

Alice selected a needle that Peter insisted be placed in boiling water. When it had cooled she threaded the needle and began to sew the wound. Peter broke into a sweat but did not utter a word. When the task was completed Alice stood back to admire her work.

'You have done well,' Peter said hoarsely, reaching for his bloody shirt and jacket. 'I could never have imagined in my wildest thoughts that you and I would be spending our honeymoon under the current dire circumstances.' He reached across to touch his wife on the cheek. 'I could never have dreamed how very competent and courageous you are. I do not deserve you.'

A wry smile crossed Alice's face. 'I doubt the good ladies in London at their tea parties would be entertained by my adventures in India. Many of them would consider me a traitor to our gender.'

'True, my dear. Ladies do not shoot man-eating tigers, carry guns or act as assistants in surgical operations – let alone sew up their husbands!'

They both laughed.

'It is time for you to rest, Dr Campbell,' Alice said sternly. 'That is an order from a wife who has still not forgiven you for riding out with your reckless brother.'

Peter slid from the bench and took Alice in his arms.

'Mrs Campbell, I love you just a bit more every time I wake to see a new day.'

⋆

The troop transport had reached the southern tip of Africa and anchored at Cape Town for supplies.

Colonel Jenkins sat opposite a staff officer of major rank in the sweeping room adorned with the portraits of former governors and a young Queen Victoria at Government House. He was mystified as to why he had been called to this special meeting before the one scheduled for all officers of the expeditionary force steaming for India.

'Sir, a telegram has been received from the general staff in India,' the smartly dressed officer said. 'We have been requested to supply a rifle company in a rescue mission once the force reaches India. It is your regiment that has the honour of supplying that company.'

'Who is behind the request, Major?' Jenkins asked, suspicious about why his regiment had been singled out for what was likely a dangerous mission.

'General Outram, sir,' the major replied. 'It appears he is aware of your regiment from the Persian campaign.'

'Is the mission considered risky?' Jenkins asked.

'I must be honest and say it is,' the major said. 'It will be deep in territory overrun by the mutineers in the Bengali region. It was decided to risk only a single company should things go wrong in the rescue attempt.'

'I have an officer who is suited to this request. A captain already known to the general, one Captain Samuel Forbes. I know that Captain Forbes will jump at the opportunity to lead his men into such a venture.'

Jenkins was delighted. The pact he had made with Charles Forbes during the Crimean campaign still stood.

It had been settled that if Jenkins could ever place Captain Samuel Forbes in a situation that got him killed, Jenkins would be richly rewarded. But Clive Jenkins did not even need the substantial bounty, as his hatred for the man was such that he'd send him to his death even if he was not to be rewarded. He vividly remembered the slights he had endured when he had been under Samuel Forbes' command during the Crimean campaign. He grudgingly accepted that Forbes was an outstanding officer, but he was also a living reminder of Jenkins' own cowardice. One way or the other the captain must die, and here was the perfect opportunity.

'If that is all, Major, I will inform Captain Forbes of his mission,' Jenkins said, rising from his chair.

'There is just one other thing before I pass on detailed instructions, sir,' the major said, holding a thick package of sealed papers. 'This mission is considered to be top secret and not to be communicated to anyone else. When Captain Forbes has taken in the contents of the mission, as outlined in these orders, the papers are to be destroyed.' He passed the package to Jenkins, who smiled warmly. In his hands he held Captain Samuel Forbes' death warrant.

SIXTEEN

Ian stood in the cabin of the expeditionary force's flagship. He saluted Colonel Jenkins who was sitting behind a small desk.

'Sit down, Captain Forbes,' Jenkins said, waving to a chair adjacent to the desk. 'I have summoned you here to discuss a mission assigned to our regiment by General Outram.'

Ian was pleased to hear the name of the British general he greatly admired. Whatever the mission, he knew it must be important. On the table, Ian could see a bulky brown envelope that had been closed with a seal. Jenkins fingered it for a moment, inspecting the seal, then he pushed back his chair and stood, his head almost touching the wooden ceiling of stout ship's timbers. Both men could feel the motion of the vessel rolling on the southern seas.

'I have volunteered your company to rescue a very important man to the Empire. He is the Khan of the Bengali district, and he and his family are currently hiding out in a coastal village – as you will see when you examine the documents the general's HQ has provided. From what is known, the area is heavily infested with mutineers. It will be your job to get the Khan and his family safely to one of our warships, and from there he will be taken to London. The details are in here,' Jenkins said, and finally handed the sealed packet to Ian. 'Needless to say our meeting is strictly confidential. At the appropriate time, and not before, you will brief those included in the mission. When we reach port in India, you and your company will be transferred to another ship bound for the Bengali coast. You will destroy the contents of that packet when you have perused them.'

Jenkins sat down again and busied himself with the papers on his desk. 'Good luck, Captain Forbes,' he said without much conviction. 'If you have any questions, you know where to find me.'

'Very good, sir,' Ian replied, then he stood and saluted.

He returned to the cabin he shared with his company second-in-command, Lieutenant Ross Woods, who was a man in his forties without the financial means to purchase a captaincy. He was an experienced officer, however, and Ian was pleased to have him in his company.

Ian opened the envelope and laid the papers on his bunk to examine them in detail. He was reassured to see that he was to confide the mission to his senior NCO and whoever he appointed as his second-in-command for the actual operation ashore. Ian had already decided that employing a few chosen men of his company would be the best way to track down and extract the Khan from India. He knew that he could trust Woods to assume command whilst he and his selected men went ashore.

When Ian was satisfied that he had taken in all the intelligence the report provided, he carefully folded the papers, securing them in a small locker for which only he had a key. He would dispose of them later. Then he made his way to the deck of the ship where he knew he would find his company sergeant major.

'Sarn't Major, a good evening to you,' Ian said, joining Conan at the railing. The seas were calm and fluorescence followed the wake of the steamship.

'Evening, sah,' Conan replied, tapping his pipe on the rail. 'A grand night it is.'

'You may not think so after what I am about to tell you,' Ian said. 'Our old friend, General Outram, is requesting that a company from the regiment carry out a very secret and rather perilous mission when we get to India. Colonel Jenkins has chosen us to undertake that mission.'

'I am not surprised,' Conan grinned. 'Considering how our illustrious colonel would like to see you dead.'

'That may be so,' Ian agreed. 'But it also puts the lives of my men in harm's way. That includes you. I may have a way to exclude you from the mission.'

'Sir, you and I will come to blows if you leave me out,' Conan said with a pained expression. 'You will need me, and Owen. It's in our Celtic blood to fight.'

Ian stared at the calm seas under a rising moon and felt humbled by Conan's willingness to stand by his side. 'Maybe there will be a way to minimise the risks to the company. I will need time to figure that out. Mr Sinclair will act as my second-in-command in the mission.'

'Captain Sinclair's brother?' Conan queried. 'He has not seen any action. Do you think he is a wise choice, considering that we lost his brother at the Redan?'

'I have a feeling Mr Sinclair will acquit himself well,' Ian replied. 'He has to start somewhere, and I know if you keep an eye on him he will be as safe as any soldier can be.'

Conan nodded his understanding.

'I forgot to mention that there is one other very important reason why Mr Sinclair should accompany us,' Ian added. 'He speaks the Indian language. According to his record of service, Mr Sinclair studied the language at university before taking his commission. It seems he also had ideas of joining the honourable East India Company but decided on the army when Miles was killed. He is keen to use his language skills when we get to India.'

'What about Owen?' Conan asked.

'Sergeant Williams will remain with the company and assume the temporary role of CSM in your absence,' Ian said.

'We will miss his canny knack of finding things that sparkle and gleam,' Conan chuckled, plugging his pipe with tobacco.

'Look at it this way,' Ian said with a wry grin, 'if we fail and don't come back, he will get extra pay for your job as the future CSM.'

'The bastard,' Conan said without rancour as both men continued to gaze out at the silver path the rising moon cast on the ocean.

*

James reluctantly accompanied Samuel to the Kentish village not far from the Forbes country manor, taking a hired carriage north-east of Dover Port and booking into lodgings on the outskirts of the little community.

The next day Samuel dressed in his best suit and top hat and informed James that he would go to the village church to visit the memorial to his brother, Herbert, who had been killed in the Crimean War. Ian had said that Sir Archibald had commissioned a stained-glass window in honour of his youngest son's memory.

James expressed his concern but let his love for Samuel silence his fears.

Samuel left in a hired carriage and journeyed the short distance to the church. It was typical of so many English churches, with its graveyard bearing headstones weathered by the years, and a flower garden carefully tended by the parish priest.

Samuel walked towards the arched entry and was startled when a voice said behind him, 'Good morning, Captain Forbes.'

Samuel turned to see a man dressed in gardening clothes and guessed he was the parish priest. When he did so he noticed a sudden expression of puzzlement on the man's face.

'I am afraid that you have mistaken me, sir,' Samuel said, his heart beating hard in his chest. 'I am John Wilford from London.' Samuel used the name on his forged identity papers.

'Oh, I am sorry,' the Anglican priest said, wiping his hands on a dirty cloth. 'It is just that you bear an uncanny resemblance to a Captain Samuel Forbes, but I realise that I must be mistaken as the last I heard of Captain Forbes and his regiment was that they had been sent to India to sort out that terrible mutiny. May I offer you a cup of tea? I am Father Ogilvie.'

Samuel felt his heartbeat slow with relief. 'I thank you for your kind offer of hospitality, Father, but I am a sight-seeing visitor to your parish and do not have long to see all the local attractions.'

'I would hardly describe my church as a tourist attraction,' Father Ogilvie smiled, 'but I do have a loyal parish on Sundays for services. Even Captain Forbes' father,

Sir Archibald, attends on a regular basis since the unfortunate death of his youngest son.'

The mention of Sir Archibald's name caused Samuel a flood of memories of a young man many years earlier left at the gates of a regiment, armed with a commission he never wanted and began to hate when he faced his first battle in New Zealand against the fierce Maori warriors.

'I believe there is a memorial to Herbert's death in the church,' Samuel said.

'How is it that you know the name of Sir Archibald's son?' the priest asked. 'I thought you were a visitor to our little village.'

Samuel felt the cold sweat of fear when he realised his slip. 'Oh, I overheard the local people mention it at the tavern,' he replied, his hands suddenly clammy. He could see that the priest was staring at him, pondering Samuel's answer.

'If you accompany me I can show you Herbert Forbes' memorial window,' Ogilvie said, and Samuel followed him inside to a large, colourful stained-glass window through which the sun streamed, illuminating a red-coated soldier being taken to heaven by two winged angels. Underneath the glass was written Herbert's name and the place and year of his death. Samuel gazed with reverence at the expensive window dedicated to his brother.

'It is certainly impressive,' Samuel said.

'Sir Archibald did not spare any expense in having it crafted,' Ogilvie said. 'As a matter of fact, he will be arriving here very soon for a meeting with the church council.'

'Thank you for showing me the memorial window, Father,' Samuel said, startled by the news of Sir Archibald's imminent arrival. He was the last person Samuel wished to encounter; his father would not be so easily fooled as the parish priest. 'I must leave now.'

Samuel walked quickly out of the church, replacing his top hat and striding towards his carriage. He had hardly gone a few steps when the rattle of a second carriage sounded outside the church gate only a few paces away. As Samuel feared, it was a fine carriage drawn by two thoroughbred horses and driven by a uniformed servant. In the open back in a leather seat was a white-haired man with a face flushed red by the summer sun. Beside Sir Archibald sat his eldest son, Charles. Samuel's first impression was of how old Sir Archibald had grown since he'd last seen him at the gates of the regiment. Samuel prayed that he would reach his carriage before either man noticed him. He was relieved to see that Sir Archibald was being helped from the carriage by Charles, who handed his father a walking stick, ignoring Samuel altogether.

Samuel kept his face down and climbed into the carriage, giving the driver instructions to return to the village immediately. As the driver prepared to depart, Samuel could just make out the conversation between the three men, and felt his blood run cold when he heard Ogilvie remark that he had just had a visitor who bore a remarkable resemblance to Samuel and knew of Herbert. From the corner of his eye, Samuel could see the outstretched arm of the priest pointing to him and Charles turning to stare right at him.

*

The puff of smoke rising from the walls of Delhi heralded a large mortar being fired at the low rise where Scott and Peter stood, facing the formidable city walls.

'Time to seek cover,' Scott said and they both stepped behind a large rock. Seconds later the mortar bomb exploded a short distance from them, spattering the rock with red-hot metal and loose stones.

'They had the right angle but not the right range,' Scott said, standing and brushing down his uniform. 'Well, time to return to camp and see if that grain merchant has arrived,' he decided, striding towards their horses which were grazing on lower ground.

The British operation could not really be called a siege as the British forces were spread around only one area of the city's walls, and the mutineers were able to have reinforcements arrive elsewhere on a daily basis to fortify the city. The mutineers had concentrated their army within the city's great walls in an attempt to confront their enemy, and the commanders of the British forces could only wait and pray that reinforcements would arrive before any serious effort to take the city was made.

'Look!' Peter said, pointing to a gateway in the city wall. Scott swung around in the saddle to see a large column of Indian cavalry accompanied by infantry flowing across the plain towards the camp.

'Go!' Scott shouted as he dug his stirrups into his mount, forcing it into an urgent gallop towards the fortified lines defending the village of white army tents. The mutineers were mounting a large-scale attack on the camp, and Peter knew where he must be when the fighting commenced. Within minutes he flung himself from his horse inside the British camp. Both horse and rider were bathed in sweat from the hard ride under a fierce sun.

Already Peter could hear the roar of the defending British cannons pouring canister shot and high explosive into the waves of approaching enemy infantry.

Peter ran to a tent, flinging open the flap to see that Alice was already laying out his surgical instruments and ordering servants to fetch buckets of water, anticipating the flow of wounded from the battlefield.

'The Sikhs and Gurkhas have taken up their posts,' she said to Peter as he stripped away his officer's jacket and grabbed an apron that had been washed but still bore the stains of blood from previous surgeries. This had not been the first attack on their camp, and each time the casualties on their side whittled down their numbers. Reinforcements had to come soon or the mutineers would surely wipe them out.

Peter quickly surveyed his instruments and medicines, assessing what he had to work with. He glanced up at his wife who, although grim-faced, appeared to be as composed and ready as he. She was now his main nurse and assistant during surgery, for which she showed a genuine flair and interest. It was a shame, he felt, that women were not cut out to be surgeons. It was simply a law of nature, he explained to Alice, but privately he doubted his own convictions when he watched his wife stitching and dressing wounds. He admitted to himself that he could not have done better.

The crackle of rifled muskets and the blast of cannons filled the air around the camp. Within ten minutes the first of their patients was carried to them on a stretcher. He was a British captain whose face had been smashed by a musket ball. Blood streamed down his jacket as he was sat up on the operating table, once a stout wooden dining table.

Peter examined the officer's face but could only see an entry wound when he splashed water over the injury. He could see that the ball had smashed out the man's teeth.

'I think he has swallowed the ball,' Alice said, peering over Peter's shoulder.

'I think you are right,' he said, turning to Alice. 'Could you attend to his wound?'

Alice took the officer by the elbow, assisting him to a corner of the tent just as another casualty was littered in by two Sikh soldiers. This soldier had a stomach wound and was groaning in agony as he was laid out on the table. And then another wounded man was brought in, and Alice calmly began to organise that the wounded be laid out on stretchers in front of the tent. She went from one to the next with soothing words of comfort, a canteen of water, and an eye for who most needed her husband's surgical skills next. Those with lesser wounds she tended to with disinfectant and bandages.

The day drew on until eventually the roar of cannons and musketry died down as the mutineers withdrew from the battlefield. Outside Peter's surgery tent, amputated arms and legs had piled up and were covered by a swarm of fat feasting flies. The soldiers with the stomach wounds were inoperable and Peter used his meagre supply of opiates to ease their agony until death took them.

The sun was setting on the dusty horizon when Peter and Alice sat, exhausted and covered in drying blood, on a bench outside the surgical tent. Soldiers had been recruited to minister to the needs of the wounded and to carry away the bodies of the dead.

Peter took Alice's hand as they gazed with vacant eyes at the peaceful stars above. 'It will not always be like this,' he said in a tired voice. 'One day we will return to a sane life in London.'

Alice chose not to reply. She felt Peter would not understand that she felt exhilarated by her role helping the wounded. This experience was so far removed from the tedious garden parties and balls that would have made up her social calendar had she been at home in England. Here, what she did was as important as the role of any man, and it gave her life new meaning. Alice was in no hurry to return to her uneventful life in London.

SEVENTEEN

'That man who just left, Father Ogilvie, do you know him?' Charles asked.

'A Mr Wilford,' Ogilvie replied. 'A nice gentleman on a holiday visiting our parish. It was interesting that he knew of the window dedicated to your brother, Herbert.'

Charles took in the information and swore under his breath. Sir Archibald looked at his son with reprobation.

'What is it, Charles?' he asked.

'Did you not see the man who just departed?' Charles asked his father.

'No, I was talking to Father Ogilvie.'

'Well, if you had, you might have been looking at the Samuel we both once knew,' Charles said.

'Samuel is with the army in India,' Sir Archibald answered, confused at Charles' statement.

Charles thought hard for a moment. 'What if the man

you think of as Samuel is an imposter, someone who has conspired with the true Samuel to take his place in the army? Samuel always hated being in the military. What if he has found someone to take his place and complete his ten years of service so that he is able to claim his share of the Forbes estate?'

'Don't be foolish, Charles. What man would take Samuel's place and risk his life in such a manner? No, it is ridiculous. Besides, when Samuel returned to London it was obvious that he knew too much about the family's secrets to be an imposter. It would take a very intelligent man to be able to fool me.'

'You know, I have heard from officers in the regiment that the men call Captain Forbes "the Colonial". What if Samuel met a man with a striking resemblance to him whilst in New South Wales? It is possible that they made a pact to swap places. I say that the man you think is Samuel is an imposter, and that the real Samuel was just here.'

'It sounds preposterous to me,' Archibald said with a frown. 'You will need to provide evidence. Go and meet with the man who just left.'

'I will do that,' Charles said, and turned to Father Ogilvie. 'Did Mr Wilford say where he was staying in the village?'

'I am afraid not,' Ogilvie replied. 'There is only the one tavern in the village, so my guess is that is where you will find him.'

'Father, I will take our carriage and go immediately to the tavern.'

Without waiting for a reply, Charles strode to the carriage, instructing the driver to take him to the village tavern and leaving a befuddled Sir Archibald in his wake.

*

'There's no Mr Wilford staying here, Mr Forbes,' the tavern keeper answered. 'He might be staying at the boarding house on the northern side of the village, though.'

Charles hurried back to the carriage and directed the driver to the boarding house, where the landlady told him that a Mr Wilford and his travelling companion had just fifteen minutes ago paid their bill and left. She did not know where they were going and Charles guessed it was probably London. He knew there was no sense in pursuing them – in this parish there were too many byroads heavily covered with trees that could easily hide a small carriage.

Charles decided he must return immediately to London and make contact again with Mr Field. The truth about Captain Forbes was about to be uncovered and so, too, what Charles was convinced was his brother's fraudulent attempt to claim his inheritance. He smiled grimly as he returned to his coach. He was on the verge of exposing an ingenious plot to defraud the family fortune.

*

Samuel and James, both wrung out after their headlong flight from the village, arrived in Dover and went straight to the wharf where their ship was docked. To their horror there was no sign of it. The ship had sailed!

When they asked around the wharves they were informed that the vessel's repairs had been completed and it had sailed some hours earlier.

'What are we to do?' James asked in despair.

'We have no choice but to continue to London and make contact with Mr Solomon,' Samuel said, staring at the vacant space where their ticket to safety had been waiting for them.

'I had a bad feeling circumstances would not be in our

favour when you chose to visit your brother's memorial,' James said bitterly. 'Luck has not been on our side.'

'I am sorry, dear James,' Samuel said sadly. 'I suppose my stubbornness has brought us to this place. I should say that you warned me it would.'

'Too late for recriminations,' James replied in a resigned tone. 'Pray that Mr Solomon is disposed to assist us once again.'

⋆

It was at Ceylon that Ian's company was transferred to another steamship. His men boarded, mystified as to why they were being separated from the regiment. Only Ian, Conan and Lieutenants Woods and Sinclair knew the reason as their ship raised its anchors and steamed alone on a northerly route along the east coast of India.

The ship, disguised as a merchant vessel, was not heavily armed but did carry a detachment of Royal Marines. As the ship approached the delta of West Bengal, Ian felt it was time to gather his company of riflemen on deck to brief them on their mission. It was a viciously hot, cloudless day.

'Men, no doubt you have been wondering why you were chosen to join this ship whilst the regiment remained behind to travel to Calcutta. I can tell you now that Colonel Jenkins has chosen us for a mission to save an Indian prince of strategic importance to England. Because of the sensitive nature of what we will be doing, it has remained a secret until now. Very soon, the ship will anchor off the coast and you will be further briefed on your role in this operation. For the moment you remain with the ship under the command of Mr Woods. That is all I can tell you at present, but be assured, we will bring honour to the regiment and the Queen.'

One of the soldiers in the ranks raised his voice and called, 'Three cheers for the Colonial and the Queen.'

The cheers erupted and Ian was touched by his men's sentiments. He noted that cheers had not been offered for Colonel Jenkins.

'Sarn't Major, fall out the parade,' Ian ordered and Conan stepped forward, saluted and turned to dismiss the infantrymen back to their allocated duties.

Ian made his way to the bridge to find the ship's captain, a burly Scotsman with a gingery beard and ruddy complexion. Ian saluted the superior rank of the British naval captain.

'Well, Captain Forbes, as per orders from the Admiralty, we will drop anchor tonight about a mile from the coast. I have been able to secure all the stores you require for your mission. I will arrange to have them taken to your cabin.'

The captain ordered a young naval sailor to carry the bundle of garments to Ian's cabin, and Conan and Lieutenant Sinclair met him there.

'Gentlemen,' Ian said, pulling apart the bundle of native Indian clothing and revealing six revolvers and three wicked-looking American Bowie knives. 'This is our uniform and our weapons for the task ahead.'

Conan lifted one of the heavy Colt 1851 Navy revolvers from the bundle of clothing. 'I have always wanted one of these,' he said with pleasure.

'You get to have two of the Colts each,' Ian said. 'They are ideal for what we have to do.'

The two men picked through the clothing and dressed with advice from Lieutenant Sinclair, who was something of an authority on Indian customs, clothing, culture and language – at least from an academic point of view. Each man was able to conceal the weapons he carried, as well as the ammunition required. They then applied dark polish to their faces and hands, the only flesh exposed when the clothing was adjusted. To all intents and purposes, and if no one looked too closely, they could pass as Bengali locals. Ian had ensured that he had a good supply of rupees with him in a leather pouch.

A knock on the door of the cabin alerted Ian and his team of two that it was time to commence the dangerous mission. The Indian prince was somewhere ashore in a village not far from the coast. All Ian had was a map drawn up by a member of Outram's staff who was familiar with the area, and intelligence that was six weeks out of date. For all Ian knew, the prince and his family had been discovered by the mutineers and murdered.

They followed a marine officer above decks and were pleased to see that heavy storm clouds had masked the half-moon. Six marines sat in a landing boat waiting to ferry their passengers ashore. Ian, Conan and Lieutenant Sinclair clambered over the side on a rope ladder to join the men who would row them towards the faint lights of the coastal village a mile away. It was just after midnight and Ian experienced both exhilaration and fear for what lay ahead.

The tide was running in and the clinker-built wooden landing boat made good progress through a shallow surf, beaching on a muddy bank covered by scrub trees. In the distance they could see a fishing hut with a lantern burning in the window.

'Good luck, chaps,' the marine officer whispered. 'Better you than me.' With that, the marines hauled their boat off the mudflat, turning to row back to the ship which would withdraw out to sea beyond the horizon.

A soft wind blew through the long jagged grasses of the mudflats, and when the gentle slap of oars on water disappeared from hearing Ian realised just how alone they were in a hostile environment where wits and daring alone would have to carry the day.

'We take a chance and make contact with the natives in that hut ahead of us,' Ian said softly. 'Are there any questions?' Both men shook their heads, and the three trudged across the sticky mudflat until they came within paces of the small hut with its single door and window. Crouching behind a rack of fishing nets, Ian gave his last directions.

'We enter without displaying our pistols,' he said softly. 'Mr Sinclair will inform those inside that we mean them no harm, and request that they allow us to remain during the day. I will creep up and see who is in the hut.'

Ian made his way to the window to peer inside. Conan could see that the young officer was trembling and he recognised the fear.

'It's all right, sir,' he said. 'Captain Forbes and I have done this sort of thing before in the Crimea. The captain gets us safe home every time.'

Harry Sinclair could see Ian signal to them to approach the hut. The three stepped inside, startling a man sitting on the earthen floor mending a net. Beside him lay a woman under a blanket. Ian raised his finger to his lips to signal silence to the terrified man, now frozen with fear. Harry Sinclair said something that seemed to confuse the man, and his wife woke with a start, staring with petrified dark eyes at the three strangers.

Harry repeated his words and the man moved his head to indicate that he did not understand him. Frustrated, Harry turned to Ian.

'I'm sorry sir, but this man must speak a dialect I am not familiar with,' he apologised.

'That is not your fault, Mr Sinclair. I think I have the

universal language solution,' Ian said and reached under his baggy clothing to produce the leather purse. He retrieved a generous handful of rupees, offering them to the man, whose expression was a mixture of puzzlement and avarice. 'For you,' Ian said, pressing the coins into the man's hand. The universal language appeared to work as they could see some of the fear evaporate and composure return.

The man turned to his wife and said something.

'I think I understood some of his words,' Harry said triumphantly. 'I think he said we are crazy bandits who give away money rather than steal it!'

'See if you can tell them that we mean them no harm – unless they tell others that we are here. If they betray us, they will be killed,' Ian said.

Harry was able to get the message across and the man knelt, grabbing Harry's hands and babbling his gratitude.

Satisfied, Ian turned to Conan and Harry. 'We remain inside this hut until night comes again, and when it does, we set out on the next leg of our journey. According to the orders I received, we should meet a European contact in the next village who appears to have some protection against the local mutineers.'

While they waited out the day, the man left the hut and returned with water and food for his uninvited guests, reassuring Harry that he had informed no one of their presence.

The men spent the day cleaning their revolvers, ensuring that the powder loaded in the chambers was dry and that the fulminate percussion caps were secured on the nipples at the rear of each loaded chamber.

Ian had learned from the Bengali fisherman that the next leg of the mission would take them across a plain past a few scattered mud huts to a small village. They would travel that night knowing time was critical as the naval ship would return in forty-eight hours, sending a boat ashore under the cover of darkness to pick them up from the mudflats.

Evening was coming to the tropics, and as Ian prepared to move out he was suddenly alert to the noise of a party of men moving in their direction. Ian peeked out through a crack in the wall and felt his heart skip a beat. He could see a group of ten well-armed men moving towards them. Had they been betrayed?

EIGHTEEN

'What do we do, sir?' Harry asked.

'This reminds me of an incident when we were in the Crimea,' Conan said with a grim smile, unholstering his pistols.

'Ask the fisherman if he knows who the men are, Mr Sinclair,' Ian said.

Harry turned to the terrified fisherman and spoke with him.

'He says the men are bandits well known on this part of the coast. They take what they want – and that includes the women.'

'So they are not sepoy rebels,' Ian said. 'We have only one choice and that is to kill them all and let none get away. We have surprise and firepower on our side.'

'Do you mean we fight them?' Harry asked, open-mouthed.

'I strongly suggest you unholster your pistols, Mr Sinclair, and prepare to use them,' Ian said, pulling back the hammer of his Colts. 'We burst out on my order and start shooting as fast as we can until they are all dead. Any questions?'

The husband and wife clung together, huddled in the corner of the hut with absolute fear written on their faces. Ian took another peek at the approaching party of bandits, noting that they were armed with ancient muskets and long knives. They appeared relaxed and were even joking together as they came within ten paces of the hut. One of the men called out, and Ian guessed that he was the leader of the party.

'He is calling to the fisherman to come out with his wife,' Harry whispered, his trembling hands gripping his pistols.

'Get ready,' Ian said softly. 'Now!'

Ian was the first to burst out from behind the flimsy door, firing as he did so. Conan quickly followed, and behind him, Harry. Ian's first round brought down the bandit who had called out, and the man fell backwards as the .36 calibre lead ball took him in the chest. Such was the surprise of the attack that the rest of the party were momentarily frozen in their confusion, and Conan's rounds caused others to topple as each ball found a target. Only one man was able to raise his musket and fire wildly. A round from Harry took him out, and within seconds the sandy stretch in front of the hut was covered in bodies. Satisfied that the ten men were dead, Ian quickly reloaded, as did Conan.

'Time for us to get moving,' Ian said as the fisherman tumbled from the hut to stare wide-eyed at the mass of bodies in front of his hut. He spoke rapidly to Harry.

'What is he saying?' Ian asked.

'He is thanking us for saving him and his wife, and he says he will tell anyone who asks how they were killed that it was another bandit gang known in this district.'

The fisherman grasped Ian's knees, tears in his eyes, babbling his thanks, and Ian felt that the man could be trusted to keep their secret.

The trio checked their clothing and faces to make sure their disguise still held, then used the falling darkness to follow their course to a village a couple of miles away. They were to make contact at a specific house at the edge of the town marked with a painted red crescent on the door. Ian had Conan and Harry run for a while, then walk, followed by another run to put distance between themselves and the coast.

After a couple of exhausting hours he ordered a stop two hundred yards short of the village. They slumped to the grassy earth, getting their breathing under control. Each man took a long swig of water from his canteen, and after a few minutes Ian turned to Conan and Harry. 'I will leave you two here and reconnoitre the village. If I don't return, you are to make your way back to the coast and await the navy's pick-up.'

Harry and Conan accepted the order and Ian stood and walked towards the village.

'We had a close call back there,' Harry said. 'We were lucky to survive.'

'Luck is when you are charging the enemy across no-man's-land,' Conan said. 'Musket balls and grapeshot do not discriminate. At the hut, Captain Forbes knew exactly what he was doing and he decided the odds were on our side.'

'My brother always spoke highly of Captain Forbes,' said Harry. 'Said that he was born to be a soldier.'

'If you only knew,' Conan chuckled. 'There is more to Captain Forbes than any man will really know.'

They peered into the night until the darkness completely swallowed the figure of Ian Steele making his way cautiously into the village.

*

Far away in England Charles Forbes was once again in the private investigator's office.

'The man that I wish to meet is now going under another name,' Charles said. 'I would presume that this Mr Ian Steele has had help to forge a new identity.'

'Quite so,' Field answered. 'Whoever your man is, he must have contacts in London who have been helping him.'

'The man I seek I suspect to be my half-brother, Samuel, using the fictitious name of Ian Steele or John Wilford. It is vital that I confront him.'

'May I ask why?' Field asked.

'I think Samuel has hired a man to substitute for him in my grandfather's regiment. By doing so, and if this man completes ten years' service, Samuel will be able to claim his equal share of the family estates. As you can gather, he is doing this by fraudulent means, and if I can prove this he will no longer have a claim.'

'Ah, money,' Field said. 'One of the principal reasons for murder – along with love and revenge. I pray that you do not wish to do your half-brother any mischief when we find him.'

'Nothing of that nature will be necessary,' Charles said. 'Samuel will be exposed before the law and the matter of his inheritance curtailed.'

'That is good because I will not be party to anything unlawful. I know of a forger who may have assisted this man.'

'Who might that be?' Charles asked.

'A fellow by the name of Ikey Solomon. Our paths crossed when I was with the police. He has a somewhat fearsome reputation in the city's underworld and it is not wise to get on the wrong side of him. He has an office not far from here, and for a few pounds might be willing to discuss the matter with us.'

'I am prepared to pay if you think he could help us,' Charles said.

'If that is so, we might be able to meet with him now if that is convenient to you,' Field said and Charles agreed.

The office was within walking distance and the two men found themselves confronted by a burly and dangerous-looking man at the entrance to the building.

'Hello, Egbert,' Field said. 'I see that you are still working for Ikey.'

'Mr Field,' Egbert said with a note of respect. 'What brings you here?'

'I have a financial matter to discuss with Mr Solomon,' Field said. 'If you would do me the courtesy of taking me to him.'

Egbert told them to wait, then after a couple of minutes returned to usher them inside. It was obvious that the former detective inspector still had a reputation amongst London's underworld.

Egbert knocked on a door and a voice bade them enter.

Field stepped inside first, followed by Charles and Egbert.

Ikey did not bother to rise from behind his desk. 'Detective Inspector, a pleasure, I am sure, that you should visit my humble establishment. What can I do for you?'

Although he had not been offered a chair, Field found one, sat down and placed his hat on his lap. 'Ikey, I would like to introduce you to Mr Charles Forbes. He has a proposition for you that comes with a generous financial reward.'

'Charles Forbes,' Ikey said. 'Are you any relation to Captain Samuel Forbes?'

'Do you know my brother?' Charles asked, surprised that the Jewish businessman with the dangerous reputation would know Samuel, as Ikey belonged to a class of people no member of the Forbes family ought to mix with.

'I do. A fine gentleman.'

'What if I said that the man you think is my brother, Samuel Forbes, is an imposter?' Charles said, and noticed Ikey Solomon shift in his chair.

'I am sure you must be mistaken, Mr Forbes,' Ikey replied mildly.

'The brother I knew was a shy dreamer who desired a life as a poet. Does that sound like the man you know as Captain Forbes?'

Ikey did not respond to the question but leaned forward towards Charles. 'I was informed that you came here with an offer to pay me generously for my services,' he said. 'Tell me what you want.'

'We want to know if any of your acquaintances have been involved in forging identity documents for one John Wilford,' Field said. 'If you do, Mr Forbes will pay for that information.'

'Forgery is a serious crime, as you well know, Mr Field,' Ikey said. 'I am an honest businessman.'

'Mr Forbes is prepared to pay well,' Field reminded him. 'I am sure as a businessman in this part of the city you must have heard something about such criminal people.'

'I am sorry, Mr Forbes,' Ikey said. 'I cannot help you. Mr Field has the wrong man for such information.'

Field rose from his chair, replaced his top hat and gestured to Charles to follow him.

'We will bid you a good day, Mr Solomon,' Field said,

walking to the door with Charles in tow. 'If you do come across such intelligence in the future, I am sure Mr Forbes' offer will still stand.'

Ikey did not get up as the two men left his office. He frowned. Was the man he knew as Captain Samuel Forbes an imposter? If so, he had allowed his one and only precious daughter to be escorted to a ball by the man. It was time to make his own enquiries into Captain Samuel Forbes – whoever he was.

★

On the street, a small shower promised to become a heavy downfall. Charles and Field hurried back to the private investigator's office.

'Well, that proved to be fruitless,' Charles said irritably.

'I would not be so sure of that,' Field said. 'My copper instincts tell me that it is Ikey who is helping your brother, and who is in contact with the man you consider a charlatan. We learned all that without you having to spend a penny of any reward. At least I have a point to work from, but I must caution you, Mr Forbes, it will be expensive to bring to heel the two you believe are defrauding your family.'

'Money is not a consideration, Mr Field. The honour of the Forbes name is at stake,' Charles said in the most righteous tone he could muster.

'Ah, yes, family honour,' Field echoed with a knowing smirk.

★

Ian could hear the occasional barking of the village dogs that prowled the empty streets and lanes. He crouched, counting the buildings as per the sketch map he carried, until he settled on one that bordered the flat grass-covered plain from which he was making his observations. Amongst Ian's briefing was the information that his contact was a former Russian army officer. Ian was baffled by this as it was well known that the Tsar of Russia had ambitions to control the Indian subcontinent. Why would a former Russian army officer be assisting the British? Ian shrugged and crept forward to the mud-walled house, pistols in hands, to see the red crescent sign on the door.

Very gently he eased open the door, but it still creaked on it rusty hinges. Every nerve in his body was on edge.

'Hail Caesar,' Ian said, the code to be used to identify himself to the contact.

'*Et tu, Brute*,' a voice said softly from within the darkness of the tiny house.

Satisfied at the response, Ian stepped inside the hut, pistols raised. A light flared from a lantern. It took a few seconds for his sight to adjust and when it did he found himself mere paces from the Russian, who was pointing a British-manufactured revolver straight at him. The two men stared into each other's faces and the shock was mutual.

'You!' Ian hissed.

The Russian nodded incredulously.

NINETEEN

By the dim light of the lantern the two men faced each other, pistols drawn.

'I think I wished you well the last time we faced each other in the Crimea,' the tall, handsome man said with a slow smile, lowering his revolver. 'It is like an act of God's humour that we should meet again under these circumstances.'

Ian lowered his guns. 'I must apologise but I have forgotten your name since we met during that truce,' he said. 'I am Captain Samuel Forbes of Her Majesty's London Regiment.'

'I remember your name, Captain Forbes. I am Count Nikolai Kasatkin, formerly of the Tsar's army,' the Russian said without extending his hand. 'I presume by the code you gave that you are on a mission to retrieve the Khan and his family.'

'I am,' Ian said. 'The rest of the rescue party is a short distance from here, but first I am curious as to why a representative of the Tsar should be found in India when we well know that the Tsar has ambitions for this part of Her Majesty's Empire.'

'Good question, Captain Forbes, and I think it is worth an honest answer. I am working for the British Foreign Office, not for the Tsar. My allegiance has changed for personal reasons. One might say that an indiscretion in Moscow is not forgotten when one is a Jew, and as far as the Tsar's government is concerned, I am here to negotiate a deal with the Khan for a precious metal both Russia and England need for waging war.'

'What metal?' Ian asked.

'Lead,' Nikolai replied. 'The Khan has maps to potential rich lodes of lead in his district and is prepared to sell to us at a reasonable price. I was selected by my former masters to make contact as I speak the Indian language. It gave me the opportunity to correspond with friends in England I knew as a young student at Oxford. That was before we faced each other in that terrible war that cost us the Crimea.'

'I cannot see how an officer of the Tsar would turn traitor,' Ian said.

'I am a Russian but I am also a Jew, and my people are being persecuted in Russia. I have been granted British sanctuary on the condition that I use my position to encourage the Khan to go with us to England, where he can be convinced to turn over his mining rights to the East India Company. It is really the board of the East India Company that I deal with in this matter.'

'Never let a little mutiny get in the way of business,' Ian said with a wry smile. 'So, you and I find ourselves in this place at this time to assist the Company in rescuing a future trading partner.'

'It seems so,' the Russian count replied with a faint smile. 'Upon a successful outcome to our mutual mission I will able to purchase property discreetly through contacts in the London Jewish community.'

'One of those contacts would not be a man by the name of Ikey Solomon, would it?' Ian said on a hunch, and saw utter surprise cross the Russian's face.

'How do you know Ikey Solomon?' he asked.

'I have had dealings with the man in the past,' Ian replied.

'I have never met him,' Nikolai said. 'Is he a good man?'

'He is – if you don't cross him,' Ian said. 'Now, I will signal to my men to join us.' Ian stepped outside with the lantern and waved it gently and was soon joined by Conan and Harry.

They stepped inside the hut and eyed the tall stranger with suspicion.

'Count Kasatkin, this is Sergeant Major Curry and Lieutenant Sinclair, both of my company.'

'It is just the three of you,' Nikolai said, shaking his head. 'I was expecting at least a regiment to carry out the task of rescuing the Khan and his family.'

'You were allocated a company of my infantrymen but I decided that it was more discreet to use only the three of us, considering that this can be considered hostile territory and a large force of red-coated infantry would have drawn more attention than would be comfortable.'

For a moment the Russian pondered on Ian's choice. 'Probably a wise tactical decision,' he finally replied. 'I have been able to remain alive amongst the population because some of the leaders of the mutiny in this area believe I am here working for the Tsar to supply them with arms and ammunition. So for the moment I am safe, but I fear the mutiny leaders grow suspicious as I have not been able to fulfil my promise to provide arms. They watch me closely, but at night they prefer to remain at their camp outside the village.'

'Sir, what is going on?' Harry asked, confused that a Russian would be in league with them.

'Trust me, this man has his reasons to be on our side,' Ian said. 'If not, we will kill him.'

The count raised his eyebrows but smiled grimly. 'Another sound tactical decision, Captain Forbes,' he said, producing a bottle of clear liquid. 'Vodka,' he added, taking a swig, and handing it to Ian. 'We toast the success of our mission.' When Ian had taken a swig, he handed it to Conan and then on to Harry.

When the bottle was returned to Nikolai he raised it. 'Another toast to the friends who lie in the earth of the Crimea – Russian, British – and maybe even the French.'

The men drank another toast and then Nikolai placed the bottle on a rickety table. The room was bare: a wooden table, chair and what looked like a bed on the floor. It smelled of cattle dung, smoke and aromatic spices. It had only one entrance and a small open window for ventilation.

The count laid a small sheet of crumpled paper on the table and pulled the lantern closer. The rescue party gathered around the sketch map of the village.

'The Khan is living under the disguise of a Bengali merchant in this house,' the Russian said, pointing to a place on the map. Ian could see that it was on the other side of the village, and marked nearby was the mutineers' camp. 'I have made contact with him under the guise of purchasing goods, and he is aware that we will be coming for him at any moment. We reach him and take him, his wife and young son with us to the rendezvous point I presume you have established, Captain Forbes.'

'We have a place established on the coast and a plan for evacuation,' Ian said, gazing at the map and taking in all the places marked on it.

'Given the way you are disguised, we should not attract undue attention in the village,' Nikolai said.

Ian turned to Conan and Harry. He could see the fear on the young officer's face. 'Are you up to this, Mr Sinclair?' Ian asked.

'I am, sir,' Harry answered. 'But I must admit that I am a little fearful.'

'Good,' Ian said. 'As Sarn't Major Curry will tell you, he felt the same way when he won his Victoria Cross.' He grinned. 'It is time to go, so check your arms.'

The four men stepped cautiously from the hut. There was no moon and the village was silent, with the exception of a baby wailing a short distance away and a mother softly crooning to her child. Ian prayed that nothing would go wrong as they filed down a narrow street, revolvers at their sides.

*

Alice sat by Peter's bed, swabbing his brow with a damp, cool cloth. The fever racked his body and he glistened with sweat. Outside their tent before the walls of Delhi, she could hear the crash of cannon and the rattle of rifle and musket fire in the distance. Peter had come down with a fever earlier in the day, and was delirious before night had fallen. From all that she had learned, Alice suspected he did not have cholera but some other form of illness. Whatever it was, it caused him to alternately shake as if freezing and sweat and heat up as if on fire. Alice prayed that the fever would break and her beloved husband would recover.

The servant girl hovered at the edge of the bed, and Alice instructed her to fetch more clean water. The girl hurried away and when she returned Alice looked up to see a blood-stained Indian soldier of the Company with her.

'What is it?' Alice asked.

'Missus Alice,' the soldier said. 'We need the doctor master. Many wounded.'

Alice glanced down at Peter, who was tossing and turning deliriously. 'The doctor is not well,' she said.

'Please, missus doctor,' the blood-soaked soldier said. 'We need doctor. All doctors busy.'

Alice stood from her chair beside the bed and handed the wet cloth to the servant girl. 'Keep washing down the master.' The girl nodded her understanding. 'I will go with you, soldier,' Alice said and saw the expression of relief on the man's bearded face.

They crossed a pathway between the tents until they came to Peter's field surgery. Already Alice could see the red-coated soldiers lying on litters outside the tent, whilst other soldiers attempted to tend to them with water canteens and encouraging words. They were all Sikh and Gurkha soldiers who had manned the lines against the enemy pouring out from the city walls in another attempt to destroy the British camp.

Alice could hear a soldier crying out in his agony, and she pushed aside the tent flaps to find a young Sikh soldier laid out on the improvised operating table. She could see that the bottom half of his leg had been shattered, a bone protruding as blood welled from the wound. Two of his comrades were holding him down and they looked to Alice when she entered. From all she had witnessed working alongside Peter, she knew that the leg must be amputated. For a moment she stared at the young man, realising that he would die unless the injury was treated.

The pleading look from the men who were holding down their comrade was enough to convince Alice she had no other choice. She must do something. She looked to Peter's tools of surgery. She remembered exactly how he went about amputations.

'Hold him down hard,' she commanded, then turned to the soldier who had fetched her. 'You, hold his leg.'

Alice took a clamp and affixed it above the wound to stem the flow of blood. Then she picked up the razor-sharp crescent-shaped cutting blade and leaned over the soldier.

'Hold him!' she said loudly in an attempt to stem her own fear.

Alice began cutting and the wounded soldier arched in his pain. As if in a terrible dream she continued with the operation, hardly aware of the sound of the leg thumping onto the earthen floor after she had used the tenon saw to cut through the bone. Within minutes it was all over and the man was taken off the table to be placed on a litter outside the tent.

Alice reviewed each wounded man who was placed on the table. She knew there was nothing that could be done for the stomach or head wounds. She instructed the men who had remained after the first amputation to have these cases taken outside, to a separate tent, and asked for them to be tended until their agony was finally over. From some of the wounds she was able to retrieve musket balls and then quickly stitch the flesh and apply antiseptic solution. Before she finished, she carried out two more amputations. It felt to her that she almost always knew exactly what she was supposed to do, and that her hours of carefully observing

Peter at work had paid off. She had been able to detach herself mentally from the awful work of cutting, sawing and stitching throughout the night. She had had no time to think about Peter's condition, and she wondered now whether he had recovered or, God forbid, grown worse.

Exhausted physically and emotionally, and soaked in blood, Alice stepped out of the tent to see the first rays of the sun on the horizon. Her hands were trembling now but they had been steady and certain during those terrible hours of surgery. Around her were the litters waiting to be carried to the recovery tent. A wounded soldier who had only required her to stitch his bayonet wound stood nearby and went to her, falling to his knees and taking her hands in his own. He said something Alice could not understand, but his gesture said it all. He was thanking her for helping him, for helping them all. She smiled weakly down at him in her own appreciation for what she had done that night under the light of a single lantern.

'Good God!' a voice boomed, and Alice recognised it as one of Peter's fellow army surgeons. 'Your husband has done a fine job with the amputations,' he said as he strode towards her. 'I have just seen them come into the hospital tent. Where is Dr Campbell?'

'I am afraid that my husband is not here,' Alice said, pushing back her hair with a bloody hand. 'He is in our tent with a fever.'

'But, but . . . who operated on the Sikhs who were brought to his surgical tent?' asked the surgeon, confused, looking around as if expecting to see another doctor step forward.

'I did,' Alice answered defiantly. 'It was either that or let them die.'

For a moment the British army surgeon simply gaped at

her as if she was something from an alien world. 'Damn it, Mrs Campbell, please do not jest. Who really carried out the surgery?'

'As I said, Doctor, I did,' Alice answered.

'But you are not a qualified surgeon,' the man said. 'You are a woman.'

'Pure necessity, Doctor,' Alice said, standing her ground. 'Now, I need to wash and change my clothes.' She walked away and the surgeon stared after her in utter disbelief.

When Alice returned to her tent she saw with joy that Peter was sitting up on the edge of the bed. He still looked pale and weak, but he smiled at her – until he saw the blood.

'God almighty!' he exclaimed in shock. 'Are you hurt?' He rose shakily to his feet to take his wife in his arms.

'It is not my blood, my love,' Alice said. 'It is the blood of the men whose limbs I amputated during the last few hours.'

Peter sat back down hard on the bed, almost faint at her statement so casually delivered.

TWENTY

The four men moved cautiously through the village, ever aware of how important it was to reach the coast before first light.

'How far?' Ian whispered to Nikolai, who was leading their party.

'Just around the corner of this street,' he answered.

They turned the corner, and Ian felt his heart skip a beat. He could see two armed men standing by the house Nikolai identified as the Khan's residence. He thought from the arms they carried and the uniforms they wore that they were probably mutineers from the nearby camp.

'What do we do?' Harry whispered.

'We get rid of them,' Ian replied.

'But if we shoot them, it will alert the camp nearby,' Harry said.

'We don't shoot them,' Ian replied, drawing his razor-sharp

Bowie knife from under his clothing. 'We cut their throats.' He could see the young officer recoil at the idea.

Conan slid out his knife, waiting for Ian's instructions.

'I will distract the men,' Nikolai said, 'then you can dispatch them.'

Nikolai stepped out and walked towards the two men, who were engaged in conversation. As he emerged from the shadows the two former sepoys raised their rifled muskets to challenge him. Nikolai said something in their language and there was a small burst of laughter from the two armed men. It was obvious that they knew him, and he was able to position himself so that they turned their backs to the waiting assassins. Ian and Conan moved forward stealthily in the dark and were on the two guards before they could react. Ian placed his hand over his man's mouth and nose and brought his knife blade across his throat. The blade bit, and the man hardly had time to struggle before Ian could feel the hot blood splashing his arm. Conan had carried out a similar manoeuvre on his selected target. When the bodies ceased twitching, they let go of the dead men, who crumpled at their feet.

'What do we do with them?' Nikolai asked.

'We drag them inside the Khan's house so they are out of sight. Hopefully they won't be missed for a while, which will give us a chance to put distance between us and the mutineers.'

Nikolai knocked loudly on the door to attract the attention of those inside.

A candle flared and the door opened cautiously. Then it was opened wide and the three men tumbled through with Harry hurrying across to the house to join them. In the candlelight Ian could see that this house was relatively comfortable and clean, with ornate rugs on the floor. He could see the horrified expression on the face of a pretty young woman clutching a boy to her, and Ian realised that both he and Conan were soaked in blood.

'This is the Khan,' Nikolai said, introducing a tall and handsome young man with a regal bearing. 'This is Captain Forbes of the British army. He is here to get us to the coast and onto a British warship.'

'Then we must go quickly,' the prince said. 'We already have our few possessions packed.'

The Khan threw two bags on his shoulders and said something to his wife, who picked up a couple of smaller bags. With the small family outside, Harry and Conan dragged the bodies of the mutineers into the house and shut the front door on them.

'Let's go,' Ian said, withdrawing his two Colts in case they had to shoot their way out of the village. He was pleased to note that the residents appeared to be asleep and undisturbed by their activities.

They hurried through the streets and alleyways in the pitch dark until they came to the grassy plain on the edge of town. They would be walking towards the rising sun. Ian took the lead, navigating with his compass. By sunrise they were on the outskirts of the fishing village and Ian supervised positions in a ditch for them to hide. All they had to do now was wait till evening when the warship would stream into the coast and retrieve them.

*

'I have just come from a meeting with my commanding officer,' Major Scott Campbell said, pacing the small space of the tent his brother shared with his wife. Alice was currently absent from their quarters, tending to sick and wounded soldiers at the hospital tent. 'Alice has caused somewhat of a furore.'

'I half expected that,' Peter sighed as he filled his pipe with a plug of tobacco. 'I have returned from examining the men she operated on and, without exception, they are all recovering well.'

'But Alice acted as a surgeon without any qualification to do so,' Scott exploded. 'She is a woman. What if she had botched the amputations?'

'I have been a surgeon for many years past and cannot even remember how many limbs I have removed. What I saw of her work was as good as any qualified surgeon I know, maybe better. God knows how she was able to do what she did. Call it a miracle or, God forbid, admit that women are able to carry out the tasks of a surgeon. In a sense, Alice has been learning the art of amputation from assisting me. I do not say that qualifies her to be a surgeon, but with me bedridden with fever that night, I feel she had no other choice. Those men she operated on are still alive today thanks to her intervention – qualified or not.'

Scott ceased pacing and rubbed his brow in frustration. 'I accept what you are saying is true, brother. Alice is truly a remarkable woman, but the instruction from my commanding officer is that what she did will never happen again. I need your word Alice will never pick up an operating saw again. Give me your word and I will relay that to my commanding officer so that the matter is taken no further.'

'I will promise that Alice will not carry out any further surgical duties – other than assisting me during operations as a nurse would,' Peter said reluctantly.

Scott nodded, then bid his brother a good morning and left the tent. He was startled to see Alice standing outside and he muttered a hasty greeting and strode off.

Alice stepped into the tent.

'I have the feeling from your annoyed expression you heard the conversation with my brother,' Peter said wearily.

'I did,' Alice replied angrily. 'How stupid you men are!' she exploded. 'Would it have been preferable to have let one of the Sikh soldiers chop off limbs simply because he was a man? Or perhaps I should have left those men to die even though I had the skills to save them?'

'I am very proud of the work you did,' Peter said, walking to Alice and embracing her. Any doubts he had had that women were capable of being surgeons had long been dispelled. 'But we live in an age that cannot accept that a woman such as yourself is as capable as any one of us men. So for the moment I have had to promise the army hierarchy that you will not indulge in surgical procedures again.'

'Is stitching wounds a surgical procedure?' Alice asked sweetly.

'Well, technically, yes,' he replied. 'But if you do it out of my sight, I cannot chastise you for it, can I?' Peter grinned, knowing that the woman in his arms was incapable of following the rules of Queen Victoria's England.

*

The sun blazed down on the ditch but Ian was satisfied his party was hidden from the sight of the people in the coastal fishing village. The last of the water in the canteens had been drunk, and neither Ian nor his men had had much sleep since they had stepped ashore for the rescue mission. They dozed intermittently, gazing up at the blue skies now filling with great billowing thunderhead clouds.

Ian found himself sitting beside the Indian prince, who was staring across the shimmer of heat just above the tops of the long dry grass.

'I am curious as to why you would be fleeing your

home,' Ian said. 'I imagine you had a palace like most of the local royalty.'

The Khan turned to look at Ian. 'I have, and as soon as this mutiny is suppressed I will return to it.'

'According to the count you were about to negotiate a contract to sell lead to the Russians. Why would you wish to seek sanctuary in England?'

'I never considered trading with the Russians. The count approached me with the offer and I refused. It was then that he revealed himself to be an agent for the British. He explained that he had left Moscow under the guise of making a deal with me. He wanted to test my loyalty to the Queen, our Empress, and thanks to the wise hand of Allah, may His Name be blessed, I was able to prove my faith in the East India Company. At the same time the Sikhs in my realm wanted me dead. The count was able to put together a plan to smuggle myself and my family to a safehouse, which is where you found us. He has made contact with your General Outram to get us to England where I will sign my lead rights over to the East India Company. A small cost to save my firstborn son and the future heir to my kingdom.'

'You must be worth your weight in lead,' Ian grinned.

The Khan smiled at Ian's joke. 'You appear to be a very competent British officer,' he said. 'When I get my land back, I would like you to be a guest at my palace.'

Ian was touched by the offer and felt a great respect for the Indian prince. 'I would be honoured,' he said.

'I have met many remarkable English people,' the Khan continued. 'I recently met an Englishwoman who shot one of our fierce Bengal tigers as it was about to attack her. She has the spirit of the goddess Kali in her. Mrs Alice Campbell.'

Ian looked sharply at the Khan. 'Her husband's first

name is Peter,' he said, and now it was the Khan's turn to look surprised.

'Do you know Mrs Campbell?' he asked.

'She is my sister,' Ian replied. 'Do you know where Alice and her husband are now?'

'They travelled to Meerut with the doctor's brother, Major Campbell. That is all I know. I can see that Allah moves in mysterious ways and has guided my family under your protection.'

Ian knew that a bloody mutiny had occurred at Meerut and many Europeans had been slaughtered. He felt sick to the stomach.

The Khan saw Ian's stricken expression. 'My friend, I would not fear for the fate of your sister. She has the spirit of the tiger in her and no enemy can hurt her. You will meet with her again.'

Ian nodded his appreciation but still felt sick with apprehension.

'Sir!'

Ian turned to Harry who was peering above the top of the long grass. 'Yes, Mr Sinclair, what is it?'

'Sir, I can see a large cloud of dust on the horizon, as if raised by a number of horses.'

Ian scrambled to his knees and saw the dust rising slowly in the hot, humid air. He calculated the distance to be about a mile from their present position, and from his long experience calculating numbers of troops he guessed a party of at least fifty men on horseback.

Conan was beside Ian in an instant. 'Do you think it is the men from the village camp?' he asked anxiously.

'Could be,' Ian said, his mind already racing to find a plan of action. 'They will be on us within the next half-hour. I doubt this ditch will conceal us from them.'

'We are outnumbered and outgunned,' Nikolai said grimly.

Ian sighed and sat back down in the ditch. 'Our options are limited,' he said. 'We either stand and fight, which will mean they eventually overwhelm us. Or we surrender and put our trust in being taken prisoner. I doubt that is really an option because of what will be a slow death at their hands. There is no sense retreating to the mudflats when we don't expect to see our fellows until dusk.'

'We have faced worse odds before,' Conan said. 'Remember how we were trapped in that villa in the Crimea and it looked impossible that we would get out alive?'

Ian remembered, appreciating Conan's faith in his ability to find a solution to this dire situation.

'Mr Sinclair, you and the count must escort the Khan and his family back to the fishing village and hide until the retrieval boat arrives.' Ian turned to Conan. 'I am afraid you and I will have to remain here in the ditch and put up a show to delay whoever is coming our way.'

'That is as good as suicide, sir,' Harry protested. 'It should be me who remains to delay the enemy, not Sergeant Major Curry.'

'You obey orders, Mr Sinclair,' Ian said firmly. 'Your duty is to ensure our guests leave the country safely and our mission is completed.'

'Sir, I –' Sinclair began.

'Do it now, Mr Sinclair,' Ian commanded.

'I will remain with you, Captain Forbes,' Nikolai said quietly. 'But I will trade my pistol for Mr Sinclair's two Colts. I am sure that Mr Sinclair, as one of your officers, is more than capable of escorting the Khan and his family to safety.'

Ian frowned at the Russian. 'It is not necessary to remain,' he said. 'There is no sense in us all getting killed.'

'I was at the Redan the day you British stormed it and I thought that was to be my last day on this earth,' Nikolai said. 'Maybe we will triumph today. It could not be as bad as those final weeks at Sebastopol.'

'Sarn't Major Curry and I were also at the Redan,' Ian said with a tone of respect. 'We all survived those terrible days, so you may be right, Count Kasatkin.'

Ian extended his hand and the Russian took it.

'Go, Mr Sinclair, and raise a tankard to us if we don't make it,' Ian said, and the young British officer scrambled with the Khan and his family from the ditch, looking back once to see the three remaining men facing the long rows of mounted figures that could be discerned ahead of the dust cloud.

Ian checked his pistols, as did Conan and Nikolai.

'What I would give for my old Enfield right now,' Conan grumbled. 'I could be picking off the bastards long before they reached us.'

Ian could now see the figures on horseback, noting that they appeared to be cavalry.

'We have to wait until they are almost on top of us before we commence firing,' Ian said. 'That will give us the best chance to make every shot count and maybe make them think twice. We will spread out. A distance of around ten yards apart to give us more frontage.'

Conan extended his hand. 'Ian,' he said. 'We have come a long way from the bush of New South Wales, and in the short time we have served together, it has been an honour.'

Ian accepted the gesture, growling, 'We're not dead yet, Curry.' Deep in his heart Ian knew that was not true, as the extended line of enemy cavalry came close enough that he could see their bearded faces and the sun shining on their sabre blades. They were dead men for sure.

TWENTY-ONE

The three men crouched in the ditch as the cavalry approached at a steady pace. Ian could see that they were well trained, and a half-dozen rode ahead of the main body as a screen. He knew they might prevail for a short time, but soon enough the enemy would outflank them and a slashing blade would end their lives.

'Wait until they are almost on top of us before firing,' Ian called as a reminder.

Each man, armed with two Colt pistols chambered for six rounds, could certainly provide a devastating initial output of firepower.

Then the advancing six men on horseback were only ten paces away. Ian could see that they were not expecting any resistance from the party as their sabres were still sheathed.

'Now!'

The three men rose from the ditch, startling the enemy cavalrymen. Ian levelled his pistol and fired two shots at the horseman nearest him. He toppled from his horse, which reared, leaping the ditch to gallop riderless towards the fishing village. Ian quickly switched his aim to one of the enemy desperately scrabbling for his sword, but another two well-aimed shots brought him down.

From the corner of his eye, Ian could see that Nikolai and Conan were having the same success and only one of the riders was able to wheel about, galloping back to the main body of enemy some three hundred yards away.

Ian noticed Conan standing over one of the men he had shot. He bent down and pulled off an Enfield rifled musket the man had slung across his back. It did not have a bayonet but Conan ripped the spare ammunition from the dead body.

'Now I will teach the buggers a lesson in marksmanship,' Conan said.

Nikolai recovered a sabre, and Ian immediately reloaded as he watched the cavalrymen milling about in the distance. A flash of lightning startled the three men, and Ian immediately thought that the mutineers must have a cannon. But fat droplets from the darkening sky alerted him to the fact that a heavy storm was closing in on them.

'Brings back memories,' Conan muttered to Ian as he levelled the Enfield on the distant cavalry formation.

'Can you make out the leader?' Ian asked, squatting beside Conan as the rain began to fall.

'I think so,' Conan said, squinting down the sights and steadying his aim. He squeezed the trigger and a second later they had the satisfaction of seeing a rider fall from his horse. It seemed to unsettle their enemy, who withdrew a couple of hundred yards.

'Damn!' Conan swore. 'I missed the bugger – I was aiming for the man next to him.'

'It does not matter,' Ian said with his hand on Conan's shoulder. 'You have made them think about withdrawing out of range and now we have a little time as they get organised.'

'What do you think will be their next move?' Conan asked, already reloading the rifled musket.

'As they appear to be trained cavalrymen, I suspect that they will attempt to flank us. Maybe even launch a frontal attack to distract us as they manoeuvre to the flanks. Whatever they do, I doubt we will be able to hold them off for long,' Ian answered grimly.

Ian's prediction proved correct as the three defenders watched the formation split into three parts. Two large parties wheeled away from the centre to ride in a long arc on either side of the ditch. Nikolai stuck the blade of his captured sword in the earth, waiting with his twin revolvers, whilst Conan levelled the deadly rifled musket on another target. The rain was increasing in its ferocity but it would not save them from a swinging sabre when the enemy finally charged the ditch again. Ian knew that there were no such things as miracles and he wondered how he would die – by bullet or sword. His greatest regret was that he would not have the opportunity in this life to be with Ella Solomon again.

*

Five boats arrived early on the mudflats, three manned by Royal Marines and two loaded with a small group of men from Ian's company. Harry Sinclair stood beside the Khan and his family, waving frantically in the rain. He was seen and the boats beached on the mudflats nearby. Harry recognised Lieutenant Ross Woods and Sergeant Owen Williams as they disembarked from one of the boats.

'Good to see you, old chap,' Ross said when Sinclair approached him with the Khan and his family. 'It appears that you were successful in your mission.'

'There is not much time. We have to go back and fetch Captain Forbes,' Harry said.

A Royal Marine captain approached. 'Time to go, gentlemen,' he commanded.

'Sir, my commanding officer and the company sergeant major are just a few hundred yards behind this cluster of fishing huts. They are pinned down by a force of around fifty sepoy cavalry,' Harry said. 'We need your men to assist us in getting Captain Forbes back to the ship.'

'I am sorry, Mr Sinclair, but my orders are to rescue our esteemed guest, not to chase after anyone left behind. It is too risky.'

'Sir,' Harry pleaded, 'they are close by. I request that I take command of the men of our company who are with you.'

'My orders instruct me to take our guests aboard so that we can steam away before the rains become heavier. That is why we are early,' the marine captain reiterated. 'I am sorry, Mr Sinclair.'

'I have temporary command of the company,' Ross intervened, 'and my orders are that we go in search of Captain Forbes.'

'You will do so on your own, as my orders are that we return to the ship immediately,' the marine captain snapped.

Ross stared with contempt at the higher-ranking officer, turning his back to address the handful of men from the company still in the boats. 'Company, fall in!' he barked and the riflemen clambered out of the boats, assembling in their ranks on the mudflats.

'Lead on, Mr Sinclair,' Ross said, drawing his sword and pistol. 'Take us to Captain Forbes.'

Harry flashed a smile of gratitude, then set off through the village in the heavy rain with Lieutenant Woods and the contingent of twenty infantrymen following. But when Harry looked back he was surprised to see that the marine captain – with a contingent of twenty Royal Marines – was following them.

*

'Here they come!' Ian shouted unnecessarily as the formations galloped towards them, yelling war cries to bolster their courage.

The three men were now back to back in a triangle, as they had more chance of living for a short time in a formation of all-round defence. The thunder of hooves was muted by the noise of the storm, but the spectres of death appeared through the sheets of rain.

Conan fired a shot at the cavalrymen charging from the flank and was satisfied to see a man fall from his saddle. He dropped the rifle, which he would wield as a club when his pistols were emptied.

Ian raised his pistols at the group charging from the front, taking careful aim, knowing there would be no time to reload when the enemy arrived. A horseman was on him and the blade slashed down. Ian felt the stinging tip shred through his coat jacket, slicing his flesh in a shallow wound. In desperation, he fired both his pistols at the cavalryman who was swinging his mount around to make another pass. The shots found their mark and the horseman slumped in the saddle as his horse galloped away.

The Russian count had emptied his pistols and was standing with the captured sabre, waiting for one of the enemy to attempt close-quarter combat.

Ian knew that the ditch would soon run with their blood

and he had one final thought of Ella. Oh, how he desired to hold her one last time. The three waited for the cavalry to swamp them once and for all. Conan held the captured musket by the barrel to use it as a club, and Ian held his Bowie knife in a futile gesture of defiance. The thunder of hooves was loud enough that even the drumming rain could not conceal the terrifying sound.

They were only seconds away when Ian swore he heard the sound of nearby thunder. Momentarily confused, he watched the Indian mutineers and their horses crash into the earth as if hit by lightning. The sudden and unexpected interruption to their attack caused the surviving enemy to pull on reins, turning in confusion to confront the new threat. A second devastating volley tore into the sepoy horsemen.

'There!' Conan shouted above the roar of falling rain and gunfire. 'Over there!'

Ian swung around to see the dim outlines of kneeling men firing in their direction, whilst a second rank was standing, ready to fire whilst the kneeling rank reloaded.

'It's our boys!' Conan whooped as the cavalry broke formation to seek safety away from the deadly fire.

Miracles did happen after all, Ian thought as the riflemen advanced in line towards them with Lieutenant Woods in front, followed by Lieutenant Sinclair.

'Just like the old days in the Crimea,' Conan said, a grin from one side of his bearded face to the other. 'Ian Steele, you must be the luckiest man alive.'

'Not luck, Conan, a bloody miracle this time,' Ian grinned. 'The miracle is the boys of our company and, it appears, a few Royal Marines to boot.'

Harry hurried over to Ian. 'Sir, are you wounded?'

Ian was puzzled and then realised blood was pouring down the sleeve of his jacket. 'Nothing a few stitches won't fix,' he replied, examining the wound to his upper arm. He could see that the blade had not penetrated very deep and he tore off his sleeve to bandage the laceration. 'I must express my gratitude to you for coming back for us, Mr Sinclair,' Ian continued. 'I presume that you were able to get the Khan off the beach first.'

'Yes, sir, we were,' Sinclair replied.

'Well done, Mr Sinclair. Your brother would be proud of you,' Ian said.

'Sir, he once told me of how you would draw the Muscovites towards your position and then have the company ambush them,' Sinclair said. 'I simply used your tactics against those savage scoundrels as you would have.'

Ian did not have the heart to correct his junior officer. Those times were the result of Herbert's quick thinking, not Ian's. Maybe Herbert was now his guardian angel.

The marine captain approached. 'I say, old chap, you seem to have an uncanny loyalty from your officers and men,' he said to Ian. 'I wonder if my men would do the same for me under such circumstances.'

'It is the way of our regiment,' Ian said. 'We are all brothers, regardless of rank.'

'Mr Ross led me to disobey my orders and intervene here,' the marine captain said, gesturing to the scene of carnage where the ditch ran red with the blood of the mutineers and their mounts. 'But I realised that if Mr Ross was going to be successful, he would need the assistance of the Queen's Royal Marines.'

'I thank you for that,' Ian said, extending his hand. 'Maybe one day we will be in a position to assist you under similar circumstances.'

Around them in the torrential rain, wounded horses whinnied pitifully and wounded mutineers moaned. The

Minié bullets had caused horrific injuries, and already Lieutenant Ross was supervising the shooting of both wounded horses and enemy combatants. To the soldiers carrying out the shootings it was an act of mercy and not barbarity.

'It is time that we left and returned to our rum ration,' the marine captain said.

Ian heartily agreed as he attempted to bring his suddenly shaking legs and hands under control. He realised that they had probably been mere seconds from death before the timely intervention of the small but lethal British contingent.

Ian turned to the Russian count. 'Are you coming with us?' he asked.

Nikolai nodded. 'I do not think I will be welcome back at the village and your government has promised me sanctuary. I think it is time for me to leave India behind and travel to London.'

*

Aboard the warship steaming south, Ian gratefully accepted the tin cup of rum from Conan. The decks were lashed by monsoonal rain and the ship wallowed in the rising sea, but Ian did not care that he was soaked to the skin as he stood gazing back at the distant coastline cloaked by the night.

'Another close-run thing,' he muttered as he raised his tin cup to drink the dark liquid.

'Luck of the Irish,' Conan said, swallowing his ration.

'Sir, the Khan would like to see you below decks,' a soldier of the company said, miserable that he had been forced to go above into the storm and be drenched to the skin.

Ian glanced at Conan with a questioning expression and followed the soldier below, attempting to shake off the wet and make himself presentable. He was brought to a cabin that had once been occupied by the ship's captain. The soldier knocked and the Khan bid them enter.

Ian stepped inside the cabin which was just large enough to accommodate three people. He saw the Khan's wife sitting on the bunk with her son beside her, and the Khan standing by a desk.

'Captain Forbes, I requested your presence to thank you. I know that your decision to remain behind was one that the odds said you would not survive. You did that to ensure that my family and I survived. Such an act of courage should be recognised. In your army I believe the Queen has issued a new medal, the Victoria Cross, which I believe you have truly earned. But I do not have the power to grant you the medal.' The Khan reached into one of the leather sacks he and his family had carried with them from the village. When he pulled his hand out Ian could see the sparkle of red rubies and green emeralds under the light of the lantern swinging from the ceiling.

'These are for you, Captain Forbes,' the Khan said, offering the precious stones.

'I was only doing my duty, sir,' Ian said, transfixed by the beautiful sparkling gems. 'I do not expect any financial reward for carrying out the Queen's commands.'

'Please take them, Captain Forbes. My son is worth more than every stone I carry with us. If you, Sergeant Major Curry and Count Kasatkin had not offered to stay behind, we may not have survived. I will personally thank your sergeant major and the count in turn. Consider the rubies and emeralds my medals to you in recognition of your bravery.'

The Khan dropped the precious stones in Ian's hands.

'Thank you, sir,' Ian said with genuine gratitude. 'It is not necessary, but gratefully accepted.'

Ian left the cabin gripping the cold stones in his hand. Only hours earlier he had not believed he would live out the day, and here he was with a small fortune of emeralds and rubies! He had always dreamed of fame and fortune. War had provided him with fortune and a certain degree of fame amongst the men of the regiment. But what lay ahead when his company re-joined the regiment in India? Fame and fortune would not save him on the battlefield. More importantly, what had been the fate of his beloved Canadian friend, Dr Peter Campbell, and Alice, Peter's wife and sister of the real Samuel Forbes?

Ian met with Conan on the deck. 'Did the Khan reward you?' Conan asked.

'He did, and he will also reward you with riches well beyond anything the army can pay you in the next ten years,' Ian replied, displaying the handful of glittering stones. 'We will split the money we receive four ways, as is our custom.'

'Four ways?' Conan queried.

'Yes, a share will go to Molly,' Ian replied.

'Yes, it is only fair,' Conan agreed. 'Our situation may look dire from time to time, but at least I am making more money as a soldier in the Queen's army than I would have made back home in a lifetime of robbing travellers.'

Ian grinned. 'Soldiering has made an honest man of you, Conan Curry.'

TWENTY-TWO

Samuel felt trapped. He had come so close to being exposed by Charles and now, hiding out in yet another London boarding house with James, he knew that they must get out of England. This time their accommodation was less salubrious but cash payment meant no questions as to their identities.

The room he shared with James felt like a prison cell. It was barely an attic but it was a place that would not attract Charles' attention as it catered to workers from out of London and not those of aristocratic breeding.

'We have to do something,' James said. 'I think I will go mad if we remain in this place.'

'There is nothing stopping you from returning to New York,' Samuel said, pacing the small room. 'My brother is not hunting you.'

James walked over to Samuel. 'You know I would never leave you,' he said gently. 'We face this situation together.'

Samuel smiled sadly, touching James' cheek. 'I love you and it pains me to see you caught up in a mess of my making.'

'I think our best option to leave England is for us to make contact with that Jewish man. He seems to have the ability to help us.'

'Mr Solomon,' Samuel said. 'I do not completely trust him. He is a criminal whose main ambition in life is to make money. He has no reason to be our friend.'

'If money is his friend, I can pay,' James replied.

Samuel slumped on one of the single beds and sighed. He knew James was right. They were trapped and the dubious Jewish businessman was their only hope.

*

Charles Field had been paid enough money by his generous client, Charles Forbes, to hire a network of immigration officials at London's seaports, and even a round-the-clock surveillance of Ikey Solomon's office. Like a spider at the centre of a web, Field was able to respond to any filament that might vibrate, indicating the fly had been caught. He had no personal animosity to the man he hunted; it was purely business. But he did have a personal stake in the case. Ikey Solomon had always been able to thumb his nose at the police, and Field, when he'd been a detective inspector, had repeatedly failed to have him put away . Here he was presented with an opportunity to catch his old adversary in the illegal act of aiding and abetting a man falsely pretending to be someone else. Catching Ikey Solomon would be the icing on the cake of an already highly lucrative case.

*

Samuel and James arrived in the afternoon at Ikey's office and were met at the door by Egbert. They explained that they wished to speak with his boss and were prepared to pay for the consultation. Egbert left them and went upstairs while Samuel and James remained nervously on the street, glancing at the people passing by.

'Mr Solomon says he will see you,' Egbert said and the three men climbed the stairs to the office. They were ushered in and found Ikey standing by a window peering out over the city's rooftops. Smoke spouted from the many chimney and a lay like a blanket across the city.

'Gentlemen,' said Ikey, turning around. 'I did not expect to see you back in London after all my hard work in assisting you to leave for New York. I have since had a visit from a Charles Forbes purporting to be your brother, and my old friend, Inspector Field. Why are you trying to pull the wool over my eyes, Mr Steele? I am not a man who has much patience for people lying to me.'

'It is a long story, Mr Solomon,' Samuel said. 'I am sure you are a man who is too busy for stories, but if you help us leave England once again – a kindness we will pay for generously – I can promise we will not return.'

'The man who recommended my services to you, Captain Samuel Forbes, is a man I thought I could trust in a world of lying scoundrels. But is it true that you are the real Samuel Forbes and that he is in fact Mr Ian Steele?'

'Would it matter if it were?' Samuel countered.

'I need you to be straight with me,' Ikey replied. 'As I said, I do not like being lied to.'

'I can vouch for the integrity of Ian Steele, the man you know as Captain Forbes. I assure you the reason he and I switched places is quite separate from our dealings with you,' Samuel said. 'Now, my friend and I need to get out of England as soon as –'

Suddenly Egbert burst through the door. 'Mr Solomon,

one of those kids hanging around across the street has run off.'

'Gone to get Mr Field, no doubt,' Ikey said. 'You don't have much time,' he said to Samuel and James, 'and you won't be leaving through the front entrance.' He leaned over his desk and scribbled something on a piece of paper, thrusting it at Samuel.

'This is the person you will contact in the future if you require my services,' he said. 'Do not attempt to contact me here. I do not wish for any more attention from Inspector Field. Now, follow me.'

Samuel slipped the scrap of paper into his trouser pocket and hurried after Ikey. He and James were led down a hallway with empty offices either side until they reached the end, where Ikey seemed to magically make the wall slide sideways, revealing a set of steps down into the dark.

'Go down there and follow the tunnel until you get to a fork, then turn left. This will take you out behind this building to an empty warehouse. You can then leave without being seen on this side of the street.'

Samuel and James did not question Ikey, who quickly closed the sliding door behind them, throwing them into pitch blackness. Very carefully, the two men inched down the steps, touching the wall for balance as they went. In the dark they could hear rats scurrying away from their footsteps. It was obvious that this was a last-measure escape route from Ikey's building and rarely used. It stank of sewage and must. A dim light glowed ahead from an overhead manhole in the street, and when they came to the fork they took the left-hand turn and found themselves inside a small warehouse frequented only by pigeons and spiders.

'This way,' James whispered.

They walked to the door which led out onto the street. It took a few moments to orient themselves but both men walked casually along until they located a familiar side street that would direct them back to their lodgings.

When they were safely in their attic room, Samuel removed the slip of paper from his pocket. He read the name of the middleman who was to be their contact with Mr Solomon. But it was not a man, Samuel noted with surprise. It was a woman by the name of Miss Molly Williams, confectioner.

*

Henry Havelock, now a general in the Queen's army, had received the telegram that Cawnpore had fallen to the rebels and that the majority of the British civilians – men, women and children – had been massacred by sepoy troops. Those who had survived the initial slaughter under a flag of truce were rounded up and ordered to be killed. But even the mutinous Indian soldiers refused to carry out the order, so butchers were employed to kill the surviving civilians, dismembering the bodies as they would sheep or goats.

The general had a secret fund to pay local spies, and his intelligence service was a well-oiled machine. He pored over one report from a loyal Indian shopkeeper who provided his staff the mutineer's numbers and dispositions in the Cawnpore region.

'Sir, Captain Forbes is outside as you requested,' a major of his staff said through the tent flap of Havelock's field HQ.

'Bid him enter,' Havelock said, pushing away from the field table and standing to receive Ian.

Ian stepped inside, saluted smartly and stood to attention.

Havelock thrust out his hand, surprising Ian.

'My hand in gratitude is about all I can offer you, Captain Forbes, for successfully rescuing the Khan.'

'I was doing my duty, sir,' Ian replied as he let go the firm grip.

'I have been informed by General Outram that you continually prove your courage and resourcefulness. It should be you commanding your regiment and not that popinjay, Jenkins. As it is, I will be sending your regiment in the advance on Cawnpore. Colonel Jenkins has been given his orders to help provide reinforcements there.'

'Sir, I can promise you that the regiment will gather glory in any contact we have with the mutinous sepoys,' Ian said.

'I know it will with officers such as yourself in command of the men.' Havelock sighed. 'I also have information on the welfare and whereabouts of the surgeon you wrote to my headquarters about. Dr Campbell and his wife are well, and with the contingent we have outside the walls of Delhi. I even heard a rumour that Mrs Campbell successfully carried out surgery, amputating limbs. However, I know that could not be true as she is a woman, and we both know such a gory procedure is beyond the sensibilities of a delicate English lady.'

Ian could see that the general had the hint of a smile on his face and sensed Havelock believed the rumours to be true. 'My sister is a remarkable lady, sir,' Ian said diplomatically.

'Last reports said that she and Dr Campbell have been carrying out their duties under rather arduous conditions, so hopefully we will recapture the city soon.'

'Sir, my gratitude for your enquiries,' Ian said. 'Cawnpore is on the road to Delhi, and I hope that I soon have the opportunity to meet with them.'

'First Cawnpore and then Delhi,' Havelock said with a nod.

Ian left the tent and marched back to the regiment's lines nearby where he was met by his company sergeant major whose gloomy expression said it all.

'Sir,' said Conan, 'the commanding officer desires to meet with you immediately.'

'How could I guess,' Ian sighed.

Ian made his way to the regimental HQ tent where he was saluted by the two soldiers on guard. A young officer appointed to Jenkins' staff stepped out of the tent and also saluted. Ian returned the salute.

'Sir, the colonel will see you now,' the young officer said, ushering him inside.

Ian saluted and stood to attention. 'Sir, you wished to see me?'

Jenkins rose from his desk and stood with his hands behind his back. From the scowl on his face Ian knew things were not going to go well for him.

'I have finished speaking with your second-in-command, Mr Sinclair, and your CSM about the mysterious rescue mission General Outram sent you on, and neither would divulge any information. They said they had been sworn to secrecy and only you were authorised to speak about it. As your commanding officer I am now ordering you to give me a full report on the matter.'

'Sir, with all due respect, I think you should first speak to General Havelock before I comply with your request,' Ian answered, and noticed the scowl on his commanding officer's face deepen.

'I am not about to disturb the general as he is a busy man,' Jenkins said in frustration.

'I am not sure of that, sir,' Ian said smugly. 'I have just come from his HQ and he had time to have a chat with me.' He knew his statement would take the wind out of Jenkins' sails.

'You are insolent, Captain Forbes,' Jenkins snarled. 'And you appear to have the luck of the devil on your side. I won't be forgetting your arrogant behaviour. You are dismissed.'

Ian saluted, turned on his heel and marched out of the tent with a smile on his face.

TWENTY-THREE

Samuel had developed a nervous tic at the corner of his eye, and the strain of remaining in the nondescript boarding house in London was taking a toll on his relationship with James. James had snapped that they may as well be living in a cage, and Samuel felt the guilt of having dragged him into this game of cat and mouse with his brother.

Right now James was out purchasing a newspaper, so Samuel wrote a note to inform him that he would be away for a short time. He did not want to cause the man he loved any more anguish if he should be caught.

Samuel slipped out of the boarding house, hailed a hansom cab and directed the driver to Molly's shop in a better part of London. As he walked through the door he was assailed by the pleasant scent of confectionary. Behind the counter, weighing out bags of boiled lollies, was a young woman, barely into her teens.

'Miss Molly Williams?' Samuel asked.

'No. The mistress is in her office,' the girl said with a pleasant smile.

'May I speak with her?' Samuel asked politely.

The girl looked him up and down. 'I will see if Miss Williams is taking visitors.'

She disappeared and a minute later returned. 'Miss Williams wishes to know who is requesting to speak with her and on what business.'

'I am an acquaintance of Mr Ikey Solomon and he gave me Miss Williams' name,' Samuel said, and the girl disappeared and this time returned with a young woman with a pretty face and firm figure. For a moment Molly stared at Samuel with a look of both confusion and recognition.

'You can come to my office,' Molly said. 'May I ask your name, sir?'

'Hubert Smith,' Samuel improvised.

Molly led him into a small office piled with stores for the shop. She closed the door behind them and gestured to a chair near her overflowing desk.

'You are not Mr Smith, but I suspect that you are one Samuel Forbes,' Molly said. 'Your resemblance to Ian Steele is remarkable.'

Samuel was taken off guard by this woman's recognition and the mention of Ian's real identity.

'How did you know?' Samuel asked.

'My man told me the story of how you and Captain Steele traded places,' Molly said. 'Captain Steele is a wonderful and remarkable man, and his secret is safe with me. Now, Ikey Solomon sent you to me for a reason.'

'I need some assistance to leave England,' said Samuel, 'and as soon as possible.'

'I see,' Molly said. 'It is well known on the streets that

you are being sought by Inspector Field's investigative service, and from my knowledge of Inspector Field, he is a man who always solves his cases.'

'I am a little confused as to how a lady of your standing knows the likes of Mr Solomon. You appear to be a successful person in your own business.'

'It is a long story, but I once worked for Ikey as his book-keeper, and he looked out for me, so now I try to repay that kindness by returning a favour when I can. Ikey is a good man, despite what some might say about him. Now, we should get down to business.

'Field is meticulous, so we have to presume he has all the ports covered with his spies.' Molly looked thoughtful. 'But probably not those ports in Wales,' she concluded. 'I know people there who can smuggle you aboard a ship leaving one of the Welsh ports, but you will need money.'

'We have money,' Samuel replied. 'Our fate is in your hands, Miss Williams.'

'I am not doing this for your sake,' Molly said. 'I am doing this to ensure that Captain Steele's real identity is not revealed. While you remain in England you put him in jeopardy. Come back to my shop tomorrow night after I close and I will have something arranged.'

Samuel thanked her and purchased a bag of Turkish delight on the way out. Feeling much relieved, he stepped onto the street and was fortunate to hail a passing hansom cab.

*

Havelock's intelligence service informed him that a leader by the name of Nana Sahib had emerged after the defeat of the Cawnpore garrison. The Moslem leader had declared himself Peishwa of the Mahrattas. This self-proclaimed sovereign had almost destroyed a smaller force of British soldiers under a Major Renaud's command as they advanced towards Cawnpore. Now he aimed to take the city of Allahabad and then advance on Calcutta where he would establish his Moghul dynasty.

The British general knew from reports that the self-proclaimed Peishwa had at least three and a half thousand well-trained sepoy infantry, reinforced with eager recruits, and had many artillery guns taken from the British. Opposed to his force were a mere four hundred British troops and three hundred untested Sikh soldiers, as well as a small force of irregular cavalry. Havelock's great fear was that the Sikh troops might desert when they made contact with the vastly larger enemy force confronting them. Major Renaud, who had survived the slaughter of his troops, knew he was faced with a terrible decision, but it was one that had to be made. Did he withdraw his outnumbered force, or would he command it to stand and fight?

The decision was made to stand and fight the superior force.

*

The blistering sun was taking a toll on Ian's men. This was the time of year when the sun would appear in the Indian skies between downpours of monsoonal rain to savage everything below with its blazing rays.

The column had trudged through a dismal landscape of stunted trees and shimmering plains with Ian at the vanguard of his company. Before they'd left, Colonel Jenkins had feigned great disappointment that only Ian's company and not the whole regiment would be joining the attack on Cawnpore, but the cowardly colonel's relief at avoiding combat was palpable. Rumours already abounded that the small force marching towards Cawnpore would encounter a large number of enemy and likely be massacred.

They had marched fifteen miles under the unforgiving sun and Ian could see that his company was flagging. The oxen carts creaked behind the column, filled with men struck down with heatstroke, and even the army medical staff begged the column's commander to rest the men. But Major Renaud chose to push on, until finally the sun set across the dreary plains of scrub and the men were given orders to pitch tents and rest.

Ian walked amongst his exhausted soldiers, sharing a joke here and there, asking about their health. He always received the same answer: they could go on. He sat down in a small copse of scrubby trees with a small fire to heat his water for his ration of tea. He was joined by Conan, who squatted down beside him.

'How do you think the men are holding up?' Ian asked, swishing the tea leaves into the boiling water with a twig.

'They would follow the Colonial into hell if he asked them,' Conan replied, producing his battered metal cup to share Ian's tea. 'The lads think that serving under you means they cannot be killed.'

'If only that were true,' Ian said wearily. 'I have orders that we strike tents just before midnight. Try to get a couple of hours' sleep.'

Conan rose with his mug of tea and walked into the night, leaving Ian alone with his thoughts. Ian was aware that his company was always singled out for the most dangerous missions, and wondered how his men would react if they knew that. He felt they were misguided to put so much faith in him to keep them alive. As he sipped his brew, he reflected on the seemingly hopeless task ahead when they eventually clashed with the superior Indian force.

At 11 pm, the column struck their tents and marched in under the light of the full moon, until about an hour later they were challenged by the picquets of the force they had come to strengthen.

This did not mean any rest for Ian's company, however, as the two small forces continued marching until the sun rose the next morning, when the order was to take an overdue rest before they encountered the enemy.

*

The blast of an enemy cannon shattered the morning.

Meals being prepared were quickly discarded as the order, 'To arms!' was yelled down the lines. Soldiers scrambled to snatch up their Enfield rifles and ammunition as senior NCOs harried them into battle formations. Ian grabbed his sword and revolver, falling in with his company. He ensured that he was standing conspicuously, his sword drawn, amongst the men in the first rank.

To his front Ian could see the dust rising as a large force of Indian cavalry charged their position. Conan was moving through the ranks, chiding some for not having percussion caps on their rifles, or not being properly dressed for battle. He knew his role was to act as Ian's guard dog in battle – and he did his job well.

'Sir, there are so many of the buggers,' a frightened young new recruit said.

'Then you can't miss when you fire, Private Cummings,' Ian said. He knew the name of every man in his company, and that alone seemed to settle the soldier down.

The sudden charge of enemy cavalry came to a confused halt, no doubt because they only now realised they were facing five regiments of infantry and eight artillery guns drawn up in perfect order. The Indian mutineers were well aware of how deadly the British army was on the battlefield when they were organised for combat, and they instinctively slowed in the attack.

Ian could feel the tightness in his stomach that he experienced before every battle. He was careful that his men not discern the slight tremble of his hand as he held his sword aloft. He knew they looked to him with blind faith in his ability to keep them alive and he did not want them to lose confidence just as they stepped into battle.

The Indian cavalry fell back and a couple of cannon were pushed forward, along with the Indian infantry.

'Steady, lads!' Conan roared down the ranks as they witnessed the smoke erupt from the mouth of the artillery pieces, and seconds later heard the sound. It was important that the British formations display a vision of resolute red-coated ranks to the Indian mutineers.

A junior officer from the task force HQ hurried to Ian. 'Sir, the general requests your company to occupy a copse to our front.'

Ian acknowledged the order and passed it on to his NCOs, who hurriedly arranged his company of riflemen to advance to the copse of trees Ian had indicated. Ian knew that they were being pushed forward to act as skirmishers, using the Enfield's range to inflict casualties on the enemy before they could come into range of the Indian smooth-bore muskets. Ian's company had only just arrived in position in the stand of trees and deployed into fighting formation when the Indian infantry charged their position.

Ian gave the order and a volley of well-aimed Minié bullets struck down the forward troops charging towards them in the trees. Ian trusted that his hours of training his men would lead them to fire and reload quickly. The first volley was followed by disciplined volleys, pouring the deadly and devastating bullets into the waves of advancing enemy infantry.

Gun smoke filled the still air like a London fog, partially concealing the plain to their front. Ian roared encouragement as the withering fire continued. Private Cummings was only feet away and Ian observed how calmly he fired and reloaded the long rifled musket. If the enemy came close enough, Ian knew he would have to give the order to fix bayonets, although this made loading the rifles harder. For the moment the well-aimed rifle fire was doing the job of slowing down the attack.

Above the constant loud crash of rifles, Ian could hear the blast of artillery not far away and knew it was British guns. The smoke continued to billow around the copse, obscuring the enemy to their front, but it was now Ian's job to defend the gunners from the mutineers as the artillery shells tore huge gaps in their ranks.

Conan was beside Ian, holding spare ramrods, and young Private Cummings fired off a shot. In his haste to do so he had left the ramrod in the barrel and it flew away like a spear.

'That will come out of your pay, Private Cummings,' Conan growled in the young soldier's ear. 'Take one of these.' Conan thrust the spare ramrod into the soldier's hand, who accepted it sheepishly.

'Sorry, sir,' Cummings said, cursing himself for his mistake.

Swamps either side of the hard ground to their front channelled the attackers, while the British cavalry used the strips of firm earth to advance.

Ian did not know how long his men continued to fire but suspected it was for at least ten minutes. He could see that the longer range of the Enfield rifled muskets was devastating the advancing infantry, and he sensed that the smaller British force was getting the upper hand. Thirst, smoke, noise and heat were Ian's impressions of the battle.

The artillery guns were being limbered and Ian saw them dragged further forward onto the firmer areas of the nearby swampy ground, to be unlimbered and put into action closer to the enemy forces, firing at almost point-blank range. They particularly targeted the brass and iron cannons of the mutineers, putting three of the Indian guns out of action.

Part of the enemy force was situated in a small village behind a cluster of garden enclosures made of mud bricks. The British artillery rounds smashed through the walls, killing and wounding anyone in their lethal path.

Ian noticed that the attacking infantry had withered away in the face of the deadly volleys of his riflemen, and he ordered a ceasefire to conserve valuable powder and shot. As he gave the order another junior staff officer appeared.

'Sir, the general has ordered an advance to the front,' he said breathlessly. 'Your company is to reinforce Major Renaud on a hill he has captured to our right.' Ian could see the British redcoats on the hill indicated by the staff officer.

'Tell the general we will move to Major Renaud's position now,' Ian replied, and the officer saluted and dashed back to HQ.

Ian turned to Conan. 'Sarn't Major, form up the company to advance to that hill over there,' he said, and Conan immediately issued the order. Platoon commanders and their senior NCOs expertly fell in and hurried forward. Ian observed the exhaustion of his men in the heat of the day. The fact that they had had little sleep the night before and no breakfast only exacerbated the situation. Still, they reached the hill held by Major Renaud, and Ian reported his arrival.

'Sir, what are your orders?'

'Good show, Captain Forbes,' the weary major replied, wiping his brow with the back of his cuff. 'We will have to advance through a swamp down there.'

Ian followed the major's outstretched hand.

'Company, advance to the front!' Ian bellowed, and the men stepped forward off the hillock into the swampy ground, moving towards the village of mud huts.

They were only yards from the first of the small walls when Ian saw the Indian artillery gun being wheeled into a position to fire point blank at his and Major Renaud's troops. Acting quickly, he drew his pistol and sprinted towards the crew of three Indians manning the gun. He was firing at such close range that his bullets took the lives of two of the enemy serving the gun. But the third man desperately reached to fire the upper hole on the cannon. Ian knew that the gun was probably filled with canister shot, an artillery round that acted like a giant shotgun for close-range defence. He leapt the wall with a strength he did not know he possessed, and before the taper could touch the hole, he had driven his sword into the man's chest. He fell and Ian fell on top of him. When Ian attempted to scramble to his feet, he was aware that Conan was beside him.

'You orright?' the sergeant major asked, helping Ian to his feet. 'Bloody stupid thing to do.'

'There was no time,' Ian gasped. His lungs felt like they were on fire. His company were pouring over the low walls and advancing towards the village.

'Fix bayonets!' Conan roared and the men paused to slide the long knife-like bayonets onto the end of their rifles before continuing the advance. All around them lay the dead and dying Indian mutineers. As Ian's company advanced they were able to clear the town of fleeing enemy without sustaining any further battle casualties. Ian noticed some of his men collapse, though, the victims of heat exhaustion rather than enemy action. But his priority was to clear the town, and he could not spare any soldiers to tend the sick.

Soon they were through the town, driving the enemy before them.

Ian ensured his men were in their battle formations when they broke out onto the plain on the other side of the village. It was then that he saw a large formation of Indian cavalry make a determined charge against their own outnumbered cavalry on the company's flank. He was acutely aware that should the Indian mutineers succeed, they could then attack along the flank of his own force and, at such close range, obliterate them. From the corner of his eye, he could see that the British artillerymen had been able to bring up a couple of guns and were already setting them up to fire into the Indian formation.

Ian was weak from the physical effort of battle and his throat was parched. Despite this, he bellowed his order.

'Riflemen, cavalry to the right. Form ranks!'

Above the din of the scattered firing and the triumphant shouts of the enemy, Ian's order carried, and at the same time the two cannons roared their defiance into the men and horses about to attack their own weakened cavalry.

The volley of rifle fire rippled along the rifles of the company line, bringing down both horses and men. The combined artillery and rifle fire proved to be too much for the Indian cavalry who only mere moments earlier had sensed an easy victory. In disarray, they turned and fled the battlefield. Off to their left, Ian could see the swirling tartan skirts of the Scottish infantry regiment break through. He knew then that they had done the impossible and won the day.

But at what cost?

TWENTY-FOUR

Already the familiar sickly sweet stench of death rose in the hot air from the already fly-covered bloated enemy bodies scattered about the battlefield. Ian barely noticed it anymore.

'I don't know how we survived,' Conan said, surveying the carnage of the battlefield. 'They had us outnumbered.'

'But we had the Enfield,' Ian said.

'Never in my wildest nightmares back home could I have ever imagined I would be standing here today wearing a bloody British red coat. My Irish ancestors will not welcome me to heaven when I die.'

'Put it this way, Sarn't Major, we don't get to choose where we are born – but we have a choice in where we die in the business of soldiering for the Queen.'

'That is not very cheerful.' Conan smiled under his thick beard. 'I am hoping to depart for the next world in a soft bed with Molly holding my hand.'

'Maybe that will happen,' Ian said. 'In the meantime, I need you to make a rollcall to see if any of our lads have been killed or wounded.'

'Sah,' Conan replied and marched away. When he returned with a long face Ian knew they had taken casualties.

'Two dead, sir,' he said. 'Struck down by the sun. I heard from an officer that we lost twelve all up to the effects of the sun – and none from enemy action. I also heard this is the first successful encounter with the mutineers.'

'Not for the twelve poor souls who will not be going home,' Ian replied.

'What is the name of this place?' Conan asked, his pencil poised to record their geographic location.

'Futtehpore,' Ian replied. 'But I doubt any will remember the name – except the men who were here today.'

The twelve soldiers who had succumbed to heatstroke were buried on the battlefield with military honours. Their graves were marked, but in time they would disappear forever in the Indian earth.

★

Alice Campbell stood gazing at the massive walls of the city they besieged. The sun was setting and she reflected on the moment. She was so far from the genteel salons of London and the gossip of her friends. Here she stood with the blood of her patients on her worn dress. The past was little more than a ghost and she knew she could never go back to being the protected and pampered young woman she had once been. In that moment she felt an affinity with Miss Florence Nightingale, who had ministered to the wounded of the Crimean War.

'Well, my dear,' Peter said, approaching his wife. 'I have some good news. A trader came through camp and for sixteen rupees I was able to purchase a dozen bottles of tar bund beer, and also a bottle of Harvey's Sauce, as well as a good selection of tinned foods. We shall dine in luxury tonight.'

Peter placed his hands on his wife's shoulders and stood for the moment also gazing at the massive and seemingly impregnable Delhi walls. 'A penny for your thoughts?'

'What becomes of us after this dreadful war is over?' she sighed. 'I do not desire to return to London and the family home.'

'We will do whatever it is you desire,' Peter said, gently turning his wife to face him.

'I wish to travel with you to see the world,' Alice said. 'I would like to see your Canada – and even the Australian colonies where my Uncle George has a sheep farm.'

'Is that all?' Peter asked with a twisted smile.

'No, I wish to travel to Africa, and to Egypt after that.'

'Well, Canada is achievable, but you must remember that I am a simple surgeon on a simple surgeon's income.'

'You are not a simple surgeon,' Alice said. 'I have been beside you when so many poor souls have been saved by your God-given skills.'

'But I have never shot a tiger.' Peter laughed, realising it had been a long time since he had laughed. 'Maybe we could hunt lion in Africa.'

'No, I will never again kill such a beautiful and noble creature. Sometimes the spirit of the tiger haunts my dreams,' Alice said sadly. 'After all that travel, I will be content to find some part of this world to settle down with my country doctor and raise a family.'

Peter did not reply but gazed at the great walls of the city which harboured a vast army of men ready to kill them at the first opportunity. He knew that they were still outnumbered and outgunned by the Indian mutineers, although word had arrived in the camp that General Havelock was having success against the mutineers just south-west of their current location. For now, all they had was the stark reality of the present. At least that promised a feast for dinner. For the moment, that was enough.

★

Charles Forbes was frustrated and angry. He forced himself not to pace in the private investigator's office but stood with his hands behind his back, glaring out a window at the smog hanging over the city.

'I am afraid at this stage, Mr Forbes, that our man has disappeared. If it is any consolation, I believe he and his companion are still in the city, as my contacts on the docks have not reported them attempting to leave London.'

'What if my brother is cunning enough to depart the country from another port?' Charles asked, turning towards Field.

'Ah, to prevent that happening you would have to be prepared to pay a lot more,' Field said. 'Your money would need to buy eyes and ears in every port in the British Isles.'

'I am prepared to pay,' Charles said.

'Then I will be able to put a watch on Scotland and Wales – as well as all our ports in England,' Field said.

'But if they identify my brother, how could you detain him if he attempts to leave from, say, a Scottish port?'

'I still have many contacts in my old job,' Field said. 'After all, this appears to be a case of fraud and the local constabulary can be enlisted to arrest the man you say is your brother. I have prepared posters from the photograph you gave me to be distributed across the country – with a cash reward for any information that locates him. Your brother's face is now familiar to many police constables and members of the public.'

For the first time, Charles smiled. 'I can see that my money will be well spent,' he said. 'There will be a generous bonus if you succeed.'

'I always do, Mr Forbes,' Field said. 'I always do.'

★

Samuel Forbes truly regretted not leaving England when he had had the opportunity. Now he felt like a hunted animal, and the tic at the side of his eye grew more persistent as he walked towards Molly's shop, where he was ushered into the back office.

'I have written to my cousin in Cardiff and he has agreed to help you, but he will require payment for his troubles,' Molly said. 'He will arrange a ship to take you to America.'

'I thank you for helping us,' Samuel said.

'I am doing this for Captain Steele,' Molly replied. 'You will need to be ready to take a locomotive train to Bristol this Friday, and then travel by coach to Cardiff,' she said, passing Samuel a piece of paper. 'This has all the information you will require to make contact with my cousin. From there he will be able to book you passage once you pay him. I will bid you a good voyage.'

Thanking Molly again, Samuel slipped the paper into his pocket.

Molly watched him depart and reflected on how strange life had become since the day a young colonial had first set foot in the rundown tenement she'd shared with her brothers, Owen and Edwin. Fate had brought them all together, and Captain Steele was enmeshed in their lives now. Edwin was dead – killed on the bloody battlefield of the Crimea – and the man she loved above all others, Sergeant Major Conan Curry VC, was far away in India, serving alongside Captain Steele. Molly was growing wealthy from the two shops she now owned, serving the finest confectionary to wealthy patrons. They had all experienced such a dramatic change in their lives, and at the centre of it all was the enigmatic Captain Ian Steele.

*

Rarely did Ian have personal contact with his commanding officer. As their animosity was mutual, he only found himself in Colonel Jenkins' presence at the officers' mess when they dined or at formal regimental briefings usually conducted by the regimental second-in-command, Major Dawkins, whom Ian respected for his competence. Whenever Jenkins had him summoned to his office, Ian knew he was in trouble of some kind.

Ian stood to attention in Jenkins' tent. He could hear the senior NCOs barking orders to the soldiers outside as they drilled, and the clatter of a field kitchen nearby. It was a very hot day and the sweat trickled down both men's faces.

'Captain Forbes,' Jenkins said, and Ian could see that he had an open letter on his desk. 'I have received disturbing correspondence from London that you may be an imposter.'

Ian could see the grim look of victory on Jenkins' face.

'May I ask who has levelled such a preposterous and malicious accusation against my good name?' he asked, feigning indignation.

'None other than your alleged brother, Charles Forbes,' Jenkins answered smugly. 'Now, I ask why such an honourable man as Charles Forbes would intimate that you are not who you say you are?'

Ian could feel the sweat trickle down inside his jacket and knew that somehow Charles had come into contact with Samuel in London.

'My brother has never liked me,' Ian replied. 'I suspect that this is his way of causing mischief. I would suggest that you write to my father, Sir Archibald, before this matter gets out of hand.'

Jenkins leaned forward in his camp chair and stared at Ian. 'I know that you are Outram and Havelock's golden boy, God knows why, but they will not always be around to protect you. I am being posted back to London to attend the newly established staff college there and I will make personal contact with Charles and ensure we sort out this matter. Until then you will remain with your company, but Major Dawkins, who will assume command in my absence, will be reporting to me on your conduct. That is all, Captain Forbes – if that is your real name. You are dismissed.'

Ian saluted and stepped outside the tent into the blast of Indian heat, experiencing the familiar trembling in his hands and the feeling his legs would give way. Somehow he made it back to his tent where he slumped on his camp bed, cursing Samuel for putting them both in this dangerous situation. At least he had General Havelock's tacit protection, and Jenkins had enough sense not to upset the brilliant general. However, when Jenkins returned to England he would certainly make contact with Charles, and if Charles had managed to find Samuel, Ian knew his time would be over as the Queen's colonial.

*

Samuel and James arrived at the Paddington railway station in the very early morning to purchase their tickets to Bristol. The train was scheduled to leave at 4.30 am and arrive in

Bristol at 10 pm. The two men were dressed in their finest suits, wearing expensive top hats and looking the part of first-class travellers. The fares were expensive but at least they would receive a private cabin with padded seats and windows through which to gaze at the passing countryside. As it was proving to be a warm day the windows would also provide a cooling breeze.

They carried only hand luggage, which meant they did not have to be separated from their bags by the railway porters. On each carriage roof sat a guard in the tradition of horse carriages, and the men could see that the Brunswick green train engine had an open cabin for the railway engineers, who would have to suffer any kind of weather they might encounter on the journey. Their own carriage was painted in chocolate and cream colours, with open carriages being towed behind for the third-class working men and women. The movement of the working class was driven by the massive coal and iron industries of the Welsh valleys, but the railways preferred to transport the wealthier patrons with money to spare, drawn to the tourist pleasures of Bristol.

Samuel and James boarded their carriage and settled opposite each other. 'At least we will be able to take in the scenery of my country before we depart England.' Samuel sighed, lighting up a cigar as the engine pulled out of the station, billowing thick, acrid coal smoke into the fading darkness of the summer morning.

'What if someone was loitering at the railway station to identify us?' James asked in a concerned voice.

'I don't think my brother has the means to have someone watching every train station in the country,' Samuel replied. 'I suspect he has the ports in London under watch, but our contact in Cardiff will be able to put us on a ship leaving the Bristol Channel, which is a long way from London and

Mr Field. I have arranged for us to be accommodated at a hotel in Bristol tonight, and tomorrow we take our journey to Cardiff on a coach, so just relax and take in our beautiful and historic countryside, old chap. There is nothing we have to concern ourselves with now.'

James tried to settle back in his seat but could not dismiss the nagging feeling that they were still being hunted.

TWENTY-FIVE

All had gone smoothly. Samuel and James had stopped overnight at a fashionable hotel in Bristol and the next morning purchased a fare on a coach to Cardiff, where they were able to find the address of their Welsh contact.

Samuel and James were disappointed to see that the Welsh town was a dirty, disease-ridden place thanks to the sudden industrialisation produced by its ironworks and export of coal. So many English and Irish workers had flooded the place that it had shantytowns filled with the desperately poor. Samuel knew his own family had shares in the new industries and felt a twinge of guilt when he took in the poverty of the workers and unemployed in the town bordered by the beautiful and rolling hills of Wales.

Molly's cousin lived in a tiny tenement house in a row of such places built by the big mining and industrial companies to house their workers.

The two men had walked from the coach depot with directions from those they met on the street.

Samuel knocked on the door and it was opened by a smallish man whose skin appeared to be ingrained with dirt. He was of an indeterminate age, balding, and his clothes were almost ragged.

'I am Samuel and this is James,' Samuel said. 'Your cousin, Molly, informed us that you would know why we are here.'

'Come in, sirs,' the man said, opening the door wide to allow them entrance. 'I know of your plight and have made preparations for you to ship out of Cardiff,' he said. 'My name is Kevin Jones.'

Samuel glanced around the tiny house. The strong stench of boiled cabbage filled the room. A woman with a wizened face and of similarly indeterminate age appeared. 'This is Mrs Jones,' Kevin said awkwardly, and Samuel's guilt increased at the sight of these malnourished people. He was aware that the rich, and he was one of them, lived off their poverty, making huge profits from their labour and enjoying lives of excessive luxury.

'I believe that you will require some payment now,' Samuel said, reaching into his coat pocket and peeling off a wad of English pounds. He handed them to Kevin, whose eyes widened at the amount.

'Sir, this is more than I agreed with Molly. It is very generous,' he said. He attempted to pass back an amount of the currency, but Samuel raised his hand.

'It is what I wish to offer for the trouble you have gone to in assisting us,' he said with a gentle smile, aware that James was frowning. Their supply of ready cash was diminishing, although they had more than enough money when they returned to New York.

'My wife can make us a pot of tea and you are welcome to share a meal with us,' Kevin said.

'I thank you for your kind offer,' Samuel said, the stench of the overcooked cabbage still in his nostrils, 'but James and I will take up temporary accommodation in one of your hotels until it is time for us to depart.'

'That will be later tonight, so you will not need to arrange accommodation in the town,' Kevin said. 'I have been able to get you both a berth on a coal ship leaving on the high tide. Here are your papers for the passage, which contain all the particulars of the ship, berth and time to board. It is steaming to a port in Canada, and from there you will be able to make your way to America. I hope that is to your liking.'

Samuel accepted the papers with thanks, hardly glancing at them, and asked, 'Do you recommend any establishment in town we might partake of an ale and meal before we depart?'

Kevin thought for a moment, suggesting the best place for a meal for gentlemen who were able to pay.

The two men thanked the couple again, and departed the tenement with directions to the hotel.

*

It was a chance in a million!

Ewen Owens stood amidst the tobacco smoke, staring at the two well-dressed gentlemen imbibing in the bar. Owen gripped his ale and shuffled closer to the pair, who appeared oblivious to him.

Ewen knew from the accent that one of the two men was an American, and the other bore a striking resemblance to the poster Ewen carried in his ragged coat pocket. It had to be Samuel Forbes. He tried to remember what he was to do next to claim his reward. Yes, that was it – Mr Field had instructed that the local constabulary were to be contacted to arrest Mr Forbes on a charge of fraud. But Ewen was afraid that if he left the hotel, the subject of the search might disappear into the crowded city.

Ewen knew that he must remain and observe the wanted pair and find out where they were staying. It was frustrating as he did not trust any of the other patrons to deliver a message to the local police. This was his prize, and he calculated that he could personally lead the constables to wherever the men were residing. Two hours went past and night was arriving. Ewen had used the last of his pennies to buy ale as he sat in a corner watching the two men as a hawk would a coop of chickens.

A bell rang and the two men finished their drinks and went into the dining room.

Ewen felt it was safe to leave and fetch the constables now, as the men would be occupied with dinner for a while.

*

'Samuel, I swear that man sitting in the corner was watching us,' James said when they entered the dining room laid out with fine linen and polished cutlery and already filling with well-dressed men and women.

'You are just being paranoid, dear James,' Samuel countered. 'We are safe in Cardiff.'

James turned and, walking to the door of the dining room, looked back at the bar. 'Don't you think it is strange that the man I observed left the hotel at just the moment we came in to dine?' he said. 'I do not wish to take any chances. I think we ought to leave now.'

Samuel was a little tipsy from the alcohol he had consumed over the last couple of hours. Maybe James was right, he pondered. He had made the mistake of being complacent before. Nowhere in the British Isles seemed to be safe from his brother's reach. 'Your instincts may be right, my dear,' Samuel said. 'I think it is time that we found a back entrance from this establishment and made our way to Mr Jones' residence.'

On the street the sun was setting over the smoggy town and already sinking behind the green hills. James and Samuel walked quickly towards the row of tenements, and when they reached Kevin Jones' house it was his wife who opened the door.

'My husband is not here,' she said, not inviting the two men into her house. 'He has gone to the docks.'

'Damn!' Samuel muttered. He was feeling more and more paranoid. The coal ship they were to take passage on was not due to depart for another two hours.

'James, I think that we should make our way to our ship and board early.'

'A goddamned good idea,' James agreed with relief. 'In my opinion, the sooner we are aboard the better.' James wanted to add that it had been Samuel's reckless and impulsive nature that had brought them to this point of fleeing like felons from the law, but he restrained himself. After all, aboard their passage to Canada they would be beyond Charles' clutches. They were mere hours from escaping both the British law and Charles.

*

Ewen led two uniformed constables and a sergeant to the hotel, but when they arrived they were told by the publican that the Englishman and American had left without dining. It seemed they had left the establishment via the kitchen door.

'Well, Owens, where do you think they have disappeared to?' the police sergeant asked irritably.

Ewen screwed up his face in frustration. The generous reward was slipping through his fingers. 'From what I understand, the two men are attempting to flee the British Isles. Maybe they have a berth on one of our ships departing tonight? I think we should go to the docks.'

'You had better be right, Ewen Owens, or I will consider doing you for wasting police time,' the sergeant replied. 'There are a lot of ships at the docks.'

'It would have to be one of the cargo ships steaming out of the country,' Ewen said. 'That narrows things down.' He knew the docks like the back of his hand and there was nowhere for the wanted man to hide.

*

In an elite gambling club in London, Colonel Clive Jenkins, recently returned to London from India, sat across the table from Charles Forbes, examining his hand of cards. The game was of secondary importance, however, a way of going unnoticed amongst the rakish gentlemen of the British aristocracy.

'Your brother is a hard man to kill,' Jenkins said quietly, staring at his cards.

'As I informed you, the man in your command is not my brother,' Charles said, and Jenkins looked at him sharply.

'Then who is he, old chap?' Jenkins asked.

'I have very strong reasons to believe that my brother has swapped roles with some unknown person, probably from the Australian colonies,' Charles said. 'However, I have just received a telegraph that the real Samuel Forbes has been sighted in Cardiff, and that the local constabulary will arrest him on fraud charges. When that happens, the imposter, your so-called Captain Forbes, will be revealed for who he really is. I am sure then you will be able to have him court-martialled. Does the army execute imposters pretending to hold the Queen's commission?'

'If what you say can be proved, Captain Samuel Forbes will definitely be drummed out of the army, but I doubt it will lead to his execution. He has friends on General Havelock's staff, and an impressive record of military service.'

'No matter,' Charles replied. 'As long as he is exposed.'

'It will be my greatest pleasure to have the man in my regiment paraded as an imposter and dishonourably discharged from the army,' Jenkins said. 'But what if he is killed before I return from staff college? Does the bounty still exist on his life, old chap?'

'A gentleman's agreement is to be honoured,' Charles replied, laying down his hand on the table with a smirk of satisfaction.

*

The Cardiff dock was a hub of noise and suspended coal dust. Lights illuminated areas where grubby men toiled to ensure the black gold was loaded aboard freighters, and the noise of metal chains and shouting workmen filled the early evening.

Samuel and James made their way towards the gangway of the ship that Kevin had named as their transport to Canada.

'Stop!'

The command rang out and was followed by a whistle blast. Samuel turned to see three uniformed policemen hurrying towards them, in the company of a civilian. It was obvious they were in deep trouble.

Already the appearance of the Cardiff constabulary had drawn the attention of the men working on the docks, and they paused in their labour to see what the excitement was all about.

'Stop those men!' the sergeant commanded.

'What do we do?' James asked in panic.

'We run,' Samuel said, and broke into a sprint.

Both men discarded their hand luggage to run faster, knowing that the most valuable items they had were the money belts around their waists which contained their supply of English banknotes. The situation looked hopeless when they reached the end of the wharf and turned to see the police only yards away.

'Jump!' Samuel said, grabbing James' arm and hauling him from the edge of the wharf into the dark water many feet below. They hit with a hard splash and disappeared beneath the murky salty water. Samuel was still holding James' arm as they descended into the depths. Samuel kicked out, desperately forcing his way to the surface, dragging James with him. James spat out a mouthful of dirty water when they broke the surface.

'I can't swim,' James gasped.

'I can,' Samuel spluttered, grateful he had learned when he was in the colony of New South Wales.

The weight of their shoes and jackets was dragging them beneath the surface, so Samuel quickly kicked off his shoes and struggled out of his jacket. He required all his strength to keep James afloat and when Samuel glanced up at the wharf he could see the faces of the police above peering down at them.

'You men, come to the shore immediately,' the sergeant yelled. 'You are to be arrested.'

'Like hell,' Samuel muttered to James, who bobbed in

the water while Samuel held him as best as he could with one arm. Drowning was fast becoming a possibility in the cold, filthy waters.

'We are going to swim around the bow of the ship to the other side where they cannot see us,' Samuel said in desperation. He knew they could not stay in the water for long, especially as night was beginning to fall, and if they did not drown they would be captured. It appeared that Charles had finally won. Samuel's greatest regret now was that Ian would suffer for his foolish desire to return to England. The situation was hopeless, but Samuel began swimming anyway, dragging James with him.

Somehow he was able to get them both to the far side of the hulking ship where they were hidden from the shore. But he could not find anything to hold on to, and he knew his strength was rapidly fading in the icy waters.

'I'll get you in,' came a voice from behind, and in the dim light Samuel could just make out a small rowboat with Kevin at the oars. Relief flowed through him. 'Just keep to the shadow of the ship.'

Samuel dragged James with him to the shadow, out of sight of the police on the shore. Kevin reached down and gripped James by the collar of his shirt as Samuel helped push him up and over the side of the boat. James struggled into the small craft, coughing up water. Using the last of his diminishing strength to aid him, Samuel dragged himself into the boat and slumped down beside James.

From the shore they could hear the shouts of the police trying to catch sight of them.

'Thank you,' Samuel finally gasped. 'I thought that we would drown. How is it that you became our guardian angel?'

'I was at the docks, and as soon as I saw what was happening with the peelers after you, I guessed you were in trouble. When I saw you jump into the water I ran to fetch a rowboat nearby, belongs to a friend of mine. I doubt you will be able to return to the wharf to board your ship, but all is not lost, boyos. I think I can still get you a berth. I am going to row out into the channel where the lights from the shore do not reach and take you to an iron ship that is ready to up anchor. Do you still have money?'

Samuel touched his money belt. His cash would be a bit soggy but it was still currency of the realm. 'I do,' he replied, and Kevin set out with a strong stroke, rowing the boat towards a well-lit freighter raising steam.

Samuel started to feel the night air chill his sodden clothes and beside him he could feel James shivering. After fifteen minutes they reached the side of the vessel, just as the anchors were rattling up the ship's side. Kevin called out and a rope ladder was thrown to the small boat below. He told the faces above that he needed to speak with the ship's captain about a couple of unexpected passengers prepared to pay well for a berth.

'I know the captain,' Kevin said, 'and if you mention my name while producing a generous amount of English pounds, I am sure he will find a passage for you both.' With that, Kevin extended his hand.

Samuel took it and hoped his firm grip conveyed his gratitude. 'We cannot thank you enough. I hope that we may meet again under better circumstances,' he said, releasing Kevin's hand and grasping the rope ladder.

Both he and James were able to clamber to the ship's deck, where they were met by a bearded sailor who looked more like a pirate. Nevertheless he identified himself as the ship's captain and said he had come down from the bridge to find out why his ship was being hailed by a man in a rowboat.

'Hope you got a bit of money to pay your fare,' he said.

'We do. Mr Kevin Jones highly recommended your ship,' Samuel said. 'Where is this ship bound?'

'First stop, Cape Town, and then the colony of West Australia,' the captain replied. 'Afterwards we steam to New South Wales to deliver our cargo. Have you ever been to the Australian colonies?'

Samuel just grinned.

The ship slid into the running waters of the channel, tooting its horn to indicate that it was departing on a long sea voyage, and leaving Ewen Owens on the wharf using language not acceptable in polite company.

Part Three

A Tale of Two Cities: Delhi and Lucknow

TWENTY-SIX

Alice stood on the stony ridge amongst the small encampment of army tents wearing a ragged dress stained with dried blood. The air was still filled with the stench of rotting bodies, but she barely noticed these days. If it was not raining, it was hot and humid, and the ground was a world of sticky, stinking mud.

As she stood gazing at the relief column approaching from the north, Alice saw horses pulling artillery twenty-four-pounder guns along a rutted track towards their camp. She had grown to know one artillery gun from another and had often stood beside her husband treating the results of their devastating cannonballs. Even so, it was cholera that remained the gravest threat due to the unsanitary conditions. Peter had insisted that water brought up from the stream be boiled before consumption, but Alice spent much of her time visiting those sick soldiers who had ignored her husband's advice.

Alice knew that these guns and the men marching beside them were coming to their aid. A frontal infantry assault on the impressive city walls was akin to suicide – the defenders outnumbered them and were well armed – but a combined infantry and artillery attack could make a breakthrough.

The mutineers had continued their forays against the British force on the ridge, but each attack had been repulsed by the mixed force of British soldiers and loyal Indian troops. Scott had informed Peter and Alice that the mutineers were being reinforced with what were known as Moslem *mujahidin*, holy warriors, and intelligence sources indicated that Delhi was to be established as a major centre in a resurrected Moghul empire.

'Impressive, aren't they?' Scott said, striding towards Alice. 'We now have six twenty-four-pounders, eight eighteen-pounder long guns, six eight-inch howitzers, and four ten-inch mortars. Enough artillery to concentrate on breaching the city walls. Alas, it will be the gunners, sappers and infantry who will lead the eventual attack on the town, but my squadron will follow up once they are inside the walls.'

Just then the explosive blast of British guns opened fire from the southern edge of the ridge.

'Counter battery fire,' Scott said. 'Our gunners are neutralising the closest enemy guns in one of the bastions outside the eastern city walls. We want the damned rascals to think that will be the direction of our eventual main assault.'

Suddenly, Alice doubled over and vomited, causing Scott to leap forward to her. She straightened up and wiped her mouth with the back of her tattered sleeve.

'Are you ill?' Scott asked, and his first thought was that he was seeing the onset of cholera.

'If being with child is an illness, then you could say so,' Alice said with a weak smile.

Startled, Scott could only blink his surprise. 'Does my brother know?' he asked awkwardly.

'Peter is aware of my condition,' Alice answered and Scott frowned.

'This is not the place for a woman who is with child,' he chided. 'As a medical man, my brother should know that.'

'It is a bit late now,' Alice smiled. 'Besides, for centuries women have borne children in times of war. Why should I be any different?'

'Well, let me extend my congratulations then,' Scott said gruffly. 'Let us pray that the birth comes when we are back in England.'

England, Alice thought. England was just a vague memory now, and this world of war was all she knew with its pestilence, death and dying.

Scott made his way back to HQ for a briefing, leaving Alice alone to listen to the guns roar and watch the smoke rise in the distance as the cannonballs found their mark. She was relieved that she could not hear the screaming of the men they hit – even if they were the enemy – and returned to her tent for a short nap before she joined Peter in his makeshift surgery. There were bandages to be boiled and rolled, surgical instruments to sharpen. There was a kind of simplicity to her life now, but she also thought about her pregnancy with great fear. Under these terrible circumstances, would she be able to carry the life within her to term?

*

Lucknow was now the objective of Havelock's small mixed force of British and Indian troops. First, however, the city of Cawnpore had to be taken from the rebels and the days of fighting in the surrounding countryside had taken a great toll on the Queen's soldiers. Bursting artillery fire, volleys of musketry and terrible bayonet charges under a fierce Indian sun had taken their share of lives in Ian's company at the walls of Cawnpore. But they had taken the city.

The British forces bivouacked on the Indian plain and sentries were posted. Ian's batman assisted him in setting up his tent in the meagre shade of some scrubby trees.

'I have the list of men reporting sick,' Conan said, passing Ian the company roll book.

'Cholera?' Ian asked, and Conan nodded. 'That bloody disease is taking a greater toll on our ranks than the mutineers,' Ian growled.

'The lads are still in good spirits,' Conan said. 'They trust you.'

'I fear that my decisions will one day cost them their lives,' Ian quietly admitted.

'They all took the Queen's shilling knowing that a soldier's life means the risk of being killed one day,' Conan replied.

Ian shrugged. How many times in the bloody hand-to-hand fighting for Cawnpore had he come close to death? He was fortunate that at night in his tent no one witnessed the feverish nightmares; the twitching, crying and sweating. These were the unseen wounds of a soldier exposed to combat.

Colour Sergeant Paddy Leslie approached, saluted and stood to attention.

'At ease, Colour Sergeant,' Ian said, returning the salute. 'You wish to speak to me?'

'Yes, sah,' Leslie said, glancing at Conan. 'It is a private matter.'

'I need to check on the lads settling in for the night,' Conan said and walked off.

'What is it?' Ian asked.

'It's about Sergeant Williams, sah. He has assaulted one of his men and is drunk in his tent.'

Ian was startled by the colour sergeant's revelation. He had always observed Owen's behaviour as a senior non-commissioned officer to be in line with the highest traditions of the service. He made his way to Owen's tent and found his friend sitting on an ammunition box, a bottle of gin in his hand. Owen looked at Ian through bleary eyes and remained sitting.

'Stand up, Sergeant Williams,' Ian barked.

Owen rose unsteadily to his feet in a semblance of attention, still holding the half-empty bottle of spirits. 'What is this that I hear of you assaulting one of the lads?'

'Dunno what you mean,' Owen slurred.

'Don't know what you mean, sir,' Ian said.

'Sir,' Owen added reluctantly. 'If that is what I should call you. I know all about you, *sir.* I know who you really are.'

'What are you talking about?' Ian frowned.

'Molly told me that your real name is Ian Steele and that you were once a colonial blacksmith. Between you and Curry, I reckon you have been cheating me on the loot. All you colonials are a thieving lot.'

Ian was shocked by Owen's revelation. How had Molly learned his secret? The suspicion that Conan must have told her crept into his thoughts. Who else knew? He could see there was a dramatic change in Owen, and it shocked him, but he did not understand what had caused it. It was as if he had a mental sickness – like those Ian had seen driven mad by the horrors of war.

'You well know that everything has been equally divided,' Ian said.

'What about the jewels you took when we were in the Crimea? You didn't share those with me and my brother.'

Ian acknowledged that he was right, but the Williams brothers had found their own small fortune in the Russian baggage train they had looted.

'We all collected valuables in the Crimea,' said Ian calmly. 'We have all contributed on an equal basis since then.'

'I don't believe you . . . sir,' Owen said, swaying on his feet. 'You and that colonial Paddy are working together against me. But it don't matter, because I know this war will get me killed anyway.'

'You have been reported for assaulting a soldier and here I find you drunk. No matter the circumstances of our friendship, I am obliged to have you punished in order to maintain discipline in the company,' Ian said.

'What are you going to do with me?' Owen asked.

'I am forced to have you stripped of your rank,' Ian said sadly. 'You have to get a grip, Owen, or you will get yourself killed. You will surrender that gin bottle to me now, and you will also remain in your quarters until you sober up.'

Owen hesitated but passed the bottle to Ian, who turned on his heel and stepped outside the tent. Colour Sergeant Leslie was hovering nearby.

'Make sure Private Williams remains in his tent until you deem him sober enough to join the ranks, Colour Sergeant,' Ian said, emptying the remaining gin on the dry soil of the Indian plain.

Ian found Conan supervising the cleaning of regimental kit and gestured him to follow a short distance away.

'You saw Owen?' Conan asked quietly.

'I am afraid something has happened to Owen,' Ian said worriedly, and quickly described to Conan the scene he had just witnessed. 'It is possible that the fighting has unnerved him. I have stripped him of his sergeant's rank rather than see him flogged before the regiment on a punishment parade.'

'From what the lads told me, Owen punched a soldier to get hold of the bottle of grog,' Conan said. 'Maybe the sun has got to him. A few of the lads have told me that they see Owen talking to himself – or to people he says are talking to him in his head.

'I think the fighting and killing has got to him. Owen was never born to be a soldier. I know that because I convinced him to join up. At the time I thought we had little choice if we wanted to stay out of the hands of the peelers back in London. I think Owen resents me for making that decision.'

'How does he know my real identity?' Ian asked, staring directly into Conan's face and watching as he paled.

'I told Molly,' Conan said, stricken that he had broken his mate's confidence. 'She swore she would tell no one.'

'Well, it seems she told her brother. When I meet the Queen at a tea party, I may as well tell her I am an imposter, too. Although I am sure she already knows.'

'I'm sorry,' Conan said, truly repentant. 'Molly must have thought that as our friend, Owen already knew. I am sure both she and Owen will keep their mouths shut.'

'I hope you are right because Owen thinks that you and I are in a conspiracy to take his share of the war booty,' Ian said. 'Keep a close eye on him. He told me he thinks he will be killed in this campaign, and expressing such thoughts is likely to make him careless in what he tells people. He may think he has nothing to lose.'

'I'll kill him myself if he opens his mouth about who you really are,' Conan growled.

Conan stepped back, saluted and marched away, leaving Ian to ponder how hard it was becoming to remain Captain Samuel Forbes when so many people knew the truth.

*

Charles Forbes reluctantly paid out the last of the commission to Charles Field.

'I am sorry that you have spent so much on this search for your brother,' Field said as the pound notes were placed on his desk. 'He has proven to be a very resourceful man.'

'Do you know where the ship he escaped on was bound?' Charles asked.

'I was informed that the ship was carrying a supply of iron to South Africa, and its final cargo to the colony of New South Wales. From there I presume that your brother and his friend will take a ship across the Pacific to the United States.'

'New South Wales, you say,' Charles mused with a flicker of hope. New South Wales was where his uncle, Sir George Forbes, had a sheep property. Surely Samuel would not be able to resist visiting the man who was his real father.

Charles leaned back in his chair. 'Tell me, Mr Field, do you have contacts in the colonies?'

Field had finished counting the money and looked with surprise at his client. 'A detective I once worked with migrated to Sydney Town,' he replied. 'What do you have in mind?'

Charles removed a wad of currency from his pocket, peeled off some notes and placed them on the desk in front of Field.

'If you could get an urgent letter to your former colleague I am sure our business arrangement will continue, Mr Field,' Charles said, his determination to unmask the conspiracy stronger than ever. 'If your agent in the colony can prove that Samuel is actually in New South Wales, then that would mean the man serving in the regiment is an imposter.'

'The Australian colonies are a long way from here,' Field said.

'I have the exact details of where my brother is likely to be found. You know I am prepared to be generous and this is my advance on our venture.'

Field stared for a short moment at the money on his desk, then reached for it.

'I will endeavour to contact my man in the colony,' he said. 'But I do not promise anything.'

'My brother will feel safe and secure so far away,' Charles said. 'He will not in his wildest imagination think that I can reach across the ocean to him.'

Field stared at his client and could see the obsession blazing in his eyes. What else was this man capable of? He did not want to reflect on that any further; as a detective inspector he had once hunted murderers. He did not now wish to be employed by one.

TWENTY-SEVEN

The sound of artillery guns hardly disturbed Alice's sleep as they fired relentlessly day and night. Her baby had been conceived to the sound of their thunder, although now the gunfire was growing more intensive. Alice came awake under her mosquito net in the early hours of the morning and realised Peter was not beside her. This immediately made her think that something of great importance was occurring. She slipped quickly from the bed and dressed.

Bugles sounded and Alice could hear that the camp was coming awake with the jangle of saddlery and the neighing and snorting of cavalry horses. Men were shouting orders and outside the tent she could see the flaring lights of burning tapers.

Scott had informed her weeks earlier that the gunners had been directing a heavy bombardment on the enemy bastions outside the city walls in an effort to neutralise them before the inevitable assault on the city. The guns would also breach the walls, and then it would be up to the engineers, infantry and cavalry to finish the job.

Last night Alice had watched the columns of East India Company and British troops with their loyal Indian regiments moving out in grim silence. Scott had waved to her and shouted, 'Cheerio, old girl. Tell my brother I hope I don't meet him on his operating table.'

Alice had waved back, his ominous words echoing in her mind. It seemed that, one way or another, the fate of Delhi was in the balance on this day. A cold tremor ran through her and she hurried to the operating tent where she found Peter cleaning his surgical tools in boiling water.

'You should be resting,' Peter said when he saw her.

'I am not sick, Peter, I am pregnant, and I think you will need me when the sun rises on this day,' Alice replied firmly, looking to the pile of rags that would become bandages.

'I think you are right,' Peter said, wiping his wet hands on the apron he wore to absorb the blood. 'Scott told me that five columns have been organised to attack the city. He said not to worry about him as he was in the third column, acting as a liaison officer for the fifth column, for when the breaches had been made. He assured me that he would be safe. He said that they will be attacking from the north.'

Alice had grown very fond of her dashing brother-in-law, so different from her quiet husband, and if he was killed she knew she would mourn deeply for his loss.

'I will roll bandages and have tea and chapattis brought to us for breakfast,' Alice said, and then they fell silent as they prepared for the stream of wounded that would inevitably come once the attack commenced.

⋆

Major Scott Campbell sat astride his mount, frustrated by the delay. The assault had been scheduled for dawn, but the enemy had replaced some of the breaches with sandbags, and the British artillery was once again required to smash the hastily repaired fortifications.

He watched the first glimmers of the sun's rays creep above the flat horizon as his column waited behind a former residence of the old Moghul kings a quarter of a mile from the city walls to their south. Scott was not with his squadron, which had remained with the fifth column in reserve. The plan was that once the engineers and infantry had entered the city the cavalry would sweep in behind to help clear the narrow streets and alleyways of any resistance.

'It will be a damned hot day,' commented an infantry major sitting on his horse beside Scott. 'And I don't just mean the weather.'

The crash of artillery shells slamming into the city appeared to taper away and both men knew what that meant. The sun was now above the horizon and they had a clear view of the walls. Heavy smoke from the guns drifted on a light breeze.

'Well, old chap, this is it for me,' the British major sighed, dismounting from his horse and handing the reins to an Indian servant.

Scott also dismounted, disobeying his orders to act in a liaison capacity as he knew there were junior officers who could take this role. He cast about to see a lieutenant, pale faced and trembling.

'Mr Giles, you are now the liaison officer for the fifth column.'

'Sir,' the startled young officer replied. 'What do I do?'

'You remain in place close to the colonel, and he will direct you to carry orders to the fifth when required,' Scott said, and could see the expression of relief on the young man's clean-shaven face. The young officer would not have to go forward in what appeared to be a suicidal attack on the city.

The infantry major drew both his pistol and sword. Scott, who was not about to be left out of this chance for glory, did so too, although something inside told him that he was a fool.

'Welcome to the infantry, Campbell,' the infantry major grinned. 'Not as fancy as being astride a horse, galloping through the enemy ranks.'

Scott watched as the engineers moved forward to blow the Kashmiri gate open on the city's north wall. It was an extremely hazardous mission as the British engineer officers and Indian sappers would be under constant fire from the defenders on the wall when they carried the explosives forward. Under a withering fire, the British and Indian engineers were to place four gunpowder charges, reinforced by sandbags, concentrating the blast at the gate. The engineers advanced, and many were wounded or killed in the process of lighting the fuses, but their bravery was rewarded when the explosion demolished the gate.

Scott waited beside the infantry major, and a bugle sounded for the charge through the gap created by the courageous engineers. He surged forward, yelling at the top of his voice, brandishing his sabre and gripping his revolver. Men were falling before they reached the wall but Scott ignored the casualties mounting around him. The red haze of battle was on him as he panted and sweated under the heat of the early morning sun. Something whipped through his sleeve but Scott hardly registered the musket ball coming so close.

He stumbled over the rubble mixed with the smashed bodies of the engineers and found himself in the city, where the British force was met with further heavy fire from nearby houses. Scott realised that he was in the lead and had become separated from the infantry major. He cast around to see if any threats showed themselves and noticed the blood-soaked body of the major sprawled only a few paces away. The soldiers around their fallen officer hesitated, but Scott roared at them to continue the attack on the enemy, who were shooting at them from loopholes in the walls of the surrounding buildings. The men responded to his leadership, and Scott continued at a trot towards an alley which he suddenly realised was manned by four enemy infantrymen.

He whipped up his pistol arm and emptied his six shots into the four men. Two fell but the remaining two charged forward with bayonets fixed. Scott balanced on his feet and met the first bayonet lunged at him, deftly deflecting the sharp point from entering his belly. With practised skill he brought the razor-sharp sabre around to slice through the Indian's neck, severing his head from his body. A burst of blood spurted like a fountain from the headless man, soaking Scott. The second enemy soldier hesitated at the terrible sight. Scott did not pause and in a blurred movement sliced his sabre down on the sepoy's head, splitting it asunder. Four dead mutineers lay at his feet, but when he looked up he felt his stomach knot. From the other end of the alley he could see around twenty mutineers running towards him with bayonets fixed. He knew he could not fight his way out of this situation in the narrow confines of the alleyway. He was seconds from certain death when he felt himself brushed aside. A dozen red-coated soldiers pushed past him, levelling their rifled muskets at the advancing enemy. Well disciplined, they fired a volley, each bullet finding a target, and in some cases passing through one body to hit another. The attack was halted, and before the enemy could consolidate, the redcoats charged with fixed bayonets any mutineers still standing. The clash was bloody but brief. Men screamed, grunted, swore, and some even cried in the hand-to-hand fight to the death.

Scott quickly reloaded his revolver with powder and ball in a whirl of noise, heat, confusion and death. Smoke poured from burning buildings and muskets crashed all around. Chips of stinging stone spattered his face as stray musket balls hit nearby walls, but Scott hardly felt them. The red-coated soldiers retreated back to Scott, their faces and hands covered in blood. In all he counted eleven soldiers with two suffering wounds requiring a surgeon's knife.

'What now, sah?' a corporal asked, and Scott had to think. As a cavalryman, it would be simple: keep moving forward until they were through the enemy ranks.

'Get those two wounded men back to the surgeon. One man can assist them while we continue forward to capture the palace.'

'Very good, sah,' the corporal answered. He was an older man and Scott could see in his expression the years of service.

'What is your name, Corporal?' Scott asked.

'Corporal Welsh, sah,' the man answered.

'Well, Corporal Welsh, let us do some mischief to these mutineers.'

The corporal grinned under his face blackened by gunpowder. 'C'mon lads,' he said, turning to the private soldiers gripping their muskets and Enfield rifles. 'You 'eard the officer.'

Scott advanced down the alley with his loaded pistol and sabre. The soldiers followed, ready for the next encounter. As they advanced towards the royal palace, the other British columns entered the city, and also encountered fierce resistance. Many officers were killed, and some disorder ensued from a lack of leadership. At least Scott was able to provide leadership in his little sector of the battle, but he was starting to regret that he had not entered the city on his horse with his squadron. At least a horse provided him the mobility to escape the enemy, who were mostly on foot.

They broke out of the alley into a plaza where Scott could hear the crackle of musketry. When he scanned the open ground he saw the ranks of mutineers on the far side readying themselves to fire a volley at the British soldiers who had taken up a position in the open a hundred yards away. The mutineers were in the process of loading their cumbersome muskets but they had been previously trained by the British occupiers and knew their drills well.

Scott quickly appraised the situation, realising that his small force had not been noticed.

'Form a single rank!' he roared, and the well-disciplined redcoats fell quickly into a line slightly to the front and flank of the mutineers.

'Present! Fire!'

The soldiers stood, firing a volley into the mutineer infantrymen on the other side of the plaza. Their musket balls, and a few Minié balls from the Enfields, tore through the two ranks of the enemy. The volley caused confusion in the enemy ranks, and they discharged their muskets without properly levelling them.

'Ready bayonets! Charge!'

Immediately, Scott's small detail of redcoats charged across the open plaza. Yelling and cursing, they caused panic in the demoralised enemy ranks and the flashing bayonets of the British tore into exposed bellies, chests and throats as men cursed, cried and grunted their last breaths.

Scott brought his pistol up to a big, bearded Indian who was waving a large sword in the air. He thrust the muzzle into the man's face, firing as he did so. The heavy lead ball shattered bone, and flesh and blood splashed back into Scott's face as the man fell. Scott was almost felled by the body of an enemy soldier falling against him from a bayonet thrust in his chest. He stumbled but quickly regained his feet, glancing around for any immediate threat. He was pleased to see that the charge across the open plaza had succeeded, and only panting, shocked red-coated troops remained standing amongst the dead and dying Indian rebels.

'Sir, I must extend my gratitude to you for your timely intervention,' said a young lieutenant with a blackened face and blood-soaked uniform. Desultory fire was still coming from isolated enemy marksmen in the surrounding buildings. 'Lieutenant Johnson of the Foot Regiment, at your service.'

'Major Campbell, Bengali cavalry,' Scott replied, and suddenly registered his raging thirst. He reached for his water canteen on his belt and a searing pain shot through his left wrist.

Scott spun around in shock, noticing at the same time that Lieutenant Johnson had already issued orders for his men to take cover. Scott felt Corporal Welsh grip his jacket and yank him to the cover of a stone wall at the edge of the plaza, shielding him against other marksmen in the surrounding houses.

Scott stared down at his hand and saw his mangled wrist. Blood was flowing from the wound and pain coursed through his body.

'Here, sah,' said the British NCO. 'I will wrap your wrist.' He produced a clean linen cloth and commenced wrapping the wound, although blood quickly soaked the cloth. The pain was numbing Scott's mind as he fought off the desire to scream.

'Corporal, you take our men to join Mr Johnson's unit.

Leave me and I will make my own way back for medical treatment,' Scott ordered through gritted teeth.

'Sah, I can help you back to our lines,' the corporal protested. 'The lads will be all right with Mr Johnson.'

'Thank you, Corporal Welsh, but I can see your lads will need you, and I can walk,' Scott grimaced.

'Very good, sah,' the NCO answered. 'Good luck, sah.'

Corporal Welsh fell in with the main contingent of the advancing force preparing to clear the enemy from the houses around them. Their muskets were primed and their bayonets fixed for the inevitable hand-to-hand fighting.

Scott gripped his loaded pistol in his right hand and looked back to the mouth of the alley he had cleared minutes earlier. He knew that he would have to retrace his steps lest he become confused in the winding streets of the city. Around him he could hear the firing of small arms and artillery, and the shouts in English and Indian dialects of men using their last words in defiance of death. He was still experiencing a terrible thirst and slipped his revolver into the leather holster as he again attempted to retrieve his canteen. The water partly revived his body and when he had finished slaking his thirst, he carried on.

Scott stepped over the bodies of the mutineers he and his small squad had killed only minutes earlier, although it felt like a lifetime ago. When he reached the area before the breach in the wall he saw a red-coated soldier lying on his back, groaning as he held in his own intestines. Scott looked around and could see that the army had advanced, leaving the critically wounded soldier to his fate. Scott knelt beside the man and saw how young he was. He guessed he must have been around sixteen years old.

'I will get you to the surgeon, Private,' Scott said, ignoring the intense pain of his own wound.

'Too late for me,' the soldier said, staring up at the blue skies. 'Could you tell me ma that I died like a soldier?' He gasped and closed his eyes. Scott could see that his stomach wound was beyond medical care, and he would die in agony under the blazing sun alone.

'I will tell your family you died heroically storming the walls of Delhi,' Scott said, and while the young soldier's eyes were closed, he shot him in the head, ending his agony.

Scott rose and stumbled towards the smashed gate to leave the city.

★

By midmorning a steady stream of wounded was arriving at Peter's tent for surgery. The big, lead balls of the enemy's muskets caused horrific wounds, smashing bone as they entered the body. There were others with bayonet wounds and sword cuts, and Peter worked feverishly to amputate limbs that were beyond repair. Alice went amongst those waiting on stretchers outside in the blazing sun, carrying canteens of boiled water to quench their thirsts, and examined the extent of wounds, prioritising those she knew her husband might save.

Alice bent over one older soldier who had sustained a musket shot to the chest. She knew there was no sense in attempting to extract the ball, as bloody froth formed around his mouth and his skin had paled under his tanned, bearded face.

She felt the grip of his hand in her own as he stared at the vultures swirling in clouds over the camp. 'I'm slain,' he whispered, closing his eyes. Alice could see that he was dead, and slowly rose to attend the next man.

'I said I would be back.'

Alice turned to see Scott standing a few paces away, holding his arm. She could see the blood-soaked bandage around his left wrist.

'Oh my God!' she said, stepping towards him. 'How bad is your wound?'

'I am hoping that Peter can tell me,' Scott replied through gritted teeth, and slowly sank to his knees.

TWENTY-EIGHT

The two medical orderlies assisting Peter were older soldiers unfit for combative operations, and they carried the amputated arms and legs of soldiers out of the large surgical tent and discarded them in a pile outside. While Scott waited for his turn, he glanced at the tangle of limbs, wondering if his left hand would soon be added to the already stinking and decomposing flesh now covered with myriad crawling flies.

Scott stepped inside the tent, dread written in his agonised expression. Peter looked up from a patient whose life he could not save, and the orderlies removed the body from the table.

'I hope you have time to look to my rather minor wound,' Scott said, attempting a smile that turned into a grimace.

Peter could see the blood-soaked bandage and the blood dripping from it.

'Good God, old man!' Peter said, wiping his bloody hands on his apron. 'What have you done to yourself?'

Scott stepped forward, raising his arm so that Peter could examine the shattered wrist. Peter gently unwrapped the bandage to reveal the extent of the wound.

'I think it just needs a few stitches and then I will be able to join the lads again,' Scott suggested, but Peter knew better. He could see fragments of bone mixed with the pulverised wrist joint, all barely held together by a few strips of raw flesh. It was obvious that the wound was beyond repair and the hand required amputation.

'I need you to get on the table,' Peter said. 'The only way I can save your life is to remove your hand at the wrist.'

Scott looked with despair into his brother's eyes. 'Are you sure you cannot sew my hand back together?' he asked, and Peter shook his head.

'I promise it will be quick, and with further treatment you should recover well.'

Scott lay down on the table smeared with blood and Peter nodded to his two attendants who stepped forward and put their hands firmly on the cavalry officer's shoulder and arm. Peter fetched an extremely sharp knife, silently thanking God that from what he could observe he would not have to use a surgical saw to cut through bone.

Before Scott could react, Peter gripped the useless hand and, with a deft movement, sliced through the flesh that retained hand to arm. The hand came off and Scott let out a strangled cry of pain. Peter quickly passed the amputated flesh to one of the orderlies who discreetly placed it in a new pile of limbs collecting in the corner of the tent, awaiting disposal outside.

Peter quickly and expertly went about cleansing the open

wound with a mix of water and carbolic acid. His brother attempted to sit up.

'Take it easy, old boy,' Peter said gently, tears in his eyes. He had always thought he was immune to the terrible suffering of his patients, but this was different. This was his own brother who had always lived life to the fullest. Now he had lost his hand and his life would change forever.

Alice appeared in the tent.

'Alice will help you back to your quarters,' Peter said after bandaging the wrist. 'She will care for you until you have recovered.'

Alice helped Scott from the surgical tent to his own, and there made sure he lay down on his cot.

'I need some medicine,' Scott groaned. 'You will find it in my chest.'

Alice opened the lid to the big chest and saw a bottle of whisky on top of his kit. Alice removed the stopper and poured an amount into a tin mug, handing it to Scott.

'You should be drinking water and trying to sleep,' she chided gently.

He grinned weakly and took a long gulp of the alcohol. 'Leave the bottle by my bed,' he said, using his right hand to place the mug beside him and pouring another shot from the bottle.

'I will return whenever my duties allow,' Alice said. 'Your bandages will need to be changed daily.'

'You are an angel in my life,' Scott said. 'The best thing my brother ever did was marry you, and if he had not, I would have married you myself.'

'I am sure that one day you will meet a good woman,' Alice replied. 'You are still a dashing figure, and I am sure we will be able to fit you with a wooden hand when your wound heals.'

'Ah, a one-handed cavalry officer,' Scott sighed.

'You will be up and leading your men in no time,' Alice said, wiping Scott's brow with a wet cloth.

Scott gripped Alice's arm. 'Do you really believe that?' he asked.

Alice nodded. 'Now get some sleep and I pray that the pain will recede with rest,' she said.

Scott lay back and stared at the ceiling of the tent. They both knew that infection could still easily take his life in this Indian climate. Alice pulled down the mosquito net to keep off the clouds of flies gathering to the smell of blood. She said a quiet prayer that her brother-in-law would live.

She hurried back to the wounded men lying on stretchers outside the surgery tent and calmly went about her work of assessing who would be next on her husband's operating table, and comforting those she knew would die.

*

Private Owen Williams sat on a wooden crate in the bivouac on the road to Lucknow, cleaning his rifle. Around him, soldiers smoked pipes, played cards and exchanged gossip about the battle ahead. They ignored Owen, whose morose manner did not encourage company. He stewed in his thoughts about the betrayal of the two men he had once thought were his friends. He was sure they were keeping his share of the loot. Captain Samuel Forbes was an imposter, and both he and Conan Curry were colonials from New South Wales, so neither of them could be trusted. Owen promised the voices inside his head that he would get even with them – one way or another.

'Hey, Taffy,' called one of the soldiers sitting in a small circle a few feet away. 'Want to join us in a hand or two of cards? Winner gets a bottle of gin.'

Owen put down his rifle and accepted the offer. Despite once being their sergeant, the men had accepted him back into their ranks, and a bottle of gin was worth gambling for. Even as the cards were dealt Owen fumed about the betrayal of trust by the fancypants Captain Steele. When Colonel Jenkins returned to the regiment Owen would parade before him and expose the upstart colonial officer for who he really was. Owen did not trust the current acting regimental commander because he seemed to respect Ian Steele as a very competent officer. But Owen knew from their campaign in the Crimea that Colonel Jenkins would listen to him.

*

Colonel Jenkins was pleased to be on leave from the staff college. He found military matters boring and the invitation to Lady Rebecca Montegue's manor was a breath of fresh air. He arrived in his personal coach in the mid-afternoon and knew that he would not be returning before breakfast. India had kept him away from what was most important in life: his future marriage to Rebecca, whose wealth, coupled with her influential political contacts, would help him achieve the highest office in the land.

The occasion was an afternoon tea held in the manicured gardens of the country estate while the last flowers of the English summer still bloomed. Jenkins was greeted by a butler who ushered him into a garden of colourful pavilions erected on the sprawling lawns of Rebecca's grand mansion. Jenkins could see that there were many civilian and military guests. Amongst the civilians he recognised prominent members of parliament, wealthy bankers and captains of industry.

Rebecca radiated beauty and charm when she walked over to greet Jenkins.

'A rather lavish afternoon party,' he said.

'Thank you, Clive,' Rebecca replied. 'I thought this would be a good opportunity to show you off to some very important people.'

'Ah,' Jenkins said, bowing and kissing Rebecca's hand. 'You are the one who should be teaching strategy and tactics.'

'Come,' Rebecca said, and Jenkins followed her towards a small group of high-ranking army and naval officers in their dress uniforms, adorned with the medals of their service. Jenkins was dressed in a civilian suit with top hat.

'Ah, Lady Montegue,' said one of the naval officers when she and Jenkins approached. He gave a small bow of respect, and then focused on Clive Jenkins. 'I have heard that you are currently attending the new staff college, Colonel Jenkins. Not sure if all that book work and theory is really necessary to be a good soldier. We sailors learn about warfare from experience rather than books.'

'Times are changing, Sir Rodney,' Jenkins replied politely. 'New weapons are changing the way we manoeuvre on the battlefield.'

'I am surprised that you made leave from your regiment when it is engaged on a campaign in India, old boy,' a whiskered general commented, and Jenkins identified him as a close friend of General Havelock. 'I would have suspected that to choose a place at staff college under such circumstances would have been a second priority to that of leading your men in the field.'

Jenkins felt uncomfortable. It was almost as if he was being accused of desertion, or worse, cowardice. He glanced at Rebecca and he could see her frowning.

'If you really wish to know why Colonel Jenkins returned to England it was because he missed my company, gentlemen,' Rebecca said, slipping her arm through Jenkins'. 'I must apologise and take the colonel to meet my other guests. I will bid you gentlemen a good afternoon. I am sure you will agree that the French champagne is of excellent quality.'

The small group of military officers raised their glasses as a salute to Rebecca as she led Jenkins away to meet with a couple of members of the House of Lords. All Jenkins received from the two older politicians was praise for his esteemed military service. Jenkins felt much more comfortable in their company, chatting about the demise of morals in this modern world of too many liberal ideas.

The afternoon drew towards evening and the coaches arrived to return the guests to their respective homes in London, leaving Rebecca and Clive Jenkins to their own company.

'It has been a grand day, thank you,' Jenkins said, sipping the last of his champagne.

'I planned the function as soon as I learned that you were returning to England,' Rebecca said. 'You were not born to be a soldier, rather a man destined to lead this country into the future.'

'I could be insulted by your observation,' Jenkins said, 'but I know that a union between us is destined for greatness. I often wonder, though, if you love me or simply see that you can mould me into the man of your dreams.'

'Love is irrelevant,' Rebecca said. 'But I am fond of you, and that is a good basis for a partnership.'

'So, you will marry me after all,' Jenkins said, and felt quite content that he would possess this rare beauty with great ambition.

'When you are no longer playing soldiers, I will,' Rebecca said, turning to walk to her manor as the servants scurried about clearing up after the visitors. 'But I will expect you to do me one great favour before we wed. I want you to destroy Sir Archibald Forbes' son, Charles, who I know is a friend of yours.'

Jenkins was stunned by Rebecca's request. 'Charles!' he exclaimed in shock. 'Why do you wish me to destroy the man?'

'Because I have asked you to,' Rebecca replied. 'If you have any real feelings for me, you will ensure that you use all in your power to destroy Charles Forbes.'

'I do not understand,' Jenkins said, shaking his head in his confusion.

'I want him killed,' Rebecca said without flinching. 'He has done me a great wrong that I do not wish to disclose at the moment, but I trust that in your love for me you will carry out my wishes.'

*

That night Jenkins lay beside Rebecca in the huge double bed, staring at the dark ceiling. He could not sleep. What kind of woman was he marrying? Behind her beauty lay a woman as ruthless as any enemy he had ever encountered on the battlefield. What had Charles Forbes done to her that would warrant his destruction, even his death?

Jenkins was a weak man and he knew it. He was not about to question Rebecca as to her motives. He thought about the conspiracy that he and Charles had entered into to have Samuel killed, and wondered how this orderly society he belonged to could be crawling with vipers – both male and female.

Rebecca stirred beside him, rolling over to face him. In the trickle of moonlight through the panes of the bedroom window he swore he could see a smile of satisfaction on her face. For once Jenkins wished he was back in India facing the dangers of an enemy he understood, but he knew he was a slave to this beautiful woman beside him. After all, he knew she had the potential to make him prime minister.

TWENTY-NINE

Torrential rain fell the night after the battle, and the British survivors huddled in misery in the open, waiting for the sun to rise. Colour Sergeant Leslie moved amongst the cold and wet troops, offering a word of encouragement and a joke where possible. When he came across Private Owen Williams sitting alone, the man was mumbling incoherently and stabbing at the muddy earth with a long bayonet. Colour Sergeant Paddy Leslie had seen this behaviour many times in his long years with the British army. It was something the horror of war did to many soldiers' minds, and he could see that Private Owen Williams had reached that point where the mind no longer controlled the body. The army's cure for such a state was harsh corporal punishment, but Paddy Leslie had never seen that cure any soldier of the malaise induced by combat.

'Taffy, get control of yourself,' Leslie snapped as the rain beat down on them.

For a moment Owen paused to stare at the ground. 'Got to go home, Colour Sergeant,' he said. 'Sarn't Major Curry is out to get me – and so is Captain Forbes.'

Leslie crouched down beside Owen. 'You have to snap out of this, Private Williams, or you will find yourself tied to the triangle for a lashing.'

'I don't care anymore,' Owen said, tears streaming down his face. 'I just want to go home. I don't want to die here.'

Leslie stood, shaking his head. He realised that the soldier was beyond reasoning with and only hoped that when the sun rose he might be thinking more clearly. The word spreading through the regiment was that in the morning they expected to see action near the fortified village of Unao. Leslie knew that he should report Private Williams' condition, but he had a soft spot for the man he had recruited for the war against the Russians in the Crimea. Owen Williams had been a brave and excellent soldier then, but time had clearly taken a toll on his mind. With cholera and heatstroke impacting so highly on the small force, every man who could hold a rifle was needed to fight under General Havelock on his advance towards Lucknow, a mere thirty-six miles away. Colour Sergeant Leslie walked away in the rain, leaving the afflicted soldier to continue stabbing the muddy earth with his bayonet.

★

The sun rose on the following morning to beat down on the heads of the assembled British force. Captain Ian Steele called for the roll to be read and was satisfied to see that all his company was on parade, albeit wet and weary. On either flank of the regiment other British units were assembling, and laid out before them across a swamp were the walled houses outside Unao. A raised road ran through the swamp to the fortified town, and using his telescope Ian could see that the houses had firing loopholes in the walls.

'What is happening today?' Conan asked.

'General Havelock is sending in the Scots along the causeway,' Ian replied, lowering his telescope. Already fire pouring from the defences was ripping into the Scottish ranks and men were falling. Ian could see the terrible price the Highlanders were paying for the assault, but he closed his mind to their casualties as he knew that before the day ended it would be his regiment's turn to face the defences. Havelock's staff had calculated that there were around fifteen thousand mutineers up against their small force of around fifteen hundred.

The enemy artillery opened fire, adding grape and round shot into the advancing Scots soldiers, who were roaring the ancient slogans of the Highlands as they advanced into the wall of lead and iron.

'Poor bastards,' Conan said softly. 'Straight into a frontal assault against an entrenched enemy.'

'Rather them than us,' Ian replied, wiping sweat from his forehead with the back of his hand. The heat was becoming oppressive and Ian wondered how many of his men would succumb to the invisible enemy that dogged them alongside the cholera. 'We are being held in reserve but as the enemy outnumber us I know we will see our share of action. I will brief the junior officers and senior NCOs in five minutes.'

Conan acknowledged the unspoken order to spread the word about the briefing, and afterward the officers and NCOs marched smartly back to their sections to continue with preparations. Only Colour Sergeant Leslie lingered.

'What is it, Colour Sergeant?' Ian asked.

'Sir, it is a matter about Private Williams,' he replied. 'Is there a chance he could be kept back with the regimental HQ when we commence the advance?'

'Why does Private Williams need to be kept out of the advance?' Ian frowned.

'I think he needs a rest from being in the ranks,' Leslie said. 'His mind has been touched and I don't think he will live if he advances as a skirmisher. I have seen this before when a soldier loses his mind.'

Ian thought for a moment, accepting the senior NCO's many years of soldiering. 'I will get the CSM to pass on to Private Williams that he is to be assigned to regimental HQ as a runner for the company.'

'Thank you, sir,' Leslie said, then saluted and returned to his young lieutenant, who would be carrying the colours into battle.

Even as Ian's company went about their duties, the Scots Highlanders were progressing along the causeway towards the fortified town with their two artillery guns supporting them. The town had deep ditches and new earthworks to overcome in the assault. The battle had well and truly begun and in the next few hours they would either win against the seemingly impossible odds, or forever remain in Indian soil if they lost.

Soon enough the remnants of the courageous Scottish brigade were on the first line of the defenders, pushing through with bayonets and entering the town of Unao. The British forces were aided by the fact that the nearby flooded plains prevented the numerically larger Indian cavalry threatening their flanks.

A runner was sent from Havelock's HQ to the regiment, and the order was passed down to the company commanders.

Ian turned to his men.

'Fix bayonets!' A rattle of long knives being attached to the end of rifled muskets sounded, and Ian roared the next order. 'Company will advance. Advance!'

Leading the way, he stepped onto the causeway to follow the unflinching Scots into the town. The company acted as the vanguard for the regiment and soon Ian's men were in the narrow streets, fighting a desperate battle of musket fire and hand-to-hand bayonet combat, as the mutineers quickly deserted their positions. Smoke filled the hot, humid air but Ian noted his men were going about their work well, ever alert to snipers in houses and on rooftops. After many hours clearing Unao they were past the houses and marketplaces and facing their next obstacle: a village called Busserut Gunge which was also heavily fortified.

As night was approaching, Havelock gave the order to bivouac and consolidate the positions they had taken. The small British force had suffered many casualties in the initial assault, and the British general well knew he would take many more on the morrow.

After a rollcall of the butcher's bill, Ian ensured his company had time to take a meal and to check one another for signs of cholera and heatstroke, and for his officers and senior NCOs to be briefed on the next day's fighting. Exhausted as all were, they listened, and very few questions were asked as to their duties. It would be another night of little sleep as men contemplated what lay ahead of them.

When the sun rose, Ian was summoned to a regimental briefing and the orders were issued. They were to participate in a second battle for the village of Busserut Gunge. It, too, had the obstacle of a swamp, and a narrow causeway and bridge leading to it. The mutineers had also reinforced the village with earthworks, protecting their artillery and infantry.

Ian's company was to attack from the left flank.

Weary men looked to their kit and rifled muskets as sergeants and corporals checked the men for their fitness to fight. Cholera continued to stalk the soldiers as surely as the enemy.

Conan joined Ian who was standing alone, deep in his thoughts.

'Reporting that the company is ready to advance, sir,' he said smartly, and Ian lifted his telescope to survey the narrow causeway and village ahead.

'Very good, Sarn't Major,' Ian replied, staring gloomily at their target. Around him the other companies of the regiment deployed into their formations and Owen joined them.

'Order to move out, sir,' Owen said to Ian.

'How are you finding your tasks as the messenger at HQ, Owen?' Conan asked.

'Can't complain,' Owen answered, but his tone was cold, and Conan was hurt by the sullen reply.

'Very good, Private Williams,' Ian said. 'Inform the general staff that we are advancing now.'

Owen saluted, turned and marched back to General Havelock's HQ behind the ranks of infantry.

'He does not appear to be very happy,' Conan remarked.

'I had no pleasure in reducing him to the ranks,' Ian said. 'I am hoping he will redeem himself and get his rank back. But right now we have a fight on our hands. Sarn't Major, fall in with the colour party.'

Conan saluted and fell back with the regimental standard.

For just a moment, Ian hesitated. Behind him he could feel the tension of the men waiting. 'Company will fix bayonets!' he roared. The click of bayonets fitted to the ends of the rifled musket barrels was ominous as it meant the terrible struggle of man on man in a fight to the death. 'Company will advance! Advance!'

Ian stepped off. He did not hold his sword but a rifle instead, despite the orders issued that all officers would lead with swords drawn. In a holster was his six-shot cap and ball Beaumont Adams revolver, and tucked in his belt was Samuel's pistol. His sheathed sword was strapped to his belt.

The company of infantry moved in their orderly ranks towards the causeway, and the Indian rebels commenced firing at them with muskets and artillery.

Ian gave his next order before his voice could be drowned out by the rising noise of battle.

'Company, at the double, charge!'

And so the men following Ian passed through the doorway into a place called death.

*

Colonel Clive Jenkins was in London and pondering the task Rebecca had assigned him. He sat in a deep leather chair in the lounge of his club, sipping a gin and tonic. Around him other exclusive members quietly read *The Times*, following the mutiny in India before turning to the financial section to observe its impact on their stocks and shares.

'Sir, your guest, Mr Charles Forbes, is here,' said one of the club's uniformed employees.

'Fetch him to me,' Jenkins said. 'And bring me another G and T. Also a whisky straight for Mr Forbes.'

When Charles arrived, he sat down in one of the big leather armchairs opposite Jenkins.

'Good to see you, old chap,' Jenkins said. 'If I remember correctly, whisky is your poison, so I have taken the liberty of ordering one for you.'

'A little early for me, but I thank you for your courtesy,' Charles replied. 'Your invitation to meet this early in the morning is rather unusual, Colonel Jenkins.'

'I know you are a busy man, Mr Forbes, but this matter is important,' Jenkins replied. 'How well do you know Lady Rebecca Montegue?'

Charles accepted the tumbler of whisky brought to him on a silver platter by the waiter. He was startled by the question, so directly asked. 'I have only been in the company of Lady Montegue at social occasions – I barely know her – although she has a striking resemblance to a village girl I once knew.'

This revelation caused the hair on the back of Jenkins' neck to rise. He did not know why, but there was something in the statement that made him suspect he'd found the seed for Rebecca's intense dislike of this man.

'You say that the woman you knew has a remarkable resemblance to Lady Montegue,' Jenkins said as casually as he could. 'Where is she now?'

'I was last informed that she had run away from the village near our country manor,' Charles replied with a frown. 'No one has had any news of her whereabouts since; she might be dead for all I know. As a matter of interest, the woman was reputedly pregnant to my brother . . . or should I say, to the man pretending to be my brother, the man you command as Captain Samuel Forbes.'

Jenkins raised his eyebrows at this snippet of gossip. 'What is the name of this woman?'

'Her name was Jane Wilberforce,' Charles said, taking another sip of the whisky.

'You say she was with child to Captain Forbes,' Jenkins said. 'How did you know that?'

Charles paused. 'Your questions seem a little strange, Colonel,' he frowned. 'Why are you so interested?'

Jenkins could see that he had hit a raw nerve with Charles and decided it was best to discontinue his line of questioning.

'Because of Captain Forbes,' Jenkins replied. 'Know your enemy, as they say.'

His response seemed to settle Charles, and their conversation turned to matters financial. Two more drinks and Charles excused himself to attend a luncheon with members of a bank board.

Jenkins watched him leave and ordered another gin and tonic. There were clearly intricate threads that would need to be tied together before he could understand why Lady Rebecca Montegue wanted to see Charles Forbes dead.

THIRTY

Thirst, fear and adrenaline surged through Ian's body as he led the charge on the earthworks. Grapeshot from a cannon blasted past him and two soldiers screamed in agony as the big metal balls ripped through them. A third soldier took the full impact of five balls and was ripped into bloody scraps of flesh and cloth. But Ian kept going; he could see the raised earth just a few yards ahead. His rifle was levelled and the bayonet readied to find a soft target of stomach, throat or chest.

He scrambled to the clinging clay of the sloped front wall and caught a glimpse of one of the mutineers. Before he could lunge with his bayonet the target was gone, and Ian rolled onto his side to unholster his revolver. Rifle in one hand and revolver in the other, he flung himself over the wall onto a startled Indian soldier. Once on his feet, Ian levelled the pistol, firing point blank into the man's face, causing the rebel to fall backwards.

Around him Ian could see the rest of his surviving company tumble down amongst the Indians who had not had time to flee the artillery guns they had manned. Maddened by the terrible wounds the guns had inflicted on their comrades, the British soldiers bayoneted and shot any enemy they encountered, asking no quarter and giving none either.

Ian glanced around and saw that the regimental colours were fluttering from the staff and was pleased to see Colour Sergeant Leslie standing alongside the colour ensign with Conan. The firing tapered off except for an odd shot from his men at the backs of the retreating mutineers.

'We've done it, sir,' Colour Sergeant Leslie said. 'We've put the beggars to flight.'

Ian's ears were ringing as he clambered to the top of the earthworks and looked back down the causeway where he could see the trail of smashed and broken red-coated soldiers. The victory, like so many others on the road to Lucknow, had come at significant cost.

From here Ian could see Private Owen Williams running towards him.

'Sir, General Havelock requires your attendance at his HQ,' Owen said breathlessly. Ian acknowledged the instruction and passed temporary command to one of his senior lieutenants to organise the consolidation of the positions they had taken.

Ian arrived at the headquarters under an open tent where senior officers stood around a table jabbing with their fingers at points on a map. Ian waited patiently, noticing his fellow senior officers of the various units of Havelock's force. Like Ian, they stood back, faces blackened by the gunpowder of battle, their eyes weary and their expressions grim. Eventually Havelock ceased conversing with his brigade staff officers and turned to the assembled officers.

'Gentlemen, my order of the day is that all regiments withdraw from their current positions and fall back on Unao for the night. I have decided that due to our casualties we do not have sufficient force to continue our advance on Lucknow. From Unao we will march to Cawnpore, as I have received a message from the garrison there that they have come under a fresh threat from hostile forces gathering in strength in the countryside. But we can remember that we have fought seven battles and been victorious in each one against greater odds. In the last two days we have captured nineteen cannons, but I have been informed that it is estimated that we have only twelve hundred able-bodied men left. It is my intention to gather reinforcements before we advance. For now, we need to get our sick and wounded to a place where they may be treated. God be with you all, gentlemen.'

Ian listened and agreed with General Havelock's summation of the situation. He was also aware how important it was to advance on the Indian city of Cawnpore once again where a force of British soldiers was holding out in a compound within the walls. Not only were there British and loyal Indian forces facing starvation within the city, but also many civilian men, women and children.

*

Colonel Clive Jenkins wore his dress uniform to the dinner held in honour of the British prime minister at Rebecca's London residence. Rebecca was resplendent in her finest clothes and jewels.

As they waited to welcome the distinguished guests, Jenkins mulled over the conversation he had had with Charles Forbes and broke the silence by saying, 'I met with Mr Forbes this day and he informed me that his brother,

Captain Forbes, knew a village girl, a Miss Jane Wilberforce, whom he supposedly got with child. Did you know this Jane Wilberforce?' He could see Rebecca tense at his question.

'Why do you ask?' Rebecca countered.

'It is just that Charles mentioned how much this village girl resembled you – as if you could pass for sisters – and I feel this may account for your interest in Charles Forbes,' Jenkins replied.

'I did not ask you to meet with Charles Forbes,' Rebecca said stiffly. 'I asked you to ensure he was either disgraced or made to disappear forever.'

'You are asking me to risk everything for this foolish notion and yet you do not do me the service of telling me why,' Jenkins said. 'You have me bewitched, and you know I will do anything for you, but this is asking something that could see my neck stretched.'

'Jane was my twin sister,' Rebecca said quietly. 'We were separated at birth, and it was only in the last few months before her mysterious disappearance that I was told of her existence, although I always had a strange and inexplicable feeling that I was not alone. I found Jane living in the village, and she reluctantly told me that she was Charles Forbes' mistress but that she had found love with Charles' brother, Samuel. Jane's last contact with Samuel was when he was in the Crimea and she wrote that she was expecting his child. After that, my sister simply vanished from the face of the earth. Both Samuel and I strongly suspect that Charles was behind her disappearance, which I can only imagine means that he killed her. If you truly love me you will act as my avenging angel and bring justice for my sister.'

Stunned, Jenkins listened to the hatred for Charles Forbes that was clear in Rebecca's voice. 'Do you have proof that Charles killed your sister?' he asked.

Rebecca turned towards him with a cold stare. 'I do not need to have legal proof. I know he is responsible for my sister's death. Call it intuition.'

Jenkins did not attempt to argue with her zeal. All he knew was that if he did not agree to help her get vengeance then she would sever her ties with him. Jenkins accepted that he must find a way of either ruining Charles Forbes or killing him. Neither would be easy, and there remained the matter of the pact he and Charles had made to have Captain Samuel Forbes eliminated. The latter task of seeing off Samuel Forbes – or whoever he may be – was personal to Jenkins, as the infernal man had witnessed Jenkins' cowardice on the battlefields of the Crimea.

Just then the carriage of the prime minister was announced. As soon as the formal greetings were over, Rebecca manoeuvred Jenkins into the prime minister's company and Jenkins, a hero of the Crimea and recently in India with his regiment, was quizzed on his views on the current campaign to quell the mutiny.

Jenkins was quick to ingratiate himself with the highest level of political power, all the while knowing that it was Rebecca pulling the strings. He knew he needed her, and this reinforced his thoughts of plotting the demise of Charles Forbes. Had Charles not displayed his murderous aspirations when he'd asked Jenkins' help get rid of his so-called brother for his own convenience? Surely such a man had the capacity to kill in his own right? It was a small consolation to Jenkins that he would not be killing an innocent man. But a voice echoed in his thoughts, telling him that he was a coward and that killing Charles Forbes was beyond him.

*

Nana Sahib had mustered forces at the town of Bithoor, sending his cavalry into the outer suburbs of Cawnpore. Ian's company fired on them from the cover of the city's buildings, causing them to retreat under the British riflemen's deadly accuracy. The same story was repeated in other sections of Cawnpore with the result that the enemy commander fell back with his army, but the audacious display against the city captured by the British proved that the mutineers were far from a defeated force.

As usual the heat beat down on the defenders, and Ian found a small scrap of shade beside one of the mudbrick buildings in the city. He flopped down, reaching for his water canteen, and was joined by his company sergeant major.

'No casualties to report amongst our lads in that skirmish, but a few of the mutineers never made it out of the city,' Conan said wearily.

'Good show, Sarn't Major.' Ian sighed as the warm water took away his immediate thirst. His head throbbed, and he forced himself not to allow the listless state he was experiencing to detract from his duties as company commander. Along the low mudbrick wall they had used as a defence he could see his men taking out pipes and lighting them as they chattered amongst themselves, boasting of their marksmanship in the recent melee.

'Oh, the mail arrived and I picked up a letter for you from regimental HQ,' Conan said, reaching inside his jacket to retrieve the precious envelope. 'Somebody back in England must love you.' He grinned, passing the letter to Ian. 'I don't know how any woman could, though.'

'Have you heard from Molly?' Ian asked, holding the precious correspondence and recognising Ella's handwriting.

'I have. She asks after your health. She has written that the two shops are doing a grand trade. It seems she is the bright one in the Williams family. I will leave you to your letter.' Conan rose to walk down the ranks of men sitting with their backs to the wall and enquired gruffly as to their welfare.

Ian carefully opened the envelope, extracting the delicate sheet of paper. He began to read with a serene smile on his face, but halfway through the one-page letter his smile turned to a stricken expression and his hands began to tremble. Ella had written that she was sorry to have to tell him in such an impersonal way that she had met another man who had her father's approval. He was a Russian aristocrat of the Jewish faith by the name of Nikolai Kasatkin who had recently escaped the Russian Tsar via India. Surely Ian remembered him because she believed he had rescued Nikolai during a dangerous mission. He was now a partner in certain enterprises with her father, and the love had grown slowly between them. She wished Ian well and prayed that he would be safe.

For a fleeting moment Ian remembered how he and Nikolai had met during a truce in the Crimean War; he could never have imagined then that the same man would take the heart of the woman he had come to love beyond his own life. He sat staring into the blinding heat rising as a shimmering wave in the street. He tried to convince himself it would never have worked between them when their lives were divided by his soldiering career and their religions. But he had not really believed that this would have been an insurmountable barrier to their love.

Tears trickled down Ian's face, smearing the gunpowder residue and leaving furrows in the black soot stains. He could not remember the last time he had cried. For so long in his life he had been told by his father that tears were the realm of women and not men. Men had to remain stoic in the face of sorrow. But the tears came and Ian wondered if they were all for the loss of Ella – or for something deeper: that of a life of peace beyond war.

Then the order came that General Havelock was to resume his advance towards Lucknow, and the contents of the letter seemed irrelevant as Ian once again faced his possible death.

*

Private Williams could not get the voices out of his head. Captain Forbes and Sergeant Major Curry were plotting to have him killed so that they did not have to share any of the spoils of war. He knew he must do something to protect himself. A stray musket ball would do the trick, and satisfy the nagging of the voices in his head. It was so easy to make a death look like a genuine battle wound. And Owen was one of the best marksmen in the regiment. He would be able to carry out the killings when the time was right.

THIRTY-ONE

After a ferocious struggle, the Indian city of Delhi had been taken by the British forces.

Dr Peter Campbell had immediately sought out one of the better residences that had not been completely vandalised and had it converted to a surgery. The house had accommodation in the upstairs portion for him and his wife and their Indian housemaid who had loyally followed them from Meerut.

Amongst Peter's first patients was Scott, for treatment to the stump at the end of his left wrist. The wound had miraculously avoided infection and, under the clean bandages, was healing. Peter was able to remove the stitches, but the stump still throbbed and the pain was excruciating if Scott bumped it.

'Well, old chap, it is not the end of the world,' Peter attempted to reassure his brother as he examined the wound closely. 'Back in England there are people who design artificial hands.'

'I'm an officer on active service, and I cannot be away from the men of my squadron,' Scott moaned. 'I can't wait till we return to England.'

Alice entered her husband's surgery.

'Did I hear that you need an artificial hand?' she asked with the hint of a smile. She held out something wrapped in a cloth. 'I happen to know a Gurkha soldier who is renowned for his wood carving and he kindly made this for me.' She unwrapped the article from the cloth and passed it to Scott.

'Good God!' Peter exclaimed. 'It looks almost real. Alice, you are a miracle worker.'

Frowning, Scott held the wooden hand with its leather straps in his good hand. 'It does not replace the function of my real hand,' he said with a surly tone.

Alice smiled broadly, suddenly producing a second wooden hand, but this one had the fingers curled with a hollow between them. 'I took the liberty of borrowing your sabre and having the soldier make measurements. I think that you will be able to slide the hilt of your sword into the adapted hand.'

Scott gazed with astonishment at the second wooden hand. 'It just might work,' he said, placing the first hand on the table and taking the sword hand from Alice.

Peter picked up the first hand to examine it. 'I will need to carve out the wrist end and apply padding for the hand to fit the stump,' he concluded.

'Make the sword hand your priority, brother,' Scott said, beaming with renewed pleasure. 'I can use my right hand to hold my pistol and the left my sword. I cannot thank you enough, Alice.' He rose to his feet to kiss her on the forehead. 'There is no time to waste,' he continued. 'I wish to show my fellow officers that I will ride again at the head of the squadron.'

Peter went about preparing the sword hand and carefully fitted it to his brother's wrist, using the leather straps to secure it to his forearm. Scott winced with the pain when the padding came into contact with the bandaged wrist and he broke into a sweat, but he refused to admit to his distress.

'With time the pain will subside,' Peter reassured him, and his brother nodded.

Scott did not dally at his brother's surgery but went immediately to the officers' mess, a large tent with tables covered in white linen and set with his regiment's silverware that travelled with the army on campaign in the baggage train. Silver candle holders flickered light in the dissipating heat of the day as the sun slipped below the horizon. Scott showed off his new hand to the admiration of his fellow officers.

Dinner was served by Indian waiters, and afterwards, when the table was cleared, a few officers of Scott's cavalry regiment retired to smoke cigars and chat with tumblers of a good Madeira port that also travelled with the officers' mess baggage train.

Scott stood outside the mess in the company of fellow cavalry major and close friend, Major Jason Cambridge, who had a reputation for being a reckless adventurer. Cambridge came from a family that had acquired their wealth through the establishment of textile factories in England, relying heavily on cheap Indian cotton. For a moment both men simply stared at the evening sky filling with stars.

'I say, old chap,' Cambridge said, puffing on his thick cigar and watching the blue smoke curl away on the still evening air, 'I have an idea where you might try out that new hand of yours. I have planned a little foray out to a village about twelve miles from here. I have learned it is occupied by a number of sepoys. Fifty of my men and I leave tonight.'

'I have heard nothing about such an operation,' Scott said.

'Ah, but that is the point,' Cambridge said quietly. 'It has not been officially sanctioned by the colonel.'

Scott looked sharply at his friend. 'You mean that you have not received permission to carry out your plan?'

'My men are getting restless just sitting around in the city, and I feel that they need a bit of action to keep them sharp.'

'There has to be a bit more to it than that to warrant this foolish idea of yours,' Scott said.

'Between you and me, old boy, my Indian informant has told me there may be buried treasure in the village, and he will be able to guide us tonight so that we are in place as the sun rises for us to fall on any sepoys occupying the town. I doubt they will be in a mood to stand and fight after the thrashing we gave them here. It is up to you whether you accept my invitation to join us. I would not blame you if you declined the offer, what with that bung hand of yours and all.'

Scott shook his head. 'When do we leave?'

Cambridge flicked the stub of his cigar into the night. 'Right now.'

*

The guards had been quietly informed that a party of cavalry would be leaving the city walls on a mission. That it was not sanctioned was not revealed. Scott sat astride his mount, his good hand holding the reins as the patrol left in single file, following their Indian guide towards the village.

They rode in silence with just one break to eat the cold roast chicken with chapattis they carried as rations, then resumed the silent advance on the unsuspecting village. Hours later, with the sun just breaking the horizon across the vast plain, they saw the thatched-roofed mudbrick houses of the small Indian village.

Scott sat astride his mount and observed the blue smoke curling from early morning cooking fires.

'Look!' Scott said to Cambridge. 'They have two brass cannon at the edge of the village.'

'By Jove, they are not even manned,' Cambridge said, and suddenly three sepoys appeared wandering from the village onto the plain only a short distance away. The three enemy immediately recognised that the mounted force of British and Sikh troops was not friendly and turned to flee back to the huts. Cambridge shouted his order, and already his party of fifty men were dividing into two groups – one tasked to ride in a flanking move around the village, taking up their places to block any withdrawal, whilst the other column charged through the village itself.

Scott knew the deadly effect of brass cannon firing grapeshot at cavalry and took it upon himself to immediately charge the two unmanned artillery pieces as he saw half-a-dozen mutineers scrambling to man the guns. Cambridge ignored the possible deadly threat, leaning over the neck of his horse, sabre in hand, and led the rest of his men onto the main street of the small town.

Foolishly the mutineers had not thrown up earthworks and Cambridge's charge was directed at the panicked sepoys desperately seeking to mount their horses and escape the flashing sabres. The sharp blades came slashing down on the dismounted sepoys, carving away terrible wounds on them.

Scott had been able to retrieve his pistol from the holster and, using his knees, turned his horse towards the men attempting to swing around the two brass cannons. He realised that he was alone in his desperate attempt to foil the Indian gunners but was on the gun position before the enemy could put the cannon into action.

Wild-eyed, they stared up at the British officer, three of them falling as his revolver fired at almost point-blank range. The survivors fled in panic from this mounted bringer of death. Single-handed he had captured the guns, and from the village nearby he could hear the screams of men as they were cut down.

Then it was all over. The cavalrymen herded their prisoners before them back into the village with Cambridge riding ahead, triumphantly waving his bloody sabre over his head. Cambridge had not lost a single man in the attack and they had taken fifty prisoners, two brass cannon and a small herd of Indian horses as their prize.

'Good show, old chap,' Cambridge said when he rode over to Scott, the dead gunners sprawled beside the artillery pieces. 'I see they could have done us some mischief if you had not taken it on yourself to silence them.'

'It had to be done,' Scott said with a growl. 'I am surprised you did not make the capture of the guns a priority in your assault on the village.'

'Can't think of everything, old chap,' Cambridge replied, dismissing the obvious rebuke. 'But now we have our mission to complete. The men are currently occupied going through the cummerbunds of the dead and captured for coins and other trinkets. The Indian guide is going to take you and I to a house where he says a chest has been buried. Are you in, Major Campbell?'

Scott reluctantly left his two captured brass cannons and followed his colleague to a walled house with what must have once been a pretty garden around it. He dismounted and the guide jabbered excitedly at a portion of the garden where the soil had clearly been disturbed. A shovel was found and Cambridge began to dig. His efforts were rewarded when they heard the distinctive clunk of metal striking something hard and Cambridge continued digging until he had cleared away the loose dirt from around a large wooden chest. The three men stood above the exposed chest, thoughts of great riches swirling through their minds.

Cambridge and the Indian guide hoisted the chest from the soil, placing it on the edge of the hole. It had no lock and Cambridge swung open the lid. The three men strained at once to gaze inside at their booty of war.

'Good God!' Cambridge exclaimed. 'All that effort for nothing.'

Scott stared at the pile of papers and stamps the chest held. Not even a single rupee inside. 'Oh well,' Scott sighed in his bitter disappointment. 'The papers may have some intelligence value to the general's staff.'

Cambridge wiped his brow which was streaming with sweat. 'We might have been better off joining the lads and looting the enemy of their coins.'

'We will have to explain our unauthorised raid on the village when we return,' Scott cautioned. 'At least our success might soften their ire.'

'I will order the men to round up the captured horses, prisoners and have the two cannons towed back with us,' Cambridge said. 'Maybe the chest does contain something of military importance.'

Scott left the walled house, riding out to where Cambridge's men were standing guard over the horses that had been taken in the raid. A fine roan mare caught Scott's eye, and he decided she would not be handed over to the army back in Delhi for use as badly needed replacements for the cavalry. He dismounted and walked over to the horse. She appeared to have a good temperament and Scott stroked her nose.

'You may as well take her, old chap,' Cambridge said from astride his mount. 'Otherwise the bloody contractors will keep her.'

Scott took her by the bridle and led her away.

The British cavalry returned to Delhi, pushing their prisoners and the captured horses ahead of them, with the captured cannons towed behind.

Scott rode beside Cambridge, leading the roan mare on a short rope.

'Who is going to explain to the general about our little adventure?' he asked.

'I will,' Cambridge replied. 'I think his annoyance will be lessened when he sees what we achieved.'

'It still does not explain why we carried out an unauthorised mission,' Scott reminded him.

'Military success trumps disobedience in the army,' Cambridge replied, spurring his horse in the direction of the general's HQ. Scott hoped his friend was right. Losing his hand was bad enough; losing his commission to a possible court-martial would be more than he could stand.

Scott broke away from the column and rode with the mare towards his brother's surgery in the city. He arrived just as the sun had set and he could see the light from lanterns within. Scott secured the two horses and made his way upstairs to find Peter and Alice sitting down to dine.

'Where have you been these last twenty-four hours?' Peter asked accusingly, rising from the table. 'Rumour around the city is that you and Major Cambridge decided to desert with fifty of Cambridge's cavalry.'

'Damned rumours. They seem to err on the most salacious side of any mistruth. No, I accompanied Major Cambridge on an impromptu mission to seek out the enemy only a few miles from here, and as a result we had a resounding victory that entailed no injury to ourselves but much to the mutineers. As a matter of fact, I personally captured two of their cannons and we brought back around fifty prisoners. Not bad when one considers they outnumbered us by at least three to one. I hope that you can spare another plate at the table because I am damned hungry.'

'Of course,' Alice said and called for their maid. 'You should not have sallied forth with your wound still healing.'

Scott turned to his sister-in-law. 'Ah, dear Alice, only concern and not accusation from you.' He smiled. 'I have brought back a present for you from our small adventure. So, before we dine I would like to present my gift downstairs.' He could see the look of both surprise and curiosity in her face.

Peter and Alice followed Scott and in the dim light of the darkening sky Scott took the reins of the roan mare and handed them to Alice. 'I thought you might enjoy a mount to get around the city,' he said with a broad smile. 'She is yours, dear Alice.'

Alice stood frozen, stunned by the wonderful gift. She had always been an excellent horsewoman and had a good eye for a well-bred horse. She could see that the mare was of extremely good quality. She reached up to stroke the animal's nose.

'She is magnificent, but such a fine gift is more than I deserve,' Alice said, tears of joy already welling in her eyes. 'I cannot accept such a beautiful present.'

'Both your husband and I would agree that you deserve much more for the grand service you have rendered to the sick and wounded on this campaign. Let us just say she is also a gift from the British army for your sterling efforts.'

Peter stepped forward, extending his hand to his brother. 'Thank you, brother,' he said. 'Alice will accept your gift, as we can both see how much it means to her.'

Scott gripped his brother's hand, experiencing the love in the gesture.

The mare had seemed to take an instant liking to Alice, nuzzling close to her.

'You need to give your horse a name,' Scott said.

'I will call her Molly,' Alice said. 'In honour of a remarkable young lady I once met.'

Cambridge was correct in his assumption that their small victory trumped their disobedience. The matter was quickly forgotten as the general staff pored through the captured documents worth much in enemy intelligence.

THIRTY-TWO

Charles Forbes left his office in London on the Friday morning and took his carriage to the Forbes manor in Kent. Inside the coach Charles leaned back to sip on a brandy flask and smoke a thick Cuban cigar. The coach clattered through the cobblestoned streets until it was out of the city and into the country lanes.

He stopped at a country inn for lunch and an ale or two, and then the journey continued through fields of grain, past copses of trees and the occasional low hill, until in the late afternoon they passed through the village nearest the manor. Charles felt the warmth of knowing that when he arrived home he would make arrangements for one of the maids to come to his bedroom that night.

The coach passed the small hill and its copse of ancient trees. Knowing what was buried in the circle of stones caused Charles a twinge of nervousness.

Suddenly, something smacked into the padding of the leather seat opposite him, and at the same time he swore he heard the report of a gun being fired as the horses reared in their harnesses.

'Go!' Charles screamed to the confused coachman, who instantly obeyed, bringing the horses under control. As the coach clattered away as fast as the horses could manage, Charles cowered in the cabin. It was obvious that someone had shot at him from near the ancient place of the Druids. A wave of terror rolled over Charles. It was as if the ghost of Jane Wilberforce had reached out to kill him.

The coach quickly reached the avenue leading to the Forbes manor and came to a stop at the front entrance.

'Did you see who shot at us?' Charles screamed at the coachman as he tumbled out.

'No, sir,' the coachman replied. 'But I heard the shot. It weren't no musket. I heard muskets when I was in the army and it weren't no musket for sure. Are you hurt?'

'No, but the projectile passed only inches from my head,' Charles replied, his body still shaking with shock and fear. He glanced back at the carriage. 'Coachman, I want you to extract the ball from the leather and bring it to me.'

'Yes, sir, I will do that.'

Charles walked with shaking legs towards the front entrance, where the butler met him. 'You look ill, Master Charles. Did something happen on your journey here?'

Charles did not answer, brushing past the old servant in search of the liquor cabinet in the billiard room. Thoughts of his carnal conquest for the night shrivelled in his mind as he found a decanter of whisky, poured himself a stiff drink, and swallowed the liquid in one gulp in an attempt to steady his trembling hands. Someone had tried to kill him! Who would want to do that – besides the imposter posing as his half-brother?

'Sir, the coachman wishes to see you,' the butler said in a calm voice.

'Send him in.' Charles waved to the servant as he poured another whisky.

The coachman entered the room with his cap in one hand, something clasped in the other. He opened his palm to reveal a strange-looking projectile Charles had never seen before. He was very aware of musket balls from his time hunting on the estate, but this was different. Charles rolled the projectile in his hand, feeling its lethal weight.

'It's a Minié ball,' the coachman offered. 'I seen them just before I got out of the army. The lads have been using the Enfield rifled musket for a couple of years now. They tell me it is deadly accurate as the Minié round engages the rifling in the barrel and spins when it comes out.'

'Yes, yes,' Charles said irritably, experiencing a shudder of fear as he stared at the misshapen, cone-shaped projectile. He sensed that such a round hitting a man's body would inflict terrible damage. 'You say it is only the army that has the Enfield?'

'Yes, sir, as far as I know,' the coachman replied, twisting his cap in his hand.

'You can go,' Charles said curtly, angry at his own fear.

Could it be that Samuel's imposter was back in England? As far as Charles knew he was still in India. Who else would wish him dead? It could not be Samuel because the last report was that he was on a ship bound for the Australian colonies. Besides, the Samuel he knew did not have it in him to carry out such an act.

That night Charles slept alone, trembling at how close he had come to being killed and still mystified as to who would want him dead. He was at a complete loss for an answer and knew that he would once again need the services of Mr Charles Field, private investigator. Charles knew it would not pay to involve the police. He had far too much to hide.

⋆

It was spring when Samuel Forbes arrived in the southern hemisphere.

The lumbering cargo steamer slipped into an industrial dock in Sydney Harbour amongst the tall masts of graceful clipper ships. It was a balmy morning of fluffy white clouds and blue skies.

Samuel stood beside James at the railing of the ship, taking in this blossoming city. 'We are finally home,' he sighed, despite the acrid stench of a nearby tannery.

'For a short time,' James said. 'It is even risky for us to visit Sir George at Wallaroo farm, you know.'

'I doubt that Charles' reach stretches this far,' Samuel said. 'After I visit my father to pay my respects, we can depart for New York.'

James nodded his head, not entirely reassured. He was aware that fast clipper ships spanned the distance between England and the Australian colonies, and even as they steamed across the Indian Ocean they had watched from time to time those graceful ships pass them by. What if Charles had been so determined to bring down Samuel that he had sent someone from England to find him? After all, the destination of the English registered freighter would have been discovered in Wales by anyone who was interested – and Charles had proved himself interested indeed.

The gangplank was lowered and the customs officers waited at their tables for anyone coming ashore. Samuel and James had little trouble passing through customs as they now produced their real passports, and the name of Forbes was well known to the officials working the docks because of the large amounts of wool Sir George Forbes exported to the English mills.

'Welcome home, Mr Forbes,' said one of the customs officers, signing off on his passport.

'Thank you,' Samuel replied and thought about what 'home' meant. Living in America did not truly feel like home. Samuel was English and he actually felt more at home in this English colony, despite its lack of European culture. But Sydney Town was taking on many commonalties with London, with its grand sandstone buildings rising into the sky. It now had theatres, public libraries and cafes, although it still had none of the genteel sophistication they had left behind in London.

The two travellers passed from the docks into the bustling streets of Sydney where they found stables and hired a horse and buggy to take them to James' vacant cottage at the fringes of the city. He had purchased the cottage on a previous visit to discreetly entertain his small circle of select friends, and this had led to it being a special place for he and Samuel. There they spent the night, and in the morning set out to travel west to the estate of Sir George Forbes.

Back in Sydney, a customs officer met with a lean, tough-looking man with a knife scar marring his face. Their meeting took place in a public house in the notorious Rocks area overlooking the busy harbour.

'They came through yesterday,' the customs officer said in the smoke-filled bar. 'They used their real names and passports.'

The man slipped a note from the wad he carried and passed it to the customs man.

The wait had been worth it, and somewhere far away a client of Mr Charles Field was prepared to pay a lot of money to expose the identity of Samuel Forbes. The man had once been a police constable of dubious reputation. The brutal murder of a young prostitute might have been linked to him had he remained in England, so he had fled to the Australian colonies. Field had discovered his plan to leave before he set foot on the passenger ship and made him promise to remain in contact should Field ever need a favour on the other side of the world.

The man in his early forties now went under the name of Harold Salt, working odd jobs around Sydney for those involved in petty crime. The letter that had arrived on the clipper ship weeks earlier promised a rich reward for carrying out a small task for one of Mr Field's clients. It was an easy job with little risk. Salt even knew from the information in the letter where he was most likely to locate Mr Samuel Forbes. He would in all probability visit his uncle, Sir George Forbes, at the estate of Wallaroo west of Sydney. The job was as good as done.

⋆

After the securing of Cawnpore once again, Ian attended the briefing by Major General James Outram for the relief of the besieged British garrison in Lucknow. The small garrison had turned a compound into a fortress within the fortress walls of the Indian city and had come under many attacks over the months of the rebellion. Yet against almost overwhelming odds they still held out. The besieged force consisted of British military as well as civilian men, women and children and was on the verge of defeat according to the reports smuggled out.

Although overall command for the relief was granted

to General Outram, General Havelock would accompany the column on the march towards Lucknow. The relieving force was to be divided into two brigades, and Ian's regiment would be at the vanguard of the advance.

Inside his tent Ian prepared orders for his company. The sun was going down but the ever-present heat caused him to sweat beneath his jacket. He paused in his writing to gaze at the vast rain-sodden plains of spindly scrub. How many battles had they fought? They all seemed to blur when he tried to remember. Names meant very little now as they simply continued the endless advance. Ian continually put himself at the forefront of any attack and sheer luck had kept him relatively unscathed, but he knew luck was a fickle thing, and he wondered if he would ever return to England. Since Ella's letter he was not sure he even wanted to return.

'Sir, permission to enter?'

Ian glanced up to see Conan.

'What is it, Sarn't Major?' Ian asked wearily.

'I was able to purloin some medicine for you,' Conan grinned. 'I have noticed lately that you have not been your cheery old self.' He produced a small bottle of rum.

'You know I have never been cheery, Conan, but the rum is the best medicine I can think of right now,' Ian replied with a wan smile.

Conan pulled up an empty ammunition case, sat down and took the top off the bottle, passing it to Ian.

'To us surviving Lucknow,' Ian said, raising the bottle as a toast then swallowing a large mouthful. It felt good and he passed it back to Conan, who silently raised the bottle in response.

'I have a request,' Conan said. 'Private Williams wishes to re-join the company.'

'Do you think he is fit to do so?' Ian asked.

'I think it would do him good to be back with the lads. Company runner does not suit one of our best marksmen,' Conan said.

'You have my approval then,' Ian said.

The two men finished the bottle between them, chatting as friends rather than soldiers, and never imagining that Conan's decision had played into the madness of Private Williams.

*

Even as Conan and Ian sat in the tent sharing the rum, Owen finished cleaning his rifle as the voices continued to nag him. He could not decide whether they were angels or demons come to him. They reminded him over and over that Conan Curry and Ian Steele were evil and had to be killed. Owen told the voices he knew that, and had returned to the company so he would be in a position to shoot them during the next battle. In the confusion of an engagement with the enemy, no one would know from whence came the bullets.

Owen lifted his Enfield to his shoulder and gazed down the sights at the company commander's tent. He could see through the flap the two men sitting together, sharing a bottle and conspiring to kill him. This was not the time, he told the voices.

But the time was coming, he reassured them.

THIRTY-THREE

Ian Steele passed his telescope to Conan.

'There it is,' he said as Conan observed the walled city of Lucknow.

The British forces were about to commence their assault. They were six British and one Sikh battalion with three artillery batteries, but only one hundred and sixty-eight volunteer cavalry. From general to private soldier, all knew they were still vastly outnumbered by the mutineers inside the city walls. They were also surrounded by fields of water as a result of the heavy rains, and this severely restricted the use of the small force of British cavalry.

Behind Ian stood his company of riflemen, waiting patiently for the order to advance along a road that would funnel them into long columns. That would make them vulnerable to enemy artillery fire before they even reached a walled park only four miles south of the besieged British force within the walls. However, in their haste to return to the defences of Lucknow the mutineers had failed to destroy bridges, and the order came down to advance. This time Ian's regiment was not at the vanguard of the initial assault, and he was grateful for that fact as he had a terrible dread this battle had a lot in common with the one he had known attacking the Redan in the Crimea.

They reached the walled garden known as Alambagh without any serious resistance, and the captured area provided a good base to leave their baggage train. It was also an opportunity for senior commanders to plan their next move, which did not look promising because of the water-logged fields surrounding the city. The only firm ground led them to a bridge crossing the Charbagh canal.

For the assault, volunteers were called for to organise what was known as a forlorn hope to storm the bridge and open the way into the city. The terrible title echoed those from the Napoleonic wars when volunteers were promised promotion and rewards if they succeeded. In fact, it was a suicide mission and the men who stepped forward knew this.

Ian did not volunteer. Nor did he encourage men from his company. But volunteers stepped forward from other regiments in the desperate hope that they would live to reap the rewards.

The attack went in at company strength, and the volunteer force succeeded in seizing the bridge at a cost of nine out of ten men killed or wounded. Those watching the courageous soldiers storming the bridge stood in silent horror as the enemy cut down the forlorn hope. The bridge was slippery with blood as litter bearers desperately sought out any wounded and the remaining British force advanced under heavy enemy fire.

★

Private Owen Williams heard the voices in his head screaming at him to kill as he advanced with the company across the blood-soaked bridge, his rifle with bayonet fixed. He was just behind Conan and Ian and he knew this would prove the best opportunity as they entered the confusion of fighting. No one would notice a couple of bullets from his Enfield strike down the company commander and the CSM. It was now or never.

⋆

As usual Ian carried his two pistols, Enfield rifle and sword. The rifle was slung on his back and he held his sword and revolver ready for use in the close confines of the alleys they now found themselves in. The musket fire pouring into their close-packed ranks from rooftops was murderous, and Ian screamed encouragement to his men with orders to clear the windows and rooftops. The accuracy of the Enfield proved itself when the better marksmen in the company were able to stand off, shooting at any puffs of smoke betraying a fired musket. As soon as the musketeers rose to reload they were killed by the lethal Minié bullets.

Ian hardly felt any fear. He had resigned himself to dying today and only cared that he killed as many of the enemy as he could before he died. He was aware that Conan was always at his elbow with his Enfield; firing, reloading and firing again. Conan did not even have to think about these steps as the weapon was now a part of him.

The air was thick with gun smoke, and the noise of men fighting and dying filled the air. All Ian knew was how thirsty he was but he could not take his focus even for a split second from their advance down the alley, which was bordered by two-storeyed mudbrick houses.

Five Indian mutineers suddenly rose from behind an overturned oxcart when they turned a corner. Ian was in front of his men and directly in the path of any fire. It was impossible for the Indian rebels to miss at twenty paces. Ian froze, waiting for the lead ball that would kill or maim him, but he felt himself crashing into the hard-packed earth instead and realised that someone had tackled him. The volley smashed into two soldiers behind him, and when he rolled over he saw Conan's blackened face. 'Sorry, sir,' Conan said, scrambling to his feet as the enemy musketeers lowered themselves behind their barricade to reload for the next volley.

But they were too slow, and Ian's men scrambled over the upturned cart and drive their bayonets into the small party of defenders. Ian and Conan were just behind their men and pushed past the barricade to advance into another alleyway. Ian was aware that he was leaving a trail of his dead and wounded behind him, as the remainder of the company continued to fight for every house and street. All around them in other streets and alleys the other regiments were doing the same and suffering the same heavy losses incurred in street fighting against a determined enemy that vastly outnumbered them. Time seemed to stand still for Ian, although he was aware that he was still alive, and so too was Conan.

A volley of musket fire erupted from a two-storeyed building to their left, spattering earth and hitting Ian's men. Ian could see that the fire had come from the rooftop and immediately launched himself through a doorway, followed by Conan and Owen trailing behind. Revolver in one hand and sword in the other, Ian glanced around the darkened room to see a sepoy raising his musket, and fired three shots into him. The sepoy fell without discharging his weapon. Then Ian saw the narrow stairway leading to the next level and cautiously began to ascend, every nerve in his body straining to sense what lay ahead. He could see that the next level was as dark as the lower one, but before his eyes could adjust, a shot hit him and flung him face down on the steps. His sword clattered off the stairs, falling below. From the source of the pain Ian was aware that he had been hit just under the armpit.

'Owen, you fool, you've shot Captain Forbes!' Conan's voice yelled from the bottom of the stairs.

Ian felt for the wound and realised with relief that the bullet had ripped through the flesh under his left arm and exited cleanly. Then the pain came and Ian struggled to regain his feet just as a figure with an axe appeared above him. The second shot came from Conan's rifle and the enemy soldier pitched forward, falling heavily into the room below.

Conan scrambled up the steps to Ian's side, helping him to his feet.

'We have to clear the rooftop,' Ian gasped as the pain swamped him.

The two surged forward to the second level of the house where they encountered two more of the enemy. Conan leapt ahead of Ian with his rifle, bayoneting one of the men attempting to rush at them with his own bayonet-tipped musket. The two men met and the sepoy's bayonet caught Conan a glancing slash along his side. Ignoring his wound, Conan's bayonet pierced the Indian in the chest, and Conan twisted his bayonet savagely, ensuring maximum internal damage. The Indian soldier screamed in pain as Conan used all his strength to extract the long pointed blade. Ian had already emptied his revolver into the second enemy, and the two British soldiers panted with the sudden surge of adrenaline. They were both wounded but still alive.

Ian and Conan knew the task was not finished as above them they could see an opening in the ceiling, with a ladder leading to the roof. Private Owen Williams was not to be seen as they prepared to carry out clearing the roof of enemy musketeers.

Conan glanced at Ian. 'Are you all right, sir?' he asked, seeing the dark stain of blood spreading around Ian's wound at the front of the red jacket.

'Let's get this job done,' Ian said through gritted teeth. He still had the use of his left arm, although it hurt to move it. There was not time to reload, and Ian slipped the Enfield off his back where it had been slung. It was loaded and primed to fire.

Suddenly the square of light from the opening was blocked, and Ian realised that one of the Indian mutineers was staring down at them from the rooftop. Without considering the pain, Ian lifted his rifle and fired upwards. He knew it was more luck than accuracy, but the heavy Minié bullet smashed the Indian's face to pulp and he did not have time to scream in his death.

Owen had finally joined them in the room and Conan had turned to say something to him when the grenade fell through the hatch above. It hit the floor, and the round metal ball with the smoke trailing from the hand-lit fuse hung in the air. The three men stared in horror at the explosive device as it lay on the floor between them.

Owen did not hesitate. He threw himself on the object as it exploded, flinging his body in the air as he absorbed the full blast and metal shrapnel fragments.

Ian could hear a scream of 'NO!' and realised that it was coming from his own mouth. His ears were ringing from the concussion caused by the enemy grenade in the confined room.

Conan knelt beside the torn body of the man who would have been his brother-in-law, desperately trying to lift him in his arms.

Another face appeared in the hatch but disappeared quickly.

Enraged, Conan lowered Owen's mutilated and smoking body to the floor and began ascending the ladder without any thought for the danger to himself. Ian was behind him as he poked his head out to survey the rooftop and ducked as a musket ball smashed into the edge of the opening. Without hesitating, Conan pulled himself onto the rooftop.

The rooftop defender did not have time to fire a second shot as Conan launched himself across the short distance, grappling at the soldier fumbling to reload his musket.

Roaring obscenities, Conan grabbed the smaller man by the throat, causing him to drop his musket and fling his hands up to release Conan's grip. But Conan now gripped him in a bear hug, pushing him towards the edge of the roof. He headbutted the Indian soldier, stunning him enough to make him stagger. Conan broke away and shoved the Indian soldier with all his strength towards the edge of the roof, where the man toppled to the hard earth many feet below.

Ian had joined Conan on the rooftop and was sweeping the area for any other defenders, but they could see they had cleared the obstacle to the company's advance below. Both men sat down, hands trembling with the pain of their wounds as the adrenaline surge abated. Below them the fighting continued, but for the moment they sat quietly.

'Owen is gone,' Conan said flatly.

'I will recommend him for a medal,' Ian replied. 'His courageous sacrifice saved our lives.'

'For a fleeting moment back there I could have sworn Owen shot at you deliberately,' Conan said, staring at the pillars of smoke rising from many buildings in the distance. 'There was no threat when he fired, and he was too good a soldier to accidentally shoot you. I heard rumours that he had it in for you and I, but what he did back there just proves that they were false. He died a hero.'

'I will write to Molly and tell her so,' Ian said. 'How bad is your wound?' He indicated the blood on Conan's uniform.

'It hurts a bit but nothing serious from what I can feel,' Conan replied. 'However, I think you should see the surgeon about your wound.'

'In good time,' Ian said. 'I have a duty to show the lads that my luck still stands. We will come back for Owen's body when we take the city.' Ian reached for his water canteen and gulped it dry.

After a moment he reloaded his revolver and rifle then descended from the roof to the room where Owen's mangled body lay. The explosion had ripped him open, and his intestines bulged from his body. Ian paused to salute Owen's body, which was already covered by a swarm of flies.

On the street they re-joined the rearguard of the company and were met by Lieutenant Upton, one of Ian's platoon commanders.

'You are wounded, sir,' Upton said, seeing the blood on Ian's uniform.

'Nothing of consequence, Mr Upton,' Ian replied. 'To your knowledge, what is the status of the company?'

'I think we have lost a third of the men, sir,' Upton replied. 'I have arranged for our wounded to get treatment with the surgeons back at the baggage park. From what the sergeants have told me, we have cleared the enemy from this section of the city and it appears that they have retreated to other defensive positions.'

'Good show, Mr Upton,' Ian said in a tired voice.

'What do we do now, sir?' Upton asked. Ian could still hear the sounds of sporadic fighting from nearby streets and alleys.

'I will send a runner to regimental HQ to wait for further orders,' Ian said. 'In the meantime, make sure those who are able take up defensive positions in the event of a counterattack. Block the alley here with anything you can, and see to the men. Make sure they have shade and water.'

'Yes, sir,' the junior officer replied, hurrying away to carry out Ian's orders, gathering the survivors into a fortified position, using oxcarts and furniture to form barricades.

Ian was not sure of their situation until the runner returned. The orders from their regimental commander, Major Dawkins, were to pull back and re-join the remainder of the regiment a few streets away. Night was falling, and the battle to break the siege of Lucknow had not yet been won.

Ian was able to walk amongst his men who were cheered to see that their respected commander, although wounded, was still alive. This meant a lot to the men of Ian's company. Already the word had gone through the ranks that the commander of their task force, Colonel Neill, had been killed by a musket ball in the narrow streets of the city that day.

THIRTY-FOUR

That evening, Ian reluctantly returned for medical attention to the walled garden being used as the base for the assaults on the city.

The surgeon examined his wound and muttered that another couple of inches and the ball would have shattered Ian's upper arm, which would have resulted in amputation. However, all that was required was that he wash out the wound, stitch it and apply a thick bandage.

Ian thanked him and returned to his company, who were settling in for the night in the outskirts of the city taken by force of arms that day.

'The lads are a bit quiet tonight,' Ian observed to Conan.

'Most lost good friends today,' Conan said as they observed the men sitting in small groups, smoking their pipes or lying on the ground, attempting to sleep in the flickering light cast by small campfires.

'I heard that we were able to break the siege,' Conan continued, packing his pipe and lighting it.

'I also heard that our people being besieged have discovered a fresh stock of supplies so can continue to hold out for a while longer if the rebels counterattack. But it appears they have suffered too many casualties to mount another attack at this stage. Now it appears that we are the besieged. We will be moving out at first light to reinforce the compound and enlarge the defences. The general hopes that our appearance in the city will discourage the mutineers and they will leave.'

But the general was wrong.

★

A world away across the Indian Ocean, Samuel and James arrived at Wallaroo homestead. It was springtime in the southern hemisphere and wildflowers bloomed across the uncultivated open fields around the property.

Sir George Forbes greeted their arrival with joy and tears.

'Welcome home, son,' he said, embracing Samuel on the veranda of the house as servants carried the luggage from the carriage. 'We have been too long apart and have much to speak about.'

Sir George turned to James and shook his hand. 'You must have a lot to tell of your adventures in the Americas.'

Samuel and James glanced at each other with knowing looks. There would be a lot more to tell of than their time in New York.

★

The war went on in Lucknow. The defence of the compound by the original besieged force was expanded, and its control remained under that of Colonel John Inglis, whilst

General Outram took over the larger perimeter. Messages were able to go in and out of the newly established fortifications, but day and night the enemy continued its musket and artillery fire on Outram's freshly dug-in troops.

Tunnelling became a way of life on both sides as the Indian rebels attempted to place explosive mines beneath the British defences. In turn the British defenders sank twenty-one shafts to counter the Indian mine tunnels. It became an underground war, each side attempting to intercept the other's tunnels, but the British were able to keep one step ahead of their Indian foe, whose numbers were calculated at between thirty and sixty thousand troops, opposing their small force of a few thousand.

Ian's depleted company had been left out of the tunnelling duties but manned the outer defences. The continuous skirmishing had taken a toll on Ian, who spent sleepless nights thinking of Ella and listening to the constant artillery barrages and crackle of musket fire. As the company sergeant major, Conan carried out his duties like an immoveable rock and gained the utter respect of the men.

Ian's wound was healing, but it still pained him to use his left arm. News occasionally arrived of battles being fought across northern India, and all were optimistic that the Queen's Indian Empire was slowly being won back, but at a heavy cost. The East India Company was already being called to account in the hallowed halls of Britain's parliament, and it appeared that the Company would lose its monopoly and the British government would step in to rule the vast country with its own appointed civil servants.

For Ian and his men, this news held little interest as they simply fought each day to stay alive against an enemy determined to retake the city. Manning the defensive barriers was both tedious and terrifying as the monotony of sentry duty was often broken by near suicidal frontal attacks on the British forces, who found themselves in a position similar to the small force they had come to relieve in Lucknow. Ian knew from the briefings that they desperately needed a relief force to arrive and break the stalemate. Courage and fortitude alone would not win the day as the rebel forces continued to muster troops outside the city walls.

Occasionally Ian led small parties of his men on night raids to neutralise enemy artillery gun positions. The results were good and the guns were taken out of action, but Ian's men were being worn down by exhaustion and the nervous condition caused by constant fear. Rations were at a stretching point and hunger was starting to become evident in the thinning faces of the British soldiers.

Relief eventually arrived, with Sir Colin Campbell's force of five thousand seven hundred infantry, six hundred cavalry and thirty guns. The tough and dependable Scots soldiers were greeted with cheers by the weary British defenders.

The Scots had eventually broken through the ranks of the rebels outside the city, but the battle was far from over.

Ian was called to meet with General Havelock at his HQ in the compound, a heavily shelled building with fallen masonry lying all about.

He was greeted warmly by the general, who offered him a tumbler of rum.

'I was informed earlier of your wound, Captain Forbes,' he said, 'I commend your sense of duty to your men in remaining by their side.'

'The wound is healing, sir,' Ian said, gratefully feeling the soothing effect of the rum in his stomach. Alcohol was a rare thing as supplies ran short.

'I have asked you here because it has been decided that we must evacuate the women and children from the city.

We all agree that whilst the mutineers remain entrenched, our women and children are in great danger, and Colonel Inglis has been tasked with organising their evacuation. I am assigning your company to escort the civilians out of the city. We want to get them back to Cawnpore, and I know I can rely on you to ensure they arrive safely. There will be other officers with you for this mission, good men who have proven themselves during the siege. The journey is fraught with danger from the enemy forces roaming the countryside, but I am confident your riflemen can deal with that. We have lancers on the road who will also assist you. Here are your written orders.'

The general passed Ian an envelope which contained his authority and the details of the evacuation plan drawn up by Colonel Inglis.

Ian accepted the envelope, saluted the soldier he very much admired, and left the crumbling building. He barely flinched when an explosive shell landed a mere fifty paces away, scattering the courtyard with shrapnel.

Ian then went to brief his company.

'Lads, we are finally getting out of here,' he said simply, and saw the look of happiness in the expressions of the men left in the company. He had only thirty-three soldiers left who were fit to march and fight. Their faces were grimy from days of being covered in spent gunpowder, their uniforms in tatters, but their morale was still high under his leadership.

'Your parade, Sarn't Major,' Ian said, turning to Conan who was standing to attention nearby. Conan called for the salute, and Ian returned it before walking away.

In the early hours of the morning, he gathered his kit for the march and found the letter Ella had sent him informing him of her love for the Russian aristocrat. How long had it been since he had seen her in person? Ten months – a year. Time had lost much of its meaning when some days seemed to stretch forever, and at other times during an action, seconds became hours.

Always he could picture her warm smile and remember the scent of her body from that one night they spent together. The memory of their lovemaking had eased the discomfort of the long nights he'd spent shivering in the torrential rains on the Indian plains or marching under a blazing sun. Thoughts of Ella had crept to him as he retreated into a rare quiet place in his mind, away from the battlefields drenched in blood. But that was all gone now.

Ian sighed. Why did he carry the written reminder of love lost?

'Sir, the lads are ready to march.'

'Thank you, Sarn't Major,' Ian replied, tucking the letter inside his jacket. 'I will join you.'

Conan saluted and Ian let all thoughts of Ella pass from his mind as he followed Conan to join what was left of his battered company.

His men assembled either side of the column of carriages and oxcarts drawn by loyal Indians in lieu of horses and carrying women, children and servants as they prepared to leave the city. In the early dawn light Ian was met by the acting commanding officer of his regiment.

'We will be joining you at Cawnpore,' Dawkins said. 'I wish you Godspeed, Captain Forbes. I know our refugees are in good hands.' The major extended his hand. If only Major Dawkins was able to retain command, Ian thought as he shook hands.

'Thank you, sir,' Ian said. 'I have total faith that my men would lay down their lives to protect the women and children.'

He saluted and Dawkins strode away.

Then the mounted lancers joined the line of refugees departing the city and Ian marched forwards, his Enfield at the ready. He was acutely aware that amongst those he was designated to protect was the young wife of Lucknow's legendary defender, Colonel John Inglis.

They had hardly passed through the outer gate of the city when a sporadic fire opened up on the column from positions off the road.

'Move quickly!' Ian roared to the Indians drawing the vehicles, although they hardly needed urging. Musket balls spattered dirt, slamming into the sides of the oxcarts and carriages. Already Conan had deployed his sharpshooters to locate and fire on the enemy snipers. The enemy fire tapered away as one by one the Enfield bullets reached out to tear into soft flesh.

After the first ambush they were fired at on two more occasions. However, between Ian's men and the mounted lancers they were able to clear the road, and eventually in the late afternoon they reached a house standing in a large garden. Immediately Ian and his men were assailed by the stench of rotting flesh. Glancing around, Ian could see numerous partially buried bodies. He remembered the report he had read before leaving Lucknow of a battle at this place a few days earlier, where around two thousand one hundred rebels had been cut to pieces.

Conan joined Ian. 'Is this where we bivouac tonight?' he asked.

'No, we continue the march as soon as extra troops join us for the rest of the journey,' Ian replied.

At 10 pm the weary column of refugees continued the march to a place called Dil Khoosha Park. In the dark only the creak of oxcarts, the occasional whimpering of children, and the muffled sound of men marching broke the silence of the night. It was important that the train not draw undue attention from the bands of armed rebels roaming the area. Once during the trip, a halt was called, lanterns extinguished and all waited, holding their breaths as the sound of many horses could be heard in the distance. Ian's men gripped their rifles, bayonets fixed, ready for any close fighting in the darkness. But it was their reinforcements arriving, and all were able to breathe again.

Around midnight they came to the camp set up to accommodate them on the route to Cawnpore. Ian had his company settled in for the night with sentries posted and was surprised to see tea, bread and butter distributed to his men. It was a luxury they had not seen in months and Conan was even able to scrounge a couple of bottles of beer.

'Not enough to share with the lads,' he said, holding up the bottles, 'but a reward for senior NCOs and officers of the company – at least the sarn't major and the company commander.'

Ian gestured for Conan to enter his tent and in the dark they removed the tops from the bottles.

Ian raised his bottle. 'To dear friends lost and comrades forever to remain in the earth of India.'

'Hear, hear,' Conan said, and drank down every last drop of the precious amber liquid.

As he did so, he thought of all those people he had loved who had died since he had left the colony of New South Wales. First it had been his brother murdered on the ship that had brought them to London; then Edwin, Molly's brother, killed in the Crimean War, and now Owen, killed in India. He did not want to think of who else might be lost before he could return to England and the woman he loved.

The march for Cawnpore was continued and when they reached the city, Ian turned to look down the straggling column of refugees in the knowledge that they had not lost a single man, woman or child on the march.

THIRTY-FIVE

At Cawnpore Ian and his company paraded with the rest of the regiment. Ian had lost two-thirds of his company to cholera, dysentery and enemy action, but none on the march to Cawnpore. Major Dawkins reviewed what was left of the regiment on a dusty improvised parade ground in a former park.

'Men, you have acquitted yourselves in the finest traditions of the Queen's army. Your courage and loyalty will not be forgotten, and I have good news. Tomorrow, we march out for our barracks in England.' Ian could hear behind him a slight murmur of approval from the troops. 'Silence!' Conan growled, loud enough to dampen any further expression of joy.

'In London we will need to recruit to re-establish our strength for future campaigns,' Major Dawkins continued. He turned to his regimental sergeant major. 'You can dismiss the men to their duties, Sarn't Major,' he said and a general salute was called before the commanding officer left the parade.

Ian raised his sword in salute, and the parade was given the order to fall out. As he turned to march off he reflected on the fact that he would be leaving India without seeing Alice and Peter again. He had heard nothing from them for months and could only pray that they had survived the fighting at Delhi, not to mention the spread of disease and the fury of the sun, and that he would be reunited with them in England.

Conan had already began organising the men of the company to pack, and Ian found his written orders for the march out of Cawnpore at his temporary office. He read that the civilian survivors of the Lucknow siege and his regiment were to be evacuated back to the port of Calcutta and from there they would ship out for England.

In the early hours of the next day the regiment assembled, and Ian's company was given the honour of leading the soldiers from Cawnpore with the regimental colours unfurled.

Conan marched beside Ian at the head of the column as the sun rose over the Indian plains.

'I hope that we never see this accursed place ever again,' he muttered. And Ian could do nothing but agree.

*

In a village tavern nestled in the shadow of the Blue Mountains in the colony of New South Wales, a stranger sat at a sawn-log table with a tankard of ale before him. Across from him sat one of the workers from Wallaroo farm.

'So you reckon that one of the men who arrived recently at the farm is Samuel Forbes?' Harold Salt said, taking a swig from the warm ale. 'How can you be sure?'

'Because I knew Mr Forbes before he left a few years ago,' the farmhand said, enjoying the free ale the stranger had bought him.

'Would you sign a paper swearing to that?' Salt asked.

'What's in it for me?' the farmhand countered.

'A shilling – just to sign a piece of paper,' Salt replied, thrusting a sheet of paper across the table with the shilling coin.

'I can't read or write,' the farmhand said, staring at the paper.

'Just give me your name and then you can put your cross next to it,' Salt said. In anticipation Salt had already written a declaration that Samuel Forbes was currently residing at Wallaroo with Sir George Forbes. All he needed was a witness to the document.

The farmhand gave his name, residential address and occupation, which Salt wrote down, and then made a cross next to it.

'What's this all about?' he asked as Salt neatly folded the paper and slipped it into the pocket of his jacket.

'Nothing for you to worry about,' Salt smiled, swigging down the rest of his ale.

Harold Salt departed the small village on his horse, taking the winding track back down to Sydney Town. He had not taken to the Australian countryside as he was a man who had lived his life in the smoggy confines of London and then Sydney, where he was at home amongst the alleys and mean streets, not the wide-open spaces and dense bushland.

⋆

Alice's pregnancy was beginning to show, and Peter was worried about her. Alice had suffered one miscarriage already and he knew that she needed a specialist doctor to ensure that this pregnancy ran its full course. He had approached the military hierarchy in Delhi and put forward his case to return to England with his wife. Reluctant as they were to release their best army surgeon, they agreed, and another surgeon would be sent out from England to replace him.

Peter broke the good news to Alice in their quarters and was surprised at her reaction.

'We have a place here,' Alice said. 'You have your surgery, and I know how much good you are doing – not only for the army but for the poor people of Delhi. I can have our baby here.'

'I am not a missionary,' Peter replied, rubbing his forehead in frustration. 'My first concern is for your welfare in these difficult times. I insist that we return to London. As it is, my brother has been recalled by the East India Company to return to London to report on affairs here, so we would travel together.'

Alice sat down on a divan Peter had been able to purchase from a wealthy Indian merchant. 'I suppose there is merit in what you argue,' she sighed. 'I must think of the welfare of our baby.'

Alice could not tell even her beloved husband that she feared her experiences in India had changed her forever. She had witnessed and experienced so much in this exotic and alien country, how would she be able to sit amongst her contemporaries in London's lavish drawing rooms and feel anything in common with her cloistered, pampered friends? But she could see the deep concern in her husband's face and knew that he, too, would miss the adventure of India – despite the fact he had also experienced so much death and destruction. She knew that India and the tiger would forever remain in her dreams – and sometimes in her nightmares.

'We will return to London,' she said finally.

*

Charles Forbes had hardly had a sound night's sleep since the attempt on his life. He was haunted by a recurring nightmare that Jane Wilberforce had risen from the grave, armed with an Enfield rifled musket. Even those he knew from his club remarked on his health. He was losing weight and had the look of a haunted man.

Word had arrived that Samuel's regiment was returning to England from India, and this added to his deep fears, as the man posing as his brother was a recognised war hero and dangerous enemy. Charles Forbes was a shadow of the arrogant and narcissistic man he had been.

It was over a hand of cards at his club that Charles confided to Clive Jenkins the attempt on his life weeks earlier.

'Good God, man, you must report the matter to the police,' Jenkins said.

'I would rather leave the police out it for reasons of my own,' Charles replied.

The news of the attempt on Charles' life disturbed Jenkins because he was not responsible for it. As the two men played cards in the smoke-filled room, Jenkins found his mind reeling with one question. Who else wanted Charles Forbes dead?

*

In the far-flung colony of New South Wales, a horseman was riding towards Sydney to post a signed report to London. Harold Salt reckoned he was about halfway to Sydney and it was time to take a break and boil a billy of tea.

He tied his horse to a tree and went in search of small sticks to make his fire, and when he reached down to pick up some dry twigs beside a rotting log he felt something sharp strike his wrist. He stumbled back and intense pain set in almost immediately. He watched in horror as the big brown snake slithered over the rotting trunk of the fallen tree.

Holding his punctured wrist, he fell on his backside in terror. Harold knew why he hated the colonies of the Australian continent. Everything that crawled and slithered was deadly poisonous. He tried to rise to his feet but fell back, sweating profusely, weakened by panic and poison.

He lay on his back, gripping his wrist as the toxic venom surged through his body. He knew it was senseless to try to ride away. He would surely be dead before his horse had taken more than a few paces. He could hardly believe that he was going to die here, alone, surrounded by the damned eucalypts of this savage continent. He closed his eyes and dreamed of London, awaiting the inevitable.

Five days later, a traveller was drawn by the stench of rotting flesh to a blackened and bloated body. After taking anything of value and pulling a few personal papers from pockets, the traveller buried Harold Salt beside the track. He did not consider the papers to have any value, so he discarded them in the bush and then continued his journey to Sydney.

*

It was Christmas Day and the regiment began boarding their steamer at the busy Calcutta wharves. The atmosphere was euphoric amongst the battle-weary soldiers looking forward to being reunited with friends and family in London.

Ian and Conan stood on the dock supervising the company's embarkation.

'Festive greetings,' Conan said. 'Permission to have a smoke?'

'Why not,' Ian replied. 'It's Christmas Day, Sarn't Major.'

Conan retrieved his battered pipe, plugged it with rough-cut tobacco and lit the bowl's contents, puffing smoke into the humid breeze drifting across the waters.

'When do we sail?' Conan asked, gazing at the last of the red-coated soldiers climbing the gangplank.

'As soon as we have taken aboard a party of civilians, I believe,' Ian answered. 'Then we depart for merry old England, but not in time for plum pudding and roast goose.'

'In my opinion, the best Christmas gift is still being alive and getting out of here,' Conan said. 'But just as good would be sitting with Molly in the kitchen, sharing a port wine in front of the stove while the snow falls outside.'

'I think you might still be in her bed if we were back in London,' Ian grinned.

'What about you, sir? What would you be doing if we were back in England?' Conan asked, and the smile on Ian's face faded.

'No doubt I would be recovering from a heavy night of drinking and remembering the hot Christmas Days we spent back in New South Wales with my ma and da.'

'There is no lady waiting for you when we return?' Conan asked.

'I am afraid not,' Ian sighed. 'No special gifts for Christmas this year.'

'Ah, I see we may have company,' Conan said, gazing at a small convoy of oxcarts arriving, and a carriage drawn by two Indian horses. Ian hardly took any notice, so deep was he in his melancholic thoughts.

'Begorah!' Conan exclaimed, catching Ian's attention. 'Sir, look who it is!'

Ian looked towards the carriage Conan was pointing to, and felt his heart almost stop beating in his chest. He gaped, blinking to make sure that he was seeing correctly.

The obviously pregnant woman was being helped from the carriage by a man Ian knew very well. Without hesitating, he strode up to the carriage.

'Alice, Peter, how the devil are you?' he asked, and saw Alice and Peter turn their heads towards him. Alice immediately burst into tears, and Peter quickly stepped forward, grasping Ian's hand.

'God almighty!' Peter said, gripping Ian's hand as if never to let it go. 'Is it really you, old man?'

Alice pushed aside her husband to embrace Ian, and the tears spilled down her cheeks. 'Sam, I hardly dared believe we would meet again in this life,' she sobbed. Ian noticed a tall and dashing major in Alice and Peter's company.

'My brother, Major Scott Campbell,' Peter said. Ian saluted and Scott returned the salute before extending his hand. His other hand, Ian could see, was a wooden prosthesis.

'Pleased to meet you, old chap,' Scott said with a broad smile. 'My brother has told me so many stories about you that I thought you might be his imaginary friend.'

'Peter never told me about you,' Ian grinned. 'I suppose that is because you are obviously a cavalryman and not infantry.'

Christmas Day 1858, aboard the steamer departing Calcutta, turned out to be one of the happiest Ian could remember. They were even able to feast on a brace of roast duck, followed by tinned plum pudding and precious bottles of beer.

As the steamer plied the calm waters of the ocean late that night, Ian stood alone on the deck, leaning on the railing, smoking his last cigar. He gazed at the moon's bright trail, reflecting on the importance of family and friends in his war-torn life. He knew what lay behind him, but he did not know what lay ahead. All he knew was that he was a commissioned officer in Queen Victoria's army, destined to continue to fight her imperial wars until either he was killed in some backwater of the empire or completed his ten-year contract with the real Samuel Forbes.

★

It was cold. Snow fell gently onto the streets of London. The horse and coach came to a stop outside one of the tenements cloaked in the darkness of night. The appearance of such a grand coach in this part of London, where bank clerks, civil servants and moderately prosperous merchants lived, was a rare sight.

A young woman, swaddled in the warmth of expensive furs, stepped from the coach and went to the front door of the tenement while her coach driver waited atop his seat.

She glanced around before knocking on the door, which was opened by a burly man she knew well.

'Miss Ella, come in,' Egbert said, opening the door to her.

Ella stepped inside the warmth of the modest tenement house, shaking off the cold from outside.

'Can the missus make you a cup of tea?' Egbert asked politely.

'Thank you, Bert,' Ella replied, 'but I must not be long away from home. I have come to see my baby.'

'Just come with me,' Egbert said, and Ella followed him into a small room where his wife sat by a baby's cot. Meg was in her late thirties and still retained some of the beauty of her youth.

'The little fellow is in fine health,' she said, turning to Ella. 'He is a bonny baby.'

Ella stepped forward to gaze down at the face of the baby in the cot and felt as if her heart would burst with the pain she was suffering for her loss. Without asking, Ella reached down to cradle the sleeping baby in her arms, tears welling in her eyes.

'Does your father know you are here?' Egbert asked nervously.

'He does not,' Ella replied, gazing into the face of the child she and Ian had created, and who had been taken from her in the first hour after his birth. Her father had bitterly suggested to her that the baby's father was a man he knew as Ian Steele and, fearing Ikey's reaction and the potential consequences for Ian, Ella had denied it. She couldn't tell if he believed her or not.

Exhausted from the labour, Ella had asked to see her baby. Her memory of the moments after the birth were hazy but someone had taken the child from her and left her alone in the room with her father. Ikey told her that the baby had been weak and sickly and had stopped breathing suddenly. The doctor confirmed her father's story and said that the tiny corpse had already been taken away. Ella instinctively knew that the two men were lying, but she was too weak to do anything about it. She wondered whether her father had smothered the infant, but prayed he would not commit such a crime. She had heard rumours that her father had ordered men killed, but she also knew he had a reputation for protecting women and children.

Within a couple of days Ella had recuperated enough to leave the bed and she played a hunch. Just after the birth of her baby she had noticed Egbert hovering in the background.

Ella had cornered the tough and burly employee and pleaded with him to tell her what had happened to her baby.

Egbert had always cared for Ella; he had witnessed her grow from a child to a beautiful young woman. He felt paternal towards her and could not bear to see her so distressed so he admitted that the baby boy was in the care of him and his wife, Meg. Egbert explained that her father had passed the baby to them as he knew Egbert and Meg did not have a child of their own, and he had promised he would provide financial support for the little family.

Egbert knew from his many years with Ikey that the big man had a soft heart – despite his fearsome exterior. He had agreed to include Ella in the infant's world but had made her swear on pain of his own demise to keep their connection a secret. Ikey might have a soft heart but he did not stand for his orders being disobeyed.

Ella knew she could not oppose her powerful father and was content for the moment to be able to visit her baby. Now she crooned to the baby in her arms, wondering how the future would unfold for them both.

'Have you given him a name?' Ella asked.

'No, not yet,' Meg replied.

'I would like him to be called Josiah,' Ella said. 'Like my baby's father, Josiah was a great warrior.'

'It is a fine name,' Egbert said as Ella gently placed the swaddled baby back in the cot.

Ella stumbled from Egbert's tenement, tears streaking her face. For Christians the following day would mark the birth of their prophet, Jesus. Ella wondered if the man she had loved and lost had survived his war in India. And if he had, how would he react to learning that he was a father? But Ella also knew there was little chance that the man she had loved would ever discover the truth.

EPILOGUE

1859

Spring had come to the fields and farms of England. Fruit trees were flowering and lambs were being born, but in the city of London the stench of industrialisation still lingered in the warm air.

Outside the great synagogue at Aldergate the small crowd did not allow the acrid smell to spoil their enjoyment of the occasion. Weddings always attracted a crowd, and this one was special as the daughter of a well-known and colourful businessman was marrying a handsome Russian count.

Amongst the crowd of onlookers stood Ian Steele wearing civilian clothing. He could not explain to himself why he had chosen to come today, but here he was. A hush fell on the waiting crowd as the new bride and bridegroom exited the synagogue to step into an open coach drawn by a set of fine greys. Ian experienced an emptiness as he gazed at Ella. She was beautiful and radiant, and Nikolai handsome.

Why had he dared hope that he could have been with Ella when everything was against them?

'It was never meant to be between you and my princess, Captain Forbes,' came the voice of Ikey Solomon. Ian had not seen him leave the bridal party.

Ian turned to face the big, bearded man dressed in a very expensive suit and wearing the traditional Jewish skullcap.

'Your daughter is the picture of a beautiful bride,' Ian replied.

'She certainly is,' said Ikey. 'I have always known that my Ella was sweet on you, but we both know it could never have come to anything.'

Ian nodded. 'You are right, I know.'

'I saw you from across the street and wanted to speak with you,' Ikey said. 'You have always been an honourable and honest man with me, so I am asking a favour of you.'

'If it is within my ability to grant it, I will do so,' Ian replied.

'My new son-in-law has accepted my offer to join the family business, and I want you to promise me that no animosity will arise between you and him. If you can grant me that promise, I can assure you I will return the favour if you ever ask.'

'I can promise you that there will be no animosity between us, Mr Solomon,' Ian said, feeling the bone-crushing grip of the big man's hand.

'Thank you, Captain Forbes . . . or should I say, Captain Steele,' Ikey said, releasing his hand. 'I value good men in my life.'

Ian watched as Ikey walked back across the road. It seemed half of England knew who he really was. It was a revelation that made him deeply uncomfortable.

He hailed a hansom cab and directed it to take him to

the barracks in London. There he was obliged to meet with Colonel Jenkins, who had resumed his command of the regiment. He was riding on the tributes showered on the regiment for its courageous service in India. The fact that he had not been with his men under fire but instead lounging at staff college in England seemed to be overlooked by the press, who hailed his service to the public anyway.

Already the rumour was spreading through the officers' mess and the barracks rooms that the regiment was to be shipped to China or Africa to confront the enemies of the empire. Another war in another country. As the hansom cab clopped through the streets of London, Ian reflected that his life was destined to be lived or lost in the far-flung parts of the British Empire, leading his riflemen. Love and marriage were but an idle dream for a man such as he, certainly until his agreement with Samuel came to a conclusion or was exposed.

He consoled himself with the fact that he had accrued a small fortune from his military enterprises. He could disappear back to the Australian colonies and establish himself as a rich and successful man.

Yet his beloved company of infantrymen was as close to a family as he had ever had, each and every man like a brother to him. Leaving them behind was something he could not imagine. It seemed he was destined forever to be travelling from one battlefield to another until his time for travel in this world was ended once and for all.

AUTHOR NOTES

Captain Ian Steele's regiment is purely fictional, but the events portrayed in *The Queen's Tiger* are real. I have been fortunate that many of the historical sources have been preserved in books, now reproduced on the internet, as the original manuscripts are almost non-existent.

As such I was able to refer to *Memoirs of Major General Henry Havelock K.C.B* by John Clark Marshman, originally published in London in 1867 by Longmans, Green & Co, for the material concerning the obscure Anglo-Persian war. The reproduction originated from the University of California Libraries network. It was interesting to discover within the pages of that biography that the Persian referred to themselves as belonging to the land of Iran.

The Indian Mutiny is better known, but to Indian historians today it is viewed as the first revolutionary war of independence from the British colonists. It is also my amateur opinion that what started as a military mutiny soon turned into an Indian rebellion for independence. Its failure to do so appears to be the lack of overall agreement between Hindus and Moslems for a united country. That would be an issue echoing down the years leading to the partition of India and Pakistan in the twentieth century.

For background to the sepoy mutiny I referred to the memoirs of Colonel A.R.D MacKenzie CB, from his biography published in Allabadad in 1891 by Pioneer Press, titled *Mutiny Memoirs: Being Personal Reminiscences of the Great Sepoy Revolt of 1857.* This was found through the University of Pittsburgh. Colonel MacKenzie was an eyewitness to the events that unfolded at Meerut, and the character of Lieutenant Craigie is a real person.

The events at the siege of Lucknow are taken in part from the diary of a truly remarkable woman, Lady Julia Inglis, wife of the military commander, who held out against overwhelming odds until relieved as portrayed in *The Queen's Tiger.* I recommend going on the net and searching for *A Celebration of Women Writers* to read her full account of the Lucknow siege and her vital role in assisting her husband.

The private investigator in this novel, Charles Field, is a portrayal of the real Charles Frederick Field, who was once a noted detective inspector with the Metropolitan Police and friend of Charles Dickens, and who became a noted private investigator after leaving the police force. I doubt that Inspector Field would have approved of the character of Charles Forbes in his real life.

It is worth mentioning that the Enfield rifled musket, and its projectile, the Minié bullet, would feature heavily in the American Civil War and change the course of history for both the British Empire and the Union of the United States.

Something that stood out in my research was the competency of two British generals, Havelock and Outram. Both men are largely overlooked by military historians, who continue to concentrate on Wellington. The event of my fictional characters rescuing General Outram is based on an actual incident – although the original account did not explain why he did so, so I have filled the gap to explain the general's gratitude to Captain Steele.

Needless to say, there are no shortages of campaigns for Captain Steele and his company of riflemen to march to in the many virtually forgotten battlefields trod by the British army in the nineteenth century.

And no, the next in this series will *not* have the title *The Queen's Corgi*!

ACKNOWLEDGEMENTS

As always, my thanks go to my publisher, Cate Paterson, who has been there from the first book. Completing this project would not have been possible without the work of Julia Stiles, Libby Turner, Brianne Collins, Rebecca Hamilton, LeeAnne Walker, Tracey Cheetham, Lucy Inglis and Milly Ivanovic.

I would also like to acknowledge the following people who have contributed to my writing year: From the USA, John Kounas, in Australia, Kevin Jones OAM and family, Dr Louis Trichard and Christine, Peter and Kaye Lowe, John and June Riggall, Kristie Hildebrand, John Carroll, Rod Henshaw, Geoff Simmons, Mick and Andrea Prowse, John Wong and family, Rod and Brett Hardy, Jan Dean, Betty Irons OAM, Chuck and Jan Digney, Bob Mansfield and all members of the Gulmarrad Rural Fire Service Brigade.

I will extend that thank you to all volunteer emergency service volunteers in the Clarence Valley – and beyond.

To my family of cousins; the Paynes and Duffys. To my brother, Tom Watt and family, as well as my sister Lindy Barclay and husband, Jock, and family, Ty McKee, Kaz and family.

Best wishes go to a few of my author mates, Dave Sabben MG, Simon Higgins, Tony Park and Greg Barron.

HISTORIANS AT WORK

What Did the Internment of Japanese Americans Mean?

Readings Selected and Introduced by

Alice Yang Murray

University of California, Santa Cruz

Selections by

Roger Daniels

Peter Irons

Michi Weglyn

Gary Y. Okihiro

Valerie J. Matsumoto

Bedford / St. Martin's *Boston* ♦ *New York*

For Bedford/St. Martin's
Executive Editor for History and Political Science: Katherine E. Kurzman
Developmental Editor: Mary T. Stone
Senior Production Supervisor: Dennis Conroy
Marketing Manager: Charles Cavaliere
Project Management: Books By Design, Inc.
Text Design: Claire Seng-Niemoeller
Cover Design: Zenobia Rivetna
Cover Art: Eviction Order. Detailed instructions on eviction procedures. Posted in San Francisco, CA, April 1, 1942. Authorized by Executive Order #9066. Courtesy of the National Japanese American Historical Society.
Evacuation Day. Mother and child en route to detention camp. Bainbridge Island, Washington, March 30, 1942. National Japanese American Historical Society archive, courtesy of the Museum of History and Industry, Seattle, Washington.
Composition: G&S Typesetters, Inc.
Printing and Binding: Haddon Craftsmen, an R. R. Donnelley & Sons Company

President: Charles H. Christensen
Editorial Director: Joan E. Feinberg
Director of Marketing: Karen R. Melton
Director of Editing, Design, and Production: Marcia Cohen
Manager, Publishing Services: Emily Berleth

Library of Congress Catalog Card Number: 99-63689

Manufactured in the United States of America.

5 4 3 2
f e d c b

For information, write: Bedford/St. Martin's, 75 Arlington Street, Boston, MA 02116 (617-399-4000)

ISBN: 0-312-20829-4 (paperback)
0-312-22816-3 (hardcover)

Acknowledgments

Acnowledgments and copyrights are continued at the back of the book on page 163, which constitutes an extension of the copyright page.
Map of Assembly and Relocation Centers, from *Years of Infamy: The Untold Story of America's Concentration Camps* (New York: Morrow Quill Paperbacks, 1976), 6. Reprinted with permission from the California State Polytechnic University, Pomona, which has established the Michi and Walter Weglyn Chair for Multicultural Studies to honor the memory of Michi and Walter Weglyn and their dedicated efforts to seek justice for all persons of Japanese ancestry who were unjustly incarcerated during World War II.

Foreword

The short, inexpensive, and tightly focused books in the Historians at Work series set out to show students what historians do by turning closed specialist debate into an open discussion about important and interesting historical problems. These volumes invite students to confront the issues historians grapple with while providing enough support so that students can form their own opinions and join the debate. The books convey the intellectual excitement of "doing history" that should be at the core of any undergraduate study of the discipline. Each volume starts with a contemporary historical question that is posed in the book's title. The question focuses on either an important historical document (the Declaration of Independence, the Emancipation Proclamation) or a major problem or event (the beginnings of American slavery, the Pueblo Revolt of 1680) in American history. An introduction supplies the basic historical context students need and then traces the ongoing debate among historians, showing both how old questions have yielded new answers and how new questions have arisen. Following this two-part introduction are four to six interpretive selections by top scholars, reprinted in their entirety from journals and books, including endnotes. Each selection is either a very recent piece or a classic argument that is still in play and is headed by a question that relates it to the book's core problem. Volumes that focus on a document reprint it in the opening materials so that students can read arguments alongside the evidence and reasoning on which they rest.

One purpose of these books is to show students that they *can* engage with sophisticated writing and arguments. To help them do so, each selection includes apparatus that provides context for engaged reading and critical thinking. An informative headnote introduces the angle of inquiry that the reading explores and closes with Questions for a Closer Reading, which invite students to probe the selection's assumptions, evidence, and argument. At the end of the book, Making Connections questions offer students ways to read the essays against one another, showing how interesting problems emerge from the debate. Suggestions for Further Reading conclude each book, pointing interested students toward relevant materials for extended study.

Historical discourse is rarely a matter of simple opposition. These volumes show how ideas develop and how answers change, as minor themes turn into major considerations. The Historians at Work volumes bring together thoughtful statements in an ongoing conversation about topics that continue to engender debate, drawing students into the historical discussion with enough context and support to participate themselves. These books aim to show how serious scholars have made sense of the past and why what they do is both enjoyable and worthwhile.

EDWARD COUNTRYMAN

Preface

On October 9, 1990, Attorney General Richard Thornburgh presented an official government apology to Mamoru Eto, a Japanese American who was interned during World War II. In 1942, Eto was one of 120,000 Japanese Americans uprooted from their homes and incarcerated behind barbed wire. In 1990, the wheelchair-bound 107-year-old traveled from a Los Angeles nursing home to Washington, D.C., to become the first recipient of a payment from a federal redress program. "By finally admitting a wrong," Thornburgh told Eto and the eight other elderly internees who were present, "a nation does not destroy its integrity but, rather, reinforces the sincerity of its commitment to the Constitution and hence to its people." The attorney general then handed each of them a check for $20,000. In a written statement accompanying all redress payments, President George Bush declared, "We can never fully right the wrongs of the past, but we can take a clear stand for justice and recognize that serious injustices were done to Japanese Americans during World War II."

Although many factors contributed to the government's recognition in 1990 of the injustice of internment, historical research played a major role. In fact, the first three authors in this collection were important activists in the redress movement of the 1970s and 1980s. Roger Daniels, Peter Irons, and Michi Weglyn testified before the government and spoke to Japanese American community groups to mobilize support for redress. In their published work and public appearances, these scholars challenged America's heroic image during World War II by denouncing the rationale for internment and describing internees' suffering during and after the war. In these accounts, the government's decision to intern Japanese Americans, two-thirds of whom were American-born citizens, could not be justified or excused as a tragic mistake caused by wartime hysteria. Using a variety of government sources, including newly declassified documents, these scholars revealed in great detail how the advocates of internment were influenced by racism, greed, and political expediency.

As researchers and activists, Daniels, Irons, and Weglyn changed American history. They not only provided evidence for redress lobbyists, but they also took part in the campaign. They helped convince politicians, judges, and the press to acknowledge the injustice of internment. Perhaps most important, however, was their impact on the Japanese American community. For decades after the war, many former internees repressed memories of the war because they blamed themselves for the incarceration. By indicting the motives and policies of the architects of internment, these scholars encouraged former internees to shift the burden of guilt from themselves to the government, to remember what happened during the war, and to share those memories with the public. In other words, these historians not only transformed views of the causes of internment, they also changed the understanding of the consequences of the incarceration. There was a "snowball" effect as former internees who heard others recount life behind barbed wire decided to describe their own painful experiences. Increasing numbers of former internees began demanding redress and helped sustain the movement in the 1980s.

The redress movement in turn helped create new sources on the history of Japanese American responses to internment. The final two selections in this collection, by Gary Y. Okihiro and Valerie Matsumoto, provide further evidence of the relationship between history, politics, and scholarship. When Okihiro tried to research a history of resistance in the camps in the 1970s, he had to reinterpret government sources because few former internees were willing to talk with researchers about the war. Because of the redress movement, more Japanese Americans became comfortable speaking about their experiences and working with oral historians. In fact, Valerie Matsumoto began her research at the behest of a community in California that wanted to preserve a record of its history. These two selections illustrate how a critical reexamination of wartime sources and the collection of recent oral history sources can shed new light on the diversity of Japanese American experiences in the internment camps.

The design of this book reflects two considerations. First, I want to provide students with a wide range of influential scholarship on the causes and consequences of internment. Students can use this collection to compare the sources, methods, and interpretations of researchers in the fields of political, constitutional, cultural, and social history. Second, I wish to draw students' attention to the process of producing historical research and knowledge. The introduction to each selection discusses the background and perspectives of the author to help students think about how the researcher's intellectual, social, and political commitments might have shaped his or her views of the past and approach to the study of internment. I hope that this will encourage students to contemplate the relationship between politics and scholarship and to explore connections between intellectual agendas, scholarly careers, and political activism.

Acknowledgments

I am grateful to Jack N. Rakove for suggesting that I do this volume and to Katherine E. Kurzman, Bedford/St. Martin's executive editor for history and political science, for recognizing the importance of including internment in the Historians at Work series. Katherine and developmental editor Mary T. Stone provided encouragement and unfailing support as I completed the manuscript. I appreciate the professionalism and commitment of the entire staff at Bedford/St. Martin's: publisher Charles H. Christensen, associate publisher Joan E. Feinberg, managing editor Emily Berleth, art director Donna Dennison, and Books By Design coordinator Nancy Benjamin. I was able to interview many of the historians in this collection because of a grant from the Civil Liberties Public Education Fund. Many historians also gave generous and perceptive advice on the book. My sincere thanks to John Cheng, Karen Dunn-Haley, Ariela Gross, Leslie Harris, Brian Hayashi, Victor Jew, Renee Romano, Wendy Wall, and Jun Xing for helping me develop my prospectus for the book. The manuscript benefited greatly from the insightful suggestions of Donald Collins, Arthur A. Hansen, Victor Jew, Wendy Kozol, K. Scott Wong, and two anonymous readers. Their questions and comments were invaluable in improving the final manuscript. Donald Collins deserves special mention for allowing me to use his copies of negatives of several photos from the National Archives. Roger Daniels and Gary Okihiro granted me permission to reprint their scholarship without a fee and took the time to review my description of their lives. I am truly grateful to have had the support and assistance of so many professional colleagues. Finally, I thank Steve Murray and David Yang-Murray for their love and moral support as I completed this book.

ALICE YANG MURRAY

A Note for Students

Every piece of written history starts when somebody becomes curious and asks questions. The very first problem is who, or what, to study. A historian might ask an old question yet again, after deciding that existing answers are not good enough. But brand-new questions can emerge about old, familiar topics, particularly in light of new findings or directions in research, such as the rise of women's history in the late 1970s.

In one sense history is all that happened in the past. In another it is the universe of potential evidence that the past has bequeathed. But written history does not exist until a historian collects and probes that evidence (*research*), makes sense of it (*interpretation*), and shows to others what he or she has seen so that they can see it too (*writing*). Good history begins with respecting people's complexity, not with any kind of preordained certainty. It might well mean using modern techniques that were unknown at the time, such as Freudian psychology or statistical assessment by computer. But good historians always approach the past on its own terms, taking careful stock of the period's cultural norms and people's assumptions or expectations, no matter how different from contemporary attitudes. Even a few decades can offer a surprisingly large gap to bridge, as each generation discovers when it evaluates the accomplishments of those who have come before.

To write history well requires three qualities. One is the courage to try to understand people whom we never can meet — unless our subject is very recent — and to explain events that no one can re-create. The second quality is the humility to realize that we can never entirely appreciate either the people or the events under study. However much evidence is compiled and however smart the questions posed, the past remains too large to contain. It will always continue to surprise.

The third quality historians need is the curiosity that turns sterile facts into clues about a world that once was just as alive, passionate, frightening, and exciting as our own, yet in different ways. Today we know how past events "turned out." But the people taking part had no such knowledge. Good history recaptures those people's fears, hopes, frustrations, failures, and achievements; it tells about people who faced the predicaments and choices that still confront us as we begin the twenty-first century.

All the essays collected in this volume bear on a single, shared problem that the authors agree is important, however differently they may choose to respond to it. On its own, each essay reveals a fine mind coming to grips with a worthwhile question. Taken together, the essays give a sense of just how complex the human situation can be. That point — that human situations are complex — applies just as much to life today as to the lives led in the past. History has no absolute "lessons" to teach; it follows no invariable "laws." But knowing about another time might be of some help as we struggle to live within our own.

EDWARD COUNTRYMAN

Contents

Foreword *iii*

Preface *v*

A Note for Students *ix*

PART ONE **Introduction** 1

The Internment of Japanese Americans *3*

From Pearl Harbor to Mass Incarceration: A Brief Narrative 3

The Internment Camps 9

Historians and Internment: From Relocation Centers to Concentration Camps 20

PART TWO **Some Current Questions** 27

1. Why were Japanese Americans interned during World War II? 29

Roger Daniels

The Decision for Mass Evacuation

"The myth of military necessity was used as a fig leaf for a particular variant of American racism."

2. What caused the Supreme Court to affirm the constitutionality of internment? 65

Peter Irons

Gordon Hirabayashi v. United States: "A Jap's a Jap"

"After he showed these records to Gordon Hirabayashi, Minoru Yasui, and Fred Korematsu, Irons secured their agreement to reopen their cases through the little-used legal procedure of *coram nobis,* available only to criminal defendants whose trials had been tainted by 'fundamental error' or 'manifest injustice.'"

3. Why did U.S. officials intern people of Japanese ancestry from Central and South America? 79

Michi Weglyn

Hostages

"The removals in the United States were only a part of forced uprootings which occurred almost simultaneously in Alaska, Canada, Mexico, Central America, parts of South America, and the Caribbean island of Haiti and the Dominican Republic."

4. How did some Japanese Americans resist internment? 101

Gary Y. Okihiro

Tule Lake under Martial Law: A Study in Japanese Resistance

"In contrast, it can be seen that there had been a history of resistance and there was no such dramatic break, because both groups, for and against status quo, were committed to a program of reform and the continuing fight for a recognition of their humanity."

5. What was the impact of internment on Japanese American families and communities? 121

Valerie J. Matsumoto

Amache

"They were sustained through this period by deep-rooted networks of relatives and friends, and they maintained family bonds even though many journeyed farther from home than ever before."

Making Connections 151

Suggestions for Further Reading 153

PART ONE

Introduction

The Internment of Japanese Americans

The Internment of Japanese Americans

From Pearl Harbor to Mass Incarceration: A Brief Narrative

On the morning of December 7, 1941, Japanese Americans learned the shocking news that Japan had attacked Pearl Harbor in Hawaii. Like most Americans, they were stunned by the surprise assault that destroyed America's Pacific fleet. As Americans of Japanese ancestry, however, these immigrants and their children, American citizens by virtue of their birth in the United States, also feared retaliation. Even before the smoke had cleared from the ruins at Pearl Harbor, Federal Bureau of Investigation agents began rounding up suspected "enemy aliens" throughout Hawaii and the West Coast. Most of those arrested were male immigrants put under surveillance a year before the attack because they were leaders of the ethnic community—Japanese Association officials, Buddhist priests, Japanese-language teachers, and newspaper editors. In the weeks following the declaration of war, the FBI arrested more than two thousand of these Japanese immigrants and ten thousand immigrants from Germany and Italy suspected of belonging to pro-Nazi or fascist organizations.

The FBI interrogated these immigrants and sent those considered "dangerous" to internment camps administered by the Department of Justice in places such as Santa Fe, New Mexico; Bismarck, North Dakota; and Missoula, Montana (see map). By February 16, 1942, the Justice Department camps held 2,192 Japanese, 1,393 German, and 264 Italian "enemy aliens." The largest of these camps, the one in Crystal City, Texas, also interned many of the 2,264 Japanese Latin Americans deported from their countries so that the United States might exchange them for Americans held by Japan in 1942 and 1943.

The Justice Department camps held about 10 percent of all Japanese immigrants from the West Coast. Many of these immigrants questioned the fairness of their hearings. Masuo Yasui, for example, was interned for subversion because he could not "prove" to the government prosecutor at Fort Missoula that one of his children's homework assignments, which included

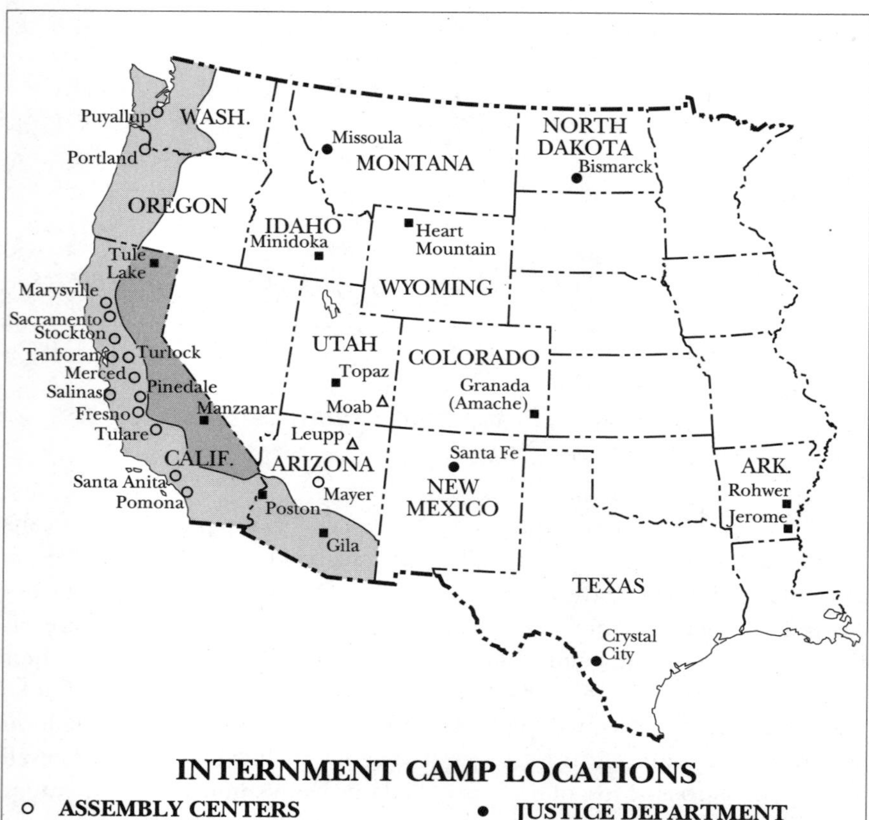

INTERNMENT CAMP LOCATIONS

○ ASSEMBLY CENTERS

Puyallup, Wash.
Portland, Ore.
Marysville, Calif.
Sacramento, Calif.
Tanforan, Calif.
Stockton, Calif.
Turlock, Calif.
Merced, Calif.
Pinedale, Calif.
Salinas, Calif.
Fresno, Calif.
Tulare, Calif.
Santa Anita, Calif.
Pomona, Calif.
Mayer, Ariz.

■ RELOCATION CENTERS

Manzanar, Calif.
Tule Lake, Calif.
Poston, Ariz.
Gila, Ariz.
Minidoka, Ida.
Heart Mountain, Wyo.
Granada, Colo.
Topaz, Utah
Rohwer, Ark.
Jerome, Ark.

● JUSTICE DEPARTMENT INTERNMENT CAMPS

Santa Fe, N. Mex.
Bismarck, N. Dak.
Crystal City, Tex.
Missoula, Mont.

△ CITIZEN ISOLATION CAMPS

Moab, Utah
Leupp, Ariz.

Military Area 1, West Coast
Military Area 2 or "Free Zone" until March 29, 1942

Map of internment camp locations. Courtesy Michi Weglyn, *Years of Infamy: The Untold Story of America's Concentration Camps.*

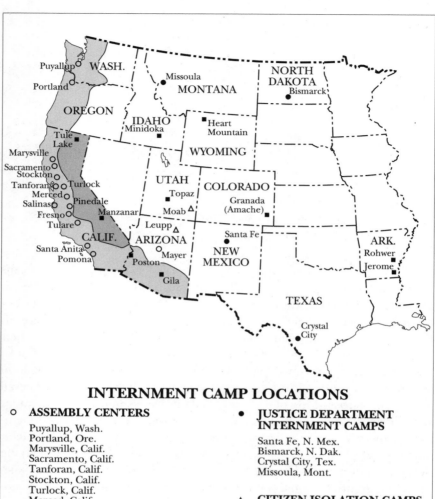

a drawing of the Panama Canal, was not evidence of his plans to blow up the canal. Wishing to return to their families, these men tried to convince the authorities that they were no threat to the war effort. All hopes of returning home, however, were dashed when they learned in March 1942 that all Japanese Americans on the West Coast would be interned in separate camps run by the War Relocation Authority (WRA).

Ultimately, 120,000 Japanese Americans, two-thirds of whom were citizens, were interned in one of ten WRA camps (see map). Why did the U.S. government decide to remove and confine people from the West Coast solely on the basis of their Japanese ancestry? Most scholars now agree that this decision was not simply the product of wartime hysteria but reflected a long history of anti-Japanese hostility fueled by economic competition and racial stereotypes. In fact, any menace posed by the Axis was much stronger on the East Coast than on the West Coast throughout 1942. Along the Atlantic coast, German submarines regularly torpedoed unconvoyed American ships. Thirteen ships were sunk in the last weeks of January and nearly sixty vessels were lost in the North Atlantic and along the eastern seaboard. By contrast, the West Coast did not suffer any attacks from the Japanese until after President Franklin Delano Roosevelt issued Executive Order 9066, authorizing the removal of Japanese Americans from the West Coast, on February 19, 1942. Four days after the order was announced, a Japanese submarine lobbed a few shells at a Santa Barbara oil field, and on September 9 a Japanese seaplane dropped two incendiary bombs on the Siskiyou National Forest in Oregon. Both of these incidents, which caused little damage and no injuries, occurred after government officials had already decided to uproot Japanese Americans from their homes and communities.

Of course, the Germans had not attacked Pearl Harbor. Yet even though many advocates of internment falsely claimed that Hawaii was full of "Jap spies and saboteurs," there was no mass removal or incarceration of people of Japanese ancestry on the islands. Why, then, did officials decide to intern all Japanese Americans living on the West Coast? Historians now emphasize the role of a century-long campaign against Asian immigrants. Anti-Asian activists, who had first mobilized against Chinese immigrants when they began arriving in California in the 1840s, employed the same "yellow peril" imagery to attack Japanese immigrants in the late nineteenth century. Japanese immigrant men were portrayed as spies, sex fiends, or cheap laborers undermining the ability of white workingmen to earn a living. Japanese immigrant women were accused of "breeding like rats" and producing "unassimilable" children, who were then forced to attend segregated schools. Envious of the success of immigrant farmers, the anti-Japanese forces persuaded several western states, beginning with California in 1913, to pass "alien land laws" denying Japanese immigrants the right to own land. In 1922, the U.S. Supreme Court ruled in *Ozawa v. U.S.* that Japanese immigrants could not become naturalized American citizens. Two years later, anti-Japanese politicians convinced Congress to terminate all immigration from Japan. The Immigration Act of 1924 was also supported by many groups wanting quotas to restrict immigration from southern and eastern Europe. Anti-Japanese exclusionists, however, made sure this legislation denied Japan even a token quota that would have allowed the entry of no more than a couple of hundred immigrants each year.

The attack on Pearl Harbor and the rapid succession of victories by Japanese forces in the Pacific rekindled the embers of anti-Japanese sentiment. On December 7, 1941, the same day as the bombing of Pearl Harbor, Japan struck the Malay Peninsula, Hong Kong, Wake and Midway Islands, and the Philippines. The Japanese invaded Thailand the next day. Guam fell on December 13, Wake Island on December 24, and Hong Kong on December 25. American forces had to abandon Manila, the capital of the Philippines, on December 27 and retreat to the Bataan peninsula.

As Americans struggled to make sense of these losses, news accounts of the attack on Pearl Harbor fanned the flames of hatred against Japanese Americans. Secretary of the Navy Frank Knox told the press of an effective "fifth column"* in Hawaii, even though his official report contained no such charges. The report remained classified, and the government did nothing to allay the fears spawned by Knox's remarks as headlines blared "Secretary of Navy Blames Fifth Column for the Raid" and "Fifth Column Treachery Told." Further misleading the public and contributing to the "official" validation of sabotage suspicions were declarations by a committee of inquiry on Pearl Harbor, led by Supreme Court Justice Owen J. Roberts, that Japanese spies had helped the enemy during the "sneak" attack. Newspapers began reporting wild rumors about the bombing of Pearl Harbor as "facts." The *Los Angeles Times*, for example, announced that Japanese fliers shot down over Pearl Harbor were wearing class rings of the University of Hawaii and Honolulu High School. The paper even claimed that a Japanese resident painted himself green and "camouflaged himself so he could hide in the foliage and aid attacking Japs."

As reports of Pearl Harbor "treachery" proliferated, West Coast politicians stoked the fires of anti-Japanese prejudice and began clamoring for the removal of Japanese immigrants and citizens. In California, Congressman Leland Ford, Mayor Fletcher Bowron of Los Angeles, Governor Culbert Olson, and California Attorney General Earl Warren demanded that Washington take action to protect the West Coast from "Jap" spies. The advocates of internment found a receptive audience in the commander of the Western Defense Command, Lieutenant General John L. DeWitt. In

**fifth column:* a covert group or faction of subversive agents.

charge of protecting West Coast security, DeWitt was more impressed by the dire warnings of California politicians and Allen Gullion, provost marshall general for the army, than by reports from Naval Intelligence, the FBI, and the Army General Staff dismissing any threat of sabotage, espionage, or invasion.

On February 14, 1942, DeWitt sent a memo to Secretary of War Henry Stimson recommending the removal of all immigrants and citizens of Japanese ancestry from the West Coast. DeWitt's memo declared, "The Japanese race is an enemy race," and "racial affinities are not severed by migration." Even second- and third-generation Japanese Americans who were citizens and "Americanized" could not be trusted, according to DeWitt, because "the racial strains are undiluted." Taking for granted that all "Japs" were disloyal, DeWitt concluded that the "very fact that no sabotage has taken place to date" was a "disturbing and confirming indication that such action will be taken."

Why did Washington accept DeWitt's recommendation? Members of the government who knew there was no need to remove Japanese Americans mounted a tepid response to the advocates of internment. FBI director J. Edgar Hoover wrote a memo to Attorney General Francis Biddle noting that the public hysteria was groundless. Biddle argued against mass exclusion at a luncheon conference with President Roosevelt. But neither one publicized their objections or criticized plans for mass removal on constitutional grounds. Once it became clear that the War Department and the president supported DeWitt's request, Biddle even proceeded to help implement the plans for mass removal.

President Roosevelt accepted Secretary of War Stimson's advice to endorse DeWitt's plans and ignored the advice of his own intelligence specialists. Roosevelt, along with the War Department and the Western Defense Command, had received a series of reports from Curtis Munson* based on information from the Honolulu FBI, British Intelligence in California, and Naval Intelligence in southern California. "For the most part," Munson wrote, "the local Japanese are loyal to the United States, or at worst, hope that by remaining quiet they can avoid concentration camps or irresponsible mobs." Japanese Americans, Munson concluded, were no more likely to be "disloyal than any other racial group in the United States with whom we went to war." Munson not only denounced proposals for mass exclusion but also urged the president or vice president to issue a statement affirming the loyalty of Japanese Americans to calm the hysteria enveloping the West Coast.

* *Curtis Munson:* a successful Chicago businessman who posed as a government official to gather information for Roosevelt's own informal intelligence operation.

Instead, Roosevelt signed Executive Order 9066 on February 19, 1942, authorizing the War Department to designate military areas from which "any and all persons may be excluded." Although this order never specifically named Japanese Americans, it soon became clear that they would be the only group targeted for mass removal. DeWitt also wanted to exclude German and Italian "enemy aliens" from the West Coast, but his civilian superiors at the War Department overruled him. They rejected a blanket removal policy that would have uprooted the immigrant parents of heroes such as Joe DiMaggio and alienated millions of voters of Italian and German ancestry. Japanese Americans, however, lacked such political clout because immigrants could not vote and few second-generation citizens had reached voting age.

Individuals of Japanese ancestry in Hawaii were spared from mass exclusion despite the fact that the islands were more vulnerable to an invasion than the West Coast. The 158,000 people of Japanese ancestry in Hawaii were, however, viewed with suspicion and suffered special restrictions under martial law. "Enemy aliens" in Hawaii were required to carry a registration card at all times and endured travel and work limitations. Almost fifteen hundred "suspects" of Japanese ancestry were arrested and interned in camps run by the U.S. Army or the Department of Justice because of their activities within the ethnic community. Yet General DeWitt's counterpart in Hawaii, General Delos Emmons, recognized that Japanese labor was critical to both the civilian and the military economies of the islands. Japanese Americans made up less than 2 percent of the population of the West Coast and could be removed without much difficulty. But removing more than 35 percent of the population of Hawaii not only would be a logistical nightmare but also would cripple many industries needed for the war effort. In Oahu, 90 percent of the carpenters, almost all of the transportation workers, and a significant proportion of the agricultural laborers were of Japanese ancestry. Thus, although Secretary of the Navy Knox demanded that "all of the Japs" be removed from Oahu and the War Department sent several requests to remove Japanese residents to the mainland, Emmons stalled and ultimately frustrated Washington's calls for mass internment.

DeWitt, by contrast, quickly implemented plans for mass exclusion on the West Coast. At first, he simply ordered Japanese Americans to leave Military Area 1, which consisted of southern Arizona and the western portions of Washington, Oregon, and California (see map). Yet "voluntary evacuation" was short-lived because public officials in the mountain states condemned the prospect of their states becoming "dumping grounds" for California "Japs." If they were too dangerous to roam freely in California, why weren't they too dangerous to let loose in Idaho and Wyoming? With the exception of Governor Ralph Carr of Colorado, the governors of these western states unanimously opposed voluntary migration and urged that Japanese Americans be placed in "concentration camps."

Consequently, at the end of March, "voluntary evacuation" was replaced with what the government called a "planned and systematic evacuation." The government used such euphemisms to mask the fact that immigrants and citizens would be incarcerated behind barbed wire. Even the three thousand Japanese Americans who had moved from Military Area 1 to Military Area 2 in the eastern half of California (see map), based on government assurances that this area would remain a "free zone," were forced into internment camps.

The Internment Camps

The government developed a two-step internment program. Japanese Americans were first transported to one of sixteen "assembly centers" near their homes and then sent to one of ten "relocation centers" in California, Arizona, Utah, Idaho, Wyoming, Colorado, or Arkansas (see map). Most Japanese Americans had less than a week's notice before being uprooted from their homes and community. Instructed to bring only what they could carry, most had little choice but to sell businesses, homes, and prized possessions for a fraction of their value. Internment also disrupted educational and career plans. But for many Japanese Americans, the stigma of suspected disloyalty and the loss of liberty inflicted the deepest wounds. As one internee later recalled, "The most valuable thing I lost was my freedom."

A few Japanese Americans defied DeWitt's orders. Lawyer Minoru Yasui, still outraged by the internment of his father, Masuo Yasui, decided to walk the streets of Portland, Oregon, at night deliberately disobeying the curfew order. After failing to get a policeman to arrest him, he turned himself in at a police station so that he could contest DeWitt's authority in court. Yasui was soon joined by Gordon Hirabayashi, a twenty-four-year-old University of Washington student, who went to an FBI office to report his refusal to comply with removal orders. The third Japanese American to wage a legal challenge did not initially plan to be a protester. Fred Korematsu had simply wanted to remain in Oakland and San Francisco to be with his Italian American fiancée. But after he was discovered and arrested for violating the Army's exclusion order, Korematsu also decided to battle the government in court. Yasui, Hirabayashi, and Korematsu forced the Supreme Court to consider the constitutionality of the government's curfew and exclusion policies. When the Court affirmed the legality of the "mass evacuation," it established a legal precedent for the wartime removal of a single ethnic group that has never been officially overturned. Only in the case of Mitsuye Endo did the justices acknowledge a limitation to the government's powers

WESTERN DEFENSE COMMAND AND FOURTH ARMY
WARTIME CIVIL CONTROL ADMINISTRATION

Presidio of San Francisco, California
April 24, 1942

INSTRUCTIONS TO ALL PERSONS OF JAPANESE ANCESTRY

Living in the Following Area:

All of those portions of the Counties of Contra Costa and Alameda, State of California, within the boundary beginning at Carquinez Strait; thence southerly on U. S. Highway No. 40 to its intersection with California State Highway No. 4, at or near Hercules; thence easterly on said Highway No. 4 to its intersection with California State Highway No. 21; thence southerly on said Highway No. 21 to its intersection with California State Highway No. 24, at Walnut Creek; thence westerly on said Highway No. 24 to the southerly limits of the City of Berkeley; thence following the said southerly city limits to San Francisco Bay; thence northerly and following the shore line of San Francisco Bay, through San Pablo Strait, and San Pablo Bay, to the point of beginning.

Pursuant to the provisions of Civilian Exclusion Order No. 19, this Headquarters, dated April 24, 1942, all persons of Japanese ancestry, both alien and non-alien, will be evacuated from the above area by 12 o'clock noon, P. W. T., Friday, May 1, 1942.

No Japanese person living in the above area will be permitted to change residence after 12 o'clock noon, P. W. T., Friday, April 24, 1942, without obtaining special permission from the representative of the Commanding General, Northern California Sector, at the Civil Control Station located at:

2345 Channing Way, Berkeley, California.

Such permits will only be granted for the purpose of uniting members of a family, or in cases of grave emergency.

The Civil Control Station is equipped to assist the Japanese population affected by this evacuation in the following ways:

1. Give advice and instructions on the evacuation.

2. Provide services with respect to the management, leasing, sale, storage or other disposition of most kinds of property, such as real estate, business and professional equipment, household goods, boats, automobiles and livestock.

3. Provide temporary residence elsewhere for all Japanese in family groups.

4. Transport persons and a limited amount of clothing and equipment to their new residence.

The Following Instructions Must Be Observed:

1. A responsible member of each family, preferably the head of the family, or the person in whose name most of the property is held, and each individual living alone, will report to the Civil Control Station to receive further instructions. This must be done between 8:00 A. M. and 5:00 P. M. on Saturday, April 25, 1942, or between 8:00 A. M. and 5:00 P. M. on Sunday, April 26, 1942.

2. Evacuees must carry with them on departure for the Assembly Center, the following property:

(a) Bedding and linens (no mattress) for each member of the family;
(b) Toilet articles for each member of the family;
(c) Extra clothing for each member of the family;
(d) Sufficient knives, forks, spoons, plates, bowls and cups for each member of the family;
(e) Essential personal effects for each member of the family.

All items carried will be securely packaged, tied and plainly marked with the name of the owner and numbered in accordance with instructions obtained at the Civil Control Station.

The size and number of packages is limited to that which can be carried by the individual or family group.

3. No pets of any kind will be permitted.

4. The United States Government through its agencies will provide for the storage at the sole risk of the owner of the more substantial household items, such as iceboxes, washing machines, pianos and other heavy furniture. Cooking utensils and other small items will be accepted for storage if crated, packed and plainly marked with the name and address of the owner. Only one name and address will be used by a given family.

5. Each family, and individual living alone, will be furnished transportation to the Assembly Center or will be authorized to travel by private automobile in a supervised group. All instructions pertaining to the movement will be obtained at the Civil Control Station.

Go to the Civil Control Station between the hours of 8:00 A. M. and 5:00 P. M., Saturday, April 25, 1942, or between the hours of 8:00 A. M. and 5:00 P. M., Sunday, April 26, 1942, to receive further instructions.

J. L. DeWITT
Lieutenant General, U. S. Army
Commanding

SEE CIVILIAN EXCLUSION ORDER NO. 19.

This "evacuation" poster uses government euphemisms for the forcible removal of Japanese Americans. Courtesy Civil Liberties Public Education Fund.

to detain Japanese Americans. On December 18, 1944, the Supreme Court ruled in the Endo case that camp administrators had "no authority to subject citizens who are concededly loyal to its leave restrictions" and made it possible for at least some Japanese Americans to return to the West Coast.

Although a few individuals went to court to fight the removal and detention orders, most Japanese Americans complied with DeWitt's instructions. Few had any idea of their destinations when they were labeled, like luggage, with numbered identification tags at designated departure points in April and early May 1942. Most of the "assembly centers" were located at racetracks and fairgrounds, and many families stayed in hastily converted horse stalls that reeked of manure. Then, at the end of May, they were sent to camps run by the WRA, where barbed wire, watchtowers, and military police reminded them that they were prisoners who could not leave without the administrators' approval. Even those who received permission to leave the camps could not return to the West Coast until the exclusion order was lifted in December 1944.

Most internment camps were located on desert or swamp-like terrain. In some camps, winter temperatures dropped to 35 degrees below zero, and summer temperatures soared as high as 115 degrees. The hot and humid summers in the Arkansas camps bred swarms of chiggers and mosquitoes. The assistant project director at Minidoka, a camp in Idaho, described the camp as "hot, dusty, [and] desolate" and remarked on the "flat land, nothing growing but sagebrush, not a tree in sight." A WRA official noted a common problem in many camps: "a dust storm nearly every day for the first two months. . . . Fine, choking dust . . . swirled over the center. Traffic was sometimes forced to a standstill because there was no visibility."

Facilities differed from camp to camp, but all were spartan. Internees were assigned to a block consisting of fourteen barracks subdivided into four or six rooms. The average room for a family of six measured twenty by twenty-five feet. Privacy within the barracks proved elusive because room dividers often stopped short of the roof. Many internees, especially older women, were mortified by the lack of partitions in the communal bathrooms. Families constantly battled the dust that seeped through the barracks planks. The WRA supplied only canvas cots, a potbellied stove, and a lightbulb hanging from the ceiling. Resourceful internees later constructed makeshift furniture from scrap lumber and cultivated their own gardens to supplement the unfamiliar and unappetizing food served in the mess halls. Standing in line became an integral part of camp life. The WRA's assistant regional director once reported counting three hundred people waiting outside a mess hall.

At first, no internee could leave the center except for an emergency, and then only if chaperoned by someone not of Japanese ancestry. Regardless

A muddy quagmire in front of the barracks at Tule Lake, California. Courtesy National Archives, photo no. 210-G-B-134.

of education or training, Japanese American workers were subordinate to WRA personnel and received vastly lower wages of $12, $16, or $19 a month. For example, a WRA librarian might earn $167 a month, whereas her Japanese American staff members were paid only $16 for doing similar work. Moreover, wages and clothing allowances were often delayed, and the WRA failed to fulfill its promise to ship household goods to arriving internees. There were even rumors that WRA staff members at several camps stole food and other supplies.

WRA policies also exacerbated pre-existing tensions between Issei (first-generation) and Nisei (second-generation) community leaders. The government named Nisei leaders in the Japanese American Citizens League (JACL) as representatives of the entire ethnic community. Even though this middle-class, second-generation organization had fewer than eight thousand members before the war, government officials were pleased by JACL ultrapatriotic statements praising "American Democracy," vowing cooperation, and expressing gratitude for benevolent internment policies. Camp administrators accepted JACL advice to limit community government positions to citizens, to ban Japanese-language schools, and to prohibit the use of the Japanese language at public meetings. Whereas JACL leaders believed that cooperation, assimilation, and regaining the right to serve in the military were necessary to combat racism, many disgruntled internees, especially the disempowered Issei, derided JACL leaders as "inu" or dogs who collaborated with the government against the interests of the community.

As hostility toward the WRA grew, some internees vented their anger against JACL leaders suspected of being informers. The arrests of individuals accused of beating up suspected "inu" generated protests against the administration at the Poston and Manzanar Camps at the end of 1942. When the project director at Poston refused to release two men arrested for an attack, internees waged a general strike that shut down most camp services. Deciding to negotiate with the strikers, camp administrators agreed to release one suspect and to try the other within the camp rather than in an Arizona court. In return, strike leaders agreed to try to stop assaults against suspected "inu" and to promote harmony with the administration.

Similar protests at Manzanar, however, ended in bloodshed. The project director summoned the military police to put down a mass demonstration calling for the release of an arrested internee. When the crowd refused to disperse, military police sprayed tear gas, which was ineffective due to the wind. A member of the crowd started a car and aimed it at the police. While witnesses disagree about whether the police began firing before or after the car was started, all agree that they opened fire directly on the crowd, killing two people and wounding at least nine others. Even after the administration removed JACL leaders from the camp and moved suspected agitators to isolation camps (see map), tensions remained high.

Turmoil enveloped all of the camps in February 1943, when the WRA instituted a loyalty review program with little or no notice and without a clear explanation as to how the information gathered would be used. All internees over the age of seventeen were told to fill out a "leave clearance" application, which included ambiguously worded questions that confused many internees. Ironically, the WRA mistakenly assumed that the internees would be grateful for this expedited "leave clearance" program, which would allow them to move to the Midwest or East and volunteer for military service. JACL leaders had fought for the opportunity to serve in the armed forces and praised the War Department's decision to allow Japanese Americans to volunteer for a segregated combat unit on January 28, 1943. But many other internees resented being asked to shed blood for a country that had imprisoned them.

Unaware of the depth of internee fear and anger, WRA officials were shocked by the controversy generated by two of the questions on the leave application. Question 27 required internees to say whether they were "willing to serve in the armed forces of the United States on combat duty, wherever ordered." Question 28 asked, "Will you swear unqualified allegiance to the United States of America and faithfully defend the United States from any or all attack by foreign or domestic forces, and forswear any form of allegiance or obedience to the Japanese emperor, or any other foreign government, power or organization?" Taking for granted that both questions would be answered positively, the WRA didn't contemplate how foolish it was to ask elderly Issei to serve in combat. Some Nisei suspected that question 28 was designed to trap them into admitting an "allegiance" to the emperor they never had. The injustice of asking immigrants ineligible for American citizenship to become stateless by forswearing "any form of allegiance or obedience to the Japanese emperor" was recognized only belatedly. But even after WRA officials rephrased these questions, some internees still refused to complete the "leave clearance" forms to avoid being forced to resettle. After losing their businesses and property and being told that they could not return to the West Coast, some embittered internees were skeptical that they could start over in predominantly white communities in the Midwest and East.

Although about some 68,000 internees answered the two loyalty questions with an unqualified yes, approximately 5,300 answered "no no" and about 4,600 either refused to answer or qualified their responses. One WRA staff member noted how difficult it was to distinguish

> the No of protest against discrimination, the No of protest against a father interned apart from his family, the No of bitter antagonism to subordinations in the relocation center, the No of a gang sticking together, the No of thoughtless defiance, the No of family duty, the No of hopeless confusion, the No of fear of military service, and the No of felt loyalty to Japan.

Far from measuring "loyalty" to the United States or Japan, the questionnaire, another staff member noted, "sorted people chiefly into the disillusioned and the defiant as against the compliant and the hopeful."

Some of "the compliant and the hopeful" followed WRA procedures to leave camp for military service, jobs, or college programs. But of the almost 20,000 men in the camps who were eligible for military service, only 1,200 actually volunteered from behind barbed wire. Later, at the beginning of 1944, the Selective Service began drafting Japanese Americans. More than 300 men refused to comply with the draft while they and their families were still incarcerated. Many of these draft resisters served prison terms of two to four years, but they were pardoned by President Harry Truman in 1947. Other Japanese Americans agreed to offer "proof in blood" of their loyalty to the United States. Ultimately, approximately 23,000 Nisei, more than half from Hawaii, served in the 100th Infantry Battalion, the 442nd Regimental Combat Team, and the Military Intelligence Service during World War II. Fighting seven major campaigns in Italy and France, the 442nd suffered almost 9,500 casualties (300 percent of its original complement) and became the most decorated unit in American military history for its size and length of service. Japanese American servicemen acquired more than 18,000 individual decorations, 3,600 Purple Hearts, 350 Silver Stars, and 47 Distinguished Service Crosses. When President Truman presented the 100/442nd Regimental Combat Team with an eighth Presidential Distinguished Unit Citation in 1946, he proclaimed, "You fought not only the enemy, but you fought prejudice — and you won."

Other Japanese Americans left the camps through the WRA's "seasonal leave" program, developed in the summer of 1942 to address a shortage of farmworkers. In 1942 and 1943, more than eight thousand internees obtained work release furloughs. The WRA encouraged internees who passed the "loyalty test" to resettle in the interior states after February 1943. By December 1943, the National Japanese American Student Relocation Council was able to place more than two thousand Nisei in colleges in the Midwest and East. Then, on December 17, 1944, officials announced the termination of mass exclusion one day before the Supreme Court declared in the Endo case that the United States could no longer detain loyal citizens against their will. Once allowed to go back home, more than two-thirds of the internee population chose to return to the West Coast.

A significant number of "the disillusioned and the defiant," however, remained in camps even after the war ended in August 1945. The Tule Lake camp in northern California, which had been transformed into a "segregation center" for "disloyals," did not close until March 1946. Approximately one-third of the eighteen thousand residents at Tule Lake were people the WRA deemed "disloyal"; another third were members of their families; and the final third were "Old Tuleans," who, when the camp was designated as a segregation center in 1943, chose to remain with the "disloyals" rather than be forced to move a second time. The combination of this diverse internee population and a repressive administration created an explosive atmosphere at the segregation center. On November 4, 1943, the Army was called in to quell a demonstration, took over the camp, and declared martial law, which remained in effect until January 15, 1944. In the last half of 1944, the WRA allowed "resegregationists," who demanded a separation of those wanting to leave the United States for Japan and those at Tule Lake for other reasons, to dominate the camp. Using rumors, beatings, and in one case murder, the resegregationists intimidated inmates considered "fence-

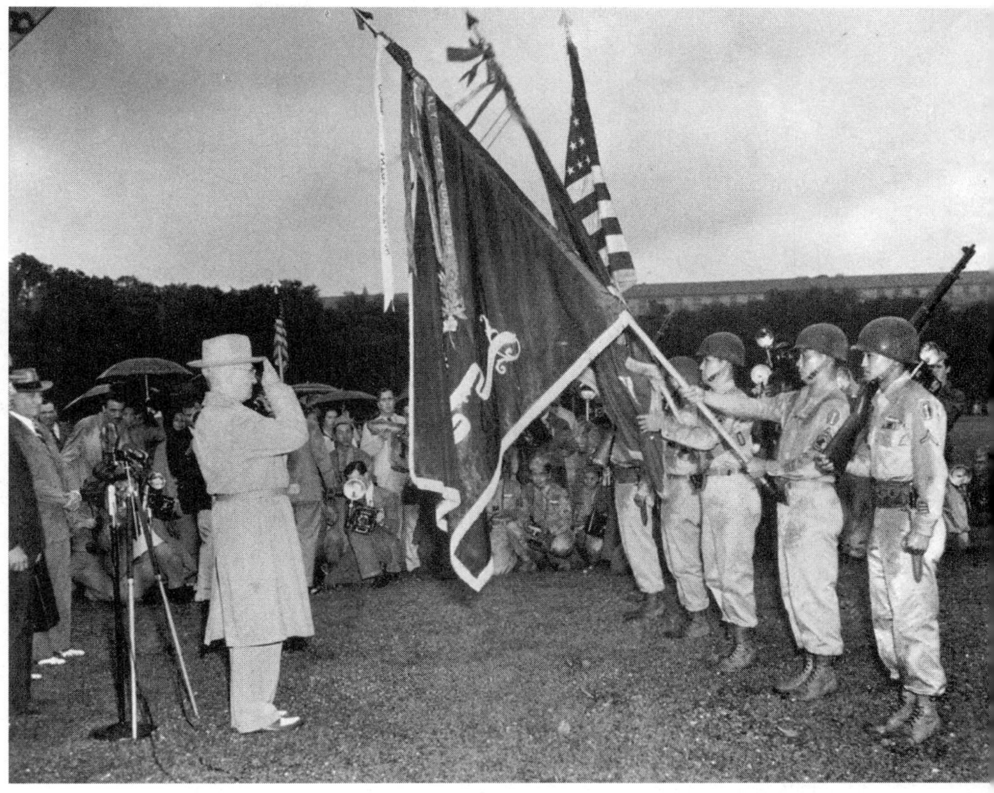

President Truman's eighth Presidential Distinguished Unit Citation to the 100/442nd. Courtesy National Japanese American Historical Society.

sitters" or "loyal" to the United States. By the time the WRA brought the camp back under control, seven of every ten adult Nisei had renounced their citizenship.

The Department of Justice received more than 6,000 applications for renunciation of citizenship and approved 5,589 of them. This number represented 12.5 percent of the 70,000 citizens interned during the war. But even before many of these applications were processed, most of the "renunciants" tried to withdraw their requests. In fact, 5,409 citizens attempted to rescind their applications but the government ignored these attempts and proceeded with plans to deport these people to Japan. In August and September 1945, the renunciants who wanted to fight for their citizenship rights organized the Tule Lake Defense Committee and hired attorney Wayne M. Collins to represent them. Collins resisted pressure from the national American Civil Liberties Union to withdraw from the case and spent more than a

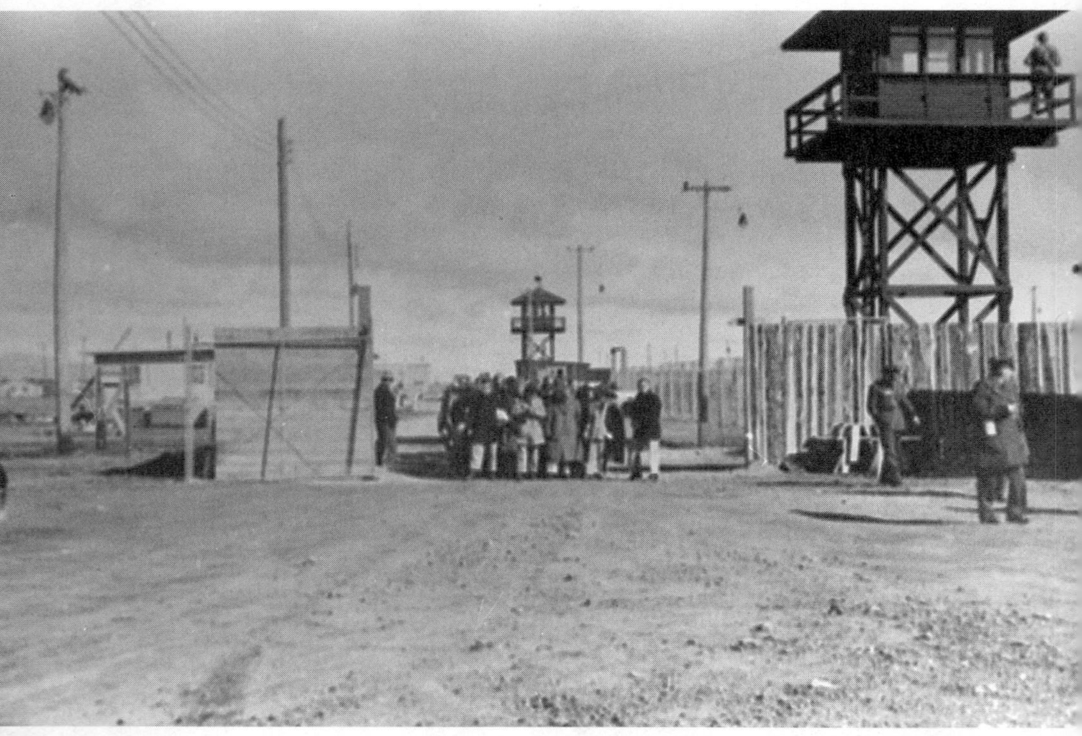

Guard tower at the Tule Lake Segregation Center. Courtesy National Archives, photo no. 210-CL-D-650-38.

decade fighting on behalf of the renunciants. In his suit, Collins argued that the Nisei had been coerced into renouncing their citizenship. He said that the government's forced removal and incarceration of Japanese Americans had subjected internees to "inhuman" treatment and extreme duress. To compound this injustice, the government had known about but had done nothing to restrain a small group of Japanese Americans at Tule Lake who terrorized many of the Nisei until they renounced their citizenship. Finally, after fourteen years, citizenship rights were restored to 4,978 Nisei.

Perhaps the most tragic example of "defiance" against the authorities was opposition to the closing of the camps. Instead of celebrating the prospect of freedom, many demoralized internees demanded that the government continue to provide for them or at least increase the amount of assistance given to resettlers. Many were afraid to leave the camps after hearing reports of how Japanese Americans outside of camp were subjected to arson, vandalism, and even gunfire. Many Issei men in their sixties didn't relish the prospect of starting over and felt that they were "entitled to receive com-

Tule Lake residents depart for Japan. Courtesy National Archives, photo no. 210-CL-R-15.

pensation from the Government for the losses which they experienced at the time of evacuation." Rejecting these calls for substantive redress, the WRA gave recalcitrant internees $25 and put them on trains back to their hometowns.

Churches and charity organizations helped "resettlers" find food and shelter, but many Issei men could find jobs only as janitors and gardeners. They had to rely on the income of their wives who worked in factories or as domestic servants. Their children, no longer barred from white-collar and professional jobs, were able to participate in the postwar economic boom. But even many "successful" Nisei bore psychological scars from the incarceration. Community activist Amy Ishii has compared internees' feelings of guilt and shame with the self-blame experienced by some rape victims. Many tried to repress memories of the camps because, as former internee Ben Takeshita later testified before a government commission in 1981, they couldn't bear remembering how internment had divided friends and family members:

> The resulting in-fighting, beatings, and verbal abuses left families torn apart, parents against children, brothers against sisters, relatives against relatives, and friends against friends. So bitter was all this that even to this day, there are many amongst us who do not speak about that period for fear that the same harsh feelings might rise up again to the surface.

Other Japanese Americans, former internee Mary Oda explained to the same commission, didn't talk about the camps to spare their children "the burden of shame and feelings of rejection by their fellow Americans."

Historians and Internment: From Relocation Centers to Concentration Camps

In the immediate postwar period, only a few Japanese American accounts of camp life, such as Mine Okubo's *Citizen 13660* (1946) and Monica Sone's *Nisei Daughter* (1953), were published. Most former internees were far too busy trying to rebuild their lives to prepare "histories" of internment. Hoping to forget the incarceration, few wrote or even read works on internment before the 1970s. Consequently, most of the histories of internment published in the two decades that followed the war were written by WRA officials and academics who had conducted research on Japanese Americans in the camps. These works paint a very different picture of the causes and consequences of internment from the one presented by studies in the 1970s. Why did the scholarship change? The studies produced in the 1970s were written by scholars influenced by the civil rights movement, protests against the Vietnam War, and the demonstrations of ethnic and racial pride that spread throughout the 1960s and 1970s. These social movements generated a different set of assumptions about the nature of government, politics, protest, and ethnic culture.

Most of the writers in the 1940s and 1950s believed that government officials might make mistakes but were generally well-intentioned. In their accounts, the decision to intern Japanese Americans is presented as a misguided policy that created hardships for those forced to leave their homes during the war. Camp administrators, according to these writers, tried to help Japanese Americans adjust to life in the camps, prove their patriotism, and assimilate into "mainstream America." Although these writers don't always agree on the extent of the success of these policies, most laud the motives and goals of camp officials. Most of their accounts praise Japanese American forbearance and cooperation with the government and lament the outbreak of protests within the camps. Even writers who express sympathy for Japanese American resisters portray such protests as unfortunate and futile.

By contrast, researchers in the 1970s had a different interpretation of why Japanese Americans were interned and how they responded to their incarceration. The view of internment presented in their accounts emphasizes a long history of government oppression against people of color. Many of these scholars argue that internment was not just a product of the war or the anti-Japanese movement on the West Coast. Instead, internment was part of a pattern of systematic government discrimination against racial groups in America. Distrusting official explanations of internment, these writers scrutinized private as well as public statements to provide a more detailed indictment of the motives of the architects of the policy. They also criticize publications from the 1940s and 1950s for perpetuating government euphemisms such as "evacuation," "assembly centers," and "relocation centers." Many insist that Japanese Americans were imprisoned in "concentration camps" during the war. They denounce camp administrators for repressing protests within the camps and promoting the assimilation of Japanese Americans. The heroes in most of these accounts are not Japanese Americans who cooperated with officials but internees who resisted the incarceration, defied camp policies, and proclaimed pride in their Japanese heritage.

These later accounts bear little resemblance to those provided by camp administrators in the 1940s. As one might expect, accounts written by officials who managed the camps are self-serving. Although they generally criticize the anti-Japanese sentiment that led to the mass removal of Japanese Americans, they invariably portrayed the camps in a positive light. In accounts such as *WRA: A Story of Human Conservation* (1946), administrators are portrayed as compassionate defenders of internees against the racists who put them in the camps and accused the WRA of "coddling" internees. The camps, such accounts claim, provided "refuge from the storms of racial prejudice and the disruptions of total war," and the WRA dispersion policies gave the Nisei "new opportunities" and "confidence in themselves."

Publications by sociologists and anthropologists employed by the WRA as "community analysts" during the war are not so effusive. The twenty-seven white social scientists whom camp officials hired to interpret and help manage the internee population did not minimize the internees' financial and emotional problems. *The Governing of Men: General Principles and Recommendations Based on Experience at a Japanese Relocation Camp* by Alexander Leighton (1945) and *Impounded People: Japanese Americans in the Relocation Centers* by Edward Spicer and others (1946) describe the harsh conditions at the camps, the internees' feelings of alienation and frustration, and the devastation wrought by the loyalty questionnaire. Yet even as these works recount a history of strikes, riots, and mass demonstrations, they present resistance as an unfortunate product of miscommunication and misunderstanding rather than a legitimate response to incarceration. Like many Americans at the time, most of these researchers took it for granted that protests were wrong and that the social scientists' role in helping control the internees was ethical. In fact, *The Governing of Men* includes a manual on managing future camps and proclaims that "communities under stress" are "ripe for change." Manzanar analyst Morris E. Opler wrote a brief for Fred Korematsu challenging the constitutionality of internment, and Tule Lake analyst Marvin K. Opler prepared a brief denouncing the unfairness of the segregation and renunciation process. Neither analyst, however, allowed his name to be printed on the brief or published any articles or books expressing his outrage at the injustice of incarceration.

Publications by the Japanese American Evacuation and Resettlement Study (JERS) are more critical of camp administrators. Under the supervision of Dorothy Thomas, a professor at the University of California, the JERS conducted field research within the camps throughout the war. Not responsible for the removal or control of Japanese Americans, the three white researchers, twelve Japanese American field-workers, and at least twelve other internees who assisted JERS research were directed simply to record events as they happened. But as Yuji Ichioka notes in *Views from Within: The Japanese American Evacuation and Resettlement Study* (1989), the assumptions and methodology of these researchers were controversial. In exchange for cooperation from the federal government, the social scientists agreed not to publish or publicly describe their findings until after the war. Thomas also compromised JERS independence by agreeing to submit monthly reports to camp administrators.

The JERS researchers could not be "detached" observers of something as wrenching as internment. Internee field-workers not only suffered the trauma of incarceration but also risked community ostracism and even violence because of the suspicion that they were FBI or WRA informants. Richard Nishimoto, the internee Thomas relied on most to help her understand the camp experience and the coauthor of *The Spoilage* (1946), concealed his JERS affiliation and actively influenced the politics at Poston. Although *The Spoilage* provides an early indictment of the WRA's discriminatory policies and incompetent supervision of militant resegregationists at Tule Lake, the study also raises several ethical questions. The book's supposedly "impartial" description of events at Tule Lake was based on field notes by Rosalie Wax (née Hankey), who later admitted, in *Doing Fieldwork: Warnings and Advice* (1971), to having deceived administrators and internees, befriended certain factional leaders, become a "fanatic" who exulted in the murder of an "accommodator," and informed on two internees to the Justice Department. Tule Lake internee Kazue Matsuda also accused Hankey of violating a promise of confidentiality, supplying false information about Matsuda's activities to the Justice Department, and ultimately causing her to be separated from her children. Ironically, despite Hankey's admiration for some Tule Lake dissident leaders, authors Thomas and Nishimoto chose the title *The Spoilage,* which further stigmatized those internees the government had pronounced "disloyal."

The second JERS study, Thomas's *The Salvage* (1952), includes fifteen life histories of Nisei resettlers interviewed by Charles Kikuchi and gave Japanese Americans a chance to describe the impact of internment on their aspirations, occupational mobility, and family relations. Though quite informative, Kikuchi's interviewees were all urban, college-educated, Christian or secular Nisei men and women. All criticized the decision to intern Japanese Americans, but many praised the benefits of postwar dispersion and assimilation. Yet one can't help but wonder whether they were truly "salvaged" when so many expressed anxiety at an association with anything "Japanese," feared talking about the camps to white Americans, and tried to suppress memories of the camps.

The final JERS study, *Prejudice, War, and the Constitution* (1954), provides an early critique of the decision to intern Japanese Americans. It documents that internment was not the product of "military necessity" and questions the Supreme Court decisions affirming the constitutionality of internment. Although it holds President Roosevelt, the War Department, and the courts "responsible" for this injustice, the only advocate of internment examined in great detail is General DeWitt. The book's dispassionate tone may reflect the fact that it was commissioned by Thomas to counter the "unscholarly" judgments in Morton Grodzins's *Americans Betrayed: Politics and the Japanese Evacuation* (1949). Grodzins had been a JERS research assistant, and his dissertation censured the racism of West Coast politicians, journalists, and economic interest groups who advocated internment. Dismayed by Grodzins's "propaganda," Thomas and a University of California investigative subcommittee urged the University of Chicago to reject his manuscript. University of Chicago Press director William Terry Couch decided to publish the book anyway and compared suppression of Grodzins's research to concealing "information concerning white treatment of the Negro from the public at large." University of California officials, fearful of appearing to censor scholarship for political reasons, backed down, and the book was published, but Couch was fired for antagonizing another university.

During the 1970s, a new generation of scholars embraced controversial interpretations and provided very different perspectives on the history of internment. These post-JERS researchers promoted "revisionist" histories that challenged earlier depictions of the causes and consequences of internment. Their studies questioned the way publications in the 1940s and 1950s emphasized a history of wartime hysteria, heroic volunteer soldiers, and beneficial assimilation. Instead, they highlighted the racism that led to the mass incarceration, the suffering and resistance within the camps, and a postwar legacy of pain and silence.

The writings in this book reflect the impact of revisionist scholarship. The first selection, an excerpt from Roger Daniels's *Concentration Camps USA* (1971), condemns the way military and government officials fabricated a "military necessity" rationale for internment. A pioneering revisionist scholar, Daniels has always insisted that Japanese Americans were confined in "concentration camps." He has repeatedly reminded readers that both President Roosevelt and Chief Justice Owen Roberts used the term "concentration camp" when talking about Japanese Americans. Daniels acknowledges that the American camp experience was very different from the Nazi Holocaust and that more Japanese Americans were born in camps than died there. Nevertheless, Daniels insists that there were important parallels. Both American and German camps confined individuals simply on the basis of ancestry, without charge or trial. Both established barbed-wire compounds and military patrols. And although Japanese Americans were never subjected to systematic execution, several inmates were shot and killed by armed guards.

Other revisionist scholars have attacked WRA policies. Richard Drinnon's *Keeper of Concentration Camps: Dillon S. Myer and American Racism* (1987) denounces the head of the WRA and the Bureau of Indian Affairs as a paternalistic, self-styled "Great White Father" bent on destroying native cultures and exemplifying the "banality of evil." JACL leaders who cooperated with the government also have come under critical scrutiny by scholars challenging JACL hagiographic accounts such as *Nisei: The Quiet Americans* (1969), *JACL: In Quest of Justice* (1982), and *They Call Me Moses Masaoka* (1987). Articles by Yuji Ichioka, Bob Kumamoto, and Paul Spickard contain evidence that JACL leaders informed on immigrant leaders to the FBI, proposed the creation of a "suicide battalion" of volunteer soldiers, and urged the WRA to limit Issei influence in the camps.

Revisionist scholars also have questioned earlier depictions of camp protests as sporadic incidents caused by misconceptions and small groups of agitators. In *Amerasia Journal,* a product of the Asian American movement, Gary Y. Okihiro, Arthur A. Hansen, and David A. Hacker have presented a history of widespread and continuous resistance within the camps. Okihiro's "Japanese Resistance in America's Concentration Camps: A Re-evaluation" (1973) proposes that "the assumptions of the revisionist histories of slave and colonized groups provide a more realistic basis for an analysis of Japanese reaction to concentration camp authority than do the older notions of Japanese 'loyalty' and helplessness." Moreover, Okihiro redefined protest to include not only organized demonstrations but also work slowdowns and the proliferation of Japanese cultural societies in the camps. Hansen and Hacker's "The Manzanar Riot: An Ethnic Perspective" (1974) extends this analysis of cultural resistance to WRA Americanization campaigns and interprets the "riot" as evidence of the internees' struggle for self-determination, the persistence of ethnic identity, and group solidarity.

Until the 1980s, revisionist scholars had to reinterpret WRA, JERS, and court records because few Japanese Americans were willing to provide oral histories of internment. The redress movement of the 1970s and 1980s exhumed former internees' buried memories of the camps. At first, the idea of redress had little support within the Japanese American community. In 1970, former internee Edison Uno persuaded the JACL to pass a resolution calling for legislation to make amends for "the worst mistakes of World War II," but the organization hesitated to take more concrete action. Grassroots activists within the JACL and other community organizations began mounting pilgrimages to former camp sites and "day of remembrance" programs to encourage former internees to share their personal histories of internment. They urged Japanese Americans to read revisionist writing, such as Michi Weglyn's *Years of Infamy* (1976). These activists also established historical landmarks at former camp sites; convinced the government to repeal Title II of the 1950 Internal Security Act, which authorized the government to maintain detention camps for suspected "saboteurs"; and successfully lobbied the U.S. government to officially revoke Executive Order 9066.

By the beginning of the 1980s, these experienced activists could mobilize significant community support for redress. Activists within the JACL successfully lobbied the government to establish the Commission on Wartime Relocation and Internment of Civilians, which held hearings on the causes and consequences of internment. These hearings, held throughout the country in 1981, encouraged Japanese Americans to share their pain and anger at the injustice of internment. More than five hundred Japanese Americans testified at the hearings. These cathartic accounts of anguish experienced during the war intensified and deepened the community's commitment to redress. After the commission called on the government to provide a formal apology and monetary compensation, Japanese Americans submitted and lobbied for redress legislation. In 1988, this effort was rewarded by the passage of the Civil Liberties Act of 1988, which provided an official apology and a payment of $20,000 to each surviving internee.

Well before the first checks were issued in 1990, the redress movement had promoted a new understanding of the history of internment by helping to unleash a flood of oral histories, memoirs, poetry, fiction, and documentaries by former internees and their children. Valerie Matsumoto's *Farming the Home Place* (1993) manifests the impact of these new oral history sources. Matsumoto's interviews helped her recover the diverse experiences of Japanese Americans from one of the few communities to retain land and property during the war. No longer relegated to being victims, patriots, or resisters, the men and women who appear in the book express a variety of feelings experienced before, during, and after the war.

Matsumoto is only one of many recent scholars who have broadened our view of internment by exploring previously neglected groups. Research by Mei Nakano, Dana Takagi, Evelyn Nakano Glenn, and Sylvia Junko Yanagisako has recognized the importance of women and gender as a category of analysis. Scholars have learned more about the Department of Justice camps thanks to John Christgau's study of "alien internees" and C. Harvey

Gardiner's research on U.S. policies toward Peruvian internees. Paul Spickard has drawn attention to the hardships of Amerasian children and non-Japanese spouses in the camps, Thomas James has examined educational policies, and Gary Okihiro has given voice to internees from Hawaii in *Cane Fires* (1991). The anthology *Japanese Americans: From Relocation to Redress* (1986) provides multiple perspectives on life before, during, and after internment. Finally, now that historians no longer feel compelled to emphasize Japanese American "loyalty" to justify redress, scholars such as Yuji Ichioka, John Stephan, and Brian Masaru Hayashi have begun to explore the pro-Japanese nationalist sentiment of some Japanese Americans and the experiences of a few who lived in Japan and worked for the Japanese government or served in the Japanese military during the war.

PART TWO

Some Current Questions

The selections that follow deal with some of the issues about the internment of Japanese Americans that now interest historians. Other questions and other selections could have been chosen, but these show the current state of the conversation. Each selection is preceded by a headnote that introduces both its specific subject and its author. After the headnote come Questions for a Closer Reading. The headnote and the questions offer signposts that will allow you to understand more readily what the author is saying. The selections are uncut and they include the original notes. The notes are also signposts for further exploration. If an issue that the author raises intrigues you, use the notes to follow it up. At the end of all the selections are more questions, under the heading Making Connections. Turn to these after you have read the selections, and use them to bring the whole discussion together. In order to answer them, you may find that you need to reread. But no historical source yields up all that is within it to a person content to read it just once.

1. Why were Japanese Americans interned during World War II?

Roger Daniels

The Decision for Mass Evacuation

Six days after Roger Daniels's fourteenth birthday, the Japanese attacked Pearl Harbor. Like most Americans, Daniels wanted to be part of a "unified national effort" to defend the country, so he misrepresented his age in 1944 and joined the merchant marine. After the war, experiences in the labor and civil rights movement led Daniels to question the "culture of consensus" that developed in the 1950s. He worked for the Congress of Industrial Organizations and the International Longshoremen's and Warehousemen's Union before becoming an undergraduate at the University of Houston. In Houston, he tried to foster exchanges between white students at his school and African American students at Texas Southern University. By the time Daniels entered the graduate history program at the University of California at Los Angeles, he knew he wanted to conduct a study on racism. His dissertation, *The Politics of Prejudice: The Anti-Japanese Movement in California and the Struggle for Japanese Exclusion,* was published in 1962. In the preface, Daniels explains his "ulterior motive" in researching campaigns to end Japanese immigration by labor unions, progressives, and other "groups supposedly dedicated to democracy": "I am persuaded that not nearly enough attention has been paid to the antidemocratic threads that make up a goodly part of the fabric of our national heritage, and that by careful studies of these threads we may discover hitherto unnoticed patterns."

Even before he finished *The Politics of Prejudice,* Daniels had decided to explore the "antidemocratic threads" that caused internment. In fact, he would later say that if more government material had been declassified, he would have published *Concentration Camps USA: Japanese Americans and World War II* (1971) as his first rather than his second book. In this period before the Freedom of Information Act of 1976, many government records were restricted. While examining Department of Justice sources, Daniels learned that he was supposed to alert archivists about any FBI documents he came across so that they could be removed from the files. But he worked out an arrangement with a helpful archivist who allowed him to view a file and then go to the bathroom (where he took notes from memory on the material) before handing it back. These notes helped him find other corroborating evidence that he could then quote. The biggest boon to Daniels's research was the assistance offered by Dr. Stetson Conn, former chief military historian of the U.S. Army. In the summer of 1969, Conn gave Daniels access to his personal notes on many items no longer available at the National Archives. Conn even underlined his notes on the phone conversations between the architects of internment that Daniels would later cite as key evidence in his condemnation of the decision.

After examining these phone conversations, memos, letters, and other sources, Daniels argued in *Concentration Camps USA* that internment was not just a "wartime mistake" but reflected "one of the central themes of American history—the theme of white supremacy, of American racism." This selection analyzes the impact of racial attitudes on officials as they considered a variety of proposals for dealing with Japanese Americans. In "The Decision for Mass Evacuation," Daniels recounts how civilians who controlled the Army developed plans to remove Japanese Americans from the West Coast. Although some politicians, journalists, and nativist groups demanded the removal of all "Japs" from the West Coast, other officials, especially within the Justice Department, expressed concern about disregarding the rights of citizens. Official military reports also discounted the need for mass removal. Even Lieutenant General John L. DeWitt vacillated in his views of internment. As Daniels notes, Major General Allen W. Gullion and his subordinate Karl Bendetsen repeatedly lobbied DeWitt and members of the War Department to support mass removal and incarceration. Other proposals, such as creating "Jap-free" zones around security installations or allowing voluntary resettlement to the central valleys of California, were considered. But ultimately, as Daniels's pioneering research demonstrates, Gullion and Bendetsen succeeded in winning over Assistant Secretary of War John McCloy and Secretary of War Henry Stimson at the beginning of February 1942. Accepting their advice, President Franklin Delano Roosevelt signed Executive Order 9066 and gave DeWitt the authority to remove and intern Japanese Americans.

The evidence Daniels uncovered played a major role in winning redress for former internees. Even before he published *Concentration Camps USA,* Daniels was active in the Japanese American community. In 1967, he was a co-organizer of the first academic conference on the causes and consequences of internment. He appeared before the U.S. Senate in 1980 to affirm that "scholarly opinion has condemned the relocation" and to call for the creation of a commission to "serve an educational purpose by reminding Americans about one of the wrongs of our past."[1]

Once the Commission on Wartime Relocation and Internment of Civilians was established, Daniels became a consultant, briefed the commissioners, wrote several memorandums, and answered staff questions. He declared monetary redress "entirely appropriate" in an introduction he wrote for a position paper submitted by the Japanese American Citizens League to the commission. Because of his expertise, the commission asked him to read and comment on the draft version of the historical text of its report. In 1982, this landmark report concluded that internment had been caused not by military necessity but by "race prejudice, war hysteria, and a failure of political leadership."[2]

Daniels, a professor of history at the University of Cincinnati since 1976, persuaded a Republican congressman from his home state to support redress legislation. An eminent scholar in Asian American and immigration history, he has written numerous books and articles, including *Asian America: Chinese and Japanese in the United States since 1850* (1988), *Prisoners without Trial: Japanese Americans and World War II* (1993), and *Coming to America: Immigration and Ethnicity in American Life* (1990). He also has served as a consultant for several documentary films and historical exhibits and has been president of the Immigration History Society and the Society for Historians of the Gilded Age and the Progressive Era.

Questions for a Closer Reading

1. According to Daniels, who were the real architects of internment? What were their motives and strategies for winning support for mass removal and incarceration?
2. Compare the assessments of Japanese Americans by advocates and opponents of mass exclusion and internment. What views had the most influence on policy decisions?
3. What alternatives to internment were proposed? Why was there such a stark difference between the treatment of people of Japanese ancestry in Hawaii and the treatment of those on the West Coast?
4. Does Daniels's research effectively contradict claims by government officials that internment was required by "military necessity"?
5. Daniels provides a much harsher view of government policies and racial attitudes than earlier scholars. Based on the research presented in this selection, would you agree with Daniels's conclusion that Japanese Americans were imprisoned in "concentration camps"?

Notes

1. Commission on Wartime Relocation and Internment of Civilians Act, Hearing before the Committee on Governmental Affairs, United States Senate, 96th Congress, Second Session on S. 1647, March 18, 1980 (Washington, D.C.: U.S. Government Printing Office, 1980), 16–17.

2. Commission on Wartime Relocation and Internment of Civilians, *Personal Justice Denied: Report of the Commission on Wartime Relocation and Internment of Civilians* (Washington, D.C.: U.S. Government Printing Office, 1982), 18.

The Decision for Mass Evacuation

December 1941 was a month of calamities which saw West Coast opinion harden against the Japanese; during January, as the war news got worse and worse and it became apparent that the Japanese audacity at Pearl Harbor would not be quickly avenged, the national climate of opinion, and Congressional opinion in particular, began to veer toward the West Coast view. That this climate had to be created is shown by an examination of the *Congressional Record.* Not only was there no concerted strong feeling exhibited against the Japanese Americans, but in the first weeks after Pearl Harbor members of the California delegation defended them publicly. (The only trace of hostility shown by a California solon in early December was a telephone call that the junior senator, Democrat Sheridan Downey, made to the Army on the night of December 7 suggesting that DeWitt prompt Governor Olson to declare some sort of curfew on "Japs.") On December 10, for example, Bertrand W. Gearhart, a four-term Republican congressman from Fresno and an officer of the American Legion, read a telegram professing loyalty to the United States from an Issei leader in his district whom Gearhart described as an "American patriot." Five days later, when John Rankin (D-Miss.), the leading nativist in the lower house, called for "deporting every Jap who claims, or has claimed, Japanese citizenship, or sympathizes with Japan in this war," he was answered by another Californian, Leland M. Ford, a Santa Monica Republican:

> These people are American-born. They cannot be deported . . . whether we like it or whether we do not. This is their country. . . . [When] they join the armed forces . . . they must take this oath of allegiance . . . and I see no particular reason at this particular time why they should not. I believe that every one of these people should make a clear, clean acknowledgement.[1]

Roger Daniels, "The Decision for Mass Evacuation," *Concentration Camps USA: Japanese Americans and World War II* (New York: Holt, Rinehart & Winston, 1971), 42–73.

Despite the lack of Congressional concern, by the end of December momentum was gathering for more drastic action against the Japanese and against enemy aliens generally. On December 30 the Justice Department made the first of many concessions to the military, concessions that had little to do either with due process or the realities of the situation. On that date Attorney General Biddle informed the Provost Marshal General's office that he had authorized the issuance of search warrants for any house in which an enemy alien lived, merely on the representation that there was reasonable cause to believe that there was contraband on the premises. Contraband had already been defined to include anything that might be used as a weapon, any explosive (many Issei farmers used dynamite to clear stumps), radio transmitters, any radio that had a shortwave band, and all but the simplest cameras. For the next few months thousands of houses where Japanese lived were subjected to random search. Although much "contraband" was found (most of it in two Issei-owned sporting goods stores), the FBI itself later stipulated that none of it was sinister in nature and reported that there was no evidence at all that any of it was intended for subversive use. But the mere fact of these searches, widely reported in the press, added to the suspicion with which the Japanese were viewed. These searches, like so much of the anti-Japanese movement, were part of a self-fulfilling prophecy: one is suspicious of the Japanese, so one searches their houses; the mere fact of the search, when noticed ("the FBI went through those Jap houses on the other side of town"), creates more suspicion.

For individual Japanese families, these searches intensified the insecurity and terror they already felt. One fifteen-year-old girl in San Jose, California reported what must have been an all-too-routine occurrence:

> One day I came home from school to find the two F.B.I. men at our front door. They asked permission to search the house. One man looked through the front rooms, while the other searched the back rooms. Trembling with fright, I followed and watched each of the men look around. The investigators examined the mattresses, and the dresser and looked under the beds. The gas range, piano, and sofa were thoroughly inspected. Since I was the only one at home, the F.B.I. questioned me, but did not procure sufficient evidence of Fifth Columnists in our family. This made me very happy, even if they did mess up the house.[2]

Concurrent with its more stringent search order, the Department of Justice and the Provost Marshal General's office decided to send representatives to DeWitt's headquarters in San Francisco; the two men sent—James Rowe, Jr., Assistant Attorney General and a former Presidential assistant, and Major (later Colonel) Karl R. Bendetsen, chief of the Aliens Division,

Provost Marshal General's office—were key and mutually antagonistic figures in the bureaucratic struggle over the fate of the West Coast Japanese. Rowe, during his short visit in California, exercised a moderating influence on the cautious General DeWitt, who often seemed to be the creature of the last strong personality with whom he had contact. Bendetsen represented a chief (Gullion) who wanted not only exclusion of the Japanese from the West Coast but also the transfer of supervisory authority over all enemy aliens in the United States from the civilian control of the Department of Justice to the military control of his office. Bendetsen soon became the voice of General DeWitt in matters concerning aliens, and was well rewarded for his efforts. A graduate of Stanford Law School, he had gone on to active duty as a captain in 1940, and in the process of evacuating the Japanese he would gain his colonel's eagles before he turned thirty-five. After Bendetsen's arrival, Gullion arranged with DeWitt that the West Coast commander go out of normal channels and deal directly with the Provost Marshal on matters concerning aliens. The result of this seemingly routine bureaucratic shuffle was highly significant; as Stetson Conn has pointed out, the consequence of this arrangement was that "the responsible Army command headquarters in Washington [that is, Chief of Staff George C. Marshall and his immediate staff] had little to do during January and February 1942 with the plans and decisions for Japanese evacuation."[3]

Telephone conversations and correspondence between DeWitt's headquarters and the Provost Marshal General's office in late December and early January reveal the tremendous pressures that the soldiers were putting on the civilians. According to General Gullion, the Justice Department's representatives, James Rowe, Jr., and Edward J. Ennis, were apologetic about the slowness of the Justice Department, an apparent criticism of their chief, the Attorney General. At about the same time Gullion was complaining that "the Attorney General is not functioning" and threatened to have Secretary Stimson complain to the President. DeWitt was, as usual, vacillating. Within the same week he told the Provost Marshal General's office that "it would be better if . . . this thing worked through the civil channels," but a few days later insisted that "I don't want to go after this thing piece meal. I want to do it on a mass basis, all at the same time."[4]

The arrival of Bendetsen at DeWitt's San Francisco headquarters seemed to strengthen the West Coast commander's resolve. Before Bendetsen left Washington he had drafted an Executive Order transferring authority over aliens to the War Department, but the Provost Marshal General's office felt that since the Justice Department's representatives were so apologetic, it "wasn't quite fair" to take over without giving them a chance to come up to the Army's standards. Shortly after his arrival in San Francisco, Bendetsen drafted a memo that quickly became the guideline for DeWitt's policy.

It called for an immediate and complete registration of all alien enemies, who were to be photographed and fingerprinted. These records were to be kept in duplicate, one set to be kept in the community in which the alien resided, the other in a central office. The purpose was to set up what Bendetsen called a "Pass and Permit System." Doubtful that the Attorney General would agree to this, Bendetsen's memo concluded with what had become the refrain of the Provost Marshal General's men: if Justice won't do it, the War Department must.

The next day, January 4, in a conference at his Presidio headquarters attended by Rowe, Bendetsen, and representatives of other federal departments and officials in local government, DeWitt made some of his position clear, stressing, as he always did to civilians, what he called the military necessity.

> We are at war and this area — eight states — has been designated as a theater of operations. I have approximately 240,000 men at my disposal. . . . [There are] approximately 288,000 enemy aliens . . . which we have to watch. . . . I have little confidence that the enemy aliens are law-abiding or loyal in any sense of the word. Some of them yes; many, no. Particularly the Japanese. I have no confidence in their loyalty whatsoever. I am speaking now of the native born Japanese — 117,000 — and 42,000 in California alone.[5]

One result of this conference was that the Department of Justice agreed to go further than it had previously: enemy aliens were to be re-registered under its auspices, the FBI would conduct large-scale "spot" raids, something DeWitt was particularly eager for, and, most significantly, a large number of restricted, or Category A, zones would be established around crucial military and defense installations on the Pacific Coast. Entry to these zones would be on a pass basis. Assistant Secretary of War John J. McCloy later described this program as "the best way to solve" the West Coast alien problem.

> . . . establish limited restricted areas around the airplane plants, the forts, and other important military installations . . . we might call these military reservations in substance and exclude everyone — whites, yellows, blacks, greens — from that area and then license back into the area those whom we felt there was no danger to be expected from . . . then we can cover the legal situation . . . in spite of the constitution. . . . You may, by that process, eliminate all the Japs [alien and citizen] but you might conceivably permit some to come back whom you are quite certain are free from any suspicion.[6]

In addition to the Category A zones, there were to be Category B zones, consisting of the rest of the coastal area, in which enemy aliens and citizen

Japanese would be allowed to live and work under rigidly prescribed conditions. Although DeWitt and the other Army people were constantly complaining about the slowness of the Justice Department, they quickly found that setting up these zones was easier said than done. DeWitt did not forward his first recommendations for Category A areas to the War Department until January 21, more than two weeks after the San Francisco conference.

On January 16 Representative Leland Ford, the Santa Monica Republican who had opposed stern treatment for the Japanese on the floor of the House in mid-December, had changed his mind. Ford had received a number of telegrams and letters from California suggesting removal of Japanese from vital coastal areas — the earliest seems to have been a January 6 telegram from Mexican American movie star Leo Carillo — and by mid-January had come around to their point of view. He urged Secretary of War Henry L. Stimson to have "all Japanese, whether citizens or not, . . . placed in inland concentration camps." Arguing that native-born Japanese either were or were not loyal to the United States, Ford developed a simple test for loyalty: any Japanese willing to go to a concentration camp was a patriot; therefore it followed that unwillingness to go was a proof of disloyalty to the United States. Stimson and his staff mulled over this letter for ten days, and then replied (in a letter drafted by Bendetsen, now back from the Pacific Coast) giving the congressman a certain amount of encouragement. "The internment of over a hundred thousand people," Stimson wrote, "involves many complex considerations." The basic responsibility, Stimson pointed out, putting the finger on his Cabinet colleague Francis Biddle, has been delegated to the Attorney General. Nevertheless, the Secretary continued, "the Army is prepared to provide internment facilities in the interior to the extent necessary." Assuring Ford that the Army was aware of the dangers on the Pacific Coast, Stimson informed him that the military were submitting suggestions to the Justice Department, and advised him to present his views to the Attorney General.[7]

The same day that Ford wrote Stimson, January 16, another federal department became involved in the fate of the West Coast Japanese. Agriculture Secretary Claude Wickard, chiefly concerned with increasing farm production — "Food Can Win the War" was his line — called a meeting in his office at which the War, Labor, Navy, Justice, and Treasury Departments were represented. He had become alarmed over investigative reports from his agents on the West Coast, who were concerned both about the fate of the Japanese and the threat to food production. Wickard had been informed that although violence against the Japanese farmers was an isolated phenomenon, greatly exaggerated by the press, nevertheless it was quite clear that the Japanese rural population was "terrified."

> They do not leave their homes at night, and will not, even in the daytime, enter certain areas populated by Filipinos. The police authorities are probably not sympathetic to the Japanese and are giving them only the minimum protection. Investigation of actual attacks on Japanese have been merely perfunctory and no prosecutions have been initiated.[8]

The federal officials then concluded that the whole "propaganda campaign" against the Japanese was essentially a conspiracy designed to place Japanese-owned and -leased farm lands into white hands; the real aim was to "eliminate Japanese competition." Wickard's West Coast representatives urged him to take positive steps both to maintain agricultural production and to preserve and protect the property and persons of the Japanese farmers.

Wickard's action was not exactly along the lines recommended by the men in the field. He did urge immediate federal action "so that the supply of vegetables for the military forces and the civilian population will not be needlessly curtailed." But Wickard also felt that the fears and suspicions of the general public — particularly the West Coast public — should be taken into account. He seemed to envision a sort of large agricultural cultural reservation in the central valleys of California on which the Japanese could "carry on their normal farming operations" after being removed from "all strategic areas." In this way, Wickard felt, the country could protect itself from "possible subversive Japanese activities," provide "limited protection to all Japanese whose conduct is above suspicion," and at the same time "avoid incidents that might provide an excuse for cruel treatment for our people in Japanese occupied territory." As for the agricultural lands in the coastal area which the Japanese had tilled, Wickard suggested that Mexicans might be brought in to replace them.[9]

Also, by mid-January, the urban Japanese, if not terrorized as were their rural cousins, were feeling more and more hopeless and demoralized. An occasional militant like James Y. Sakamoto, a Japanese American Citizens League (JACL) official in Seattle, could indignantly protest against Representative Ford's evacuation proposal which went out on the Associated Press wire on January 21.

"This is our country," Sakamoto pointed out, "we were born and raised here . . . have made our homes here . . . [and] we are ready to give our lives, if necessary, to defend the United States." Ford's drastic measures, he insisted, were not in the best interests of the nation. But even a Nisei leader like Sakamoto felt compelled to admit that there was some kind of subversive danger from the older generation of Japanese. The Seattle Nisei, he stated, were "actively cooperating" with the authorities "to uncover all subversive activity in our midst" and, if necessary, he concluded, the Nisei were "ready to stand as protective custodians over our parent generation to guard against danger to the United States arising from their midst."[10] One of the standard complaints quite properly raised by Americans in denouncing totalitarian regimes is that their police states turn children against their parents; it is rarely remarked that, in this instance at least, such too was the function of American democracy.

But for those really in charge, the agonizing distinctions between father and son, between alien and citizen, were essentially irrelevant. By mid-January, perhaps as a way of answering the points made by Representative Ford, Chief of Staff George C. Marshall ordered the Provost Marshal General's office to prepare a memorandum on the West Coast Japanese situation. Bendetsen, the natural drafter for such a report, called General DeWitt to ask what his attitude would be if "the Department of Justice still fails to do what we think they ought to do?" DeWitt, who felt that things would work out, was nevertheless apprehensive about the continuing potentialities for sabotage and other subversive activities. "We know," he told Bendetsen, "that they are communicating at sea. . . ." DeWitt actually knew no such thing, as no evidence existed of such communication, but he undoubtedly believed it. Then, in a classic leap in what Richard Hofstadter has styled the paranoid style, the West Coast commander insisted that "the fact that we have had [not even] sporadic attempts at sabotage clearly means that control is being exercised somewhere." Here then was the "heads I win, tails you lose" situation in which this one Army officer was able to place more than 100,000 innocent people. There had been no acts of sabotage, no real evidence of subversion, despite the voices that DeWitt kept hearing at sea. Yet, according to this military logician, there was a conspiracy afoot not to commit sabotage until America dropped its guard. Ergo, evacuate them quickly before the conspiracy is put into operation.[11]

The next day, January 25, the long-awaited report on the attack on Pearl Harbor made by the official committee of inquiry headed by Supreme Court Justice Owen J. Roberts was released to the press just in time for the Sunday morning papers, though it is dated two days earlier. In addition to its indictment of the general conditions of unreadiness in the Hawaiian command, the board reported, falsely, as it turned out, that the attack was greatly abetted by Japanese spies, some of whom were described as "persons having no open relations with the Japanese foreign service." It went on to criticize the laxity of counterespionage activity in the Islands, and implied that a too close adherence to the Constitution had seriously inhibited the work of the Federal Bureau of Investigation.[12] The publication of the report was naturally a sensation; it greatly stimulated already prevalent rumors that linked the disaster to wholly imaginary fifth column activities by resident Japanese. Perhaps the most popular was the yarn that University of California class rings had been found on the fingers of Japanese pilots shot down in the raid. Even more ridiculous was the story that the attacking pilots had been aided by arrows, pointing at Pearl Harbor, which had been hacked into the cane fields the night before by Japanese workers. The absurdity of this device—a large natural harbor containing dozens of war vessels, large and small, is highly visible from the air—seems to have occurred to few. The Roberts Report provided a field day for those who had long urged more repressive measures and a more effective secret police unfettered by constitutional restrictions. Congressmen like Martin Dies of Texas, then head of the House Committee on Un-American Activities, insisted, in and out of Congress, that if only people had listened to them, the disaster at Pearl Harbor could have been averted. More significantly, it gave an additional argument to those who were pressing for preventive detention and must have given pause to some who had been urging restraint.

On January 25 Secretary Stimson forwarded to Attorney General Biddle recommendations that General DeWitt had made four days earlier, calling for total exclusion of enemy aliens from eighty-six Category A zones and close control of enemy aliens in eight Category B zones on a pass and permit system. As this proposal involved only aliens, the Justice Department quickly agreed and made the first public, official announcement of a mass evacuation on January 29, to be effective almost a month later, on February 24.[13] This relatively modest proposal would have moved only about 7000 aliens in all, and fewer than 3000 of these would have been Japanese. At about the same time it announced the appointment of Tom C. Clark (who later became Attorney General under Truman and then an Associate Justice of the Supreme Court) as Co-Ordinator of the Alien Enemy Control Program within the Western Defense Command. Clark flew to the West Coast the next day.

A few days before Stimson's recommendation to Biddle, the top echelons of military command, for the first time, began to become aware of the kinds of proposals that were emanating from DeWitt's headquarters. General Mark W. Clark (then a brigadier on the General Staff and later a major commander in the European Theater) was instructed to prepare a memorandum for the President on the subject of "enemy aliens" in the Western Theater of Operations. The day after Stimson's letter to Biddle requesting the announcement of Category A and B areas, General Clark recommended that no memorandum be sent unless the Attorney General's action should "not be all that is desired." Clark's memorandum was read by Chief of Staff George C. Marshall, who noted on it "hold for me until Feb. 1." The top brass was satisfied with a very modest program, involving the forced removal, without detention, of a very few aliens. Clark's memorandum made no mention of citizens at all.[14]

But if the top brass were satisfied, DeWitt, Bendetsen, and Gullion were not. And neither were the leading public officials in California. On January 27 DeWitt had a conference with Governor Culbert Olson and related to Washington, probably accurately:

> There's a tremendous volume of public opinion now developing against the Japanese of all classes, that is aliens and non-aliens, to get them off the land, and in Southern California around Los Angeles — in that area too — they want and they are bringing pressure on the government to move all the Japanese out. As a matter of fact, it's not being instigated or developed by people who are not thinking but by the best people of California. Since the publication of the Roberts Report they feel that they are living in the midst of a lot of enemies. They don't trust the Japanese, none of them.[15]

Two days later, DeWitt talked with Olson's Republican Attorney General Earl Warren. (DeWitt thought his name was Warner.) The California Attorney General, who was then preparing to run for governor against Olson in November, was in thorough agreement with his rival that the Japanese ought to be removed. This was not surprising. Warren was heir to a long anti-Japanese tradition in California politics and the protégé of U. S. Webb, a long-time Attorney General of California (1902–1939) and the author of the 1913 California Alien Land Act. Warren had been intimately associated with the most influential nativist group in the state, the Joint Immigration Committee, but shortly after he became Attorney General in 1939 he prudently arranged to have his name taken off the Committee's letterhead, although he continued to meet with them and receive copies of all documents and notices. Because of his later prominence, some have tried to make too much of Warren's very minor role in pressing for an evacuation. He did add his voice, but it was not yet a very strong one and it is almost inconceivable that, had any other politician held his post, essentially the same result would not have ensued.[16]

On the very day of Biddle's formal announcement of the A and B zones, DeWitt and Bendetsen worked out a more sweeping scheme, which Bendetsen would present to an informal but influential meeting of congressmen the next day. After a rambling conversation — DeWitt was rarely either concise or precise — Bendetsen, always the lawyer in uniform, summed it up neatly:

> BENDETSEN. . . . As I understand it, from your viewpoint summarizing our conversation, you are of the opinion that there will have to be an evacuation on the west coast, not only of Japanese aliens but also of Japanese citizens, that is, you would include citizens along with alien enemies, and that if you

had the power of requisition over all other Federal agencies, if you were requested you would be willing on the coast to accept responsibility for the alien enemy program.

DEWITT. Yes I would. And I think it's got to come sooner or later.

BENDETSEN. Yes sir, I do too, and I think the subject may be discussed tomorrow at the congressional delegation meeting.

DEWITT. Well, you've got my viewpoint. You have it exactly.[17]

The next day, January 30, the Japanese question was discussed in two important meetings, one in the White House and one on Capitol Hill. In the Cabinet meeting fears were expressed about the potentially dangerous situation in Hawaii. General Marshall penned a short memo to General Dwight D. Eisenhower, then a member of his staff, telling him that Stimson was concerned about "dangerous Japanese in Hawaii." Justice Roberts had told the War Secretary that "this point was regarded by his board as most serious." Several Cabinet members, but particularly Navy Secretary Frank Knox, were greatly disturbed at what they considered the laxity with which the Hawaiian Japanese were treated. As early as December 19, a previous Cabinet meeting had decided that all Japanese aliens in the Hawaiian Islands should be interned, and put on some island other than Oahu, where the major military installations were located.[18]

At the other end of Pennsylvania Avenue, the focus was on the West Coast Japanese. Bendetsen, along with Rowe and Ennis from the Justice Department, attended a meeting of the Pacific Coast House delegation. (A joint meeting between the congressmen and the six senators was already scheduled for the following Monday.) The subject was what to do about the Japanese. Although Bendetsen officially reported to his superiors that he "was present as an observer," it is clear from his telephone conversations with General DeWitt, both before and after the meeting, that he went as an advocate for the policies that he and his boss, General Gullion, had been proposing. Bendetsen called DeWitt right after the meeting and told him what they both considered good news.

> They asked me to state what the position of the War Department was. I stated that I could not speak for the War Department. . . . They asked me for my own views and I stated that the position of the War Department was this: that we did not seek control of the program, that we preferred it be handled by the civil agencies. However, the War Department would be entirely willing, I believed, [to assume] the responsibility provided they accorded the War Department, and the Secretary of War, and the military commander under him, full authority to require the services of any federal agency, and required that that federal agency was required to respond.[19]

DeWitt liked this. "That's good," he responded. "I'm glad to see that action is being taken . . . that someone in authority begins to see the problem." What he particularly liked was the delegation to himself of full power over civilian agencies. He had had problems with civilians already, particularly civilians in the Federal Bureau of Investigation whose West Coast agents, as we have seen, refused to respond positively to DeWitt's imaginary alarms and excursions. As DeWitt envisioned it, "Mr. [J. Edgar] Hoover himself as head of the F.B.I. would have to function under the War Department exactly as he is functioning under the Department of Justice."

Bendetsen, naturally, encouraged DeWitt to grab for power. "Opinion is beginning to become irresistible, and I think that anything you recommend will be strongly backed up . . . by the public." DeWitt and Bendetsen agreed that protestations of loyalty from the Nisei were utterly worthless. As DeWitt put it:

> "There are going to be a lot of Japs who are going to say, 'Oh, yes, we want to go, we're good Americans and we want to go, we're good Americans and we want to do everything you say,' but those are the fellows I suspect the most."
>
> "Definitely," Bendetsen agreed. "The ones who are giving you only lip service are the ones always to be suspected."[20]

The Congressional recommendations were immediately sent to Secretary Stimson by the senior California representative, Clarence Lea, a Santa Rosa Democrat first elected in 1916. Although they did not specifically call for removal of American citizens of Japanese ancestry, the delegation did ask that mass evacuation proceed for "all enemy aliens and their families," which would have included most of the Nisei.[21] Later the same day, Provost Marshal General Gullion called DeWitt to get some details straight. He was chiefly interested in how far DeWitt proposed to move the evacuees. DeWitt did not know, but he did point out to Gullion that within California "one group wanted to move them entirely out of the state," whereas another wanted "them to be left in California." After receiving these assurances from DeWitt, Gullion began to wonder where the Army was going to put 100,000 people, and, perhaps for the first time, fleetingly realized that "a resettlement proposition is quite a proposition."[22] The following day, Bendetsen, acting for his chief, had the Adjutant General dispatch telegrams to Corps Area commanders throughout the nation asking them about possible locations for large numbers of evacuees. Bendetsen suggested some possible sites: "agricultural experimental farms, prison farms, migratory labor camps, pauper farms, state parks, abandoned CCC camps, fairgrounds."[23]

By the end of the month DeWitt was able to make his position a little clearer. When Bendetsen asked whether or not he contemplated moving citizens, DeWitt was emphatic.

> I include all Germans, all Italians who are alien enemies and all Japanese who are native-born or foreign born . . . evacuate enemy aliens in large groups at the earliest possible date . . . sentiment is being given too much importance. . . . I think we might as well eliminate talk of resettlement and handle these people as they should be handled . . . put them to work in internment camps. . . . I place the following priority. . . . First the Japanese, all prices [*?sic*] . . . as the most dangerous . . . the next group, the Germans . . . the third group, the Italians. . . . We've waited too long as it is. Get them all out.[24]

On Sunday, February 1, exactly eight weeks after Pearl Harbor, Assistant Secretary of War John J. McCloy, Gullion, and Bendetsen went to a meeting in Attorney General Francis Biddle's office. Biddle, who was seconded by James Rowe, Jr., Edward J. Ennis, and J. Edgar Hoover, had been concerned about the increasing pressure for mass evacuation, both from the military and from Congress, and about a crescendo of press criticism directed at his "pussyfooting," some of which was undoubtedly inspired by the military. Biddle presented the Army men with a draft of what he hoped would be a joint press release. Its crucial sentences, which the military refused to agree to, were

> The Department of War and the Department of Justice are in agreement that the present military situation does not *at this time* [my emphasis] require the removal of American citizens of the Japanese race. The Secretary of War, General DeWitt, the Attorney General, and the Director of the Federal Bureau of Investigation believe that appropriate steps have been and are being taken.

Biddle informed McCloy and the others that he was opposed to mass evacuation and that the Justice Department would have nothing to do with it. Rowe, remembering his early January visit to DeWitt's headquarters, said that the West Coast commander had been opposed to mass evacuation then and wondered what had changed his mind. According to Gullion, Rowe, after some uncomplimentary remarks about Bendetsen, complained about the hysterical tone of the protests from the West Coast, argued that the western congressmen were "just nuts" on the subject, and maintained that there was "no evidence whatsoever of any reason for disturbing citizens." Then Biddle insisted that the Justice Department would have nothing at all to do with any interference with civilians. Gullion, admittedly "a little sore," said: "Well, listen, Mr. Biddle, do you mean to tell me if the Army, the men on the ground, determine it is a military necessity to move citizens, Jap citizens, that you won't help us?"

After Biddle restated his position, McCloy, again according to Gullion, said to the Attorney General: "You are putting a Wall Street lawyer in a helluva box, but if it is a question of the safety of the country [and] the Constitution. . . . Why the Constitution is just a scrap of paper to me."

As the meeting broke up, it was agreed that the Army people would check with the "man on the ground," General DeWitt. As soon as they got back to their office, Gullion and Bendetsen made a joint phone call to the West Coast commander. They read him the proposed press release and, when the crucial sentences were reached, DeWitt responded immediately: "I wouldn't agree to that." When asked specifically whom he did want to evacuate, the answer was "those people who are aliens and who are Japs of American citizenship." Then Gullion cautioned DeWitt:

> Now I might suggest, General, Mr. McCloy was in the conference and he will probably be in any subsequent conference . . . he has not had all the benefit of conversations we have had with you — if you could give us something, not only in conversation but a written thing . . . stating your position.

DeWitt agreed to do this. Then Bendetsen summarized the Justice Department's point of view:

> . . . they say . . . if we recommend and it is determined that there should be an evacuation of citizens, they said hands off, that is the Army's job . . . they agree with us that it is possible from . . . a legal standpoint. . . . They agree with us that [the licensing theory] could be . . . the legal basis for exclusion. . . . However we insist that we could also say that while all whites could remain, Japs can't, if we think there is military necessity for that. They apparently want us to join with them so that if anything happens they would be able to say "this was the military recommendation."

DeWitt stated, "they are trying to cover themselves and lull the populace into a false sense of security."

When questioned about the details of the evacuation, DeWitt blustered: "I haven't gone into the details of it, but Hell, it would be no job as far as the evacuation was concerned to move 100,000 people."[25]

Actually, of course, it was a tremendous job, and even in such a relatively simple matter as the designation of Category A (prohibited to aliens) and Category B (restricted to aliens) zones, DeWitt's staff had botched the job. Bendetsen had to call Western Defense Command headquarters and point out that although they had permitted limited use by enemy aliens of the San Francisco–Oakland Bay Bridge (the bridge itself was Category B), all the approaches to the bridge were classified Category A, and thus prohibited.[26]

Two days after the conference in Biddle's office both Assistant Secretary of War McCloy and General George C. Marshall made separate calls to DeWitt. McCloy, and presumably Stimson and Marshall, had become concerned that DeWitt and the Provost Marshal's office were committing the Army to a policy that the policy makers had not yet agreed to. McCloy was blunt:

> . . . the Army, that means you in the area, should not take the position, even in your conversations with political figures out there [favoring] a wholesale withdrawal of Japanese citizens and aliens from the Coast. . . . We have about reached the point where we feel that perhaps the best solution of it is to limit the withdrawal to certain prohibited areas.

Then, incredibly to anyone who has read the transcripts of his conversations with Gullion and Bendetsen (which were apparently not then available to McCloy), General DeWitt denied that he had done any such thing: "Mr. Secretary . . . I haven't taken any position."[27]

This, of course, was a palpable lie. What the cautious commander knew, however, was that he had never put any recommendations on paper, and that General Gullion was not likely to produce the telephone transcripts because they showed him and his subordinates pressing for a policy that had not yet been officially sanctioned.

General Marshall's call was terse and businesslike; the extract of it which he furnished to the Secretary of War is worth quoting in full, both because of what it does and what it does not say.

> MARSHALL. Is there anything you want to say now about anything else? Of course we're on an open phone.
>
> DEWITT. We're on an open phone, but George I can talk a little about this alien situation out here.
>
> MARSHALL. Yes.
>
> DEWITT. I had a conference yesterday [February 2] with the Governor [Olson] and several representatives of the Department of Justice [Tom C. Clark] and the Department of Agriculture with a view to removal of the Japanese from where they are now living to other portions of the state.
>
> MARSHALL. Yes.
>
> DEWITT. And the Governor thinks it can be satisfactorily handled without having a resettlement somewhere in the central part of the United States and

removing them entirely from the state of California. As you know the people out here are very much disturbed over these aliens, and want to get them out of the several communities.

MARSHALL. Yes.

DEWITT. And I've agreed that if they can get them out of the areas limited as the combat zone, that it would be satisfactory. That would take them about 100 to 150 miles from the coast, and they're going to do that I think. They're working on it.

MARSHALL. Thank you.

DEWITT. The Department [of Justice] has a representative out here and the Department of Agriculture, and they think the plan is an excellent one. I'm only concerned with getting them away from around these aircraft factories and other places.

MARSHALL. Yes. Anything else?

DEWITT. No, that's all.

MARSHALL. Well, good luck.[28]

That same day, February 3, there was an hour-and-a-half meeting between Stimson, McCloy, Gullion, and Bendetsen. (It is not clear whether the phone conversations between McCloy and DeWitt and Marshall and DeWitt preceded, followed or straddled this meeting.) The next day Provost Marshal Gullion reported, somewhat dejectedly: ". . . the two Secretaries [Stimson and McCloy] are against any mass movement. They are pretty much against it. And they are also pretty much against interfering with citizens unless it can be done legally."[29]

What had apparently happened was that DeWitt, understanding from the McCloy and Marshall phone calls that the War Department was, as he put it, "afraid that I was going to get into a political mess," and under great pressure from Governor Olson and Tom C. Clark to allow a limited, voluntary, compromise evacuation within California, trimmed his position accordingly. Clark, a strong and vigorous personality, seemed to have great influence over the general, who described him as "a fine fellow . . . the most cooperative and forceful man I have ever had to deal with. He attacks a problem better than any civilian I have ever had contact with."[30]

Clark was clearly playing an independent role, and his position was somewhere between that of the Provost Marshal's office and that held by his own chief, the Attorney General. The plan that he sponsored or supported in the February 2 conference in Sacramento with Governor Olson and DeWitt called for a conference between Governor Olson and leading Japanese Americans which would result in a voluntary resettlement in the central valleys of California where the Japanese could augment agricultural production. As DeWitt explained the Clark-Olson plan to an unhappy Gullion:

> Well, I tell you, they are solving the problem here very satisfactorily.... I have agreed to accept any plan they propose to put those people, Japanese Americans and Japanese who are in Category A area in the Category B area on farms. . . . We haven't got anything to do with it except they are consulting me to see what areas I will let them go into. . . . Mr. Clark is very much in favor of it . . . the people are going to handle it locally through the Governor and they are going to move those people to arable and tillable land. They are going to keep them in the state. They don't want to bring in a lot of negroes and mexicans and let them take their place. . . . They just want to put them on the land out of the cities where they can raise vegetables like they are doing now.[31]

The Provost Marshal General's men were disgusted with this turn of events. Not only were their plans being thwarted by the civilians who ran the Army — Stimson and McCloy, who were thinking in terms of creating "Japless" islands of security around a few key installations like the Consolidated-Vultee aircraft plant in San Diego, the Lockheed and North American plants in Los Angeles, and the Boeing plant in Seattle — but even their former ally, General DeWitt, the all-important man on the ground who alone could make authoritative statements about "military necessity," had now deserted their cause. As Colonel Archer Lerch, Gullion's deputy, put it:

> I think I detect a decided weakening on the part of Gen. DeWitt, which I think is most unfortunate. . . . The idea suggested to Gen. DeWitt in his conference with Gov. Olson, that a satisfactory solution must be reached through a conference between the Governor and leading Jap-Americans, savors too much of the spirit of Rotary and overlooks the necessary cold-bloodedness of war.[32]

If pressure for evacuation within the Army seemed to be weakening, stronger and stronger outside forces were being brought into play. On February 2 and 3, in separate meetings, representatives and senators from all three Pacific Coast states agreed to coordinate their efforts. Serving as coordinator of these anti-Japanese efforts was Senator Hiram W. Johnson of California, who, in the mid-1920s, had masterminded a similar joint Congressional effort which brought about elimination of a Japanese quota in the Immigration Act of 1924. Johnson was actually more concerned about the defense of the West Coast — he feared a Japanese invasion — and complained bitterly to one of his political intimates that "the keenness of interest in the Japanese question far overshadowed the general proposition of our preparedness."[33]

Back in California, Governor Culbert Olson went on the air on February 4; his speech could only have further inflamed public opinion. Disseminating false information that probably came from his conference two days previously with General DeWitt and Tom Clark, he warned the already frightened people of California that

> it is known that there are Japanese residents of California who have sought to aid the Japanese enemy by way of communicating information, or have shown indications of preparation for fifth column activities.

Loyal Japanese, he insisted, could best prove their loyalty by cooperating with whatever the authorities asked them to do. Then, in a vain attempt to reassure the public, he went on to say that everything would be all right. He told of his conference with DeWitt and announced, without of course giving any specifics, that

> general plans [have been] agreed upon for the movement and placement of the entire adult Japanese population in California at productive and useful employment within the borders of our state, and under such surveillance and protection . . . as shall be deemed necessary.[34]

The next day the mayor of Los Angeles, Fletcher Bowron, outdid the governor in attempting to arouse passions. After pointing out that the largest concentration of Japanese was in Los Angeles, he turned on the venom:

> Right here in our own city are those who may spring to action at an appointed time in accordance with a prearranged plan wherein each of our little Japanese friends will know his part in the event of any possible attempted invasion or air raid.

He then argued that not only Japanese aliens but citizens of Japanese descent, some of whom were "unquestionably . . . loyal," represented a threat to Los Angeles. Disloyal Nisei, he argued, would loudly proclaim their patriotism. "Of course they would try to fool us. They did in Honolulu and in Manila, and we may expect it in California." Bowron's answer, of course, was mass internment for all Japanese, citizens and aliens alike. From favorable references to Tom Clark, he seems to have been willing to go along with the DeWitt–Olson–Clark plan of labor camps within California. Bowron also tried to take care of constitutional and ethical scruples:

> If we can send our own young men to war, it is nothing less than sickly sentimentality to say that we will do injustice to American-born Japanese to merely put them in a place of safety so that they can do no harm. . . . We [in

> Los Angeles] are the ones who will be the human sacrifices if the perfidy that characterized the attack on Pearl Harbor is ever duplicated on the American continent.

In a follow-up statement the next day, Bowron put forth the interesting proposition that one of the major reasons that Japanese could not be trusted was that Californians had discriminated against them:

> The Japanese, because they are unassimilable, because the aliens have been denied the right to own real property in California, because of [immigration discrimination against them], because of the marked differences in appearance between Japanese and Caucasians, because of the generations of training and philosophy that makes them Japanese and nothing else — all of these contributing factors set the Japanese apart as a race, regardless of how many generations have been born in America. Undoubtedly many of them intend to be loyal, but only each individual can know his own intentions, and when the final test comes, who can say but that "blood will tell"? We cannot run the risk of another Pearl Harbor episode in Southern California.[35]

And, that same week, in Sacramento, Attorney General Earl Warren presided over a meeting of some one hundred and fifty law enforcement officers, mostly sheriffs and district attorneys. According to a federal official who attended the meeting:

> In his opening remarks, Mr. Warren cautioned against hysteria but then proceeded to outline his remarks in such a fashion as to encourage hysterical thinking. . . . Mr. [Isidore] Dockweiler, Los Angeles District Attorney . . . , asserted that the United States Supreme Court had been packed with leftist and other extreme advocates of civil liberty and that it was time for the people of California to disregard the law, if necessary, to secure their protection. Mr. Dockweiler finally worked himself into such a state of hysteria that he was called to order by Mr. Warren. . . . The meeting loudly applauded the statement that the people of California had no trust in the ability and willingness of the Federal Government to proceed against enemy aliens. One high official was heard to state that he favored shooting on sight all Japanese residents of the state.[36]

Despite relative calm in the press until the end of January, a government intelligence agency (the civilian Office of Government Reports) informed Washington that "word of mouth discussions [continue] with a surprisingly large number of people expressing themselves as in favor of sending all Japanese to concentration camps." By the end of January, the press "flared up again" with demands growing "that positive action be taken by the Federal Government. This awakening of the press has increased the verbal discussions that never ceased." By early February the *Los Angeles Times,* never friendly to the Japanese Americans, . . . could no longer find human terms to describe them. All Japanese Americans, the *Times* insisted editorially, were at least potentially enemies: "A viper is nonetheless a viper wherever the egg is hatched — so a Japanese-American, born of Japanese parents — grows up to be a Japanese, not an American."

Henry McLemore, the nationally syndicated columnist, put into words the extreme reaction against Attorney General Francis Biddle, whom Californians (probably with some prompting from the military and militant congressmen) had made the chief target of their ire. Biddle, McLemore reported, couldn't even win election as "third assistant dog catcher" in California. "Californians have the feeling," he explained, "that he is the one in charge of the Japanese menace, and that he is handling it with all the severity of Lord Fauntleroy."[37]

With this kind of encouragement in the background, Provost Marshal Gullion and his associates continued to press for mass action against the West Coast Japanese despite the fact that the officers of General Headquarters, directly under Marshall, were now trying to moderate anti-Japanese sentiment among members of Congress. On February 4, an impressive array of military personnel attended the meeting of West Coast congressmen: Admiral Harold R. Stark, Chief of Naval Operations; Brigadier General Mark W. Clark of General Headquarters (who had become Marshall's "expert" on the West Coast Japanese, even though just hours before he was to appear at the meeting he had to ask Bendetsen, "Now what is this Nisei?"); Colonel Hoyt S. Vandenberg of the Army Air Corps; and Colonel Wilton B. Persons, Chief of the (Congressional) Liaison Branch. According to Colonel Persons' report, Senator Rufus Holman of Oregon was the chief spokesman, and in pressing for an evacuation, he stressed the point that the people on the West Coast were "alarmed and terrified as to their person, their employment, and their homes." Clark then gave the congressmen the first truly military appraisal of the situation that they had received. Summarizing General Headquarters' findings, he told them that they were "unduly alarmed" and speculated that, at worst, there might be a sporadic air raid or a commando attack or two, and that while an attack on Alaska "was not a fantastic idea," there was no likelihood of a real onslaught on the West Coast states.[38]

The day after General Clark's moderate presentation, the Provost Marshal began to try to bring Assistant Secretary of War McCloy around to his point of view. On February 5 he wrote McCloy that although DeWitt had changed his mind, he (Gullion) was still of the view that mass evacuation was necessary. The DeWitt–Olson–Tom Clark idea of voluntary cooperation with Japanese American leaders, the Provost Marshal General denounced as "dangerous to rely upon. . . ." In a more detailed memo the following day (February 6) he warned McCloy of the possible grave consequences of inaction:

> If our production for war is seriously delayed by sabotage in the West Coastal states, we very possibly shall lose the war. . . . From reliable reports from military and other sources, the danger of Japanese inspired sabotage is great. . . . No half-way measures based upon considerations of economic disturbance, humanitarianism, or fear of retaliation will suffice. Such measures will be "too little or too late."

This shrewd appeal—"too little and too late" was a journalistic slogan that all too accurately described the general tenor of anti-Axis military efforts to that date—was followed by a concrete program that had been drawn up by Gullion and Bendetsen, and that the Provost Marshal General formally recommended. Somewhat short of total evacuation, it still would have involved moving the vast majority of West Coast Japanese. The plan consisted of four steps, as follows:

> *Step 1.* Declare restricted areas from which all alien enemies are barred. [This had already been done by Biddle, although it would not go into effect until February 24.]
>
> *Step 2.* Internment east of the Sierra Nevadas of *all* Japanese aliens, accompanied by such citizen members of their families as may volunteer for internment. [Since a majority of the Nisei were minors this would have included most of the citizen generation.]
>
> *Step 3.* The pass and permit system for "military reservations." [This would result, according to Gullion, in excluding citizens of Japanese extraction, "without raising too many legal questions."]
>
> *Step 4.* Resettlement. [Neither Gullion nor anyone else, as we shall see, had worked this out in any detail. According to the Provost Marshal General, it was "merely an idea and not an essential part of the plan."] [39]

By February 10, however, Gullion and Bendetsen, the latter now back on the West Coast to strengthen General DeWitt's resolve, seemed to have convinced McCloy, somehow, that a mass evacuation was necessary, although Secretary Stimson still clung to the idea of creating islands around strategic locations, an idea that the Provost Marshal General's men were sure he had gotten from General Stilwell. Bendetsen insisted that safety "islands" would not prevent sabotage: "if they wanted to sabotage that area, they could set the outside area on fire. They could still cut water lines and power lines." According to Bendetsen he had been over that ground twice with McCloy, who seemed to agree, and who had told Bendetsen that he would call him back after he had had another talk with the Secretary.[40]

The next day, February 11, 1942, was the real day of decision as far as the Japanese Americans were concerned. Sometime in the early afternoon, Secretary Stimson telephoned Franklin Roosevelt at the White House. Shortly after that call, McCloy phoned Bendetsen at the Presidio to tell him the good news. According to McCloy:

> . . . we talked to the President and the President, in substance, says go ahead and do anything you think necessary . . . if it involves citizens, we will take care of them too. He says there will probably be some repercussions, but it has got to be dictated by military necessity, but as he puts it, "Be as reasonable as you can."

McCloy went on to say that he thought the President would sign an executive order giving the Army the authority to evacuate. He also indicated there was at least some residual reluctance on the part of Secretary Stimson, who wanted to make a start in Los Angeles, concentrating on areas around the big bomber plants. McCloy indicated that he thought he could convince the Secretary that the limited plan was not practicable. In his conversation with McCloy, Bendetsen had talked about evacuating some 61,000 people, but in talking to Gullion about an hour later, he spoke of evacuating approximately 101,000 people.[41]

By February 11 the Provost Marshal's men had the situation all their own way. Assistant Secretary McCloy, who had been "pretty much against" their view just a week before, had been converted, and through him, Secretary Stimson and the President, although the latter probably did not take too much persuading. Bendetsen was again in San Francisco, and helping General DeWitt draft what the Western Defense commander called "the plan that Mr. McCloy wanted me to submit." Although, in retrospect, it seems clear that the struggle for mass evacuation was over by then, not all the participants knew it yet.

Among those in the dark were the staff at General Headquarters, particularly General Mark Clark who had been assigned to make the official military report on the advisability of mass evacuation. Early on February 12 he called DeWitt, and when told that an evacuation, to include citizens of Japanese descent, was in the works, he expressed disbelief. His own official memorandum, completed at about that time, had reached opposite conclusions, and deserves quoting at length, because it alone represents official military thinking on the subject.

General Clark's report concluded:

I cannot agree with the wisdom of such a mass exodus for the following reasons:

(*a*) We will never have a perfect defense against sabotage except at the expense of other equally important efforts. The situation with regards to protecting establishments from sabotage is analogous to protecting them from air attack by antiaircraft and barrage balloons. We will never have enough of these means to fully protect these establishments. Why, then, should we make great sacrifices in other efforts in order to make them secure from sabotage?

(*b*) We must weigh the advantages and disadvantages of such a wholesale solution to this problem. We must not permit our entire offensive effort to be sabotaged in an effort to protect all establishments from ground sabotage.

5. 1 recommend the following approach to this problem:

(*a*) Ascertain and designate the critical installations to be protected in each area and list them according to their importance.

(*b*) Make up our minds as to what means are available for such protection and apply that protection as far as it will go to the most critical objectives, leaving the ones of lesser importance for future consideration, or lesser protection.

(*c*) Select the most critical ones to be protected and delimit the essential areas around them for their protection.

(*d*) Eject all enemy aliens from those areas and permit entrance of others by pass only.

(*e*) Only such installations as can be physically protected in that manner should be included in this category. For example, it is practicable to do this in the case of the Boeing Plant, Bremerton Navy Yard and many other similar vital installations. In other words we are biting off a little at a time in the solution of the problem.

(*f*) Civilian police should be used to the maximum in effecting this protection.

(*g*) Federal Bureau of Investigation should be greatly augmented in counter-subversive activity.

(*h*) Raids should be used freely and frequently.

(*i*) Ring leaders and suspects should be interned liberally.

(*j*) This alien group should be made to understand through publicity that the first overt act on their part will bring a wave of counter-measures which will make the historical efforts of the vigilantes look puny in comparison.

6. It is estimated that to evacuate large numbers of this group will require one soldier to 4 or 5 aliens. This would require between 10,000 and 15,000 soldiers to guard the group during their internment, to say nothing of the continuing burden of protecting the installations. I feel that this problem

must be attacked in a sensible manner. We must admit that we are taking some chances just as we take other chances in war. We must determine what are our really critical installations, give them thorough protection and leave the others to incidental means in the hope that we will not lose too many of them — and above all keep our eye on the ball — that is, the creating and training of an offensive army.[42]

Here was truly "stern military necessity." The General Staff officer, who probably reflected Marshall's real view, would have moved very few Japanese, not because he was a defender of civil liberty, or even understood what the probabilities for sabotage really were, but because, it did not seem to him, on balance, that the "protection" which total evacuation would provide was worth its cost in military manpower and energy. But military views, as we have seen, were not the determinants of policy; political views were. The real architects of policy were the lawyers in uniform, Gullion and Bendetsen. Their most highly placed supporters, McCloy and Stimson, were two Republican, Wall Street lawyers.

Very late in the game, and often after the fact, a very few New Dealers tried to influence the President to take a more consistently democratic approach to the Japanese. On February 3 Archibald MacLeish, then Director of the Office of Facts and Figures, a predecessor of the Office of War Information, wrote one of Roosevelt's confidential secretaries suggesting that the President might want to try to hold down passions on the West Coast. His office, he said, was "trying to keep down the pressure out there." He enclosed, for the President, a statement of Woodrow Wilson's that he thought might be useful. During the other world war, Wilson had said, in a statement highly appropriate to the West Coast situation:

> . . . I can never accept any man as a champion of liberty either for ourselves or for the world who does not reverence and obey the laws of our beloved land, whose laws we ourselves have made. He has adopted the standards of the enemies of his country, whom he affects to despise.

Getting no response from the White House, MacLeish tried the Army six days later. "Dear Jack," the libertarian poet wrote McCloy, "In my opinion great care should be taken not to reach a grave decision in the present situation on the representations of officials and pressure groups alone. The decision may have far-reaching effects."[43]

MacLeish's efforts were, of course, fruitless. Much more influential was the authoritarian voice of America's chief pundit, Walter Lippmann. Writing from San Francisco in a column published on February 12, the usually detached observer who has so often been on the unpopular side of issues, was, in this instance, merely an extension of the mass West Coast mind. In an essay entitled "The Fifth Column on the Coast," Lippmann wrote:

> . . . the Pacific Coast is in imminent danger of a combined attack from within and without. . . . It is a fact that the Japanese navy has been reconnoitering the coast more or less continuously. . . . There is an assumption [in Washington] that a citizen may not be interfered with unless he has committed an overt act. . . . The Pacific Coast is officially a combat zone: Some part of it may at any moment be a battlefield. And nobody ought to be on a battlefield who has no good reason for being there. There is plenty of room elsewhere for him to exercise his rights.

The pundit's thinkpiece drew a lot of notice. Westbrook Pegler, delighted at finding a respectable man urging what he had long urged, chortled:

> Do you get what he says? This is a high-grade fellow with a heavy sense of responsibility. . . . The Japanese in California should be under armed guard to the last man and woman right now [even Pegler didn't like to talk about children]—and to hell with habeas corpus until the danger is over. . . . If it isn't true, we can take it out on Lippmann, but on his reputation I will bet it is all true.

In the War Department, Marshall sent a copy of Lippmann's column to Stimson, and Stimson sent it to McCloy, and it was undoubtedly read in the White House.[44] It was read in the Justice Department too. Long-suffering Attorney General Francis Biddle, former law clerk to Justice Holmes, civil libertarian and New Dealer, was finally stirred to respond by Lippmann's column. In his memoirs, published in 1962, deeply regretting the whole affair, Biddle wrote:

> . . . if, instead of dealing almost exclusively with McCloy and Bendetsen, I had urged [Stimson] to resist the pressure of his subordinates, the result might have been different. But I was new to the Cabinet, and disinclined to insist on my view to an elder statesman whose wisdom and integrity I greatly respected.[45]

What Biddle did not reveal, however, was that he himself had given Stimson a kind of green light. In a letter written on February 12, the Attorney General voiced his distaste for the proposed evacuation, particularly of citizens, but assured Stimson that

> I have no doubt that the Army can legally, at any time, evacuate all persons in a specified territory if such action is deemed essential from a military point

of view. . . . No legal problem arises when Japanese citizens are evacuated, but American citizens of Japanese origin could not, in my opinion, be singled out of an area and evacuated with the other Japanese.

Then Biddle, Philadelphia lawyer that he was, told Stimson how he thought it could be done.

However, the result might be accomplished by evacuating all persons in the area and then licensing back those whom the military authorities thought were not objectionable from a military point of view.[46]

Five days later, on February 17, Biddle addressed a memorandum to the President, a memorandum that was, in effect, a last-gasp effort to stop the mass evacuation that was being planned. Biddle apparently was unaware that Roosevelt had given Stimson and McCloy the go-ahead signal almost a week before. The Attorney General opened with a statement about the various West Coast pressure groups and congressmen who were urging the evacuation. He then singled out Lippmann and Pegler, and argued that their concern about imminent invasion and sabotage was not borne out by the facts. Biddle then maintained, rather curiously, that "there [was] no dispute between the War, Navy and Justice Departments," and warned that the evacuation of 93,000 Japanese in California would disrupt agriculture, require thousands of troops, tie up transportation, and raise very difficult questions of resettlement. Then, in an apparent approval of evacuation, Biddle wrote, "If complete confusion and lowering of morale is to be avoided, so large a job must be done after careful planning."

Then, in a parting blast, directed specifically at Lippmann, Biddle attacked columnists acting as "Armchair Strategists and Junior G-Men," suggested that they were essentially "shouting FIRE! in a crowded theater," and warned that if race riots occurred, Lippmann and the others would bear a heavy responsibility.[47]

But Biddle could have directed his attack much closer to home. Not only his Cabinet colleagues but some of his subordinates were doing more than shouting. Three days before the Attorney General's letter, Tom C. Clark, of his staff, assured a Los Angeles press conference that the federal government would soon evacuate over 200,000 enemy aliens and their children, including all American-born Japanese, from areas in California vital to national defense.[48]

On February 13, the Pacific Coast Congressional delegation forwarded to the President a recommendation for evacuation that was fully in line with what Stimson and McCloy were proposing. They recommended, unanimously:

> the immediate evacuation of all persons of Japanese lineage and all others, aliens and citizens alike, whose presence shall be deemed dangerous or inimical to the defense of the United States from all strategic areas . . . such areas [should] be enlarged as expeditiously as possible until they shall encompass the entire strategic areas of the states of California, Oregon and Washington, and the Territory of Alaska.[49]

Finally, on Thursday, February 19, 1942, a day that should live in infamy, Franklin D. Roosevelt signed an Executive Order that gave the Army, through the Secretary of War, the authority that Gullion and Bendetsen had sought so long. Using as justification a military necessity for "the successful prosecution of the war," the President empowered the military to designate "military areas" from which "any or all persons may be excluded" and to provide for such persons "transportation, food, shelter, and other accommodations as may be necessary . . . until other arrangements are made." The words Japanese or Japanese Americans never even appear in the order; but it was they, and they alone, who felt its sting.[50]

The myth of military necessity was used as a fig leaf for a particular variant of American racism. On the very day that the President signed the order, a conference at General Headquarters heard and approved an opposite opinion. Army Intelligence reported, officially, that it believed "mass evacuation unnecessary." In this instance, at least, the military mind was superior to the political: the soldiers who opposed the evacuation were right and the politicians who proposed it were wrong. But, why did it happen?

Two major theories have been propounded by scholars which ought to be examined. Almost as the evacuation was taking place, administrators and faculty at the University of California at Berkeley took steps to set up a scholarly study of the relocation in all its aspects. With generous foundation support and with the cooperation of some of the federal officials most responsible for the decision (for example, John J. McCloy), the "Japanese American Evacuation and Resettlement Study" was set up under the directorship of Dorothy Swaine Thomas, then a University of California Professor of Rural Sociology and a skilled demographer. Her staff included a broad spectrum of social scientists, but curiously did not include either professional historians or archivists. Professor Thomas' own volumes did not seek to determine responsibility for the evacuation, but two volumes that flowed out of the project did: Morton Grodzins, *Americans Betrayed* (Chicago, 1949) and Jacobus tenBroek, Edward N. Barnhart, and Floyd Matson, *Prejudice, War, and the Constitution* (Berkeley and Los Angeles, 1954). Grodzins felt that the major cause of the evacuation was the pressure exerted by special interest groups within California and on the Pacific Coast generally. The "western group," he wrote, "was successful in having a program molded to its own immediate advantage made national policy." Professors tenBroek, Barnhart, and Matson vigorously disputed the Grodzins thesis: for them, the responsibility was General DeWitt's, and, they argued, his decision was based essentially on his "military estimate of the situation."[51]

Five years later a professional historian, Stetson Conn, then a civilian historian for the Department of the Army and later the Army's Chief of Military History, published an authoritative account of what really happened, as far as the military was concerned. He found in the contemporary evidence "little support for the argument that military necessity required a mass evacuation" and pointed, accurately, to the machinations of Gullion and Bendetsen and their success in bending the civilian heads of the War Department to their will.

The question that remains to be answered is why the recommendation of Stimson and McCloy was accepted by the nation. Grodzins' pressure groups were, of course, important, but even more important than the peculiar racism of a region was the general racist character of American society. The decision to evacuate the Japanese was popular, not only in California and the West, but in the entire nation, although only on the West Coast was it a major issue in early 1942.

The leader of the nation was, in the final analysis, responsible. It was Franklin Roosevelt, who in one short telephone call, passed the decision-making power to two men who had never been elected to any office, saying only, with the politician's charm and equivocation: "Be as reasonable as you can." Why did he agree? Probably for two reasons: in the first place, it was expedient; in the second place, Roosevelt himself harbored deeply felt anti-Japanese prejudices.

As to expediency, it is important to remember what the war news was like in early 1942. It was a very bad time for the military fortunes of the United States and its allies. The Japanese had landed on the island of Singapore on February 8, on New Britain on the 9th, and were advancing rapidly in Burma. Roosevelt was concerned, first of all with winning the war, and secondly with unity at home, so that he, unlike his former chief, Woodrow Wilson, could win the peace with the advice and consent of the Senate. He could read the Congressional signs well and knew that cracking down on the Japanese Americans would be popular both on the Hill and in the country generally. And the last thing he wanted was a rift with establishment Republicans like Stimson and McCloy; New Dealers like Biddle and MacLeish could be counted on not to rock the boat.

But, in addition, Franklin Roosevelt was himself convinced that Japanese, alien and citizen, were dangerous to American security. He, along with several members of his Cabinet and circle of advisers, persistently pushed for mass internment of the Hawaiian Japanese Americans long after the military had wisely rejected such a policy. And there was a kind of rationale for such a policy. If Japanese were a threat to security in California, where they represented fewer than 2 percent of the population, certainly in war-torn Hawaii, where they were more than a third of the population, they should have constituted a real menace. But it is one thing to incarcerate a tiny element of the population, as was done on the West Coast, and quite another to put away a sizable fraction of the whole. Apart from the sheer size of the problem, relatively and absolutely, there was the question of the disruption that such a mass evacuation would cause in the local economy. Referring to Oahu alone, Lieutenant General Delos C. Emmons, the Army commander there, pointed out to the War Department in January 1942 that Japanese provided the bulk of the main island's skilled labor force and were indispensable unless replaced by an equivalent labor force from the mainland. In addition, the logistical problems of internment in the islands were so great that Emmons recommended that any evacuation and relocation be to the mainland.

At the Cabinet level, however, different views were held. On February 27, for example, Navy Secretary Knox, the most vocal Japanophobe in the Cabinet, suggested rounding up all the Japanese on Oahu and putting them under Army guard on the neighboring island of Molokai, better known as a leper colony. Stimson concurred as to the danger, but insisted that if they were to be moved they be sent to the states. (The shipping situation, for all practical purposes, made this impossible.) The President, according to Stimson, clearly favored Knox's plan.[52] The President and his Navy Secretary, continued to press for this policy well into 1942, but eventually were forestalled by a strongly worded joint recommendation to the contrary signed by both Chief of Staff Marshall and Chief of Naval Operations Admiral Ernest J. King.[53] In other words, real rather than imaginary military necessity governed in Hawaii. Although Hawaii was the first real theater of war, fewer than 2,000 of the territory's 150,000 Japanese were ever deprived of their liberty.

Notes

1. Telephone conversation, Bendetsen and Meredith, December 7, 1941, Provost Marshal General, Record Group 389, National Archives: *Congressional Record,* 77th Cong., pp. 9603, 9808–09; see also pp. 9631 and 9958.

2. Contained in a collection of letters from Poston, Bancroft Library.

3. Stetson Conn, "The Decision to Evacuate the Japanese from the Pacific Coast," in Kent Roberts Greenfield, ed., *Command Decisions* (New York: Harcourt, 1959), p. 92.

4. Telephone conversations, Gullion and DeWitt, December 26, 1941; and DeWitt and Lerch, January 1, 1942, Stetson Conn, "Notes," Office, Chief of Military History, U.S. Army.

5. Notes on January 4, 1942, conference, Stetson Conn, "Notes."

6. Telephone conversation, McCloy and DeWitt, February 3, 1942, Assistant Secretary of War, Record Group 107, National Archives. For clarity, certain portions of McCloy's rambling conversation have been transposed. To the final remark quoted above, DeWitt responded, "Out here, Mr. Secretary, a Jap is a Jap to these people now."

7. Letters, Ford to Stimson, January 16, 1942; and Stimson to Ford, January 26, 1942, Secretary of War, Record Group 107, National Archives.

8. Memo, January 10, 1942, by J. Murray Thompson et al.

9. Letter, Wickard to Stimson, January 16, 1942, in Records of the Secretary of Agriculture, Foreign Relations 2–1. Aliens-Refugees 1942, Record Group 16, National Archives. For a fascinating glimpse of how the evacuation looked to a liberal Department of Agriculture staffer, see Laurence Hewes, *Boxcar in the Sand* (New York, 1957), pp. 151–175.

10. Sakamoto's statement enclosed in letter, William Hosokawa to Cordell Hull, January 23, 1942, Secretary of War, Record Group 107, National Archives.

11. Telephone conversation, Bendetsen and DeWitt, January 24, 1942, Provost Marshal General, Record Group 389, National Archives.

12. The entire report is published in *Pearl Harbor Attack: Hearings before the Joint Committee on the Investigation of the Pearl Harbor Attack,* Pt. 39, pp. 1–21 (Washington, 1946). The quotation is from p. 12.

13. Justice Department Press Release, January 29, 1942, in *House Report No. 2124,* 77th Cong., 2d Sess., p. 302. Thirty-two basic documents relating to the evacuation are conveniently assembled here.

14. Memo, Mark W. Clark to Deputy Chief of Staff, January 26, 1942, The Adjutant General, Record Group 407, National Archives.

15. Telephone conversation, DeWitt and Bendetsen, January 29, 1942, Provost Marshal General, Record Group 389, National Archives.

16. Telephone conversation, DeWitt and Gullion, January 30, 1942, Provost Marshal General, Record Group 389, National Archives.

17. Telephone conversation, DeWitt and Bendetsen, January 29, 1942, Provost Marshal General, Record Group 389, National Archives.

18. Memo, General Marshall to General Eisenhower, January 30, 1942, Secretary of War, Record Group 107, National Archives; Conn, "The Hawaiian Defenses after Pearl Harbor," p. 207, in Stetson Conn, Rose C. Engleman, and Byron Fairchild, *United States Army in World War II: The Western Hemisphere: Guarding the United States and Its Outposts* (Washington: Government Printing Office, 1964).

19. Telephone conversation, Bendetsen and DeWitt, January 30, 1942, Provost Marshal General, Record Group 389, National Archives.

20. Ibid.

21. Letter, Lea to Stimson, January 30, 1942, Secretary of War, Record Group 107, National Archives.

22. Telephone conversation, DeWitt and Gullion, January 30, 1942, Provost Marshal General, Record Group 389, National Archives.

23. Bendetson, Memo for the Adjutant General, January 31, 1942, The Adjutant General, Record Group 407, National Archives.

24. Telephone conversations, DeWitt and Gullion, January 31, 1942; and DeWitt and Gullion and Bendetsen, February 1, 1942, Provost Marshal General, Record Group 389, National Archives.

25. Ibid. and telephone conversation, Gullion and Mark W. Clark, February 4, 1942, Provost Marshal General, Record Group 389, National Archives.

26. Telephone conversation, Bendetsen and Colonel Stroh, February 2, 1942, Provost Marshal General, Record Group 389, National Archives.

27. Telephone conversation, McCloy and DeWitt, February 3, 1942, Assistant Secretary of War, Record Group 107, National Archives.

28. Telephone conversation, Marshall and DeWitt, February 3, 1942, Secretary of War, Record Group 107, National Archives.

29. Telephone conversation, Gullion and Mark W. Clark, February 4, 1942, Provost Marshal General, Record Group 389, National Archives.

30. Telephone conversation, DeWitt and Bendetsen, February 7, 1942, Provost Marshal General, Record Group 389, National Archives.

31. Telephone conversation, DeWitt and Gullion, February 5, 1942, Provost Marshal General, Record Group 389, National Archives.

32. Conn, "Japanese Evacuation from the West Coast," p. 128.

33. Letters, Johnson to Rufus Holman, February 3, 1942; and Johnson to Frank P. Doherty, February 16, 1942, Johnson Mss., Pt. III, Box 19, Bancroft Library.

34. Speech text, February 4, 1942, Carton 5, Olson Mss., Bancroft Library.

35. Bowron speech and statement in *Congressional Record,* February 9, 1942, pp. A547–48.

36. Material on the meeting of law enforcement officers from California reports of the Office of Government Reports for January and February, 1942, Record Group 44, Washington National Records Center, Suitland, Md.

37. Ibid.

38. Memo for record by Persons, February 6, 1942, Stetson Conn, "Notes," Office, Chief of Military History, U.S. Army.

39. Memo, Gullion to McCloy, February 5, 1942; letter, Gullion to McCloy, February 6, 1942, Assistant Secretary of War, Record Group 107, National Archives.

40. Telephone conversation, Gullion and Bendetsen, February 10, 1942, Provost Marshal General, Record Group 389, National Archives.

41. Conn, "Japanese Evacuation from the West Coast," pp. 131–32; telephone conversations, McCloy and Bendetsen, Bendetsen and Gullion, February 11, 1942, Stetson Conn, "Notes."

42. Mark W. Clark Memo, General Headquarters, n.d. but ca. February 12, 1942, Stetson Conn, "Notes."

43. Letters, MacLeish to Grace Tully, February 3, 1942, President's Personal File 1820, Franklin D. Roosevelt Library, Hyde Park; MacLeish to McCloy, February 9, 1942, Assistant Secretary of War, Record Group 107, National Archives.

44. Lippmann column and memo slips in Secretary of War, Record Group 107, National Archives; Pegler's column, *Washington Post,* February 15, 1942, as cited in *Congressional Record,* February 17, 1942, pp. 568–69.

45. Francis B. Biddle, *In Brief Authority* (New York: Doubleday, 1962), p. 226.

46. Letter, Biddle to Stimson, February 12, 1942, Secretary of War, Record Group 107, National Archives.

47. Letter, Biddle to Franklin D. Roosevelt, February 17, 1942, Franklin D. Roosevelt Library, Hyde Park.

48. *Los Angeles Times,* February 15, 1942.

49. "Recommendations" in Assistant Secretary of War, Record Group 107, National Archives.

50. Executive Order No. 9066, February 19, 1942, in *House Report No. 2124,* 77th Cong., 2d Sess., pp. 314–15.

51. For a good summary, see Chapter IV, "Two Theories of Responsibility," pp. 185–210 in Jacobus tenBroek, Edward N. Barnhart, and Floyd W. Matson, *Prejudice, War, and the Constitution* (Berkeley and Los Angeles: University of California Press, 1954).

52. Conn, "The Hawaiian Defenses after Pearl Harbor," pp. 207–10.

53. See, for example, letter, Knox to Franklin D. Roosevelt, October 17, 1942, copy in Secretary of War, Record Group 107, National Archives; and Franklin D. Roosevelt, autograph memo to Stimson and Marshall, November 2, 1942, Secretary of War, Record Group 107, National Archives. The King-Marshall memo, July 15, 1942, is in President's Secretary File, Franklin D. Roosevelt Library, Hyde Park.

2. What caused the Supreme Court to affirm the constitutionality of internment?

Peter Irons

Gordon Hirabayashi v. United States: "A Jap's a Jap"

During Peter Irons's first year at Antioch College, his father, a nuclear engineer who helped build H-bomb plants, died. Irons would later say, "It seems probable that I had picked up from him, very indirectly, his revulsion toward nuclear weapons and his inner agony over his role in developing them." Joining a socialist discussion group and an "informal pacifist group," Irons "wound up with a Gandhian pacifism and an admiration for native American socialism and anarcho-syndicalism." After participating in a Student Nonviolent Coordinating Committee (SNCC) conference in Atlanta in 1960, he regularly picketed suburban movie theaters that discriminated against African Americans and was arrested for sitting in at a suburban Maryland bowling alley. In October 1960, the twenty-year-old Irons sent back his draft card, explaining, "I wouldn't fight as a Gandhian," and "I felt the need to make a symbolic break with a country which oppressed blacks." Later that same month, he gave a speech and distributed a pamphlet calling for a mass draft card return before the Student Peace Union at Oberlin College. Six years later, Irons went to prison for resisting the draft. After serving a twenty-six-month sentence, he was released in February 1969.[1]

The day after he got out of prison, Irons entered graduate school. After reading Howard Zinn's *SNCC: The New Abolitionists* (1965), he began corresponding with the radical scholar, who also had a history of civil rights and antiwar activism. With Zinn's help, he was accepted into the political science program at Boston University and received his Ph.D. in 1973. After graduating from Harvard Law School in 1978, he became a member of the state and federal bars. The draft protester and convict had become a lawyer and a legal historian.

The New Deal Lawyers, Peter Irons's first book, was published in 1982. A year earlier, he had begun research on the FBI for a second book. But he was dismayed to learn that the thousands of rolls of FBI microfilm were not yet indexed. Remembering the Japanese American internment cases from his law school days, he strolled over to the Library of Congress, looked up "internment" in the card catalog, and was pleased to see few recent works listed. Taking advantage of the 1976 Freedom of Information Act, Irons ordered several boxes of documents on the internment cases from the Justice Department. Originally, as he explains in the preface to *Justice at War: The Story of the Japanese American Internment Cases* (1983), he planned to write a book about lawyers:

> My focus was less on the four test case challengers or the nine Supreme Court justices than on the forty lawyers who participated on both sides of the Japanese American cases. My interest was in examining the different legal strategies and tactics these lawyers employed in wrestling with important and unsettled issues of constitutional law, viewed against a backdrop of wartime pressures and passions.

Irons never expected that his research would help rectify a wartime injustice. But as luck would have it, the first file Irons examined contained a shocking revelation: Lawyers at the Justice Department had accused their superiors of suppressing evidence and presenting to the Supreme Court a military report containing "lies" and "intentional falsehoods." Irons found evidence that Justice Department lawyers who had prepared briefs to defend internment before the Supreme Court had learned that General John L. DeWitt and other government officials knew of intelligence reports undermining their claims of "military necessity." Lawyers such as Edward Ennis and John Burling then realized that DeWitt had deliberately excluded the FBI and Naval Intelligence reports advising against internment from his Final Report. The lawyers also discovered that DeWitt knew that the Federal Communications Commission had found no evidence of Japanese Americans using radio transmitters to signal from shore to Japanese ships. Nevertheless, DeWitt had tried to justify internment with charges of "shore-to-ship signalling." Ennis and Burling considered disclosing this information to the Supreme Court, but they ultimately bowed to War Department pressure, withheld the evidence, and misrepresented their cases before the Court.

Outraged by what he deemed a "legal scandal without precedent in the history of American law," Irons contacted the three Japanese Americans — Gordon Hirabayashi, Minoru Yasui, and Fred Korematsu — who had been convicted of violating the curfew, exclusion, and internment orders during the war. After showing them this new evidence, he agreed to represent them and filed suits to reverse their criminal convictions. Irons and a team of Japanese American lawyers used an obscure provision of federal law — a "petition for a writ of error *coram nobis*"* — to reopen their cases. The lawyers charged that the original trials had been tainted by "fundamental error" and had resulted in convictions of "manifest injustice."

The selection presented here, "*Gordon Hirabayashi v. United States:* 'A Jap's a Jap,'" reviews Hirabayashi's wartime challenge of military curfew and exclusion orders and the Supreme Court decisions upholding these orders. Irons also describes how his discovery of the "suppression of evidence" before the Supreme Court caused him to urge Hirabayashi, Yasui, and Korematsu to reopen their cases in the 1980s. This account illustrates the impact scholarship and activism can have on the public record. Irons's research and Hirabayashi's effort to clear his name helped energize the movement for redress for all former internees. In 1981, both testified about their experiences before the Commission on Wartime Relocation and Internment of Civilians. The press coverage surrounding the *coram nobis* cases also aroused more public and political support for redress.

Besides *Justice at War* and *The Courage of Their Convictions* (1988; from which this selection is taken), Irons has published *Justice Delayed: The Record of the Japanese American Internment Cases* (1989). He has served two terms on the

**coram nobis:* an order by a court of appeals to a court that rendered judgment requiring the trial court to consider facts not in the trial record that might have resulted in a different judgment if known at the time of the trial.

national board of the American Civil Liberties Union and is currently a professor of political science and director of the Earl Warren Bill of Rights Project. Like Roger Daniels, he continues to remind all Americans of the injustice of Japanese American internment in speeches, articles, books, and historical exhibits.

Gordon Hirabayashi served an eighty-day sentence following his conviction for violation of the curfew and exclusion orders in 1942. Afterward, he continued his college studies, specializing in sociology. He received a bachelor's degree in 1946, a master's degree in 1949, and a Ph.D. in 1952, all from the University of Washington. His first teaching job was at the American University of Beirut, where he served as chair of the sociology department. He later served as assistant director of the Social Research Center and headed the Department of Sociology and Anthropology at the American University in Cairo. In 1959, he accepted a position at the University of Alberta, where he served as the longtime chair of the Department of Sociology and Anthropology. A pioneer in Canadian ethnic studies, he helped develop the social sciences in Alberta and throughout Canada. Now retired, he continues to speak about his case, redress, and other human rights issues to groups across North America.

Questions for a Closer Reading

1. Why did Gordon Hirabayashi decide to defy the curfew and exclusion orders? What would you have done if you had been in his position in 1942?
2. How did Judge Lloyd Black and the members of the U.S. Supreme Court justify their decisions in Hirabayashi's case and the cases of the other wartime challengers? How did these decisions affect views of military authority, due process, and constitutional rights?
3. Imagine that Justice Department lawyers such as Edward Ennis provided full disclosure of the evidence they found to the Supreme Court. What impact do you think this might have had on the Court's decision?
4. Gordon Hirabayashi wrote an essay titled "Am I an American?" Compare the way the courts answered this question in 1943 and 1987. What changes in American society, cul-

ture, and politics might explain these different definitions of what it means to be an "American"?

5. Peter Irons's research changed Hirabayashi's life. Do you think this situation reflects the potential for historical scholarship to affect contemporary lives, or was it an unusual case? Explain.

Note

1. Michael Ferber and Staughton Lynd, *The Resistance* (Boston: Beacon Press, 1971), pp. 12–13.

Gordon Hirabayashi v. United States: "A Jap's a Jap"

On the morning of May 16, 1942, Gordon Kiyoshi Hirabayashi arrived at the FBI office in Seattle, Washington. Somewhat formal in demeanor, the University of Washington senior shook hands with Special Agent Francis V. Manion and introduced his companion, Arthur Barnett, a young lawyer and fellow member of Seattle's Quaker community. Five days earlier, Gordon had defied a military order that required "all persons of Japanese ancestry" to register for evacuation to the state fairground at Puyallup, south of Seattle. From this temporary home, where Army troops herded them into cattle stalls and tents, the uprooted Japanese Americans would be shipped to "relocation centers" in desolate areas of desert or swampland, from California to Arkansas. Forced into exile, more than 120,000 Americans of Japanese ancestry endured wartime internment in America's concentration camps, housed in tarpaper barracks and guarded by armed soldiers.

After a few minutes of small talk, Gordon handed Agent Manion a neatly typed four-page document, headed "Why I refused to register for evacuation." Gordon's statement reflected his anguish as a Quaker volunteer over

Peter Irons, *Gordon Hirabayashi v. United States:* "A Jap's a Jap," in *The Courage of Their Convictions*, ed. Peter Irons (New York: The Free Press, 1988), 37–62.

moving evacuees to the Puyallup fairground. "This order for the mass evacuation of all persons of Japanese descent denies them the right to live," he wrote. "It forces thousands of energetic, law-abiding individuals to exist in a miserable psychological, and a horrible physical, atmosphere." Gordon pointed out that native-born American citizens like himself constituted a majority of the evacuees, yet their rights "are denied on a wholesale scale without due process of law and civil liberties." His statement ended on a defiant note: "If I were to register and cooperate under those circumstances, I would be giving helpless consent to the denial of practically all of the things which give me incentive to live. I must maintain my Christian principles. I consider it my duty to maintain the democratic standards for which this nation lives. Therefore, I must refuse this order for evacuation."

After reading the statement, Manion reminded Gordon that he risked a year's imprisonment for his stand. Gordon remained adamant, even after Manion drove him to the registration center and offered a last chance to sign the forms. When they returned to the FBI office, Manion conferred with the U.S. attorney, who then filed criminal charges against Gordon for violating the evacuation order.

After placing his prisoner in the King County jail, Manion dug into Gordon's briefcase and discovered a diary that confessed his violation of the military curfew orders that kept Japanese Americans off the streets in the weeks before evacuation. "Peculiar, but I receive a lift — perhaps it is a release — when I consciously break the silly old curfew," Gordon wrote one night after escorting his friend Helen Blom to her home. Manion reported his find to the U.S. attorney, who promptly filed an additional criminal charge against Gordon for curfew violation.

The wartime internment of Japanese Americans began soon after the Japanese attack on Pearl Harbor of December 7, 1941. After an initial period of tolerance and press reminders that most residents of Japanese ancestry were "good Americans, born and educated as such," public pressure mounted for their mass removal from coastal states. Fueled by past decades of "Yellow Peril" agitation, and current fears of a follow-up "sneak attack" upon the American mainland, this campaign enlisted politicians and pundits. Los Angeles congressman Leland Ford urged in mid-January, 1942, that "all Japanese, whether citizens or not, be placed in inland concentration camps." The next month, right-wing columnist Westbrook Pegler demanded that Japanese Americans be placed "under armed guard to the last man and woman right now — and to hell with habeas corpus until the danger is over."

Despite these incendiary appeals, federal officials charged with protecting the Pacific coast from sabotage and espionage saw no reason for mass evacuation. Acting on orders from Attorney General Francis Biddle, FBI agents arrested more than two thousand Japanese aliens in the days after Pearl Harbor. Justice Department officers conducted individual loyalty hearings for this group; most were promptly released and returned to their families. The FBI also investigated hundreds of Army reports of signals to enemy submarines off the coast by lights or illicit radios, and dismissed each report as unfounded. FBI director J. Edgar Hoover reported that "the army was getting a bit hysterical" in blaming the phantom lights on Japanese Americans.

Attorney General Biddle, with Hoover's reports in hand, assured President Franklin Roosevelt on February 7 that Army officials had offered "no reasons for mass evacuation" as a military measure. Secretary of War Henry Stimson, a respected elder statesman in Roosevelt's wartime cabinet, shared Biddle's concerns: "We cannot discriminate among our citizens on the ground of racial origin," Stimson wrote in early February. Any forced removal of Japanese Americans, he noted, would tear "a tremendous hole in our constitutional system." Stimson felt that internment on racial grounds would conflict with the Due Process clause of the Fifth Amendment, which required formal charges and trial before any person could be deprived of "liberty" and confined by the government.

Within days of these statements, Biddle and Stimson capitulated to the advocates of internment. Three of Stimson's War Department subordinates combined to overcome his constitutional qualms. Stimson had asked his deputy, John J. McCloy, to frame a "final recommendation" on the treatment of Japanese Americans. McCloy, who scornfully dismissed the Constitution as "a piece of paper" which military officials could tear into shreds, later defended the internment as "retribution" for the Japanese attack on Pearl Harbor.

Colonel Karl Bendetsen, the young lawyer whom McCloy had delegated to draft the report to Stimson, exemplified the persistence of racial stereotypes: "The Japanese race is an enemy race," Bendetsen wrote over the signature of General John L. DeWitt, the West Coast Army commander. Even among those born in the United States, Bendetsen argued, "the racial strains are undiluted." General DeWitt hardly bothered to mask his racial prejudice. Regardless of citizenship, DeWitt bluntly told a congressional panel, "a Jap's a Jap."

The fate of Japanese Americans was sealed at a showdown meeting on February 17, 1942. McCloy and Bendetsen presented Attorney General Biddle with a proposed presidential order, providing that "any or all persons may be excluded" from their homes on military order. Biddle's deputy, Edward Ennis, heatedly opposed the War Department proposal on constitutional grounds, but arguments of "military necessity" finally persuaded the Attorney General. Two days later, President Roosevelt signed Executive

Order 9066 and General DeWitt assigned Colonel Bendetsen to implement the evacuation and internment plans.

Gordon Hirabayashi languished in the King County jail for five months before his trial on October 20, 1942. Judge Lloyd Black, a former state prosecutor and American Legion post commander, had already dismissed the constitutional challenge filed by Gordon's trial lawyer, Frank Walters, who argued that the Constitution barred any form of racial discrimination. Rejecting this "technical interpretation" of the Fifth Amendment, Black answered that individual rights "should not be permitted to endanger all of the constitutional rights of the whole citizenry" during wartime. Judge Black added a large dose of racism to his opinion. Branding the Japanese as "unbelievably treacherous and wholly ruthless," he conjured up "suicide parachutists" who would drop from the skies onto Seattle's aircraft factories. Black predicted that these airborne invaders would seek "human camouflage and with uncanny skill discover and take advantage of any disloyalty among their kind." The military curfew and evacuation orders, he concluded, were reasonable protections against the "diabolically clever use of infiltration tactics" by potential Japanese saboteurs.

After this opinion, Gordon's trial became a perfunctory exercise. Gordon admitted his intentional violation of the curfew and evacuation orders, and explained to the all-male, elderly jurors his belief that "I should be given the privileges of a citizen" under the Constitution, regardless of his race or ancestry. The government prosecutor, Allen Pomeroy, called Gordon's father as a prosecution witness, hoping that his halting English would remind the jurors of Gordon's ties to the Japanese enemy. Gordon's parents, brought to court from a California internment camp, spent two weeks in the King County jail on Judge Black's order.

After the trial testimony ended, Frank Walters told the jurors that "I am not representing a man who violated a valid law of the United States" and restated his attack on the racial basis of the military orders. Asking the jurors to convict Gordon, Allen Pomeroy reminded them of his Japanese ancestry and warned that "if we don't win this war with Japan there will be no trial by jury."

Judge Black sent the jurors to their deliberations with an instruction that the military orders were "valid and enforceable" laws. Whether Gordon had violated the orders was the only question for decision. Black answered for the jurors, telling them that "you are instructed to return a finding of guilty" on both criminal counts. The dutiful jurors returned in ten minutes with the proper verdicts, and Black sentenced Gordon to concurrent sentences of three months in jail for each conviction. Frank Walter stated his intention to appeal the convictions, and Gordon returned to jail after Judge Black denied his request for release on bail until the appeal was decided.

Before the U.S. Court of Appeals met in San Francisco to hear Gordon's appeal, two other internment challenges reached the appellate judges. Minoru Yasui, a young Oregon lawyer and Army reserve officer, had been convicted of curfew violation and sentenced to the maximum term of one year in jail. Before his trial, Yasui had spent nine months in solitary confinement. Fred Korematsu, a shipyard welder in the San Francisco area, had volunteered for Navy service before the Pearl Harbor attack but was rejected on medical grounds. Korematsu evaded the evacuation order for two months, hoping to remain with his Caucasian fiancée, but was caught and sentenced to a five-year probationary term in an internment camp.

The Court of Appeals met for argument on the three cases on February 19, 1943, the first anniversary of President Roosevelt's internment order. Five weeks later, the appellate judges sent the cases to the Supreme Court without decision, under the little-used procedure of "certification" of questions,* over the protest of Judge William Denman, who denounced the "war-haste" with which the cases were being rushed to judgment. Denman's colleagues confessed that the question of "whether this exercise of the war power can be reconciled with traditional standards of personal liberty and freedom guaranteed by the Constitution, is most difficult."

Before the Supreme Court met to consider the cases, government lawyers fought a spirited, but unseen, battle over the evidence the justices should consider in making their decision. Solicitor General Charles Fahy delegated the task of preparing the government's briefs to Edward Ennis, who had earlier waged a futile battle against internment. During his preparation, Ennis discovered an official report of the Office of Naval Intelligence on the loyalty of Japanese Americans. Prepared by Kenneth Ringle, a Navy commander who spoke fluent Japanese, this lengthy report concluded that "less than three percent" of the entire group posed any potential threat and noted that FBI agents had already arrested most of these suspects. The Ringle report, circulated to Army officials before the evacuation began, urged that Japanese Americans be given individual loyalty hearings and that mass internment be avoided.

Ennis recognized the significance of this document and promptly informed Solicitor General Fahy that the government had "a duty to advise the Court of the existence of the Ringle memorandum" and the Army's knowledge of its conclusions. "It occurs to me that any other course of conduct might approximate the suppression of evidence," Ennis warned his superior. Fahy ignored this red-flag request.

* *"certification of questions":* Method of taking a case from the U.S. Court of Appeals to the Supreme Court in which a former court may certify any question of law in any civil or criminal case as to which instructions are requested.

When the Supreme Court convened on May 10, 1943, Fahy suggested that doubts about the loyalty of Japanese Americans had justified the military curfew and evacuation orders. These doubts made it "not unreasonable" for military officials "to fear that in case of an invasion there would be among this group of people a number of persons who might assist the enemy." Having planted the seed of genetic guilt, Fahy left it to germinate in the minds of the nine justices.

Just a week before meeting to decide the internment cases, the justices had issued bitterly divided opinions in the *Barnette* flag-salute case. Voiding the expulsion from public schools of Jehovah's Witnesses who objected on religious grounds to compulsory flag-salute laws, the Supreme Court majority had overturned its *Gobitis* decision, issued in 1940. Chief Justice Harlan Fiske Stone, who succeeded Charles Evans Hughes in 1941, hoped to heal the wounds of this fratricidal battle and urged his colleagues to join a unanimous opinion in the internment cases. The justices had earlier returned the Korematsu case to the court of appeals for decision on a technical issue, and the Yasui case was complicated by the trial judge's ruling that the defendant had lost his American citizenship. Gordon Hirabayashi's appeal thus became the vehicle for weighing "war powers" against "due process" in the constitutional scale.

Speaking first at the conference table, Stone placed a heavy thumb on the scale. Admitting that the military orders imposed "discrimination" on American citizens on racial grounds, he suggested that the Pearl Harbor attack showed the "earmarks of treachery" among Japanese Americans. Military officials had simply responded to the "grave danger" of sabotage and espionage by "disloyal members" of this minority. Stone also convinced his colleagues to leave the more troublesome evacuation issue for later decision. Only Justice Frank Murphy reserved his decision when Stone polled the court; every other justice voted to sustain Gordon's conviction for curfew violation.

The Chief Justice assumed the task of writing for the court, hoping to put his prestige behind the decision. Stone acknowledged that racial discrimination was "odious to a free people" and had "often been held to be a denial of equal protection" by the Supreme Court. During wartime, however, "the successful prosecution of the war" may justify measures which "place citizens of one ancestry in a different category from others." Stone suggested that Japanese Americans had failed to become "an integral part of the white population" and stressed their "attachments to Japan and its institutions." Stone's evidence for these assertions included "irritation" at laws that barred Japanese immigrants from American citizenship and the fact that many children attended "Japanese language schools" to maintain their cultural heritage. Military officials who feared a "fifth column" of disloyal

Japanese Americans were entitled, Stone concluded, to impose a curfew on "residents having ethnic affiliations with an invading enemy."

Before the Hirabayashi opinion was issued, Frank Murphy wrote a scathing dissent from Stone's racial assumptions. The court's only Catholic, Murphy noted that many immigrants sent their children to parochial and foreign-language schools, without any loss of loyalty. The issue to Murphy was not the curfew but "the gigantic round-up" of American citizens, in which he found "a melancholy resemblance to the treatment accorded to members of the Jewish race" by America's wartime enemies. This reference to Nazi concentration camps upset Justice Felix Frankfurter, who warned Murphy that any dissent would be "playing into the hands of the enemy." Faced with this appeal to patriotism, Murphy withdrew his dissent and filed a concurring opinion that placed the curfew order on "the very brink of constitutional power."

Eighteen months later, when the Supreme Court met to decide the Korematsu case, the tides of war had shifted and the continued detention of Japanese Americans struck many — including Army officials — as unnecessary. Nonetheless, Justice Hugo Black wrote for six members of the Court in upholding General DeWitt's evacuation orders. Black took pains to deny that Fred Korematsu's treatment reflected "hostility to him or his race," holding that it was based on "evidence of disloyalty" among Japanese Americans. One of the three dissenters, Justice Robert Jackson, disparaged Black's "evidence" as nothing more than the "self-serving statement" of General DeWitt, whose official report on the internment program had labeled Japanese Americans as members of an "enemy race." Justice Murphy revised his reluctant concurrence in the Hirabayashi case into an impassioned dissent in the Korematsu case. The forced exclusion of American citizens from their homes, Murphy wrote, "goes over 'the very brink of constitutional power' and falls into the ugly abyss of racism."

The surrender of Japan in 1945 did not end the internment of Japanese Americans: More than a year passed before the last concentration camp closed its gates. Slowly and fearfully, members of this "disloyal" minority returned to their homes, although many left the Pacific coast for new lives in the Midwest and East. Beginning in most cases from scratch, the former prisoners opened stores and farms, and sent their children to prestigious colleges and to success in business and professional careers. But the psychic scars of internment remained.

Four decades passed before Japanese Americans found a collective voice for their wartime trauma. Pressed by young people who joined the civil-rights and anti-war movements of the sixties and seventies, survivors of the concentration camps abandoned the Japanese tradition of "gaman" — "keep it inside"—and shared their feelings of hurt and shame. Moving from personal anguish to political action, Japanese Americans organized a "redress" movement and persuaded Congress in 1981 to establish a blue-ribbon panel to review the internment program and propose remedies for legal wrongs. After hearing testimony, often tearful, from 750 witnesses, and reviewing thousands of government documents, the Commission on Wartime Relocation and Internment of Civilians agreed that the internment "was not justified by military necessity" but had resulted from "race prejudice, war hysteria and a failure of political leadership." With only one dissent, the commissioners asked Congress to provide compensation of $20,000 for each internment survivor.

Another goal of the redress movement was to secure judicial reversal of the criminal convictions the Supreme Court had upheld in 1943 and 1944. Research by commission staff members and Peter Irons, a lawyer and legal historian, uncovered federal records that disclosed the "suppression of evidence" to the courts and the racist basis of the mass internment. After he showed these records to Gordon Hirabayashi, Minoru Yasui, and Fred Korematsu, Irons secured their agreement to reopen their cases through the little-used legal procedure of *coram nobis,** available only to criminal defendants whose trials had been tainted by "fundamental error" or "manifest injustice."

Aided by teams of volunteer lawyers, most of them children of former internees, Irons drafted *coram nobis* petitions which were filed in January 1983 with federal courts in Seattle, Portland, and San Francisco. Based entirely on government records, the lengthy petitions asked the courts to vacate the wartime convictions and make judicial findings on the government's misconduct. The government answered the petitions with a two-page response which labeled the internment as an "unfortunate episode" in American history. Although government lawyers denied any misconduct, they did not challenge the charges of suppressing crucial evidence.

The Korematsu case became the first to reach decision, in October 1983. After hearing lawyers on both sides, Judge Marilyn Patel asked Fred Korematsu to address the court. "As long as my record stands in federal court," he quietly stated, "any American citizen can be held in prison or concentration camps without a trial or a hearing." Ruling from the bench, Judge Patel labeled the government's position as "tantamount to a confession of error" and erased Fred's conviction from the court's records. Ruling in January 1984, Judge Robert Belloni of the federal court in Portland, Oregon, vacated Minoru Yasui's conviction, although he declined to make findings on the petition's misconduct charges.

*See note p. 67.

Gordon Hirabayashi waited until June 1985 for a hearing on his petition. By this time, government lawyers had decided to defend the wartime internment. Judge Donald Voorhees presided at the two-week hearing in the same Seattle courthouse in which Gordon was tried in 1942. Government lawyer Victor Stone called a parade of former FBI and intelligence officials to support claims that General DeWitt's wartime orders were "rational" responses to threats of espionage and sabotage. One official labeled Japanese Americans as "the most likely friends of the enemy" and another recalled "espionage nets" along the Pacific coast. Under examination by Gordon's lawyers, none of the government witnesses could point to a single documented instance of wartime espionage by Japanese Americans.

The star witness at Gordon's hearing was Edward Ennis, the former Justice Department lawyer who had objected to the "suppression of evidence" before the Supreme Court in 1943. Four decades later, Ennis repeated his objections and stated that John McCloy and Karl Bendetsen of the War Department had "deceived" him about the Army's false espionage charges. These wartime actions, Voorhees ruled in February 1986, constituted "error of the most fundamental character" and required vacation of Gordon's conviction for violating DeWitt's evacuation order. However, Voorhees described the curfew as a "relatively mild" restriction and upheld Gordon's conviction on this count.

Neither side was satisfied with this Solomonic outcome, the mirror image of the Supreme Court decisions of 1943, and both sets of lawyers filed appeals of Judge Voorhees' rulings. After hearing arguments and reading lengthy briefs, a three-judge panel of the Ninth Circuit Court of Appeals issued a unanimous opinion on September 24, 1987. Judge Mary Schroeder wrote for the court, concluding from the evidence presented to Judge Voorhees, that "General DeWitt was a racist" and that his military orders were "based upon racism rather than military necessity." Disagreeing with Judge Voorhees that "the curfew was a lesser restriction on freedom" than evacuation, the appellate judges vacated Gordon's remaining criminal conviction.

Government lawyers conceded defeat after this blunt rebuff and declined to file a final appeal with the Supreme Court. Gordon Hirabayashi, a college student in 1942 and now an emeritus professor, credited his victory to the new generation of Japanese Americans. "I was just one of the cogs" in the crusade for vindication, he reflected. "This was truly the people's case."

3. Why did U.S. officials intern people of Japanese ancestry from Central and South America?

Michi Weglyn

Hostages

As a Nisei teenager during World War II, Michi Nishiura Weglyn trusted President Franklin Roosevelt's rationale that internment was in the best interests of the country. Even though she contracted tuberculosis at the Gila River camp, Weglyn didn't resent the government for putting her behind barbed wire. In the preface to *Years of Infamy: The Untold Story of America's Concentration Camps* (1976), Weglyn recalls her feelings during the war. Like many young internees, she blamed herself rather than the government and wanted to eradicate "the stain of dishonor we collectively felt for the treachery of Pearl Harbor." Internment, Weglyn believed, "was the only way to prove our loyalty to a country which we loved with the same depth of feeling that children in Japan were then being brought up to love their proud island nation."

Twenty-five years later, Weglyn reconsidered her views of internment and out of curiosity began examining archival documents. "Among once impounded papers," she came "face to face with facts" that left her "greatly pained." She spent seven years conducting research at the National Archives, the Library of Congress, and the Pentagon. Sometimes the revelations made her physically sick for days. Weglyn describes this period of the late 1960s and early 1970s, when stories of protest against the Vietnam War and the Watergate break-in and cover-up filled the news, as a time when "angry charges of government duplicity and 'credibility gaps' were being hurled at heads of state." Her research convinced her that "the gaps of the evacuation era appeared more like chasms." She resolved to write a book when she heard this statement by Attorney General Ramsey Clark claim "We have never had, do not now have and will not ever have concentration camps here."[1] She felt a responsibility to "those whose honor was so wrongly impugned, many of whom died without vindication." At first, publishers praised Weglyn's scholarship but called her book, *Years of Infamy,* "objectionable" because of its harsh indictment of government leaders. According to Weglyn, William Morrow published the book in 1976 because the climate had changed with Watergate and the Pentagon Papers.

This selection from *Years of Infamy* draws attention to the little-known plight of Latin Americans of Japanese ancestry whom the U.S. government interned to exchange for Americans held captive by the Japanese. Using letters, memos, and other official records, Weglyn documents the State Department's role in transporting and imprisoning 2,264 people of Japanese ancestry from Central and South America. Why was the State Department interested in Japanese Latin Americans? By early 1942, the United States and Japan had begun negotiating to exchange nationals, both officials and private citizens, imprisoned by both sides. State Department officials used Japanese Latin Americans for these exchanges, sending 1,100 of them to Japan in July 1942 and another 1,300 in September 1943.

Twelve Latin American countries sent people of Japanese ancestry to U.S. camps, but 80 percent of them came from Peru. Due to a long history of economic competition and cultural prejudice, the Peruvian government wanted to expel all Japanese nationals from the country. Technically, the United States approved the removal of only "dangerous" enemy aliens, but the program was remarkably arbitrary, and both Japanese immigrants and Peruvian citizens of Japanese ancestry were often seized for no apparent reason. Some were deported in place of wealthy Japanese Peruvians who had bribed the police. John Emmerson, third secretary of the American Embassy in Peru, who helped compile the deportation lists, later acknowledged, "During my period of service in the embassy, we found no reliable evidence of planned or contemplated acts of sabotage, subversion, or espionage."[2]

Japanese Latin Americans were not sent to the camps run by the War Relocation Authority (WRA), which held most of the Japanese Americans from the West Coast. Instead, like the "enemy aliens" rounded up by the FBI after Pearl Harbor, they were sent to camps run by the Justice Department and were treated as prisoners of war. Compounding the injustice, the U.S. government made sure that Japanese Latin Americans were classified as "illegal aliens" when they entered the country, even though their passports and visas had been confiscated en route to America. This designation paved the way for the United States to deport these people to Japan after the war. Many Japanese Latin Americans did not want to go to Japan, a country devastated by war and a land many of them had never seen. In this selection, Weglyn shows how such individuals chose to fight deportation through the courts and were able to remain in the United States.

Many former internees first learned about government racism and misconduct during the war from Weglyn's *Years of Infamy*. Activist Raymond Okamura hailed the way Weglyn, a "theatrical designer with no historical training," found an "astonishing number of facts previously de-emphasized, ignored, or censored." Crediting her with shattering the "previous image of WRA-benevolence-inmate cooperation," Okamura pronounced the book a "major breakthrough for the telling of Japanese American history from a Japanese American perspective."[3] In addition, Weglyn's book gave many Japanese Americans the courage to speak out publicly about their experiences. In a review published in the *Pacific Citizen* on February 6, 1976, Mary Karasawa described how she felt the "need to really talk" about internment after she finished reading the book:

> I don't think anyone who lived through the "camp experience" will be able to finish reading this book without experiencing every range of human emotion — much of which has been lying dormant for the past 30 years. . . . You will swear, you will cry, you will feel bitter, but you will surely begin to see the pieces of the puzzle come together.[4]

Years of Infamy also helped stimulate redress activism throughout the country. In 1976, the Japanese American Citizens League (JACL) gave Weglyn its Biennium Award and praised the way her book "therapeutically expiates the demon of shame and guilt among Japanese Americans." The league also noted that her "extensive documentation is a valuable resource in JACL's effort to realize reparations legislation." Throughout the history of the redress movement, leaders of various factions have paid tribute to Weglyn for inspiring their activism. After receiving many letters that thanked her for reviving memories of the camps, Weglyn publicly urged "all who have lived in shame and silence for many years" to "begin to speak more openly" about the "government's crimes . . . so that it can never happen again."[5] During the 1970s and 1980s, increasing numbers of former internees responded to Weglyn's call, culminating in the testimony of more than five hundred Japanese Americans at the Commission on Wartime Relocation and Internment of Civilians hearings in 1981.

Weglyn continued to fight for the forgotten victims of internment after passage of the 1988 redress legislation, which excluded Japanese Latin Americans. She publicly denounced government claims that Japanese Latin Americans were ineligible because of their "illegal alien" status or because responsibility for their plight lay with the Latin American governments. Her research and advocacy helped fuel the *Mochizuki* class action lawsuit, which led the government in 1999 to offer a settlement of $5,000 to each surviving Japanese Latin American. Although this amount was far short of the $20,000 paid to Japanese American internees, it at least acknowledged U.S. culpability in their internment.

Long considered a leader of the Japanese American community in New York City, Weglyn was awarded an honorary doctorate from Hunter College in June 1990 for her contributions to the Asian American community. In June 1993, California State Polytechnic University at Pomona established an endowed chair, the Michi and Walter Weglyn Chair for Multicultural Studies, in honor of the Weglyns. In February 1998, academics, politicians, and activists in Los Angeles presented her with the Fighting Spirit Award for her work on behalf of Japanese Americans. When Michi

Weglyn passed away on April 25, 1999, at the age of seventy-two, services were held throughout the country to commemorate her community service.

Questions for a Closer Reading

1. Weglyn begins the selection by speculating that officials may have viewed Japanese Latin Americans as a "reprisal reserve" for Americans mistreated by the Japanese. Do you think this is plausible? Why or why not?
2. Weglyn provides a global perspective on internment. Compare the motives and policies of Canada, Latin America, Alaska, and the rest of the United States. Within the United States, how did the internment experience in a Justice Department camp compare with the experience in a WRA camp?
3. Why did the State Department and the Justice Department work together to try to deport Japanese Latin Americans at the end of the war? How was this countered by the internees and by Wayne Collins?
4. The Commission on Wartime Relocation and Internment of Civilians called the history of Japanese Latin Americans "one of the strange, unhappy, largely forgotten stories of World War II." Yet the commission did not propose redress for Japanese Latin Americans, who were excluded from redress legislation. Do you agree with this decision? Why or why not? If you were a former internee offered the government's settlement of $5,000, would you take it or continue to fight in court? Could you use the research in this article to bolster your claims?
5. Japanese American activists praised Weglyn for providing a Japanese American perspective on the history of internment. Why do you think this research by a former internee might have helped Japanese Americans break their decades of silence about the wartime incarceration?

Notes

1. *The Sacramento Bee,* June 27, 1976.

2. Commission on Wartime Relocation and Internment of Civilians, *Personal Justice Denied: Report of the Commission on Wartime Relocation and Internment of Civilians* (Washington, D.C.: US Government Printing Office, 1982), p. 314.

3. Raymond Okamura, "The Concentration Camp Experience from a Japanese American Perspective," *Counterpoint: Perspectives on Asian America,* ed. Emma Gee (Los Angeles: Asian American Studies Center, University of California at Los Angeles, 1976), p. 30.
4. *Pacific Citizen,* February 6, 1976.
5. *Hokubei Mainichi,* May 19, 1976.

Hostages

I'm for catching every Japanese in America, Alaska, and Hawaii now and putting them in concentration camps. . . . Damn them! Let's get rid of them now!

— CONGRESSMAN JOHN RANKIN,
Congressional Record, December 15, 1941

1.

Since much of Munson's documentation for the President* reads more like a tribute to those of Japanese ancestry than a need for locking them up, the question remains: Had the President, having perceived the racist character of the American public, deliberately acquiesced to the clearly punitive action knowing it would be rousingly effective for the flagging home-front morale?

Or could factors other than political expedience, perhaps a more critical wartime exigency, have entered into and inspired the sudden decision

*Weglyn is referring to what historians have called the "Munson Report," a secret government intelligence report on the loyalty of Japanese Americans delivered to President Roosevelt, the State Department, the War Department, and the Navy in early November 1941. Curtis B. Munson, a successful Chicago businessman, posed as a government official to gather information from FBI and Naval Intelligence sources for an informal intelligence system developed for President Roosevelt. The report concluded, "For the most part the local Japanese are loyal to the United States, or at worst, hope that by remaining quiet they can avoid concentration camps or irresponsible mobs. We do not believe that they would be at least any more disloyal than any other racial group in the United States with whom we went to war."

Michi Weglyn, "Hostages," in *Years of Infamy: The Untold Story of America's Concentration Camps* (New York: Morrow Quill Paperbacks, a Division of William Morrow and Company, Inc., 1976), 54–66.

calling for mass action — made as it was at a time when the Allied cause in the Pacific was plummeting, one reversal following another in seemingly endless succession?

A bit of personal conjecture: Shocked and mortified by the unexpected skill and tenacity of the foe (as the Administration might have been), with America's very survival in jeopardy, what could better insure the more considerate treatment of American captives, the unknown thousands then being trapped daily in the islands and territories falling to the enemy like dominoes, than a substantial *hostage reserve?* And would not a readily available *reprisal reserve* prove crucial should America's war fortune continue to crumble: should the scare propaganda of "imminent invasion" become an actual, living nightmare of rampaging hordes of yellow "barbarians" overrunning and making "free fire zones" of American villages and hamlets — looting, raping, murdering, slaughtering. . . .

In an earlier crisis situation which had exacerbated U.S.-Japan relations to the near-breaking point, the very sagacity of such a contingency plan had been forthrightly brought to the attention of the President by Congressman John D. Dingell of Michigan. On August 18, 1941, months before the outbreak of hostilities, the Congressman had hastened to advise the President:

> Reports contained in the Press indicate that Japan has barred the departure of one hundred American citizens and it is indicated that the detention is in reprisal for the freezing of Japanese assets in the United States of America.
>
> I want to suggest without encroaching upon the privilege of the Executive or without infringing upon the privileges of the State Department that if it is the intention of Japan to enter into a reprisal contest that we remind Nippon that unless assurances are received that Japan will facilitate and permit the voluntary departure of this group of one hundred Americans within forty-eight hours, the Government of the United States will cause the forceful detention or imprisonment in a concentration camp of ten thousand alien Japanese in Hawaii; the ratio of Japanese hostages held by America being one hundred for every American detained by the Mikado's Government.
>
> It would be well to further remind Japan that there are perhaps one hundred fifty thousand additional alien Japanese in the United States who will be held in a reprisal reserve whose status will depend upon Japan's next aggressive move. I feel that the United States is in an ideal position to accept Japan's challenge.
>
> God bless you, Mr. President.[1]

Within two months after the crippling blow dealt by the Japanese at Pearl Harbor, a fast-deteriorating situation in the soon untenable Philippine campaign moved [Secretary of War Henry] Stimson to call for threats of reprisals on Japanese nationals in America "to insure proper treatment" of U.S. citizens trapped in enemy territory. On February 5, the very day when mass evacuation-internment plans began to be drawn up and formalized within the War Department,[2] Stimson wrote [Secretary of State Cordell] Hull:

> General MacArthur has reported in a radiogram, a copy of which is enclosed, that American and British civilians in areas of the Philippines occupied by the Japanese are being subjected to extremely harsh treatment. The unnecessary harsh and rigid measures imposed, in sharp contrast to the moderate treatment of metropolitan Filipinos, are unquestionably designed to discredit the white race.
>
> I request that you strongly protest this unjustified treatment of civilians, and suggest that you present a threat of reprisals against the many Japanese nationals now enjoying negligible restrictions in the United States, to insure proper treatment of our nationals in the Philippines.[3]

If a reprisal reserve urgency had indeed precipitated the sudden decision for internment, the emphasis, as the tide of the war reversed itself, switched to the buildup of a "barter reserve": one sizable enough to allow for the earliest possible repatriation of American detainees, even at the price of a disproportionate number of Japanese nationals in exchange. Behind this willingness on the part of the State Department *to give more than they expected back* may have lurked profound concern that unless meaningful concessions were to be made in the matter of POW exchanges, the whole procedure would get mired in resistance and inertia to the jeopardy of thousands subject to terrible suffering in enemy prison camps.

As revealed in a letter from the Secretary of the Navy to President Roosevelt, the Secretary of State, in Knox's estimate, was being overly disconcerted by the belief that German authorities intended to hold on indefinitely to American detainees "as hostages for captured Germans whom we might prosecute under the war criminal procedure."[4] A similar alarmist concern may have been entertained by Secretary of State Hull as to the intent of Japanese authorities.

The use of the Nisei as part and parcel of this human barter was not totally ruled out in the realm of official thinking. By curious circumstance, such intent on the part of U.S. authorities became starkly evident in the latter part of 1942 and early 1943, when numerous Nisei, to their shocked indignation, were informed by Colonel Karl Bendetsen in a form letter: "Certain Japanese persons are currently being considered for repatriation [expatriation] to Japan. You and those members of your family listed above, are being so considered."[5]

2.

The removals in the United States were only a part of forced uprootings which occurred almost simultaneously in Alaska, Canada, Mexico, Central America, parts of South America, and the Caribbean island of Haiti and the Dominican Republic.

Canada's decision to round up and remove its tiny (23,000) West Coast minority, 75 percent of whom were citizens of Canada, preceded America's by about a month and may have had a decisive influence on the War Department's decision to proceed similarly . . . but, in many ways, discriminatory measures imposed on the Canadian Japanese were more arbitrary and severe. An order of January 14, 1942, calling for the removal of all enemy alien males over sixteen years of age from the area west of the Cascade Mountains resulted in men being separated from women in the initial stage of the evacuation. But a follow-up decree of February 27 demanded total evacuation, citizens as well as aliens, most of whom were removed to work camps and mining "ghost towns" in mountain valleys of the Canadian interior. Property and possessions not disposed of were quickly confiscated and sold off at public auctions since evacuees were expected to assume some of the internment expenses from the proceeds. Canadian Japanese were not permitted to return to British Columbia and their home communities until March 1949, seven years after the evacuation.[6]

Of the 151 Alaskan Japanese plucked from their homes and life pursuits under color of Executive Order 9066, around fifty were seal- and whale-hunting half-Indians and half-Eskimos (*one-half* "Japanese blood" was the criterion in Alaska), some of whom were to associate with Japanese for the first time in the camps. Except for a "few fortunate ones with second-generation fathers,"[7] families were left fatherless since male nationals suffered mass indiscriminate internment in various Justice Department detention centers. Most ended up in the camp maintained exclusively for Japanese alien detainees in Lordsburg, New Mexico. Remaining family members were airlifted to the state of Washington (following a short initial stay at Fort Richardson, Alaska) and penned up temporarily in the Puyallup Assembly Center near Seattle. In the mass Japanese American exodus out of the prohibited military area during the summer of 1942, the evacuees from Alaska wound up in the relocation center of Minidoka in Idaho.

In Mexico, the Japanese residing in small settlements near the American border and coastal areas (along a sixty-two-mile zone) were forced to liquidate their property and move inland, some to "clearing houses" and resettlement camps, a number of them to concentration camps in Perote, Puebla, and Vera Cruz.

Even less selectivity was exercised in the case of the Japanese then scattered throughout the Central American republics. Many were simply "picked up" by reason of their "hostile origin" and handed over to U.S. authorities, who, in turn, arranged for their transportation by sea or air to the U.S. mainland.

Such gunpoint "relocations" to American concentration camps became quite commonplace on the South American continent in the days and months following the Pearl Harbor attack. The reason: Considerable pressure had been applied by the U.S. State Department on various republics of the Western Hemisphere to impound, with the option of handing over to American authorities for care and custody, persons who might be considered "potentially dangerous" to hemispheric security, with special emphasis on the Japanese. More than a month before the war's outbreak, plans for this unusual wartime action began to take shape. On October 20, 1941, U.S. Ambassador to Panama Edwin C. Wilson informed Under Secretary of State Sumner Welles:

> My strictly confidential despatch No. 300 of October 20, 1941, for the Secretary and Under Secretary, transmits memoranda of my conversations with the Foreign Minister regarding the question of internment of Japanese in the event that we suddenly find ourselves at war with Japan.
>
> The attitude of the Panamanian Government is thoroughly cooperative. The final memorandum sets out the points approved by the Panamanian Cabinet for dealing with this matter. Briefly, their thought is this: Immediately following action by the United States to intern Japanese in the United States, Panama would arrest Japanese on Panamanian territory and intern them on Taboga Island. They would be guarded by Panamanian guards and would have the status of Panamanian interns. *All expenses and costs of internment and guarding to be paid by the United States.* The United States Government would agree to hold Panama harmless against any claims which might arise as a result of internment.
>
> I believe it essential that you instruct me by telegraph at once to assure the Foreign Minister that the points which he set out to cover this matter meet the approval of our Government.[8] [Italics mine.]

Funds which would be immediately needed, as in the construction of a prison camp which would serve as a staging area for transshipments to U.S. detention facilities, were to be provided by the Commanding General of the Caribbean Defense Command.[9] And from Chief of Staff General George Marshall came the suggestion that a more liberal interpretation of persons to be detained be considered. On October 28, 1941, he wrote Under Secretary Welles:

> It is gratifying to know that Panama is prepared to intern Japanese aliens immediately following similar action by the United States.

I suggest, however, that the agreement be enlarged to provide for internment by the Panamanian Government of all persons believed dangerous, who are regarded by the United States as enemy aliens, under similar conditions.[10]

Similarly encouraged to undermine in advance any possibility of Japanese sabotage, subversion, or fifth-column treachery was Panama's neighbor republic of Costa Rica. On December 8, 1941, upon America's declaration of war on Japan, the U.S. Legation in Costa Rica wired the State Department: . . . ORDERS FOR INTERNMENT OF ALL JAPANESE IN COSTA RICA HAVE BEEN ISSUED.[11]

At a Conference of Foreign Ministers of the American Republics held in Rio de Janeiro in January 1942, a special inter-American agency (the Emergency Committee for Political Defense) to coordinate hemispheric security measures was organized, with headquarters subsequently established in Montevideo. The Emergency Committee adopted, without delay, a resolution which had been drafted by the U.S. Department of Justice in conjunction with the Department of State which stressed the need for prompt preventive detention of dangerous Axis nationals and for the "deportation of such persons to another American republic for detention when adequate local detention facilities are lacking."[12] States interested in the collaborative effort were assured that not only detention accommodations but also shipping facilities would be provided by the United States "at its own expense."[13] The State Department offered an additional incentive: It would include any of the official and civilian nationals of the participating republics in whatever exchange arrangements the U.S. would subsequently make with Axis powers.

More than a dozen American states cooperated. Among them: Bolivia, Colombia, Costa Rica, the Dominican Republic, Ecuador, El Salvador, Guatemala, Haiti, Honduras, Mexico, Nicaragua, Panama, Peru, and Venezuela.[14] Three states, Brazil, Uruguay, and Paraguay, instituted their own detention programs (Paraguay, for one, promptly arrested the two Japanese residing within her borders). Since Argentina and Chile held back breaking off diplomatic relations with the Axis powers until much later, both nations took no part in the hemispheric imprisonments.

In time, the State Department was able to claim that "the belligerent republics of the Caribbean area have sent us subversive aliens without limitation concerning their disposition"; but four republics—Venezuela, Colombia, Ecuador, and Mexico—exacted "explicit guarantees" before turning over internees.[15] Panama liberally granted the U.S. "full freedom to negotiate with Japan and agrees to the use of Japanese internees . . . for exchange of any non-official citizen of an American belligerent country."[16]

The concept of hemispheric removals had its origin in the State Department, but responsibility for the success of the operation was shared by the Departments of War, Navy, and Justice.[17] With the safety of the Panama Canal a veritable life-or-death matter after the near annihilation of the Pacific Fleet, it appears that all concerned acted on the conviction that the threat to continental security was so grave as to outweigh the momentary misuse of executive, military, and judicial power.

As a direct result of the hemispheric nations' agreement to "cooperate jointly for their mutual protection," over two thousand deportees of Japanese ancestry were to swell the already impressive U.S. barter reserve by ending up in scattered mainland detention camps, whose existence was virtually unknown then to the American public. . . . Though the deportees were legally in State Department custody, the custodial program for them was supervised by the Immigration and Naturalization Service of the U.S. Justice Department.

3.

As for persons of Japanese ancestry residing in the democratic republic of Peru, racial antagonism fed by resentment of the foreign element as being exceedingly successful economic competitors had more to do with the Peruvian Government's spirited cooperation than its concern for the defense of the Hemisphere. The steady economic encroachment of the resident Japanese and their alleged imperviousness to assimilation had aroused increasing nativist hostility; and anti-Japanese legislation and restrictive ordinances of the West Coast type had been copied through the years, culminating with the revocation, by executive action, of citizenship rights of Nisei possessing dual citizenship. Racial feelings against the Japanese minority, abetted by the press, had burst into occasional mob action even before the Pearl Harbor attack. And much of the blame for the cut-off of Japanese immigration in 1936 had been attributed to the "social unrest" stirred up by the unwanted minority because, in the words of Foreign Minister Ulloa, "their conditions and methods of working have produced pernicious competition for the Peruvian workers and businessmen."

Accordingly, 80 percent of the Latin-American deportees of Japanese ancestry was to be contributed by the government of Peru, an enthusiasm stimulated not only by the opportunity presented to expropriate property and business (Law No. 9586 of April 10 authorized seizure of Axis property) but also to rid the realm of an undesirable element. On July 20, 1942, Henry Norweb, the U.S. Ambassador to Peru, informed the State Department of President Manuel Prado's manifest fervor in this regard:

> The second matter in which the President [Prado] is very much interested is the possibility of getting rid of the Japanese in Peru. He would like to settle this problem permanently, which means that he is thinking in terms of repatriating thousands of Japanese. He asked Colonel Lord to let him know about the prospects of additional shipping facilities from the United States. In any arrangement that might be made for internment of Japanese in the States, Peru would like to be sure that these Japanese would not be returned to Peru later on. The President's goal apparently is the substantial elimination of the Japanese colony in Peru.[18]

Pressure in the name of "mutual protection" had obviously paid off. Only three months earlier, a dispatch from the American Embassy in Lima had underscored the gravity of the subversion potential inherent in the Peruvian Japanese, "whose strength and ability have, in the past, been vastly underestimated and whose fanatic spirit has neither been understood nor taken seriously. . . . there appears to be little realization of the actual danger and a reluctance on the part of the Government to take positive measures." Recommendations from the Legation included the removal of key Japanese leaders, the encouragement of "propaganda intended to call attention of the Peruvians to the Japanese dangers," and suggestion that covert assistance might even be rendered by U.S. authorities: "Ways may be found to provide . . . material without of course permitting the source to become known as the Embassy."[19]

In light of such concerns among Embassy officials of the Lima Legation, the Peruvian President's unexpected eagerness to cooperate to the fullest came as a welcome turn of events and as an instant go-ahead for the core of U.S. advisers to assist in widening the scope of Peruvian expulsions. An intradepartmental State Department memo noted ways in which the operation might be expedited:

> President Prado has officially stated his willingness to have this deportation program carried through. . . . The suggestion that Japanese be removed from strategic areas should be followed and this should be carried on by *well-paid* police; even if this necessitates a loan from this government. All police charged with supervision of Japanese should be well paid. [Legation had warned that Peruvian law officers "are susceptible to Japanese bribes . . . their alertness cannot be depended upon."] The suggestion that Japanese be expelled whether they are naturalized Peruvians or not might be met by a denaturalization law.[20]

Arrests were made in swift, silent raids by the Peruvian police, who first confined detainees in local jails, then turned them over to the custody of U.S. military authorities. Then began the strange odyssey which would take them northward to the United States mainland: "We were taken to the port of Callao and embarked on an American transport under strict guard and with machine gun pointed at us by American soldiers."[21] As it was found that immunity from deportation could be "bought" by a generous bribe unless the removal was swiftly expedited, Army Air Transport planes were used in a number of cases involving the "extremely dangerous," usually the wealthier and influential Peruvian Japanese considered high-priority trade bait. After a short stopover in the Panama-based internment camp used as a staging area, deportees were shipped on to various Department of Justice detention centers in the States, after landing at a Gulf Coast or West Coast port.

More fortunate prisoners enjoyed reunion with family members at the Crystal City Internment Camp in Texas, the only "family camp" operated by the Justice Department where detainees were dealt with as "prisoners of war." Even the voluntary prisoners. The latter were mostly women and children. A total of 1,094 of them, officially designated as "voluntary detainees," answered the State Department's "invitation" to place themselves in war-duration voluntary incarceration with the 1,024 men who had been seized and spirited to the mainland by the U.S. military.

The question of whether the reunion program had been undertaken as a direct means of swelling the U.S. barter stockpile or whether the entire procedure represented a "humanitarian" concession on the part of the State and Justice departments is a matter still shrouded in mystery.[22]

By late October of 1942, fears concerning hemispheric security had greatly diminished. A pounding U.S. counteroffensive in the Solomons had finally begun to check the thrust of the Japanese juggernaut in the Pacific. And with the mass transportation of the coastal subnation to the inland camps nearing completion, Hull hastened to advise the President of what, to the Secretary of State, were still overriding reasons why there should be no letup in the hemispheric removal—at least of "all the Japanese . . . for internment in the United States."

> There are in China 3,300 American citizens who desire to return to the United States. Many of them are substantial persons who have represented important American business and commercial interests and a large number of missionaries. They are scattered all through that part of China occupied by the Japanese. Some of them are at liberty, some of them are in concentration camps, and some of them have limited liberty, but all of them subject to momentary cruel and harsh treatment by their oppressors. Under our agreement with Japan which is still operating, we will be able to remove these people. It will take two more trips of the *Gripsholm** to do so. In exchange for them we will have to send out Japanese in the same quantity. . . .

**Gripsholm:* a Swedish motor ship that transported people of Japanese ancestry from the United States to Japan during the war.

> In addition, there are 3,000 non-resident American citizens in the Philippines. We have no agreement for their exchange but it has been intimated that Japan might consider an exchange of them. It would be very gratifying if we could obtain those people from Japanese control and return them to the United States. But to do so we would have to exchange Japanese for them. That would take two more round trips of the *Gripsholm.*
>
> Still, in addition, there are 700 civilians interned in Japan proper captured at Guam and Wake. It is probable that we might arrange for their return. But in order to obtain them we would have to release Japanese. . . .
>
> With the foregoing as a predicate, I propose the following course of action:
>
> . . . Continue our exchange agreement with the Japanese until the Americans are out of China, Japan and the Philippines — so far as possible. . . .
>
> Continue our efforts to remove all the Japanese from these American Republic countries for internment in the United States.
>
> Continue our efforts to remove from South and Central America all the dangerous Germans and Italians still there, together with their families. . . .[23] [Reparagraphed by author of this selection]

In the Secretary of State's recommended course of action, the precise wording of the directive is significant: Note the qualifying prerequisite, *dangerous,* in reference to hostages-to-be of German and Italian nationalities. In Hull's implied suggestion of more discriminating treatment of non-Oriental Axis nationals, while calling for wholesale removal — dangerous or harmless — of "all the Japanese," evidence again lies tellingly exposed of racial bias then lurking in high and rarefied places in the nation's capital.

4.

By early 1943, the Justice Department, in its custodial role in the hemispheric operation, had become greatly alarmed at the number of internees being sent up. Worse, it had come to its attention that many being held under the Alien Enemies Act were not enemy Japanese but Peruvian nationals, thus aliens of a friendly nation; and that little or no evidence supported the Peruvian Government's contention that their deportees were dangerous. "Some of the cases seem to be mistakes," Attorney General Biddle wrote the Secretary of State on January 11, 1943.[24]

Biddle insisted on more conclusive proof that the deportees were in fact "the dangerous leaders among the Japanese population in Peru," and he proposed sending his own representative to Peru and other donor nations to help sort out the people to be sent up. Since barter negotiations between Washington and Tokyo had then come to a standstill, Biddle balked at going along with the indiscriminate internment of bodies being sent up in ever-growing numbers from Peru, insisting that his department had merely agreed to "expediting *temporary* custody" pending repatriation.

The State Department's primary concern was that the competence and sincerity of the donor states would be impugned if Biddle were to challenge the veracity of their criterion of "dangerousness." But the State Department finally gave in, and Raymond W. Ickes (of the Central and South American division of the Alien Enemy Control unit) of the Justice Department was permitted to make on-the-spot reviews of all pending deportee cases. Ickes found little evidence anywhere to support the claims of the participating republics that individuals being held—or targeted—for deportation were "in any true sense of the word security subjects." On turning down the deportation from Venezuela of thirty Japanese, he advised the U.S. Legation in Caracas:

> This is the very thing that we have to guard against, particularly in the case of Peru, where attempts have been made to send job lots of Japanese to the States merely because the Peruvians wanted their businesses and not because there was any adverse evidence against them.[25]

All deportations to the United States thereafter ceased.

With the coming of peace, the once felicitous relationship between the U.S. and Peru suffered another setback. While the State Department proceeded to return various ex-hostages to their respective homelands, the government of Peru refused to allow reentry in the case of Japanese. Only a few select citizens were permitted readmission, mostly native-Peruvian wives and Peruvian-citizen children.

The Justice Department thereupon pressed ahead with an extraordinary piece of injustice on the onetime kidnapees no longer needed to ransom off U.S. detainees. With certain hierarchal changes in the Department (FDR's death on April 12, 1945, had resulted in Tom Clark, a Truman appointee, becoming Attorney General on September 27, 1945), all were scheduled for removal to Japan despite vigorous protest that a sizable number of them had no ties in a country many had never visited; wives and children of many were in fact still living in Peru.[26] The grounds for the second "deportation" of the Peruvian kidnapees was that they lacked proper credentials: they had entered the U.S. illegally, without visas and without passports.[27]

From despair arising from their prolonged detention without the possibility of return to their homeland or release, a contingent of some 1,700 Peruvian Japanese (700 men and their dependents) allowed themselves, between November 1945 and February 1946,[28] to be "voluntarily" unloaded on Japan. Many had acquiesced to this drastic federal action in the belief that reunion with families left behind in Peru could not otherwise be achieved.

Awaiting a similarly grim fate were 365 remaining Peruvian rejects, whose desperate plight came to the attention of Wayne Collins, a San Francisco attorney then conducting a one-man war against the Justice Department in trying to extricate thousands of Nisei caught in their "renunciation trap" . . . , another one of the extreme consequences of the evacuation tragedy.

To abort U.S. plans to "dump" this residual Peruvian group on a defeated, war-pulverized enemy hardly able to care for its own starving masses, Collins filed two test proceedings in habeas corpus on June 25, 1946, in a U.S. District Court in San Francisco after the Immigration Department contended that suspension of deportation on a like basis as Caucasians was not permitted, and a subsequent appeal directly to the Attorney General and the President came to no avail.[29] With the removal program brought, by court action, to a forced halt, the detainees were placed in "relaxed internment"— many of them at Seabrook Farms, New Jersey, the well-known frozen food processing plant where the labor of German POWs had been utilized during the war years, and where evacuee groups from many camps were given employment.

Collins, with the aid of the Northern California office of the American Civil Liberties Union, also sought to bring to public attention what both contended was a "legalized kidnaping" program masterminded by the State Department and sanctioned by the nation's chief guardian of decency and legality, the Attorney General, whose office and the State Department now disclaimed any responsibility for the plight of the unfortunate people.

Interior Secretary Harold Ickes (father of Raymond W. Ickes), the only high-level officer of the FDR Administration to speak out in criticism of the State and Justice departments' highly clandestine proceedings, took issue with Attorney General Clark, then seeking the U.S. Vice-Presidency spot by paying glowing homage to the nation's democratic ideals of human rights and individual liberty. This did not sit well with former Cabinet officer Ickes, who knew, through and through, the wartime injustices perpetrated on the Issei and Nisei throughout the Western Hemisphere, which, even then, were being perpetuated by Attorney General Clark's zealous pursuance of postwar deportations of "disloyals" and scores of defenseless aliens under arbitrary classification as "dangerous."[30]

Ickes was sharply outspoken:

> What the country demands from the Attorney General is less self-serving lip-service and more action. . . .
>
> The Attorney General, in the fashion of the Russian Secret Police, maintains a top-secret list of individuals and organizations supposed to be subversive or disloyal. What are the criteria for judging whether a person is disloyal? . . .

> I cannot begin . . . even to call the role of our maimed, mutilated, and missing civil liberties, but the United States, more than two years after the war, is holding in internment some 293 naturalized Peruvians of Japanese descent, who were taken by force by our State and Justice Departments from their homes in Peru.[31]

The resolution of the Peruvian-Japanese dilemma was to take years of unprecedented legal maneuvering on the part of lawyer Collins to untangle the mess in which so many charged with not one specifiable offense found themselves — their lives often mangled beyond repair through the prolonged splitting of families.

Changes in U.S. laws eventually enabled the Peruvian Japanese to apply for suspension of deportation if it could be shown that deportation to Japan would result in serious economic hardship and if "continued residence" in the United States of at least ten years could be proved — with years spent in various concentration camps counting also as "residence."

Peru finally permitted reentry of the deportees in the mid-1950s, but less than one hundred returned. By then the job of reconstructing their lives had begun elsewhere.

Three hundred of the 365 rescued by Collins chose to remain in the United States. An impressive number became American citizens under the amended U.S. naturalization law of 1952, which finally gave immigrants of Asian ancestry the right to become Americans.[32]

Notes

1. Letter, John D. Dingell to Roosevelt, August 18, 1941, OF 197, FDR Library. Dingell was grossly mistaken in claiming that there were 150,000 "additional alien Japanese in the United States." The 1940 census shows 126,947 Japanese Americans in the continental U.S., *only 47,305 of them aliens.* Two-thirds of the minority (79,642) were native-born U.S. citizens.

2. Three rough drafts (all dated "2/5/42") recommending "steps to be taken in connection with the alien enemy-potential saboteur" problem provide evidence of being precursors to the document, Executive Order 9066, which would authorize the West Coast and other mass evacuations on U.S. soil. An early draft reads: "Initially, exclusions to be essentially by class, viz. on the Pacific Coast all Japanese (except, perhaps, for a few token Japs to sustain the legality)." The drafts' opening sentences vary somewhat: (1) "Colonel Bendetsen recommends . . ."; (2) "I recommend . . ."; (3) "The War Department recommends . . .". Unnumbered documents from records of the Office of Assistant Secretary of War, RG 107, National Archives. See also pp. 69, 94, and 95.

3. Letter, Henry L. Stimson to Cordell Hull, February 5, 1942, Department of State File 740.00115 Pacific War/153, RG 59, National Archives.

4. Letter, Frank Knox to Roosevelt, August 16, 1943, PSF: War Department, FDR Library. Hull had asked for the go-ahead which would have authorized repatriation

of 266 U.S. citizens in return for approximately 750 German nationals being held in the U.S.

5. Wartime Civil Control Administration Form R-104. The State Department's Repatriation Section of the Special War Problems Division maintained a list of 100,000 names of "individuals of the Japanese race in the United States" along with "their correct addresses, and with the necessary information concerning their identification, whereabouts, and repatriability" (*Department of State Bulletin,* August 6, 1944, p. 142). Tokyo was explicit as to persons to be exchanged, therefore much misunderstanding resulted among detainees from the department's desire to fulfill the Japanese Government's "priority list."

6. "New Day for Nisei Canadians," *Pacific Citizen,* February 12, 1949. Canada had refused to induct the Nisei during wartime, and only in 1947 were citizens of Japanese descent given the right to vote. . . .

7. Letter, M.H. to Hon. Ernest Gruening, October 20, 1942, RG 210, National Archives, in which a Nisei youth implores Governor Gruening of Alaska to help alleviate the plight of the Alaskan Nisei separated from fathers: "You no doubt already know that there are more than 120 Alaskans in this camp. . . . Of this number about 50 are children under the age of 18 years. The problem arises from the fact that the Alaskan children . . . are without their paternal guidance. Not a single normal family head is with his respective families."

8. Letter, Edwin C. Wilson to Sumner Welles, October 20, 1941, Department of State File 740.00115 Pacific War/1 1/3, RG 59, National Archives.

9. Wire, Cordell Hull to Ambassador (Wilson), December 12, 1941, Department of State File 740.00115 Pacific War/6, RG 59, National Archives. The U.S. Ambassador to Panama was instructed by Hull to see that the Commanding General "furnish the necessary military guard and medical services until such time as the Panamanian officials assume full control of the camp."

10. Letter, George Marshall to Sumner Welles, October 28, 1941, Department of State File 740.00115 Pacific War/1 2/3, RG 59, National Archives.

11. Telegram #375, Arthur Bliss Lane to State Department, December 8, 1941, Department of State File 740.00115 Pacific War/9, RG 59, National Archives.

12. *Department of State Building,* August 6, 1944, p. 146. The Emergency Committee for Political Defense served to augment removal pressure being applied by the State Department. "It is hoped that pressure from this Committee . . . may increase the effectiveness of Mexican cooperation in the relatively near future," stated a dispatch to Cordell Hull which criticized the government's "apathy." Memorandum, Harold D. Finley (First Secretary to Embassy) to the Secretary of State, January 19, 1942, Department of State File 740.00115 Pacific War/53, RG 59, National Archives.

13. Ibid., p. 147. The Special War Problems Division of the Department of State handled all shipping arrangements. In most instances, Army transports were utilized to bring up detainees.

14. See Edward N. Barnhart's "Japanese Internees from Peru," *Pacific Historical Review,* Vol. 31, May 1962, p. 172, fn. 13. Though not mentioned by Barnhart, Mexico and Venezuela were also participants. Barnhart claims that, in all, "over 600 German nationals and a few men of Italian and other nationality" were also removed to U.S. detention facilities from these countries.

15. *Department of State Bulletin,* op. cit., p. 147. Alien deportees were still considered to be under the "jurisdiction" of the donor state, which meant that prior approval was required as to the disposition of each case.

16. Wire, Ambassador Wilson to Secretary of State, May 16, 1942, Department of State File 740.00115 Pacific War/548, RG 59, National Archives. . . .

17. *Department of State Bulletin,* op. cit., p. 146. The legislative branch of the government was apparently kept in the dark. As for the President, Warren Page Rucker in his well-documented unpublished M.A. thesis ("United States–Peruvian Policy toward Peruvian-Japanese Persons during World War II," University of Virginia, 1970) maintains: ". . . there seems little doubt . . . that he [FDR] was aware of the internment of the Peruvian-Japanese and that it met with his approval."

18. Letter, Henry Norweb to Sumner Welles, July 20, 1942, Department of State File 740.00115 Pacific War/1002 2/6, RG 59, National Archives. The Japanese colony in Peru was then estimated to number between 25,000 and 30,000.

10. Taken from Enclosure 1 (Memorandum to Ambassador Norweb from John K. Emmerson, Third Secretary of Embassy, April 18, 1942) to dispatch No. 3422 to State Department, April 21, 1942, Department of State File 894.20223/124, RG 59, National Archives. Norweb, in the accompanying dispatch to Hull, endorsed the recommendations as "sound and well presented."

20. Memorandum, Philip W. Bonsal to Selden Chapin, September 26, 1942, Department of State File 740.00115 Pacific War/1002 5/6, RG 59, National Archives.

21. Letter, V.K.T. to Spanish Ambassador, June 30, 1944, unnumbered document from Department of State File, RG 59, National Archives. Charges of abusive treatment were filed by a number of deportees over the years. . . .

22. Tokyo protests had stressed the inhumanity of the removals, which left families "abandoned and without resources." There is reason to believe that, as a direct result of Tokyo threats of "adequate counter measures," the family reunion program had been instituted. Tokyo was subsequently informed that initially "the facilities used for the transportation . . . were not adapted to the transportation of women and children" but that the U.S. intended to bring them over "at the earliest practicable opportunity." Memorandum, State Department to Spanish Embassy, April 19, 1943, Department of State File 740.00115 Pacific War/1549, RG 59, National Archives. Interestingly, commercial airlines and steamship lines were used in the transport of family members. . . .

23. Letter, Cordell Hull to Roosevelt, August 27, 1942, OF 20, FDR Library. At the time, mail, medicine, and other relief supplies could be sent to civilians and American POWs in Japanese hands only by way of the exchange vessels.

24. Letter, Francis Biddle to Secretary of State, January 11, 1943, Department of State File 740.00115 Pacific War/1276, RG 59, National Archives. The Alien Enemies Act (of 1798) provides that whenever there is a declared war between the U.S. and any foreign nation, "all natives, citizens, denizens, or subjects of the hostile nation," fourteen years or older, can be "apprehended, restrained, secured, and removed as alien enemies."

25. As quoted in a memorandum to the Secretary of State from Frank P. Corrigan of the U.S. Embassy in Caracas, August 21, 1943, Department of State File 740.00115 Pacific War/1845, RG 59, National Archives.

26. The drastic U.S. removal policy gained impetus from a resolution adopted at an Inter-American Conference in the spring of 1945. The resolution had recommended the adoption of measures "to prevent any person whose deportation was necessary for reasons of security of the continent from further residing in this hemisphere, if such residence would be prejudicial to the future security or welfare of the Americas." A Presidential Proclamation (Truman) of September 8, 1945, imple-

mented the resolution by directing the Justice Department to assist the Secretary of State (Byrnes) in effectuating removal of all enemy aliens to lands belonging to the enemy governments "to which or to the principles of which they had adhered" and of others then in the U.S. "without admission under the immigration laws." See Department of State File 711.62115 AR/8-3145, RG 59, National Archives.

27. The impossibility of a case-by-case review may also have led to the decision for summary removals. According to a State Department memo: ". . . unless we can get Peru to take the Japanese back, we shall be forced to repatriate all of them to Japan, since we have no information which would enable us to make a case-by-case review. In the very great majority of the cases, the Japanese were sent here only on the say-so of the Peruvian Government." Memorandum, J. B. Bingham to Braden and Acheson, December 13, 1945, Department of State File FW 711.62115 AR/12-1345, RG 59, National Archives.

28. Alfred Steinberg, "'Blunder' Maroons Peruvian Japanese in the U.S.," *Washington Post,* September 26, 1948. Author Barnhart ("Japanese Internees from Peru") maintains that the group removed during this period totaled 1,700, which is at variance with the State Department claim of 1,440 who "voluntarily returned to Japan." Letter to author from Georgia D. Hill, Office of the Chief of Military History, December 19, 1972. There had been 476 Peruvian-Japanese included in the second exchange of prisoners with Japan (September, 1943). See "Japanese in Peru" by John K. Emmerson, October 9, 1943, Department of State File 894.20223/196, National Archives.

29. Memorandum, Wayne Collins to author, postmarked June 28, 1973. Aliens among the residual group of 365 had been informed on March 26, 1946: ". . . deportation proceedings are to be instituted immediately in the cases of all who do not file applications for voluntary repatriation. Require all to make their intentions known within twenty-four hours." (Wire to officer in charge of Crystal City from the Immigration and Naturalization Service, excerpted from the Rucker study.) Collins maintains that the earlier removal of 1,700 deportees had been in no way voluntary "even if each was asked and signified his or her desire to be transported to Japan. They were being held as alien enemies under the Alien Enemies Act and couldn't escape the internment unless they agreed to be sent to Japan. That is a perfect picture of duress and lacks every essential of voluntariness."

30. Ickes wrote in his *New York Post* column (as reported in the *Pacific Citizen,* June 29, 1946) that the record of Japanese aliens in the United States during the war as "loyal Americans" is "unblemished," and that "the immediate problem is one of halting the brutal deportation of alien Japanese who have suffered so much at the hands of 'free and democratic' America." Collins successfully halted deportation of 163 longtime residents of fine standing found to be illegal entrants and of numerous Japanese nationals who had lost their admission status as a result of the war.

31. "Town Meeting of the Air" broadcast of December 2, 1947, in *The Town Hall,* XIII, No. 32 (December 12, 1947).

32. The deportees became eligible for naturalization under Public Law 751 (68 Stat., 1044), of August 31, 1954, which entitled the Peruvian-Japanese to a certification of "authorized entry" into the United States (Barnhart, op. cit., p. 176). The Peruvian-Japanese were "specifically denied restitution for damages by a House bill [H.R. 3999 *Adjudication of Certain Claims of Persons of Japanese Ancestry,* 80th Congress, 1st sess.] passed in July of 1947." (Rucker, op. cit., p. 65.)

4. How did some Japanese Americans resist internment?

Gary Y. Okihiro

Tule Lake under Martial Law: A Study in Japanese Resistance

Whereas the selections by Roger Daniels, Peter Irons, and Michi Weglyn analyze the motives and policies of government officials, recent scholarship has focused on Japanese American responses to mass incarceration. The author of this selection, Gary Okihiro, was one of the first revisionist historians to reinterpret protest within the internment camps. Born in 1945, Okihiro grew up in Hawaii far away from the Tule Lake Segregation Center in California. But Okihiro decided to research the protests at Tule Lake because, like many historians of the 1970s, he was fascinated by the topic of resistance. Influenced by the social movements of the 1960s, these revisionist scholars began writing histories of people of color challenging racial oppression in America and the rest of the world.

Okihiro first studied African resistance to colonization. His service in the Peace Corps, in Botswana in 1968, convinced him of the need to "decolonize the writing of the past" by restoring the voices and experiences of Africans to history. In 1976, he received a Ph.D. in history from the University of California at Los Angeles after completing his dissertation, "Hunters, Herders, Cultivators, and Traders: Interaction and Change in the Kgalagadi, Nineteenth Century." As a graduate student, he also helped develop Asian American studies at UCLA and began exploring the history of internment. In 1972, he made a pilgrimage to the remains of what had been the Manzanar camp, 225 miles north of Los Angeles. In the book *Whispered Silences: Japanese Americans and*

World War II (1996), he later recalled the profound impact of this journey:

> I discovered a great truth that Manzanar spring day, when surrounded by the silences of the snow-flecked mountains, the barren desert sand, and the stone and concrete foundations; I found a quickening in the wasteland, a scent in the wind. The burial ground was overfull with life. The silences of the past, I discovered, were not empty of meaning. Our stories, if missing from the pages of history, advance other stories, other lives.[1]

Inspired to restore internees to the pages of history, Okihiro reexamined the camp records produced by the War Relocation Authority (WRA) and the Japanese American Evacuation and Resettlement Study (JERS). This research made him determined to destroy the "myth of the loyal and subject victim" promoted by earlier accounts. In the pioneering article "Japanese Resistance in America's Concentration Camps: A Re-evaluation" (1973), Okihiro urged Asian American scholars to apply the insights provided in books such as Herbert Aptheker's *American Slave Revolts* (1963) and Nicholas Halasz's *The Rattling Chains* (1966). The history of noncooperation and mass demonstrations at the Poston and Manzanar camps, he argued, demonstrated that Japanese Americans also had a vital and resilient tradition of resisting oppression.

Tule Lake, as this selection shows, provided fertile ground for a revisionist interpretation of resistance. Located in northern California, just south of the Oregon border, the camp had a turbulent history even before it became a segregation center. In August 1942, two and a half months after the camp opened, farm laborers went on strike over the lack of promised goods and salaries. Packing shed workers struck the next month, and mess hall workers staged a protest in October. Administrative blunders and a strong dissident leadership exacerbated anger at the entire "leave clearance" process, and one-third of the camp refused to register or sign the loyalty questionnaire in February 1943. The WRA then converted Tule Lake into a segregation center for those deemed disloyal in all the camps. Protests escalated, and in early November the army took over and declared martial law. Military rule, as the following selection shows, only inspired more demonstrations and resistance.

In the 1970s, few academic journals were willing to publish Okihiro's revisionist interpretations because the editors didn't consider Japanese American protests a part of American history or Western history. Okihiro found receptive editors at the newly established *Amerasia Journal* and the *Journal of Ethnic Studies.* In the mid-1970s, he abandoned his plans to write a book on Tule Lake after failing to find any interested publishers. In the 1980s and 1990s, however, ethnic studies flourished, and Okihiro was recognized as a leading scholar in the field. He edited an anthology on African, Caribbean, and African American resistance and cowrote a book on Japanese American farmers in California's Santa Clara Valley. In *Cane Fires: The Anti-Japanese Movement in Hawaii, 1865–1945* (1991), Okihiro contests the popular image of the islands as a "racial paradise." The book also drew attention to the suffering of islanders arrested by the FBI and interned in camps run by the Army and the Department of Justice during World War II. Long neglected because of the focus on WRA camps, these internees also appear in Okihiro's text accompanying Joan Myers's photographs of the remnants of the internment camps in *Whispered Silences: Japanese Americans and World War II* (1996).

After nurturing Asian American studies programs at Humboldt State University and Santa Clara University, Okihiro joined the Cornell University history department in 1989. Currently the director of the Asian American Studies Program at Cornell, he also has served as president of the Association of Asian American Studies and is editor of the *Journal of Asian American Studies.* He continues to assail "traditional" views of history, most recently in his book *Margins and Mainstreams: Asians in American History and Culture* (1994), where he says that the democratic "core values and ideals of the nation" emanate from the struggles for equality by "Asian and African Americans, Latinos and American Indians, women, and gays and lesbians."[2]

Questions for a Closer Reading

1. Okihiro criticizes the "didactic approach" of earlier internment studies that focus on moral lessons and theories of responsibility. Why does he call for a new perspective on internment? How does his research help him undermine the "myth of the model minority"?
2. How does Okihiro challenge orthodox interpretations of resistance in the camps? Do you find his reinterpretation of the causes and consequences of camp protest persuasive?
3. Okihiro describes a spectrum of protest at Tule Lake. How does he explain the differences between "the more conservative protesters who hoped for a post-war future in America" and the most militant protesters?
4. What impact did military rule have on the influence of the *Daihyo Sha Kai*? Why, according to Okihiro, did the camp split over maintaining the status quo?
5. After noting differences between groups of resisters, Okihiro maintains that, "in the final analysis," they were "united in the underlying and pervasive struggle for human rights." Do you agree with Okihiro's argument that there was no "dramatic break" in the history of resistance at Tule Lake? Why or why not?

Notes

1. *Whispered Silences: Japanese Americans and World War II,* essay by Gary Y. Okihiro, photographs by Joan Myers (Seattle: University of Washington Press, 1996), p. 241.

2. Gary Y. Okihiro, "Preface," *Margins and Mainstreams: Asians in American History* (Seattle: University of Washington Press, 1994), p. ix.

Tule Lake under Martial Law: A Study in Japanese Resistance

The wartime internment of persons of Japanese ancestry has drawn considerable attention primarily because it serves the purposes of writers whose concerns are wider than the historical experience itself. There are those who regard the internment experience as historically significant because of its instructional value. That didactic approach, which forms a basis for the orthodox interpretation of the camps, has been the hallmark of popular writers, journalists, civil rights activists, ex–War Relocation Authority (WRA) officials, and members of the Japanese American Citizens League (JACL). To them, the forced removal and internment of 110,000 persons of Japanese ancestry was America's greatest wartime mistake, and the episode is a moral lesson to the nation, teaching that constant vigilance must be maintained to safeguard the civil liberties of all citizens because it could happen again to any minority group. Accordingly, those authors display a preoccupation with theories of responsibility for the mass removal and internment, and with constitutional issues.[1]

Apart from those concerns, the authors of the orthodox interpretation wrote with polemical objects in mind. While there were a few ex–WRA administrators who had an interest in answering their critics' charge of maladministration, the basic thrust of the authors of the orthodoxy was to refute the justification that "a Jap is a Jap." Their argument was based on the findings of sociologists who studied the camp communities and observed that Japanese society was not monolithic but was composed of what they determined to be geo-generational cleavages and varying degrees of assimilation. That refinement, when combined with other factors such as the education of Kibei* in Japan, formed the basis for their explanation for

**Kibei:* a term for Japanese Americans born in the United States but sent to Japan for their education.

Gary Y. Okihiro, "Tule Lake under Martial Law: A Study in Japanese Resistance," *Journal of Ethnic Studies* 5, no. 3 (Fall 1977): 71–85.

resistance in the internment camps. Their conclusion was that not all Japanese were the same, and that although there were some who were "pro-Japan" in sentiment, the vast majority were loyal to America. While that insight was an advance over the racists' indiscriminate stereotype, it simply replaced one stereotype with another. Issei were generally seen as "pro-Japan" in sentiment, Kibei were simplistically equated with "troublemakers," and Nisei, as assimilated and "pro-American."[2]

Another stereotype and myth was that the Japanese surmounted the overwhelming odds of early White racism, confiscation of property, and internment to become America's model minority. The story of the Japanese in America, therefore, is a stirring chapter in American history in which an entire ethnic minority showed America to be a land of opportunity and of justice triumphant.[3] The internment experience is crucial to that myth of the model minority. By demonstrating the innocence of the Japanese, their forbearance and fortitude throughout internment, and their unswerving pro-American loyalty despite being deprived of their rights as citizens, the cornerstone of the myth is laid. From the fires of adversity came a people ennobled. Therefore, the visible forms of Japanese resistance in the internment camps must be explained in terms other than resistance against White racism and anti-Americanism.

The orthodox interpretation explains Japanese resistance in the internment camps by citing the inexperience of the WRA administrators and the novelty of the situation. Once those initial problems had been resolved, that explanation concludes, resistance disappeared.[4] The frustration-aggression theory underlies a second explanation for the causes of Japanese resistance in the camps. This explanation views the various forms of resistance, the strike or "riot," as expressions and releases of pent-up pressures and frustrations.[5] A third causal explanation portrays resistance as an internal geo-generational struggle between Issei and Nisei, and Japanese from California set against those from the Pacific Northwest.[6] And finally, a fourth explanation admits to the presence of pro-Axis sympathizers among the internees, notably the Kibei, but it claims that these were only a small minority within the community. According to this explanation, Japanese resistance was generated by these troublemakers who stirred up discontent and used bullying tactics to coerce others to join in their protest.[7]

A small, but growing body of writings has questioned in recent years the orthodox interpretation of the internment camp.[8] These revisionists point out that the wartime removal of Japanese cannot be removed from its prewar historical context and that the internment camps were a logical extension of the established pattern of interaction between White Americans and Yellow immigrants.[9] Further, Japanese resistance in the camps was a part of that historical legacy, its roots reaching back in time to the daily struggle for survival in a racist American West; it was continuous, and purposeful. The revisionists view the camps and Japanese resistance from the perspective of historical continuities and linkages, and they deny the orthodox interpretation of treating resistance in terms of unconnected "incidents," minority "troublemakers" and "pressure groups," and geo-generational cleavages. And finally, instead of using the internment camps to illustrate a point external to that experience as do writers of the orthodoxy, the revisionists stress that the experience is not so much a moral lesson to White America as it is a part of the history of Asians in America.

There are a number of difficulties in the revisionists' interpretation of the internment camps. A major impediment is the nature of the available sources. Early analysts of the camps all wrote from the orthodox point of view and the resource materials assembled as documents, letters, memoirs, and oral history tapes all reflect the biases of the WRA and the JACL. Until a more comprehensive and objective collection of reminiscences can be made of those who formed the camp majority, we will regrettably be limited by those myopic confines. Because of that barrier, the revisionists are unable to determine precisely the number of people who actually resisted, the degree of mobilization, the exact role of coercion, and even the forms and nature of resistance. In addition, there is a notable gap in their attempt to link resistance in the camps with Japanese resistance to white racism in pre-war America. At this stage, it is too early to speak with any degree of certainty, and the revisionists can only legitimately claim that their interpretation represents a more reasonable attempt than the orthodox view. What is needed are a number of micro-studies which demonstrate the historical validity of their claim. This is written with that object in mind.

The Spoilage, by Thomas and Nishimoto, is a landmark in the orthodox interpretation of Japanese resistance: it is a detailed study of resistance at Tule Lake internment camp, it contains all the orthodox explanations for resistance, and it sets the tone for other studies on the internment camps. Its importance requires a re-examination of the argument employed in that work. Resistance, as characterized by Thomas and Nishimoto, was sporadic and not purposeful, and it was primarily intra-internee rather than anti-administration. The authors cite four basic causes for resistance: (1) the inexperience of the administrators and the initial discomforts of settling in; (2) geo-generational differences and rivalries; (3) conflicts between the old Tuleans and incoming "segregees";[10] and (4) pressure groups of radicals and pro-Axis troublemakers.

For Thomas and Nishimoto, the proof of that interpretation is encapsulated in the vote of January 11, 1944 in which a majority of Tule Lake internees rejected status quo.[11] In that vote there is a statistically significant correlation between blocks which favored status quo and the percentage of segregees. That is, blocks which voted for status quo or the continuation of radical rule had high percentages of segregees in them. That correlation appears to support the authors' contention that protesters and segregees were essentially one and the same. Further, the rejection of status quo came after the radical leaders had been locked away in the stockade. From that, the authors conclude that when given a chance, the people turned to moderate leaders and a conciliatory solution in their desire to return to "normalcy."[12]

The events leading up to that vote in January 1944 and the vote itself, therefore, are crucial to the Thomas and Nishimoto interpretation of resistance and merit a re-examination of those events beginning with the military occupation of Tule Lake on November 4, 1943 and ending with the lifting of martial law on January 15, 1944.[13] Some highlights of that period include the incarceration of the Negotiating Committee, a vote of confidence in those imprisoned leaders despite the administration's efforts to elect new representatives, a hunger strike among the prisoners in the stockade, and the so-called return to normalcy following the vote against status quo.

Ever since the creation of Tule Lake internment camp towards June 1942, the Japanese protested various conditions considered to be unjust. There was a mess hall strike in July, a campaign for higher wages in August, and two labor strikes in August and September. The immediate basis for those protests was the people's concern that they were being doubly exploited by being placed in detention by the government and asked to work to produce their own food for sixteen dollars per month. But the underlying and more fundamental cause of the people's protests was the absurd injustice of their detention.

That was crystallized by the farm labor strike in October 1943 following the accidental death of an internee, Kashima, when a farm truck on which he was riding overturned. To most of the internees, Kashima's death was a senseless loss because he would not have died had there been no internment camp. That mood was reflected in the composition of *Daihyo Sha Kai,* the representative body of the people, in elections which were held the day following Kashima's death. The majority of the sixty-four representatives, one chosen from each block, were individuals who had the reputation of being aggressive opponents of the White administration. Largely because of that and in disregard of their representative nature, the *Daihyo Sha Kai* and the Negotiating Committee were never granted legitimacy by the administrators and instead were seen as antagonists and troublemakers.

When Dillon Myer, the National Director of the WRA, visited Tule Lake the following month, the *Daihyo Sha Kai* resolved to present their complaints directly before him since negotiating with Best, the Tule Lake director, had been shown to be futile. The local bureaucrats denied that request to speak with Myer, and the *Daihyo Sha Kai* decided to force the issue. In a massive show of support, thousands of internees surrounded the administrative building in which Myer was visiting with Best. George Kuratomi, the spokesman of the protesters, outlined to Myer the people's grievances which included Best's dishonest dealings, White racism among certain administrators, inadequate food, overcrowding, and the lack of basic cleaning equipment. But beyond those specific complaints, Kuratomi asked that "we be treated humanely from this Government, this Government of the United States."[14] Myer's response was to align himself firmly with Best and his policies and not give any encouragement to a consideration of the people's demands.

Having failed to receive an acceptable response to their grievances from the WRA, who in the minds of the people were representatives of the United States government, the protesters had no other option but to turn to the Japanese government through the Spanish Consul for redress and support. At this point, there developed a major tactical fracture within the populace. The more conservative protesters who hoped for a post-war future in America viewed the appeal to Japan as incompatible with that desire because White Americans would perceive that to be "un-American." These continued their protest but only through what they considered to be "legitimate" channels — the WRA, the Army, and the Congress. Others who saw no future for themselves and their children in a post-war America viewed the appeal to the Japanese government as their final option. Their first meeting with the Spanish Consul took place on November 3, two days after the confrontation with Myer, and despite his inability to improve the conditions of camp life, the protesters had at least found a receptive ear.

Meanwhile, there was much concern among the White administrators for their personal safety, having witnessed Japanese activism in the mass demonstration of November 1. They demanded military protection in the form of tanks and machine guns, and insisted that a man-proof fence be erected between the administration and internee areas. When Myer and Best failed to give them that reassurance, they went directly to Lt. Col. Verne Austin on November 2 and received Austin's promise that Army troops would guarantee their safety. Best, miffed that his staff went over his head, dismissed two of his most outspoken critics, and within a week twenty staff members resigned.

Best, Myer, and the WRA were confronted with not only internal criticism from their staff for their handling of the mass demonstration of November 1, but also were charged with pampering the Japanese and administrative inefficiency by White residents of the Tule Lake basin and the press, and they faced possible censure from state and national legislative investigating committees. Thus, the November 1 demonstration took on national significance, and the pressure on the WRA to stamp out the resistance seemed to come from factors other than the Japanese protesters themselves. On November 4, following a minor scuffle between a handful of Japanese and White administrators, Best called in the military, a decision which appears to have been precipitated not by the scuffle but by the other pressures mentioned above.[15]

The turning over of the camp to the military, therefore, was a hardening of position *vis-à-vis* resistance and a crackdown against protesters. But Army rule did not end resistance because it failed to rectify the causes of that resistance. Like the WRA, the Army viewed the camp in terms of pressure groups and enemy provocateurs,[16] but unlike the WRA, they were efficient in their repression of Japanese resistance. Individuals were arbitrarily arrested and detained, and there was no recourse or discussion of grievances. Still, throughout the period of military rule, the *Daihyo Sha Kai* urged restraint and open dialogue, but as conditions became progressively more oppressive, their strategy of appealing to the Japanese government was shown to be ineffective and that tactic came increasingly under fire from both extremes of the protest spectrum. On November 12, Austin announced that he no longer recognized the *Daihyo Sha Kai* as the legitimate voice of the people and the following day, he ordered the arrest and detention of members of that representative body.

A tactic employed to stamp out resistance by both the Army and the WRA was to drive a wedge between the majority whom they perceived to be basically co-operative and the minority who were the troublemakers. In a speech on November 13, the day on which the arrest and detention of members of the *Daihyo Sha Kai* began, a WRA official expressed that conspiratorial view: "It is our belief that the majority of the people in this colony do want to live in peace and harmony, that many of you are willing to work and carry on necessary services, but that a few, in order to gain power for themselves, have attempted to gain such power through force."[17]

And in accordance with that strategy of isolating the troublesome minority, the Army, on November 16, reiterated that they did not recognize the *Daihyo Sha Kai* as the legitimate representatives of the people and announced that instead, the block managers would fulfill that function. The block representatives, of whom the *Daihyo Sha Kai* consisted, were elected in free elections sponsored by the people themselves, in contrast with the block managers who had been appointed by the WRA. The Army's reason for recognizing the block managers as their contact with the people was because they are representatives of the WRA. . . ."[18]

That the Army and WRA's conspiratorial view of the camp was grossly inaccurate and that they stubbornly refused to acknowledge the pervasiveness of resistance are clearly illustrated in their meeting with the representatives of the internees on November 18.[19] Austin expressed his suspicion of Japanese motives in the opening statement, that "All discussions held here . . . will be in English throughout the meeting." The block managers, aware of their impossible position, tried to make certain that the administrators understood the mood of the people regarding the announcement of November 16 that they, and not the block representatives, were to be the link with the internees. "We represent the WRA," protested Mayeda, "and we do not represent the people in the colony." Yamatani, a member of the Temporary Communications Committee,[20] added that, "we are still supporting 100% our negotiating committee."[21]

The meeting continued with the block managers pressing the Army on their exact duties since they were henceforth to be the people's representatives. The administrators replied that they were to maintain order[22] and enforce the 6 A.M. to 7 P.M. curfew. Furukawa, a block manager, pointed out that in the past, it was the duty of the wardens and not the block managers to maintain order, and he observed that previously, when the block managers had tried to move constructively to improve the mess halls, the WRA had stifled that initiative. The block managers were trying to get through to the administrators that they were not truly representative of the people and that they did not want to be caught in the middle, being seen as *inu* ("dogs" or "collaborators") by the people for enforcing the administration's unpopular regulations and being powerless to change administrative abuses and excesses.

When the Army tried to press the block managers to commit themselves to maintaining order without giving the assurance that they would have a voice in policy-making, the block managers sought to postpone that commitment by suggesting that they wait until after the expected visit of the Spanish Consul. That led an annoyed Lt. Col. Meek to respond, "We don't need him for negotiating . . ." and, "As far as we are concerned it doesn't make any difference whether he comes or not." Austin reiterated that point and concluded by saying, "Due to conditions that exist in this camp today, the Army is not interested in dealing with the committee with whom we are dealing. We do not believe or feel that it is a representative committee."

The administrators were not interested in dialogue and in understanding the true mood of the people because they had already formed an opinion of that mood. And they were not interested in suggestions about the operation of the camp from internees who held contrary opinions. They were seeking Japanese who reflected their viewpoint and fit into their *a priori* conceptions. Because any internee who was openly critical of the existing order was considered to be subversive by the Army, many were afraid to demonstrate their true inner feelings. That repressive atmosphere created by an arbitrary administration was pointed out by Shirai when he responded,

"Everybody [is] afraid to become a representative on a committee. Afraid that you will pick us up." The pressure to conform was not the monopoly of so-called internee pressure groups, but was a consciously directed policy of the administrators.

Methodical repression of the populace by the Army began the day after that meeting of November 18. Austin, in Proclamation Number 3, required that all internees, twelve years and older, receive identification badges which they had to carry with them at all times.[23] And on November 22, a comprehensive plan was formulated for a massive search of the Japanese area to be carried out on November 26. Among the stated purposes for that search were: (a) the taking into custody of trouble-making Japanese;[24] and (b) the confiscating of contraband such as knives, clubs, guns, explosives, and signalling devices. The search was to be carried out by three groups of about 150 men, each soldier carrying full field equipment and a gas mask, and every officer having side arms, clubs, and gas grenades.

The block managers were informed of this search only on the designated day, when the raid was launched with the precision of a well-planned military maneuver. The soldiers netted 25 tons of rice and other grains, 22 barrels of *saké* mash, 400 boxes of canned goods, 20 crates of dried fruit, 20 cartons of cereal, 2 *saké* stills, a Japanese language printing press, 500 knives, 400 clubs, 2 public address systems, and 500 radio receivers.[25]

Meanwhile on November 24, Austin and Best concurred on the erecting of a stockade which would include four barracks for the incarceration of "troublemakers." Various lists of such persons were drawn up and these were methodically hunted down and placed in detention in the stockade not having been charged or given a hearing. On December 4, Austin announced to the people, "You are notified that the members of the negotiating committee now in military custody are not and will not at any time negotiate with the Army, the WRA, or anyone else and they will not return to the colony." He therefore advised that the people hold elections for a new representative committee.[26]

The same day, the block representatives met to discuss Austin's suggestion and decided that they would place the matter before the people. There were three questions on the ballot the following day, December 5. These were: (1) should the *Daihyo Sha Kai* be dissolved and new representatives be elected to negotiate with the Army?; (2) should status quo be maintained? (i.e. should we support our present block representatives and the Negotiating Committee?); and (3) should there be a general strike in support of those who were imprisoned in the stockade? The results of that day's voting were as follows: three blocks favored a general strike, three blocks voted for new elections, five blocks remained undecided, and fifty-three blocks favored status quo.[27] Despite the administrators' coercive tactics, the referendum of December 5 was evidence of an overwhelming vote of confidence in the *Daihyo Sha Kai* and the Negotiating Committee.

But the pressures against maintaining status quo continued to build up the longer the Army remained intransigent in releasing members of the Negotiating Committee from the stockade and insisted on dealing only with a new committee of internees. That hopeless deadlock was pointed out by the Spanish Consul on December 13 at a meeting with the people, when he urged that the internees elect a new negotiating committee because the present Committee was powerless to effect change while in the stockade.[28] Despite that recommendation, few of the Japanese ventured to express support publicly, fearing to be viewed as pro-administration and against the imprisoned but still *de facto* leaders of the people. Yet, by isolating the members of the Negotiating Committee from the camp, the Army made it difficult for the leaders to communicate with the people.

Between the end of December 1943 and the beginning of January 1944, a series of events occurred which brought the situation to a head. According to one account, on the morning of December 30, Lt. Schaner, the Police and Prisoner Officer, arbitrarily took Yoshiyama and Tsuda, two prisoners, from the general stockade and confined them to a small cell within the stockade enclosure.[29] Schaner himself had selected these two previously to be the spokesmen for the prisoners, and his high-handed confinement of them reinforced the arbitrary manner in which the White administrators disregarded the internees' human rights.[30] In protest of Schaner's harassment of prisoners, the stockaders refused to assemble for the roll call at 1300.

One of the prisoners, Mori, spoke with Schaner about the situation and received the latter's promise that Yoshiyama and Tsuda would be released if the prisoners cleaned up the stockade area and assembled for the evening roll call. The Japanese fulfilled those conditions but by the next morning, Yoshiyama and Tsuda still had not been released. To protest that breach of promise the prisoners refused to assemble for roll call that day, December 31, but only after armed troops were brought into the stockade later in the day did the Japanese yield and file out of their barracks.

At the roll call, Schaner again arbitrarily pointed to a prisoner, Uchida, and ordered him to be confined to the small stockade along with Yoshiyama and Tsuda. Then he challenged the Japanese, "Now if there are any more of you who would like to go with him, just step up towards the gate." After a moment's pause, one of them, Koji Todoroki, stepped forward and according to an Army eyewitness, "a murmur passed through the prisoners, followed by the entire group breaking ranks and moving in the direction of the gate."[31]

The men were forced to remain in line and stand in the snow for about three hours during which time Schaner conferred with Austin. Schaner returned to announce to the prisoners, "I was just waiting for that. You men will be put on bread and water for twenty-four hours. You men will have to learn that we mean business and will not tolerate such a demonstration."[32] Trucks then entered the stockade and removed all stores of foodstuffs. One of the Japanese brought in from the outside to help load the trucks showed a reluctance to carry out that task, and he received "a few *tender* cuffs from Lt. Smith and S/Sgt. Anderson which made him change his mind." Meanwhile, Schaner ordered a search of the prisoners' quarters, which was conducted, according to one military observer, "in a most unnecessary destructive method."[33] Many personal items were stolen from the Japanese including radios, pens, watches, cigarettes, and cash.

Following that display of flagrant abuse and disregard of their rights, the prisoners vowed to go on a hunger strike until the release of all prisoners in the stockade. One of the prisoners, Tsuda, explained why that decision was made. "The reason the men . . . are on this hunger strike is because they know not the reason they are in the stockade. They feel they have been unjustly confined and the reason given to them is that they are the potential troublemakers and strong arm men of the colony, which they feel is not true. This is the manner in which they are trying to prove their sincerity and show that they should be vindicated."[34] The prisoners were protesting the arbitrary nature of their arrest and confinement, and they were trying to point out to the administrators once again their error in seeing the camp in terms of pressure groups and enemy provocateurs.

To the internees, the entire situation was absurd and senseless. In the first place, their removal and internment was an absurd though hardly unexpected happening. The White camp administrators, while accusing the Japanese of using pressure groups, employed high-handed and terror tactics in dealing with internee protest against what they considered to be violations of their fundamental human rights. Further, the administrators stubbornly refused to examine the protesters' demands objectively, rejected out of hand the legitimacy of the people's chosen representatives, and equated any criticism of their administration with pro-Axis sentiments and saw them as subversive and destructive of the American war effort.

At the same time, those same administrators lectured to the internees about the virtues of American democracy while incarcerating those who had been elected democratically by the people and who were exercising those rights of democracy. To the Japanese, there was no rational basis for the existence of the stockade or the presence of tanks and soldiers in the camp. The entire situation could have been simply resolved had the administrators accepted the legitimacy of the *Daihyo Sha Kai,* shown sincerity in discussing camp problems, and treated the internees as people with basic human rights.[35]

The prisoners' hunger strike lasted from January 1 to January 6, 1944 without producing any tangible concessions from the administration. The administrators kept the camp population ignorant of the protest until the third day of the strike when a group of concerned internees asked Austin about "rumors" of a hunger strike among the stockade prisoners and Austin confirmed its veracity. Despite an anonymously authored call among the internees for a demonstration of solidarity with the hunger strikers, there is no evidence of any such visible show of support.[36] Instead, the available sources show that there was a growing sentiment among the populace against status quo in an attempt to break the current deadlock.

There are several interesting features in the argument employed against status quo. Keeping in mind that the official (WRA and Army) and orthodox explanation is that the movement against status quo indicated that the majority of the internees rejected the legitimacy of the *Daihyo Sha Kai* and Negotiating Committee and simply wished for a return to "normalcy," we will examine some of those features. The basic premise of the argument against status quo was that the people were being severely oppressed, both in the stockade and in the camp, since martial rule. The *Daihyo Sha Kai,* the argument continued, had failed to alleviate that oppression, both because they were not recognized by the administrators and because they were being held prisoners in the stockade. Therefore, the argument concluded, a new committee must be elected, one leading to improved camp conditions and the release of those in the stockade.

The argument here was a practical one: It was not a rejection of the *Daihyo Sha Kai* as the legitimate representatives of the people but was a recognition of the impasse and that this solution was the only option permitted by the administrators. Further, their appeal was not to American patriotism but to Japanese ethnicity. The members of the *Daihyo Sha Kai,* the argument went, were not displaying the "true Japanese spirit" because "true" Japanese would resign having failed. And the appeal concluded, "we have no other desire than to exist as a true Japanese and to return to Japan unashamed."[37]

On January 10, Austin sent out a memorandum to the block managers with instructions on the upcoming referendum which was to decide on the question of status quo. That there would arise confusion among many of the internees on the issue being voted upon was assured by Austin's instructions to the block managers. These instructions failed to be accompanied by a sample ballot, and one of them stated: "Whenever any questions should arise from the floor the chair should state that he is not in a position to answer them. The only purpose of the meeting is to have the block residents vote on the question listed on the ballots."[38] The following day, January 11, Austin held a meeting with all the block managers to discuss the voting which was to take place that night. At the meeting, he reinforced the notion that should the people vote against status quo, military oppression would end. "A great deal depends upon the manner in which these meetings are held," Austin admonished, "as to whether this colony comes back to normal, in which I believe you are all interested."[39]

That night, voting was held in the camp with the ballots simply labelled, "Against Status Quo" and "For Status Quo." The results of the voting as reported by the Army was, 4,593 against status quo, 4,120 for, and 228 undecided.[40] One internee report disputed that count and accused the administrators of rigging the election results because no internees were present at the tabulation of the votes. That report went on to claim that a true count was, thirty-one blocks for status quo, twenty-nine blocks against, four blocks undetermined, and one block abstained.[41] Also, one of the internees later testified that "the ballots were none too good and some people didn't understand the meaning of status quo."[42] But apart from the question of the validity of the results, the vote revealed the reluctance of the people to cast a vote which could be interpreted as being a repudiation of the *Daihyo Sha Kai* despite the argument that such a vote would be followed by the release of the men in the stockade and a lessening of military oppression.

In a meeting held on January 14 between those who had favored the abolishing of status quo and *Daihyo Sha Kai* members who were in the stockade, their unity of purpose was reaffirmed although they had chosen two different approaches to that one basic goal.[43] Both groups lamented the fact that the issue had split the internees. "I surely hate to see the Japanese divided," commented Inouye, "and hate to see them fighting with each other." Shimada explained why that division was brought about and why they had voted against status quo. "Let me repeat this," he asserted, "the Army would not give a chance to talk about [the] release of you people, unless normal condition was first returned." Inouye, a spokesman for the stockade prisoners, reconfirmed the unity of purpose of both groups and offered: "We realize all the things you people are going through and have told the men in the stockade that you people were working so hard for the common goal. We are just as worried as you people are."

On January 15, 1944, just four days after the status quo referendum, the Army formally turned over the administration of Tule Lake internment camp to the WRA, ostensibly after having fulfilled their mission of stamping out resistance. They had accomplished that by isolating the troublemakers from the majority of the people and were vindicated in the recent referendum which they interpreted as being a repudiation of the *Daihyo Sha Kai* and a vote for the return to "normalcy." Austin expressed his persistent belief in the orthodox view of resistance on the eve of his departure: "The block representatives were all appointees of the pressure group and while some of them were capable and responsible members of the Colony the rest were actively engaged in fomenting unrest, discord and recommending violence to those desiring a return of normalcy within the Colony."[44]

While the period of military rule is merely a limited window into Japanese resistance at Tule Lake, it is a time segment crucial to the orthodox interpretation of resistance. That interpretation maintains that it was during that repressive period that the internee majority were permitted to express themselves freely because of the incarceration of the radicals, and that expression was a rejection of status quo and the election of moderate leaders.

In contrast, it can be seen that there had been a history of resistance and there was no such dramatic break, because both groups, for and against status quo, were committed to a program of reform and the continuing fight for a recognition of their humanity. Their disagreement was in the method of resistance. One group believed that the release of prisoners in the stockade was the first step toward a peaceful relationship between internees and administrators, while the other group held that the latter would be followed by the former. Further, the vote against status quo was not necessarily a vote against the *Daihyo Sha Kai*. In fact, the leaders in that vote saw it as a practical solution to the impasse created by the administration's intransigence. And in the final analysis, both those who favored status quo and those opposed to it were united in the underlying and pervasive struggle for human rights.

Notes

1. See e.g., Morton Grodzins, *Americans Betrayed* (Chicago, 1949); Jacobus tenBroek, Edward N. Barnhart, and Floyd W. Matson, *Prejudice, War, and the Constitution* (Berkeley, 1954); and Roger Daniels, *Concentration Camps, USA* (New York, 1971).

2. See e.g., Dorothy Swaine Thomas and Richard S. Nishimoto, *The Spoilage* (Berkeley, 1946).

3. See e.g., Leonard J. Arrington, *The Price of Prejudice* (Logan, Utah, 1962); Bill Hosokawa, *Nisei: The Quiet Americans* (New York, 1969); and Harry H. L. Kitano, *Japanese Americans: The Evolution of a Subculture* (Englewood Cliffs, New Jersey, 1969).

4. Edward H. Spicer, Asael T. Hansen, Katherine Luomala, and Marvin K. Opler, *Impounded People* (Tucson, 1969), pp. 15–16, 23, 63–64; and Alexander H. Leighton, *The Governing of Men* (Princeton, 1945), pp. 90–92.

5. Carey McWilliams, *Prejudice* (Boston, 1944), pp. 173, 176; Dillon S. Myer, *Uprooted Americans* (Tucson, 1971), pp. 59–65; and Shotaro Frank Miyamoto, "A Study of the Career of Intergroup Tensions: The Collective Adjustments of Evacuees to Crises at the Tule Lake Relocation Center," Ph.D. diss., University of Chicago, 1950.

6. McWilliams, *Prejudice,* 177–78; Paul Bailey, *City in the Sun* (Los Angeles, 1971); and Thomas and Nishimoto, *The Spoilage.*

7. McWilliams, *Prejudice,* pp. 179–80; and Thomas and Nishimoto, *The Spoilage.*

8. Douglas W. Nelson, "Heart Mountain: The History of an American Concentration Camp," M.A. thesis, University of Wyoming, 1970; Gary Y. Okihiro, "Japanese Resistance in America's Concentration Camps: A Re-evaluation," *Amerasia Journal,* 2

(Fall 1973), 20–34; and Arthur A. Hansen and David A. Hacker, "The Manzanar Riot: An Ethnic Perspective," *Amerasia Journal,* 2 (Fall 1974), 112–57.

9. As done for the Chinese in Alexander Saxton's *The Indispensable Enemy* (Berkeley, 1971).

10. Tule Lake became a "segregation center" after September 1943 following the so-called loyalty registration which segregated the internees into "loyals" and "disloyals." Those who were designated as "disloyals" were termed "segregees" and transferred to Tule Lake internment camp.

11. "Status quo" was the continuation of the *Daihyo Sha Kai* and Negotiating Committee as the legitimate representatives of the people. The *Daihyo Sha Kai* had been formed in October 1943 by a free and democratic election of all the internees of Tule Lake camp. Its composition, in the words of Thomas and Nishimoto, consisted of "belligerent, vociferous individuals who had gained the reputation of being aggressive opponents of the administration. . . ." The Negotiating Committee was composed of fourteen members of the *Daihyo Sha Kai* who were nominated to serve as the larger body's mouthpiece in negotiations with the administration. Thomas and Nishimoto, *The Spoilage,* p. 117.

12. Thomas and Nishimoto, *The Spoilage,* pp. 184–86.

13. A separate paper to be published in a forthcoming edited volume covers the period before martial law.

14. "Transcript of the Meeting," November 1, 1943, in Japanese American Research Project, Collection 2010, Research Library, University of California, Los Angeles [henceforth referred to as JARP Collection], Austin Papers, Box 43 [henceforth referred to as AP], Folder 4, Document 3.

15. Oral history interview with Dillon S. Myer, May 20, 1968, in JARP Collection, AP, Box 397, No. 300.

16. The orthodox interpretation of resistance falls into this same error. Protest, by the WRA and Army, was seen as being anti-administration and disruptive. In its most extreme form, the WRA and Army viewed themselves as representatives of the American government. Resistance, therefore, was anti-American and even disruptive of the entire war effort. To the internees, protest was constructive and designed simply to gain a recognition of their fundamental human rights and for a more satisfactory life in the camps. As evidence of this contrast, see Leighton, *Governing of Men,* pp. 81–89; and Spicer et al., *Impounded,* p. 133, in which at Poston, members of the WRA staff equated the internees with the Japanese enemy.

17. Speech by Mr. Cozzens, November 13, 1943, in JARP Collection, AP, Folder 5, Document 23.

18. Notes by Lt. Forbes at a meeting held November 16, 1943, in JARP Collection, AP, Folder 5, Document 27.

19. The proceedings of this meeting were taken from Evacuee Meeting, November 18, 1943, in JARP Collection, AP, Folder 6, Document 1.

20. The Temporary Communications Committee had been appointed by the *Daihyo Sha Kai* to serve as their representatives throughout the period of their detention by the Army.

21. As noted before, the Negotiating Committee consisted of fourteen members nominated from among the *Daihyo Sha Kai* to serve as the mouthpiece of that representative body.

22. Proclamation Number 2, November 13, 1943, spelled out some of the regulations which were to be enforced. These included the prohibiting of outdoor meet-

ings without prior military approval, and no incoming or outgoing telephone or telegraph messages without administrative consent. JARP Collection, AP, Folder 5, Document 18.

23. Proclamation Number 3, November 19, 1943, in JARP Collection, AP, Folder 6, Document 4.

24. Various members of the Negotiating Committee had successfully eluded arrest by the Army by going into hiding. These included Kuratomi, Kai, and Sugimoto.

25. JARP Collection, AP, Folder 6, Documents 7, 11, 15, 17.

26. Notice to All Residents of Tule Lake Center, December 12, 1943, in JARP Collection, AP, Folder 7, Document 6.

27. JARP Collection, AP, Folder 7, Document 7. Cf. "Minutes of the Meeting of the Dai-Hyo Sha Kai of the Tule Lake Center," December 5, 1943, in the Bancroft Library collection of material relating to the evacuation and internment, University of California, Berkeley, Folder R 2.25, which records the final vote to be: three blocks for a general strike, four blocks for new elections, two blocks were undecided, and fifty-six blocks for status quo.

28. JARP Collection, AP, Folder 7, Document 17. Another indication that the internees were trying all avenues open to them was their petition to the U.S. Secretary of War, Henry L. Stimson, dated December 7, 1943. The petition summarized the events which led to the military occupation of Tule Lake and asked for administrative co-operation and dialogue. JARP Collection, AP, Folder 7, Document 32.

29. Another account states that these men were confined to the small stockade because they had laughed out loud during the calling of the roll. Yoshiyama and Tsuda, however, were not laughing at the White soldiers but at two men who were trying to load cartons of tobacco. JARP Collection, AP, Folder 8, Document 26.

30. See e.g., JARP Collection, AP, Folder 8, Document 24.

31. "Stockade Prisoners Rebellion," an investigation by S/Sgt. Sam Yeramian, December 31, 1943, in JARP Collection, AP, Folder 7, Document 30.

32. "Stockade Prisoners Rebellion."

33. "Stockade Prisoners Rebellion."

34. Interview with Hiroyoshi Tsuda, January 5, 1944, in JARP Collection, AP, Folder 8, Document 8.

35. Interview with Hiroyoshi Tsuda; and "Meeting of the Spanish Consul," November 3, 1943, in JARP Collection, AP, Folder 4, Document 4.

36. "Voice of the People," in JARP Collection, AP, Folder 8, Document 10.

37. JARP Collection, AP, Folder 8, Documents 15, 16, 17, 19, 20.

38. Memorandum, Austin to Block Managers, January 10, 1944, in JARP Collection, AP, Folder 8, Document 18. The block managers were to read a statement from a pamphlet prepared by the administration to the assembled people immediately before the voting began. Unfortunately, there is no record of what that statement said. "Minutes of a General Meeting of all Block Managers," January 11, 1944, in JARP Collection, AP, Folder 8, Document 21.

39. "Minutes of a General Meeting of all Block Managers," January 11, 1944.

40. JARP Collection, AP, Folder 8, Document 22. Despite the statistically significant correlation between blocks voting for status quo and the percentage of segregees in those blocks, the link is not necessarily a causal one.

41. "Report of Present Condition," by the Nippon Patriotic Society, in JARP Collection, AP, Folder 8, Document 29. This protest of the official count is important when one considers the 228 listed by the Army as "undecided." If, for instance, that

228 and the 247 disenfranchised stockade prisoners voted for status quo, those favoring status quo would have a majority of 4,595 to 4,593.

42. "Report of the Informal Interview of the Divisional Responsible Men and the Detained Stockade Internees," January 14, 1944, in JARP Collection, AP, Folder 8, Document 26. On the morning of the vote, soldiers rounded up some members of the *Daihyo Sha Kai* and status quo sympathizers. That may have influenced a number of the Japanese to vote in conformance with the Army's wishes. Thomas and Nishimoto, *The Spoilage,* pp. 181–82.

43. The proceedings of this meeting were taken from "Report of the Informal Interview," January 14, 1944.

44. Letter from Austin to de Amat, January 14, 1944, in JARP Collection, AP, Folder 8, Document 27.

5. What was the impact of internment on Japanese American families and communities?

Valerie J. Matsumoto

Amache

This selection by Valerie Matsumoto demonstrates how oral history sources can enrich internment historiography. Only in the past two decades have many former internees been willing to share their histories with the public. Many broke their silence because of the campaign for redress, highlighted by the 1981 Commission on Wartime Relocation and Internment of Civilians hearings and the 1988 Civil Liberties Act, which awarded surviving internees $20,000 and a national apology. The redress movement encouraged Japanese Americans to speak about the war before the government, to write memoirs, and to recount their oral histories to researchers.

Matsumoto was a history graduate student at Stanford in 1982 when she heard that an agricultural community in California's San Joaquin Valley was looking for a scholar to conduct a history project for them. She learned that this community, the Cortez colony, was one of three planned Christian colonies established by businessman Abiko Kyutaro. During the war, the colonists had hired a white manager to oversee their farms and thus were able to preserve their landholdings while interned at the Amache camp. They also maintained a large network of religious, civic, and social organizations. Ignoring WRA advice to disperse throughout the country, this community remained intact for three generations when it began looking for a historian. Excited at the prospect of working with this unique community, Matsumoto eagerly asked to be considered for the position.

Her heart sank when she heard that Cortez, unable to agree on whether to produce a film, book, exhibit, or slide show, had decided to cancel the project. "About ten minutes into the beginning of deep despair," Matsumoto realized that "the Cortez residents had not said they did not want a history project, only that they were not going to carry it out themselves."[1] She got in touch with the community and found two families willing to serve as her "home bases" as she worked around the seasonal farm schedule conducting interviews for her dissertation. Nobuzo and Miye Baba showed Matsumoto "the Growers Association building, the JACL Hall, and the two churches, and then commenced calling their neighbors to see who would agree to be interviewed." While the Babas introduced Matsumoto to many Buddhists in town, George and Helen Yuge helped her meet the Christians in the community. To facilitate contacts and set up interviews, the two families took Matsumoto to numerous events, ranging from a Boy Scouts' fund-raising pancake breakfast to a local JACL installation banquet.

Although Matsumoto also used organizational records, newspapers, and wartime memorabilia in her research, her eighty three interviews clearly yielded the richest material for the dissertation that became *Farming the Home Place* (1993). She used these oral histories to explore gender role development, generational change and continuity, ethnic support networks, and the functions of community before, during, and after the war. She also found that there was no single, "representative" response to internment. Earlier studies portraying internees as either victims or protesters de-emphasized their diverse backgrounds and experiences. Matsumoto discovered that even a seemingly homogeneous community like Cortez was divided by generational and gender issues during the war. Internment accelerated some Nisei's quest for greater independence and weakened patriarchal authority. As Issei men lost their role as family breadwinner and were barred from political positions, more Nisei refused to abide by arranged marriages. Nisei men and women also became more assertive as they left camp for the armed forces, jobs, or college.

Matsumoto's oral histories also show that the Nisei men and women from Cortez had a wide range of attitudes and responses that defy simple categorization. Earlier accounts portrayed internees as either heroic soldiers, assimilated Americans, browbeaten victims, or militant protesters. But Matsumoto found that one picture cannot capture the diverse reactions to internment. Instead, in this selection on the Amache camp, she provides a composite portrait of individuals using networks of friends and relatives to cope with internment in a variety of ways.

Matsumoto acknowledges that her relationships with her interviewees may have affected their representations of the past. "As a researcher," she explains in her introduction to *Farming the Home Place,* "I was both an insider and an outsider."

> While I did not grow up in Cortez or in a Japanese American community, my background as a Sansei woman whose parents had raised tomatoes in southern California gave me some familiarity with Japanese American culture and the rhythms of rural life. At the beginning of each interview, I was asked where my family came from and in which camp they had been interned. I replied that my grandparents came from Fukuoka-ken in southern Japan, that they and their children had farmed in northern and southern California, and that they had spent the war years in the Poston Camp in Arizona and the Topaz Camp in Utah. These facts enabled the Cortez people to locate me within the Japanese American cosmos and to confirm the presence of common bonds of understanding between us.

Never pretending to be an "objective" researcher, Matsumoto candidly admits that her perspective on Cortez was influenced by a sense that "its history and hospitality were intertwined." In an appendix to the book titled "Notes on Research," she describes trying to alleviate any anxiety her interviewees might have experienced by sending her questions (also included in the book's appendix) ahead of time and agreeing to omit any topics they disliked. Aware that she was the same age as many of her interviewees' children, she always "remained conscious of the bonds of responsibility and affection."

According to Matsumoto, "One must examine one's priorities as a scholar, and weigh the implications of one's work for the women and men whose history has formed its bedrock." In *Farming the Home Place,* an article on Nisei women during the war,[2] and an article on Nisei women writers of the 1930s,[3] Matsumoto has helped restore the voices and experiences of Japanese American women to the pages of history. She is a professor in the history department at the University of California at Los Angeles and in 1992 led an interdisciplinary seminar for UCLA faculty on integrating internment into their curricula. A mainstay of UCLA's Asian American Studies Program, she also has cultivated some of the most promising new scholars in the field.

Questions for a Closer Reading

1. Matsumoto notes that "Amache was considered to be one of the more peaceful" camps. How does she account for this? What might explain the differences between Amache and Tule Lake?
2. Using her oral histories, Matsumoto profiles a number of reactions to internment and resettlement. Compare the ways people describe life in the camp, in military service, at college, and at work outside the camp. Why do you think people had such different views and experiences?
3. What role did the internees' networks of relatives and friends play in their adjusting to internment and resettlement?
4. Matsumoto repeatedly quotes her oral histories, but she also supplements these interviews with other sources. At one point, she contrasts memories shared during interviews with wartime letters. Why might memories in oral history sources not always be reliable? How can a scholar balance the use of such sources with other kinds of evidence?
5. Matsumoto declares, "It is impossible to summarize neatly the wartime experiences and feelings of even one family or community, much less the entire Japanese American population." How does her research challenge earlier generalizations of the consequences of internment?

Notes

1. Valerie Matsumoto, "Notes on Research," *Farming the Home Place: A Japanese American Community in California, 1919–1982* (Ithaca, N.Y.: Cornell University Press, 1993), p. 220.

2. "Desperately Seeking 'Deirdre': Gender Roles, Multicultural Relations, and Nisei Women Writers of the 1930s," *Frontiers* 12, No. 1 (1991): 19–32.
3. "Japanese American Women during World War II," *Frontiers* 8, No. 1 (1984): 6–14.

Amache

At the end of August 1942, the Merced Assembly Center evacuees reached Amache, Colorado. Their last stop on the train from California was the town of Granada, Colorado, population 342, established as an Indian trading post in 1844. The evacuees were taken by truck from the railroad station to the nearby Granada Relocation Center, named Amache after the daughter of a Cheyenne Indian chief whose tribe had lived along the Arkansas River.[1]

The Amache Camp in southeastern Colorado, roughly one mile southwest of the Arkansas Valley, was one of ten "permanent" relocation centers constructed in desolate regions under the auspices of the War Relocation Authority (WRA) to house Japanese Americans. The Merced evacuees arrived five months after the first Japanese Americans had been moved from the temporary assembly centers to WRA camps. Amache was the smallest of the camps, with a capacity of 8,000 residents. Most of the camps held 10,000 and the largest, the Poston Camp in Arizona, contained 20,000 people in three units.[2] By November of 1942, all the relocation centers were filled.

Four months later — a year after President Roosevelt had signed Executive Order 9066 — Dillon S. Myer, head of the War Relocation Authority, issued a statement censuring the "unnatural" and "un-American" environment of the relocation centers. Myer particularly cited the disruption of the Japanese American family by the lack of privacy and by the absence of normal family economy and home routines, which led to a corresponding decline in parental authority. He concluded that the camps were "undesirable institutions and should be removed from the American scene as soon as possible."[3]

Valerie J. Matsumoto, "Amache," *Farming the Home Place: A Japanese American Community in California, 1919–1982* (Ithaca, N.Y.: Cornell University Press, 1993), 119–48.

The relocation camps subjected families and individuals to severe stress. In accordance with many earlier scholars and observers, the congressional Commission on Wartime Relocation and Internment of Civilians reported in 1982: "The human toll the camps were taking was enormous — physical hardship, growing anger toward the United States and deteriorating morale."[4] Previous patterns of life — and the most fundamental relationships — underwent great change. As Audrie Girdner and Anne Loftis have pointed out, "the economic and social basis of the Issei's authority had been abolished by the welfare system under which all residents lived."[5] The cramped barracks, mess-hall dining, and increased peer-group interaction meant that family members spent less and less time together. In addition to the strain on family relationships, evacuees coped with internal rivalries arising between groups from different regions of the West Coast, as well as more general concerns regarding low-paying camp jobs, isolation, and negative public sentiment on the "outside."[6]

Amache was considered to be one of the more peaceful relocation centers, located in an inland area described by Michi Weglyn as "less unnerved by racially slanted media bombardment" and farther from the hostile racial climate of Arizona and California.[7] Even at best, however, as Robert Wilson and Bill Hosokawa have stated, "camp life was abnormal — subject to uncertainty, fear, frustration, anger, emotional pressures, great physical discomfort, resentment, and beset by an abundance of rumors that fed on boredom and bitterness."[8] While pondering an uncertain future, the internees strove to meet the physically and psychologically exhausting demands of daily life in a concentration camp.

How did camp life affect the Japanese Americans? The first half of this chapter explores conditions within the Amache Camp, particularly focusing on the factors that made many evacuees eager to leave and rejoin life on the "outside." Even before the last evacuees had moved into the relocation centers, Myer and the WRA had decided to focus on resettlement out of the camps. Although the WRA's leave-clearance process proved initially cumbersome and slow, the first Japanese Americans began to trek out of the camps to the Midwest and East in 1942. The wartime demand for labor and the changes in WRA policy increased this trickle to a steady stream in 1943. The ranks of the hopeful men and women who left the camps for army duty, education, and work included a number of Cortez Nisei, whose lives beyond barbed wire illustrate the paths taken by the Nisei as well as the establishment of friend and kin networks upon which the relocating evacuees depended for emotional support and assistance.

Ernest Yoshida, a Nisei from the Cortez Colony, recalled the arduous trip to Amache. Despite the suffocating heat on the crowded train, armed guards would not allow the Japanese Americans to open windows. "We got to Bakersfield, and it got hotter and hotter. Then the train started pulling toward Tehachapi Mountain, and it got hotter, and the kids started crying." In the evening, when the Japanese Americans wanted to pull down the Pullman beds for the children to sleep on, the guards ordered them to "leave those things alone." The adults stood in the aisles so that the children could stretch out and sleep in the seats.

In the course of the two-day trip, the evacuees were permitted two twenty-minute rest breaks during which they could get off the train and stretch but were warned not to go beyond four feet from the train. "I think when we got to Arizona, they finally stopped. By that time the kids were sick and the old folks were half-dead. Then, when we got off, here are all the guards standing guard with machine guns, so that we couldn't run away. Crazy, I tell you."

Yoshida continued:

> The kids started hollering for water, and we didn't have any water. It was hot and dry. And finally we reached Granada Station . . . two days, no bath and no water. It was four o'clock [in the afternoon], so we thought we had plenty of time to get off the train and go to the camp. "No," they said, "the camp isn't ready until tomorrow morning. . . . You have to stay overnight on the train." And we said, "Where are we going to sleep? You guys won't let us take the bunks down." "Well, that's the orders—we don't know what to do about it."

The following morning, the advance group of Japanese Americans who had arrived at the Amache Camp days earlier came to pick up the new arrivals in trucks. The weary Issei and Nisei set about moving into their new barracks, looking for straw to stuff mattresses, and locating the shower rooms, latrines, and mess halls. "That night we all slept like a log. The next morning we got up, and then the same old routine — nothing to do. Maybe go to a neighbor's, play cards. And those that wanted to . . . went to the scrap pile and picked up wood, and made shelves and desks. . . . That's the way we passed the time away."[9] Ernest Yoshida, like many of the evacuated Nisei, chafed at the confines of the camp and made plans to leave as soon as possible to seek opportunities on the "outside."

The Amache Camp was located within the southern boundary of a mile-square enclosure overlooking the Arkansas River. On the west lay a cemetery, dump pile, and sewer farm, and on the east, a prairie extending into Kansas. Along the northern boundary were a hospital, warehouses, housing for the appointed staff, administration buildings, and a military police compound.[10]

Life at Amache paralleled life in the assembly center with regard to organization, although the camp population was larger and the Colorado weather more extreme — many Californians saw their first snow in Amache. As in the Merced Assembly Center, the "evacuee residential section" was divided into blocks. Each of the twenty-nine blocks had its own mess hall, laundry, latrine, shower room, and recreation hall. The center also housed several churches — Buddhist and Christian — an elementary school, and a high school, for which a special building was constructed a year after the camp opened.

Each block was comprised of twelve barracks, 20 × 120 feet, each divided into six one-room "apartments." A family of seven members or less was assigned to a room and "allowed to make it as homelike as possible."[11] The barracks eventually had brick floors, although some of the first arrivals found only dirt beneath their feet. The government sparsely furnished each apartment with steel army cots, a broom, a pot-bellied stove, and a coal bucket. Making a room "homelike" generally consisted of scavenging the lumber piles for scraps to make furniture, and partitioning spaces with blankets to provide a semblance of privacy.

Like the assembly center, the relocation camp contained a mixture of rural and urban residents. Approximately half of the Amache Camp inhabitants hailed from the Los Angeles area and had been funneled through the Santa Anita Assembly Center. These included urban merchants, doctors, lawyers, scientists, gardeners, and hotel and restaurant operators. The other half, sent from the Merced Assembly Center, were predominantly rural people from the agricultural sections of the central California valleys and the San Francisco Bay Area. Forty percent of the evacuees had been engaged in agriculture; 15 percent did domestic work; 10 percent held professional and managerial positions; 13 percent had done clerical and sales work. Sixteen percent did semiskilled labor, and 6 percent unskilled.[12] At its population peak in 1943, Amache had 7,318 residents.[13]

About 260 Cortez people entered the Amache Camp, and the majority lived in Blocks 9E and 10E. Even among old friends and relatives, living so close together necessitated a certain amount of rearranging, as Sam Kuwahara learned. "I remember helping arrange the people moving into different barracks. I was all wrong. . . . They shifted around quite a bit. We thought relatives would want to stay together—naw, they didn't want to do that [Laughs]."[14]

The residents of the city that rose so quickly and completely from the prairie continued to follow the patterns of life established at the Merced Assembly Center, filling time with work, social and religious activities, classes, athletic and cultural events, and visiting. Amache, too, was run like a model city, through a series of departments headed by Euro-American administrators, with James Lindley, formerly of the Soil Conservation Corps as project director. As in the assembly center, there existed an internal fire department and police department, staffed by Japanese Americans.

In Amache, a community council of elected representatives became an established body. This contrasted with the situation at the Merced Assembly Center, where the vacillations of the Wartime Civil Control Administration (WCCA)—and the short period of duration—had hindered such attempts. In the relocation camp, members of each block who were eighteen years and older voted for a representative to the council, which was charged with "the prescription of ordinances, regulations, and laws governing community life within the center." In addition, a judicial commission of three administrative personnel and five Japanese Americans heard and tried cases regarding the violation of rules.[15] However, scholars have questioned the efficacy of such attempts at "community self-government," contending that elected representatives had little authority to effect change, and that the policy itself—by making only citizens eligible for election—widened the divisions between Issei and Nisei, vying for leadership.[16] As the Commission on Wartime Relocation and Internment of Civilians concluded, "many evacuees regarded the system as a sham, further evidence that they were not trusted, and an example of bad faith by the WRA."[17]

Each block also had a block manager, usually Issei, to oversee administrative matters. The duties of the manager, nominated by the residents but appointed by the project director, included handling requests for housing, heating, and household supplies, and relaying announcements and instructions from the administration. The other block staff person was the personnel director, in charge of the population and occupational records files. It was his job to facilitate labor recruitment, to ensure adequate distribution of food, to keep track of migration in and out of the camp, and to record vital statistics.[18]

Amache had a large educational program, similar to the other relocation camps.[19] In January 1944, the enrollment included 199 nursery school children, 802 kindergartners and elementary school pupils, 433 junior high school students, 549 high school students, and 1,043 enrollees in the adult school. The school staff consisted of three principals, a superintendent, fifty-one WRA teachers, and forty-four Japanese American assistant teachers. Except for the high school, classes were held in remodeled barracks, and adult classes—ranging from sewing to English—met in the high school building or in special rooms of the 8H school block.

Envisioned as a longer-term project than the assembly centers, the Amache Camp had several internal enterprises: a silk-screen printing shop, cooperative stores, and a large agricultural section. Because of the WRA's early decision to encourage relocation outside of the camps and its desire not to compete with the industrial production of private business on the outside, most of the enterprises established within the relocation centers were geared to internal consumption. A notable exception was the Amache Silk Screen Shop, organized in June of 1943 at the request of the United States Navy. It was the only such project in all of the relocation centers. The forty-five evacuees who worked in the shop under the supervision of a WRA administrator contracted with the Navy to print thousands of training-aid posters. They also produced a calendar that prominently featured an Amache guard tower, as well as covers for in-camp publications.

In Amache, as in the nine other relocation camps, a cooperative handled most consumer services. The Amache Consumer's Cooperative, owned and operated by the evacuees, was established in 1943. WRA policy not only authorized such associations but prohibited the establishment of any other kind of consumer services, causing *Fortune* magazine to comment that the WRA was forbidding individual enterprise within the camps.[20] This policy appears to have been linked not only to the WRA's emphasis on relocation outside the camp, but also to anxieties regarding the maintenance of uniform wages in the camps,[21] a source of controversy among anti-Japanese forces. Barbers, clerks, and other cooperative workers all received a standard stipend according to the low WRA wage scale under which professionals received $19 a month, skilled workers were paid $16, and the unskilled $12. The Amache cooperative was supervised by a board of directors and several committees elected from among the 2,650 members. The cooperative stores and shops, housed in a U-shaped building composed of three barracks, offered clothing, shoes, and shoe repairs. In addition, there was a barber shop and beauty parlor, a canteen, a newspaper department, and a cleaning-and-pressing service.

Agriculture became the largest of the Amache enterprises. Early on, the WRA had determined that the evacuees should grow as much of their own food as possible and in that way assist in keeping camp menus to the ration cost of not more than 45 cents per person daily. Consequently, all of the camps grew vegetables and raised hogs. According to the report of a Euro-American staff officer, the Amache farm program had two main objectives: to produce as much of the crops and livestock needed to feed the evacuees and to "provide physical and mental employment acceptable to the residents."[22]

The federal government had acquired the sprawling 10,221.92 acres of the Granada project—another name for the Amache Relocation Center area—from private owners by direct purchase or condemnation. The camp center, the location of the administration buildings and barracks, occupied 640 of these acres. The two largest pieces of land were gained by condemnation: The biggest piece comprised 4,688 acres owned by Elbert S.

Rule; the second largest piece—3,712 acres known as the Koen Ranch—was bought from the American Crystal Sugar Company.[23] Some of this land had been used for pasture but no one had ever before tried to grow vegetables on it.

In this agricultural endeavor, the camp supplied evacuee labor and supervisors; the government provided water, equipment, seed, and technical personnel. Initially, the technical staff consisted of four men and later, six: a chief of agriculture, a farm superintendent, two assistant superintendents, and two labor foremen. The farmland and various enterprises such as vegetable production, livestock, and food preserving were divided into a number of operating units, each headed by a Japanese American supervisor.[24] The agricultural section operated through 1943 and 1944. Although vegetable cultivation ceased in 1945, meat production continued until the closing of the center on October 15, 1945.

The evacuees grew a variety of crops that ranged from produce such as mung bean sprouts, daikon (Japanese radish), celery, lettuce, tomatoes and tea to feed crops like alfalfa, corn, sorghum, and milo. In all, the Amache farm yielded 6,051,661 pounds of vegetables grown on 1,044 acres, as well as 1,237,463 pounds of pork and beef, of which 285,230 pounds were sold to the highest bidder and to the Denver Livestock Commission companies. About one-fourth of the feed crops grown for Amache livestock was sold to the public as surplus. Despite the initial problems of inadequate machinery and facilities, and the internees' unfamiliarity with the Colorado terrain, the Amache farm produced enough of a surplus to ship some produce to other relocation centers.

As the Euro-American staff officer observed in his report, the farm project faced "numerous problems distinctly peculiar to the unusual circumstances under which it was conceived." One of these problems involved the lack of facilities: The poultry unit had 8,000 laying hens and housing for only 3,000; this resulted in feeding difficulties and low egg production, as hens laid eggs in an open twenty-acre field. Similarly, the hog project lacked enough pens for the segregation of new pigs and was also troubled by severe epidemics. Hundreds of acres of grain and corn were lost to drought because of irrigation problems.

Labor supply, however, proved to be the most crucial problem of the Amache farm program. Soon after the farm operations started, the WRA began issuing short-term leave permits to internees. Many, especially the Nisei, anxiously desired to escape the confines of camp and to seek higher wages than the standard $16 per month offered to relocation camp farm workers. Although both women and men left, most of those who did temporary agricultural work were male. Given the wartime labor shortage, many farmers were eager to have Japanese American workers, and as the staff officer ruefully noted, this placed the camp in competition with the labor demand on the outside. "It was not unusual for the [Amache] farm to lose all of its tractor drivers over night or to have 25–50% of its trained supervisors leave within a period of two weeks. . . . When, in the spring of 1944, 29 of the 42 farm supervisors left, it created a problem little short of tragic."[25]

The staff officer's report reveals not only the patronizing attitude of government administrators but also the evacuees' resistance to low-paid camp labor and their determination to act in their own interest. Not all could be described as willing docile workers in the relocation camp. Anger and frustration led some to say, "The government brot me here. They will have to feed me. I no work."[26] The most "loyal and willing workers," the officer found, were the Issei men and women — coincidentally those least likely to be able to leave the camps in search of temporary work elsewhere. The staff officer's approval of their willingness suggested mixed motives. He lauded the effort of hundreds of Japanese American volunteers who took time from their regular nonagricultural jobs to help with the harvest, but qualified his praise: "Too many wanted to work in the melon patch and some of the crops such as sweet potatoes, pop corn, daikon and beans made poor recorded yields because the volunteers carried home a large percentage of the crop they harvested."[27]

In addition, workers sought to exert some control over the pace of their labor. For instance, workers on the Koen Ranch section ate lunch at a mess hall established in the old Koen Hotel at the center of the farm. From the administrators' point of view, this practice "discouraged the tendency for workers to remain home in the afternoons," but it also allowed some workers to "sit under the shade for two hours each day."[28]

Despite the talk of common effort and self-sustenance, the hard fact remained that the evacuees performed arduous labor for poor wages, and the crops they produced did not mean individual bonuses or improvements. Little wonder, then, that many seized the opportunity to leave in search of better "physical and mental employment." And in light of the working and living conditions in the camp, the personal reaping of melons and daikon can be seen as a small means of resistance, individual and peer sanctioned. Securing a few hours of rest in the shade meant exercising a fraction of control and choice, which in turn provided a minimal basis of self-esteem.

The conditions of work and life in the relocation center necessitated flexibility. Like the Merced Assembly Center, the Amache Camp brought together a diverse group of people, young and old, urban and rural. Although most Cortez interviewees recalled that everyone had gotten along "pretty well," it is useful to balance these memories with evidence from the past that can illuminate details ordinarily filtered out by time. The massing together of so many different people in a small camp sparked strong reactions from some of the youth, whose letters indicate that harmonious relations did not come easily or quickly. Many adjustments had to be made. For example, urban-rural tensions erupted often in the early months. One Livingston teenager wrote to a former teacher, describing the animosity between the "Livingstonians" and "Santa Anitans": "I wish we could get unity here but it seems an impossible situation. If one from L.A. gets a grudge against a certain country person, they get in a big gang of fifteen or so and just knock the dickens out of this *one* person." She went on to detail the differences in urban Nisei fashion, which astonished some of the rural onlookers: "They carry knives, too, and are proud of it. They also wear zoot suits* (pleated at the cuffs of the pants legs) and long ¾ length coat-jackets—really disgusting."[29]

Two other high school students, one from Cortez and the other from Livingston, also complained of the rowdy behavior of the Santa Anita and Tanforan Nisei who were "always fighting or making trouble for us" at camp dances. "We don't get along with them," one concluded, "because they're city slickers and we're mostly country hicks."[30] These conflicts at Amache also exemplify some of the internal dissension that arose from regional loyalties at the various camps, each of which, according to Girdner and Loftis, "had its own atmosphere, dependent on the previous experience of evacuees there."[31]

A concern common to all the centers in the eyes of administrators, scholars, and inmates was the effect of camp life on the family. Nisei sociologist Harry Kitano, interned at the Topaz Camp, has asserted that in general, "the evacuation tended toward the destruction of established family patterns of behavior."[32] Daisuke Kitagawa, a Christian Issei minister at Tule Lake, similarly reported the breakdown of traditional functions and the sense of family unity in the artificial community.[33] Both agreed that this brought about significant change in individual roles and expectations.

Notable alterations occurred in gender dynamics, with corresponding changes in family relations. A number of Issei women, accustomed to long days of work inside and outside the home, found that communally prepared meals and limited living quarters provided them with spare time. Although some experienced disorientation, many availed themselves of the opportunity to enjoy the company of their female peers and to attend adult classes ranging from handicrafts and Japanese arts to English.[34]

While these women gained an increased measure of independence, Kitano and Kitagawa observed, Issei men faced the loss of the authority and

**zoot suit:* a style of men's clothing, characterized by a flamboyant long jacket, baggy pegged pants, a long key chain, and shoes with thick soles, that was popular among rebellious young men in the 1940s.

responsibility to which they were accustomed. No longer the major breadwinners of the family, they might in some cases be earning the same wages as their wives and children. And no matter how hard the Issei man worked, Kitagawa stated, "he could not improve the living conditions of his family."[35] The Issei men also lost much of their control of community leadership, because their alien status barred them from political activity under WRA rulings. These blows, as Jeanne Wakatsuki Houston recorded in her autobiographical account, *Farewell to Manzanar,* contributed to the deterioration of morale suffered by a number of the first generation.

A major anxiety of Issei parents and the older Nisei concerned the effect of the camp environment on the younger Nisei. In the relocation centers, the federal government assumed the family's function of providing food, clothing, and shelter, which in conjunction with the physical conditions loosened the reins of family social control.[36] In 1944, Leonard Bloom reported that the peer group had replaced the family as the organizing principle, and that the arrangement of community activities along age lines reinforced this tendency. Consequently, he asserted, each family member had become a "free agent," and "children detached themselves from parental supervision, returning to the home barracks perhaps only to sleep."[37] One worried parent at Tule Lake, Professor Yamato Ishihashi, lamented the "stealing out of stores and homes, smart alec thievery which we never had among Japanese children," and declared, "We no longer control our own families."[38]

A Nisei who voiced similar concerns was Eddie Shimano, editor first of the Santa Anita center newsletter and then of the *Communique* of the relocation camp at Jerome, Arkansas. He later served with the all-Nisei 442nd Regimental Combat Team. In an article published in the liberal journal *Common Ground* in 1943, Shimano indicted the camp's work system and its education courses, but he leveled his harshest critique at the effect of camp conditions on the Japanese American youth, who, "somewhere in the evacuation . . . had lost their pride." Genevieve Carter, a psychologist at Manzanar, echoed this concern over the fear and insecurity of adolescent Nisei regarding their place in a hostile society that denied their rights as citizens.[39] Shimano particularly noted how, as a substitute for lost pride and sense of belonging, many young men from their late teens to mid-twenties had formed "pachuco gangs"* in the camps. These youths were emulated by the younger boys, who formed "junior gangs." Shimano observed, in accordance with the Cortez and Livingston teenagers, that "The pachuco gangs, easily spotted . . . by their 'uniforms' and long haircuts and zoot suits, crash

**pachuco gang:* a group of Mexican American youths who often wore zoot suits and spoke Calo, an inventive mixture of English and Spanish.

social affairs, settle all personal grudges with physical assault, and follow pretty closely the pattern set by the Dead End gangs."*[40] There are certainly parallels between the second-generation Mexican American youth of Los Angeles who, facing an "iron curtain" of discrimination, turned to close-knit peer groups for security and status, and those Nisei teenagers who, branded as enemy aliens by fellow Americans and conscious of their parents' vulnerability, banded together in the camps.[41] Journalist Carey McWilliams's interpretation of the pachucos' zoot suits as "at once a sign of rebellion and a mark of belonging" can be extended to the Nisei's style of dress.[42]

At Amache, a number of Cortez Issei parents had cause to lament the influence of gangs and the wild behavior of their sons. (They hardly imagined their children's eventual respectability within the community.) One group of boys organized to counter the forays of the Los Angeles gangs, under the leadership of a very young Cortez teenager, Takeshi Sugiura, still known today as "General."

In the camps, where individuals spent most of their time with companions of their own age and gender, peer pressure could exert enormous force. For some, groups did provide a sense of camaraderie, but for others, gangs and peer pressure left lingering scars. One Cortez Nisei still remembers with pain the humiliation of being forced to shoplift items from the canteen for the older boys.

The majority of teenagers and children did not participate in gangs and violence. Many found outlets for their energies in sports, cultural events, and religious groups. Some, like Howard Taniguchi, took part in dramatic productions. Others, like Yuri Yamamoto and her siblings, were very much involved in Christian Endeavor activities. Like the assembly center, the camp offered a variety of classes and activities. However, this was not "summer camp." The dark side of internment shadowed the lives of the Nisei and provided yet another impetus for those who wished to leave.

Regardless of age and activities, the Nisei were highly conscious of their separation from "life on the outside," and their banishment to somewhere that wasn't quite America to them. This awareness—whether angry, wistful, or bewildered—permeated their wartime writings. In this vein the 1944 Amache High School yearbook was dedicated to the Japanese American soldiers: "our brothers, our friends, our schoolmates, and our heroes—who will be 'over there' fighting for those ideals that they believe in and wish to establish and maintain for us." The yearbook was titled the *1944 Onlooker,* implying that "we are onlookers— of necessity" but also looking to the future with the hope of "being once again within the orbit of world affairs."[43]

**Dead End gang:* a group of tough neighborhood kids; the term became popular after the 1937 movie *Dead End,* which featured a gang of delinquents from New York City's East Side slum.

A Nisei woman soon to leave Amache expressed some of the evacuees' ambivalent feelings in a "love letter" to America, included at the end of the yearbook. The letter was dated April 30, 1944, two years from the very day "I ceased to be a part of you [America]." She found:

> The new surroundings and experiences occupied all my attention at first, and my loneliness for you was crowded out. . . . I crammed my hours with continuous activity so that there would not be a chance for that loneliness to enter my being and begin its steady flow through my veins.

Like other evacuees, she discovered that "This plan worked wonderfully at first, but the activities soon became a drudgery to me." She also wrote obliquely of the injustice of evacuation:

> I worship you in spite of the errors you have made. Yes, you have made errors and you have roamed on many wrong roads; but everyone makes mistakes. . . . All I ask is that you do not make the same mistake twice; that is inexcusable even in the eyes of one who loves you so.

She concluded her letter with the anticipation of her approaching return to life on the outside. "I hope that your faith in me has grown since the last time I saw you," she wrote in quiet challenge, for "that faith must grow for my faith in you to grow."[44] Many Nisei carried such hopes with them to the Midwest and East when they left the isolated world of the camp, unsure of their reception but eager to return to America.

The machinery of their return moved slowly. The WRA's leave-clearance procedures and resettlement policy evolved cumbrously in the first two years of internment. The first to leave the camps in 1942 were workers with temporary leave permits. Because of the complicated screening process, few besides college students departed on "indefinite leave." In 1943 the WRA tried to expedite the clearance procedure by broadening an army registration program, aimed at Nisei males, to include all adults. With this policy change — and despite some tragic consequences, including postwar expatriation — an increasing stream of Japanese Americans, mostly Nisei, left the camps to seek work and education, or to go off to war.[45]

In 1942 the WRA began to release temporarily Japanese Americans from assembly centers and relocation camps to do voluntary farmwork in neighboring areas hard hit by the wartime labor shortage. There was a particular demand for sugar-beet workers in Colorado. "During the harvest season a lot of farmers came into the camp to get the workers," recalled Kumekichi Taniguchi. "We went, too. We got stung."[46] After Kumekichi and a group of workers finished a back-breaking stint of beet-topping at one place, the farmer refused to pay them. Kumekichi's experience was not an unusual one. Vulnerable to exploitation, the evacuees had no real recourse to reimbursement when cheated. Their work conditions varied from situation to situation and from region to region, depending largely on the integrity of the individual farmer.

Despite their being credited with saving the sugar-beet crop of Utah, Idaho, Montana, and Wyoming, and having harvested much of Arizona's staple cotton crop, the Japanese Americans were not well received in all regions.[47] When the WRA began issuing "indefinite leave" permits, it directed the evacuees to the Midwest and East and also had to launch a public relations campaign, as Weglyn explained, "not only to mitigate evacuee fears but also to reeducate a paranoiac public to differentiate between the bitterly despised foes across the Pacific and fellow U.S. citizens."[48] A number of religious groups and service organizations — such as the American Friends Service Committee — provided invaluable aid in resettling internees.

By the fall of 1942, the likelihood of a Japanese attack on the United States had faded before Allied victories in the Pacific and, with it, the military justification for the internment of the Japanese Americans. How the WRA should proceed became the subject of complicated wrangling among civilian and army leaders.[49] The debate over whether the Nisei — then classified as enemy aliens — should be allowed to enlist in the armed forces soon meshed with the larger issue of the evacuees' return to normal life. The decision to probe their loyalty meant agonizing choices for many of the interned. As the Commission on Wartime Relocation and Internment of Civilians stated forty years later, "It is a bitter irony that the loyalty review program, which the WRA and the War Department established as the predicate for release from the camps — the first major decision in which the interests of the evacuees prevailed — was carried out without sufficient sensitivity or knowledge of the evacuees. Designed to hasten their release, the program instead became one of the most divisive, wrenching episodes of the captivity."[50]

In early 1943 army officers began to administer a questionnaire designed to determine the background and loyalties of the Nisei men; the WRA also prepared an "Application for Leave Clearance" geared to the Issei and the Nisei women. The distribution of these questionnaires to all evacuees over the age of seventeen resulted in a brutal streamlining of the clearance process. Elderly men and women, who were barred from naturalization, and American-born Nisei, who had been denied the rights of citizenship — all of whom had been recently torn from homes, businesses, and communities — were now expected to affirm their allegiance to the United States. This meant forswearing loyalty to any other country, as well as testifying to their willingness to serve in the armed forces of the country that had imprisoned them. This "colossal folly" became further compounded by the combining of the mass registration with an army recruitment drive which, as Weglyn pointed out, evidenced the restoration of one right: "the right to be shot at."[51]

The loyalty oath and army registration issue created painful dissension within many families, often between parents and sons, especially in the California and Arizona camps, which were surrounded by strong public hostility. Despite the internal conflicts, many Nisei men registered, eager to demonstrate their loyalty and willing to pay with their blood for acknowledgment as Americans. Just as registration required courage, so did the decision not to register. One Cortez Nisei who refused to go for an induction physical when called for duty by the Selective Service challenged the authorities: "If you were an able-bodied person in my situation, what would you do?" The answer was a six-month sentence in federal prison.[52]

Other Cortez Nisei — including Hiroshi Asai, Key Kobayashi, Kaoru Masuda, Ken Miyamoto, Howard Taniguchi, and Kiyoshi Yamamoto — joined the approximately 33,000 Japanese Americans, half from Hawaii and half from the mainland, who fought in World War II.[53] Like many Nisei men, they served in the highly acclaimed 442nd Regimental Combat Team and with military intelligence after receiving training at the Military Intelligence Service Language School, which graduated nearly 6,000 Nisei by the end of the war. Nisei women served as well: more than 200 joined the U.S. Cadet Nursing Corps and some 100 entered the Women's Army Corps, including 51 linguists trained as translators by the Military Intelligence Service Language School at Fort Snelling.[54]

Of the Japanese American men and women who served in many capacities during World War II, the best known are the 100th Infantry Battalion and the 442nd Regimental Combat Team who together became known as "The Purple Heart Regiment" for the allegiance they proved in blood. Their motto, "Go for broke," was a Hawaiian gambler's expression, and their emblem — chosen in preference to the War Department's original design of a yellow arm grasping a red sword — was a silver hand bearing a torch, on a field of blue. By the end of the war, they had garnered 18,143 individual awards for valor, becoming "the most decorated unit for its size and length of service in the history of the United States."[55]

The 100th Battalion had its inception in a recommendation by Hawaiian Commander Lieutenant General Delos Emmons. In February 1942, upon learning that the Department of War intended to release the Nisei from active duty, Emmons — mindful of both the Hawaiian Japanese Americans' wish to participate in military service and their role in the local workforce — suggested the formation of a Nisei unit. After more than a year of training on the mainland, the initial 1,432 men of the 100th Battalion arrived in North Africa in September 1943. They sustained heavy casualties and earned 900 Purple Hearts in the grueling Allied campaign through Italy.[56]

The 100th Battalion soon met with the 442nd Regimental Combat Team in the offensive from the Anzio beachhead in June 1944. Comprised principally of Hawaiian and mainland Nisei, the 442nd had trained primarily at Camp Shelby in Mississippi from October 1943 to February 1944. The 100th Battalion formally became part of the 442nd on June 15, 1944.[57] The officers of both the 100th and the 442nd were predominantly Euro-Americans, but all of the enlisted men were Nisei, classified by their draft boards as "4-C, Enemy Alien."

Hiro Asai, one of the Cortez Nisei who served in the 442nd, joined in 1943, went to a training camp in Florida and then to Fort Meade, Maryland. He reached France with the 442nd in the winter of 1944. They stayed at Brest, on the Atlantic Coast of Normandy, holding the line until more replacements arrived; then they received orders to ship out to Italy. They fought all the way up northern Italy, from Leghorn to near Genoa. The day before the war ended in Italy, Hiro was wounded by a hand grenade: "We were fighting from hill to hill . . . up in the mountains. . . . We were advancing so fast that they told us to hold the line until the rest of the Allied Forces could come up in line, because there would be too much of a gap." The commanding officer wanted to press on, but contented himself with sending a scouting force—Hiro's platoon—ahead to gauge enemy resistance. When they reached the "next hill" several miles away, "all hell broke loose. They started shooting us from all sides and from behind, too." Six of the platoon were wounded, but all escaped.[58]

The 100th and the 442nd fought in seven major campaigns in France and Italy, including the famed rescue of the "Lost Battalion." Ordered to reach at any cost the 211 survivors of the 141st Regiment, surrounded by Germans near Bruyères, the 442nd did so with a sacrifice of more than 200 dead and 600 wounded. By the end of the war, the 100th and the 442nd had suffered 9,486 casualties, "more than twice the assigned complement of men in the unit."[59] The exploits of the 442nd and the 100th attracted much public attention in the United States and, in the words of writer Noriko Sawada Bridges, made them "Our stepping stones to freedom."[60]

The Nisei who graduated from the Military Intelligence Service Language School (MISLS) and served in nonsegregated units in the Pacific have received less recognition, despite the critical role they played as translators, interpreters, interrogators, and cave-flushers. Major General Charles Willoughby, MacArthur's chief of intelligence, claimed that "the Nisei MIS shortened the Pacific war by two years."[61] Their activities long remained a military secret, partly for their own protection, partly to conceal from the enemy the existence of expert linguists who were translating intercepted materials and questioning prisoners.[62] Joseph D. Harrington has contended that "a grudging Pentagon" kept silent about the details of their service for three decades after the war.[63]

The MISLS, according to Masaharu Ano, was the only source of linguists for the U.S. military during World War II. The school opened in November 1941 at the Presidio in San Francisco; there the students immersed themselves in intensive study of spoken and written Japanese, document analysis and interrogation, as well as Japanese geography, culture, and military structure. In June 1942 the program moved to Camp Savage in Minnesota, spurred both by the need for larger facilities and by public hostility toward the specially recruited Nisei students. Rapid growth prompted another move to Fort Snelling, Minnesota, where the program remained until it found a permanent base in 1946 at the Presidio in Monterey, California.[64] The first MISLS graduates met with suspicion by military officers who balked at accepting them. This changed, however, after they proved their loyalty and skill in the Aleutian Islands and at Guadalcanal.[65] More than 5,000 MISLS graduates, the large majority of them Nisei, served with 130 different units of the armed forces and on loan to Allied armies.[66] After the war, they became a "language bridge" between the Allied occupation forces and the Japanese, working as translators at war crimes trials, gathering statistics for an Atomic Bomb Survey, and acting as censors.[67]

Among the highly trained MISLS graduates was Kiyoshi Yamamoto, a Cortez Nisei. Kiyoshi had finished his last year of high school in Amache and then, after discovering resistance from some state universities toward Japanese American students, he attended, like many Nisei, a church-affiliated school. After a year of studying engineering in Iowa, he received his draft notice. "I thought, 'Well, there's an opportunity to go to the language school and go to the Pacific.'" Kiyoshi passed the qualifying exam and went to the MISLS—first at Camp Savage and then Fort Snelling—for nine months of rigorous training in Japanese. "We had intensive schooling from eight to four during the day, and compulsory studies from seven to nine. We were required to go from seven to nine, but most of us studied from six to ten, so we really studied hard."[68] The MISLS teachers were all Japanese Americans—some Kibei (Nisei sent to Japan for education and then repatriated) and some Nisei—as were all of the students.

Inequities persisted at the MISLS as in other branches of the army. Kiyoshi noted that at Fort Snelling there was also "an officers' candidate school . . . and it was all *hakujin* [white people] taking Japanese. But when they graduated, they were officers. When we graduated, we were just enlisted men. . . . All we got was a few stripes."[69] Harrington reached a similar verdict, stating, "Nisei got an unfair deal regarding advancement during the war although 100 or so were commissioned in 1945 as a public relations ploy. Very few got commissions before then. . . . Despite their colossal combined achievements, few Nisei ended the war higher than Staff Sergeant, and most finished at a lower grade."[70]

After Kiyoshi had completed nine months of language studies and two months of basic training, the war with Japan ended when atomic bombs were dropped on Hiroshima and Nagasaki. "So they rushed us—we went to the Philippines first and then from the Philippines some of the boys went to the war crimes trial in Manila; some went to the signing of the peace on the *Missouri;* and some went to the war crimes trial in Tokyo."[71] Kiyoshi was sent to Tokyo where he interrogated Japanese Air Force officers and translated the index of an air force manual. During his tour of duty, he traveled in Japan and met his parents' relatives in Yamaguchi-ken: "It was a strange feeling, because they felt strange, too. They knew I was their nephew, yet serving in the occupational forces. They couldn't quite understand. But it was nice. I went to visit them twice."[72]

While Nisei like Kiyoshi Yamamoto and Hiro Asai departed from the camps to serve in the armed forces, others left the barbed wire perimeters to face new challenges on the home front.

College students were the first to depart from the camps with indefinite leave permits. Between 1942 and 1946, 4,084 of them did so with the assistance of the National Japanese American Student Relocation Council, a nongovernmental agency largely composed of concerned educators.[73] The NJASRC proved instrumental in persuading schools outside the Western Defense Zone to accept Japanese American students and helping them to obtain leave clearances.

Some of the students had graduated from the makeshift high schools set up in the camps; others were trying to continue a college education abruptly terminated by the evacuation. In 1941, on the eve of the war, 3,530 Nisei were attending college.[74] Mark Kamiya had completed one year of agricultural studies when the war began. While doing temporary work outside the Amache camp—washing, sacking, and loading potatoes and working in fields of sugar beets and cantaloupes—he began to apply for college admission. The first to accept him was Brigham Young University, but he found the racial attitudes prevailing there incompatible with his own. After taking a required course in religion in which the professor expounded on the inferiority of African Americans, Mark could stand it no longer. Three quarters after his arrival, he left. He then went to Cornell University, known for its fine agricultural department, to see if the college would accept him. Cornell denied him admission, first on the grounds that they preferred not to take out-of-state students. Mark knew that the school was practically empty. He finally asked a university administrator, "Isn't it because I'm Japanese that you don't want to accept me?" The man admitted it was true, and then said, "Well, after talking to you, I think we can accept you for one semester."[75] In anticipation, Mark took a job in a local dairy, but discovered during his eight months there that he wanted to study Hegel and Marx rather than crop rotation. After the war and his completion of an eighteen-month tour of duty in the army, he enrolled in the University of California at Berkeley and graduated with a degree in philosophy.

Nisei women comprised an unprecedented 40 percent of the relocating college students.[76] According to the U.S. Census of 1940, women constituted 32 percent of the 1,132 Nisei over the age of twenty-five who had completed one to three years of college, and 29 percent of the 1,049 who had four or more years. Among them was Mary Noda, who finished high school in Amache and then attended Colorado State University at Greeley for two years. It was her "first time away from home," and like many other students, she worried about the transition to college. "I was worried about my ability to do the work. . . . I worried so much I couldn't study."[77] The strain of adjustment to the university and life away from her family was compounded by a taxing schedule of domestic work that helped pay for her education.

Despite their uncertainties about the reception awaiting them and several early incidents of hostility, the Nisei continued to leave for schools, many in areas where they became the first Asian Americans ever seen. The previous presence of Japanese Americans in an area, however, did not necessarily make the adjustment any easier. The Japanese Americans in Colorado were among the fortunate minority who lived outside the military defense zone on the West Coast, and so escaped internment. As one Cortez Nisei remembered painfully, some of the Colorado college instructors compared the evacuated California students unfavorably with the uninterned Nisei with whom they were familiar and demanded, "Why aren't you like the Colorado Japanese?" The differences in economic concerns, clothes, poise, and self-confidence were obvious, but any answer to that insensitive question would have been painful and unspeakable during the war years.

By 1943, as the WRA's resettlement program developed, increasing numbers of Japanese Americans streamed from the relocation camps to the Midwest and East. By August 1943, almost 11,000 evacuees had left the camps on indefinite leave and by the end of 1944, approximately 35,000 — or a third of the original camp population — had gone.[78] These included predominantly single Nisei and young couples whose language skills, citizenship, and age gave them a better chance than the Issei in the labor market. Among them were a large number of women; as Leonard Bloom noted, "Japanese traditions of control over young women failed to materially affect their relocation rate."[79] Women's developing sense of independence in the camp environment and their growing awareness of their abilities as workers contributed to their self-confidence and hence their desire to leave. By the end of the war, 37 percent of the evacuees sixteen years or older had already relocated, including 63 percent of the Nisei women in that age group.[80]

Because job availability and general reception of the Japanese Americans were better in urban centers than in rural areas, most headed for the cities. Accordingly, the WRA established field offices in Chicago, Cleveland, Denver, Kansas City, Little Rock, New York, and Salt Lake City.[81] There, with the placement assistance of the WRA and various religious and service organizations, the Japanese Americans turned their energies to adjusting to life in new environments.

Although they found work in restaurants, factories, and businesses, the most numerous job requests for Japanese American women and men were in the field of domestic service. As the wartime labor shortage opened new doors for African American, Mexican American, and Euro-American women, many of them left domestic positions for better-paying work in factories and defense plants. Nisei like Yeichi and May Sakaguchi and Miye Kato filled the open positions.

Like many Japanese Americans who traveled with friends or kin, Miye Kato left Amache in September, 1943, with three other Nisei—June Taniguchi, Takako Hashimoto, and Sumi Nishihara. Miye found a domestic job in Medford, Connecticut, through a Methodist church. Two of the ministers had visited Amache and subsequently helped to relocate the Japanese Americans. "They looked after us and whenever we had free time, they would invite us over to their home. If we had any problem, we asked them."[82] June worked with Miye's sister in a girls' dormitory in Bridgeport, Connecticut, and soon Miye obtained a position with a lawyer's family there.

After a year in Bridgeport, Miye and her sister decided to go to Chicago. She recounted: "We tried hotel work, but we lasted only one day! We didn't like it at all. So we went again to find a domestic job." From Chicago they moved to Evanston, Illinois, to be closer to their brother who was stationed at Camp Savage in Minnesota. There they found work situations with families who treated them well; and there Miye stayed until her marriage to Nobuzo Baba at Amache in July 1945.[83]

While some Nisei found mutual support in journeying forth together, others ventured alone into regions where few, if any, Japanese Americans had ever traveled. After she spent two years at Greeley, Mary Noda's brother—then a teacher in Iowa—helped her find a position in North Dakota. There, at age nineteen, she taught strapping seventh- and eighth-graders in a town of 200. "It was a nice experience," she recalled. "They had never seen a Japanese American." The superintendent had been too afraid to tell anyone that the new teacher was Japanese American, but tried to mitigate the surprise by saying, "I don't know what's coming. She might be an Indian." In fact, Mary said, "People thought I was an Indian on the train." During her year in North Dakota, Mary boarded with a Russian-German immigrant woman and grew accustomed to eating meat, white bread, and potatoes three times a day. The townspeople invited her to stay on, but she returned to California in 1946 to finish her education degree at San Francisco State University.[84]

Many men and a lesser number of women — like Florice Kuwahara and Ruth Nishi Yoshida — found jobs as factory workers. Florice and Sam Kuwahara left Amache in May 1943 to work on a farm in Adams City, Colorado. After one painful week — "Whatever I earned, I was spending on liniment," recalled Sam — they moved to Denver. There Sam worked in the produce business and Florice took a job doing piecework in a garment factory. "I don't know how much they paid us, I think it was about 25 cents an hour, but by the time they took my income tax, my Social Security, and war bonds, there wasn't much left." Florice laughed and added, "Of course, that was when I just started. . . . But everything was cheap in those days."[85] Florice worked there for three years, a long record among the Nisei during the war.

Because of the varying work conditions and wages, job turnover among the Nisei was high. Ernest Yoshida's wartime work history illustrates this trend. Admitted to the Milwaukee School of Engineering in the fall of 1942, he arrived on campus only to find that most of the instructors had been drafted, and no one could teach the courses he wanted to take. The school refused to refund his tuition payment and told him he could take classes in welding, a skill he already had. Ernest encountered another Nisei in the same situation, Tad Morishige (whose cousin knew Ernie), and together they went to Chicago to seek work. On their first night there, on a lead from their landlady, they began work as stockboys at a soda-water bottling plant, for $1.82 an hour. A short time later, they found work at the Cuneo Press which printed *Time* magazine and *Newsweek*. There for six months Ernest was assistant to a "trimmer" who trimmed the sides of the magazine. Then the two Nisei began making pup-tent valves at a factory where Ernie met his future wife, Ruth Nishi. For a short time he installed radios in army jeeps, but the cold, dark workplace motivated him to apply elsewhere. After three weeks as a bottler for Canadian Club, a blended whiskey, Ernest went to a house-trailer factory where he could use his skills as a carpenter. The piece-work payment was excellent but the management's treatment deplorable. One day, a janitor's accidental push caused Ernest to lose part of a finger to a wood router from which the safety guard had been removed for the sake of speed. The boss said he was "too busy" to take him to a doctor, so, bleeding profusely, Ernest had to find a streetcar. When he quit the job, two other angry Nisei left with him.[86]

According to Hosokawa and Wilson, "The first evacuees to be hired by a firm were often the best argument for hiring additional evacuees."[87] They were not only the best argument, but also frequently the means of hiring the additional evacuees. After George Yuge found a job making ammunition boxes at a Denver defense plant, the boss, impressed by the crate-nailing skills that he developed in Cortez, asked, "Do you know any other Japanese who can do that?" "I know a few," George said, and soon Smile Kamiya and five other Nisei were hard at work hammering together boxes with him.[88]

In the midst of their travels and job hunting, like earlier groups of working-class rural migrants and foreign immigrants, the Japanese Americans relied upon a flexible support network of friends and relatives, otherwise known as chain migration. Many of them combined forces in the search for jobs and lodging, like Ernest and Tad. Their ties to associates from their former communities and the camps formed vital grapevines, passing news of work and hospitable neighborhoods as well as warnings of exploitative situations. News traveled quickly, as Ernest learned at his next job at the Fowler McCormick tractor assembly plant. After a week of sweeping the floor, he was put on the line for small tractors. Two days later, a manager promoted him to the position of line foreman and asked him to find some more Japanese Americans to work on the line. Ernest told Brush Arai, a Hawaiian friend, that he needed fifty people right away. In a week, fifty arrived from three camps: Amache, Rohwer Camp in Arkansas, and Heart Mountain Camp, Wyoming. To the delight of the management, tractor production increased from 74 to 86 on their first day of work, and within three months they had increased the production to 136 tractors a day.[89]

The Japanese Americans who resettled first not only passed along information but also provided way stations for the friends and relatives who followed. When George and Helen Yuge left the Poston Camp for Denver, they lived with Helen's father and mother-in-law, Helen's sister and brother, George's brother, Smile Kamiya, and another Nisei who later died in Italy serving with the 442nd. "It used to be like a boardinghouse." When Helen and George moved to their own home in a different part of town, one of Helen's nieces lived with them, as well as several other people. "And every Saturday night, never missed, there used to be great big poker parties," George recalled.

> I never played poker at home [before the war], but the fellows there would come, and she'd always have a big dinner for them. . . . All these Nisei GIs on furlough would congregate down at our place. Many of them we knew—they were all kids from Watsonville and Salinas and places like that. They didn't have any place to go, so they'd come over, or a friend would bring a friend. . . . Gosh, it was nothing Saturday night to have eighteen, twenty people sitting there.[90]

Although they often worked with *hakujin,* the Nisei generally socialized with other Nisei. It was their ties to Japanese American friends and family on which they drew for emotional support and understanding during the war years.

It is impossible to summarize neatly the wartime experiences and feelings of even one family or community, much less the entire Japanese American population. A small number, living beyond the Western Defense Zone, were not evacuated, but 120,000 in the zone were: some to prison camps, the majority to ten concentration camps or "relocation centers." Of these, Wilson and Hosokawa have stated, "It can be safely said that there were no happy Relocation Centers. All had their problems."[91] The Issei and Nisei did their best to make that life as bearable and regular as possible, and a large number of them — both women and men — left it as soon as they could.

Regardless of the length of their stay in the camps, all were affected by the evacuation. In addition to economic and psychological losses, internment altered family roles and accelerated the trends that differentiated the second generation from their parents. Kitano has emphasized the impact of evacuation and relocation on the acculturation of the Japanese Americans: "New exposure, new opportunities, the dissolution of old institutions and structures, and life away from the ghetto hastened change."[92] While the structure of camp life loosened parental control of children, the WRA policies transferred community leadership from the Issei to the Nisei, resulting, as several scholars have contended, in competition between the two generations and the increasing independence of the Nisei.

In addition to generational roles, as Kitagawa and others have observed, gender roles also changed. As before the war, most family members worked, but men, women, boys, and girls all received the same low wage, which increased the independence of women. Furthermore, when the relocation program began, Nisei women as well as men traveled far from their families to seek opportunities in the Midwest and East.[93]

The experiences of the Cortez people reflect the stress and hardship of camp and relocation. However, the patterns of their lives also evidence the strength of support networks formed before and during the war, and the continuity of ties of affection and responsibility. Whether they departed for military service or to pursue jobs and education, all faced adjustment to unfamiliar environments and work. They were sustained through this period by deep-rooted networks of relatives and friends, and they maintained family bonds even though many journeyed farther from home than ever before. It was a time of independence, camaraderie, and experimentation as well as frustration, insecurity, and loneliness.

By 1945, 35,000 Japanese Americans had already resettled outside the Western Defense Zone. After the War Department ended the exclusion of the Japanese Americans from the West Coast, the majority chose to return. Many individuals and families journeyed back to the areas they called "home," but the available evidence indicates that Cortez, Cressey, and Livingston are the only communities that returned *as communities,* in an organized fashion. The hardship of rebuilding and the salvaging of dreams that awaited them would prove as demanding of their resources and stamina as the initial evacuation. The new Cortez would be a different one, the structure and contours of its relationships altered by the transfer of leadership to the Nisei, the influx of newcomers — mostly women marrying into the community — and the arrival of the Sansei, the third generation.

Notes

1. Henry Kusaba, James C. Lindley, and Joe McClelland, *Amache,* a report (Amache, Colo.: Documentation Section, Reports Office, ca. 1944).
2. Robert A. Wilson and Bill Hosokowa, *East to America: A History of the Japanese in the United States* (New York: William Morrow and Company, 1980), pp. 212–13. The Poston and Manzanar camps were begun as assembly centers by the U.S. Army.
3. Dillon S. Myer, *Uprooted Americans: The Japanese Americans and the War Relocation Authority during World War II* (Tucson: University of Arizona Press, 1971), p. 158. For a critical view of Myer's role in the internment, see Richard Drinnon, *Keeper of the Concentration Camps: Dillon S. Myer and American Racism* (Berkeley: University of California Press, 1987).
4. Commission on Wartime Relocation and Internment of Civilians, *Personal Justice Denied: Report of the Commission on Wartime Relocation and Internment of Civilians* (Washington, D.C.: Government Printing Office, 1982), p. 185.
5. Audrie Girdner and Anne Loftis, *The Great Betrayal: The Evacuation of the Japanese-Americans during World War II* (Toronto: Macmillan, 1969), pp. 313–14.
6. Ibid., p. 247.
7. Michi Weglyn, *Years of Infamy: The Untold Story of America's Concentration Camps* (New York: Morrow Quill Paperbacks, a division of William Morrow and Company, 1976), p. 145.
8. Wilson and Hosokawa, p. 220.
9. Ernest Yoshida interview, Cortez, Calif., January 24, 1982.
10. Kusaba, Lindley, and McClelland, p. 5.
11. Ibid., p. 6.
12. Ibid., p. 7.
13. U.S. Department of the Interior, War Relocation Authority, *The Evacuated People: A Quantitative Description* (Washington, D.C.: Government Printing Office, 1946), p. 17. . . . The camp population fluctuated a great deal, as people transferred between camps, left for and returned from seasonal work, departed for military service, and left to seek education and work in the East and Midwest.
14. Sam Kuwahara interview, Cortez, Calif., January 25, 1982.

15. Kusaba, Lindley, and McClelland, p. 10.
16. Wilson and Hosokawa, p. 219.
17. *Personal Justice Denied,* p. 174.
18. Kusaba, Lindley, and McClelland, p. 11.
19. For an examination of education in the camps, see Thomas James, *Exile Within: The Schooling of Japanese Americans, 1942–1945* (Cambridge: Harvard University Press, 1987).
20. "Issei, Nisei, Kibei," *Fortune* (April 1944), p. 7; Myer, p. 46.
21. Myer, pp. 40–43.
22. Granada Relocation Center, Agricultural Section, Operations Division, *Historical Report* (Amache, Colo., ca. 1945), p. 1 (published by the Amache Historical Society, Torrance, Calif., in 1978).
23. The Amache Historical Society noted in their republication of the *Historical Report* that there was a great deal of inequity in payment for the Granada/Amache Project land—large companies and owners received generous reimbursement; small private owners received only a pittance.
24. Ibid., p. 1.
25. Ibid., p. 2.
26. Ibid., p. 4.
27. Ibid.
28. Ibid.
29. Letter from June Suzuki to Barbara Carpenter, from Amache, Colo., December 9, 1942; cited by Betty Frances Brown, "The Evacuation of the Japanese Population from a California Agricultural Community," M.A. thesis, Stanford University, 1944, p. 157.
30. Letter from Haruko Kubo to Pat Carpenter, from Amache, Colo., October 4, 1942; cited by Brown, p. 157.
31. Girdner and Loftis, p. 247.
32. Harry H. L. Kitano, *Japanese Americans: The Evolution of a Subculture,* 2nd ed. (Englewood Cliffs, N.J.: Prentice-Hall, 1976), p. 77.
33. Daisuke Kitagawa, *Issei and Nisei: The Internment Years* (New York: Seabury Press, 1967), p. 86.
34. Ibid., pp. 89–90.
35. Ibid., p. 90.
36. Kitano, pp. 75–76.
37. Leonard Bloom, "Familial Adjustments of Japanese-Americans to Relocation: First Phase," *American Sociological Review* 8 (October 1943): 559.
38. Girdner and Loftis, p. 317.
39. Genevieve W. Carter, "Child Care and Youth Problems in a Relocation Center," *Journal of Consulting Psychology* 8 (July–August 1944): 223–24.
40. Eddie Shimano, "Blueprint for a Slum," *Common Ground* 3 (Summer 1943): 81.
41. Carey McWilliams, *North from Mexico: The Spanish-Speaking People of the United States* (New York: Greenwood Press, 1968), pp. 240–41.
42. Ibid., p. 243.
43. *1944 Onlooker,* Foreword.
44. Betty Kanameishi, *1944 Onlooker.*
45. The disastrous consequences of this poorly thought out clearance procedure have been examined in depth by Weglyn, pp. 134–73; Wilson and Hosokawa,

pp. 226–33; Girdner and Loftis, pp. 342–43; and Dorothy S. Thomas and Richard Nishimoto, *The Spoilage: Japanese American Evacuation and Resettlement during World War II* (Berkeley: University of California Press, 1969).

46. Kumekichi Taniguchi interview, Cortez, Calif., January 26, 1982.

47. Weglyn, p. 98.

48. Ibid., p. 101.

49. "Loyalty: Leave and Segregation," in *Personal Justice Denied,* pp. 185–212.

50. Ibid., p. 186.

51. Weglyn, p. 136.

52. Some of the works dealing in depth with resistance within the camps are Roger Daniels, *Concentration Camps USA: Japanese Americans and World War II* (New York: Holt, Rinehart & Winston, 1971); Thomas and Nishimoto, *The Spoilage;* Kitagawa, *Issei and Nisei;* John Okada's novel, *No-No Boy* (Seattle: University of Washington Press, 1979); Gary Y. Okihiro, "Japanese Resistance in America's Concentration Camps: A Re-evaluation," *Amerasia Journal* 2 (1973): 20–34; Arthur A. Hansen and David A. Hacker, "The Manzanar Riot: An Ethnic Perspective," *Amerasia Journal* 2 (Fall 1974): 112–57; Douglas W. Nelson, *Heart Mountain: The History of an American Concentration Camp* (Madison: State Historical Society of Wisconsin for the Department of History, University of Wisconsin, 1976); Brian Masaru Hayashi, "'For the Sake of Our Japanese Brethren': Assimilation, Nationalism, and Protestantism among the Japanese of Los Angeles, 1895–1942," Ph.D. diss., University of California at Los Angeles, 1990.

53. Wilson and Hosokawa, p. 243.

54. Masaharu Ano, "Loyal Linguists: Nisei of World War II Learned Japanese in Minnesota," *Minnesota History* 45 (Fall 1977): 283; Mei Nakano, *Japanese American Women: Three Generations, 1890–1990* (Berkeley: Mina Press, and San Francisco: National Japanese American Historical Society, 1990), p. 170.

55. "Go for Broke" exhibition brochure, Presidio Army Museum, 1981, p. 21; Girdner and Loftis, p. 330.

56. *Personal Justice Denied,* p. 256. For fuller accounts of the 100th and the 442nd, see Masayo Umezawa Duus, *Unlikely Liberators: The Men of the 100th and 442nd,* trans. Peter Duus (Honolulu: University of Hawaii Press, 1983, 1987); and Thomas D. Murphy, *Ambassadors in Arms* (Honolulu: University of Hawaii Press, 1954).

57. *Personal Justice Denied,* p. 256. As Gary Okihiro has helpfully pointed out, a Korean American and several part-Hawaiian men also served in the 100th Battalion.

58. Hiroshi Asai interview, Cortez, Calif., February 23, 1982.

59. "Go for Broke" exhibition brochure, p. 21. The usual regimental complement is 4,500. Given their distinguished record, Hosokawa and Wilson have pointed out that it is strange that only one Nisei received the Medal of Honor. Fifty-two Nisei were awarded the next highest decoration, the Distinguished Service Cross, indicating that a number were recommended for the Medal of Honor and that the recommendations were downgraded. At the end of the war, following a Military Affairs Committee investigation, Pfc. Sadao Munemori — one of 650 who gave their lives — became the only Nisei to win the Medal of Honor in World War II. "Had the men of the 442nd been of a different color," Wilson and Hosokawa ask, "would there have been more Medal of Honor winners?" (p. 240).

60. Noriko Sawada Bridges, "To Be or Not to Be: There's No Such Option," broadside, no date. The experiences of the 442nd find parallel in those of the also segregated Chicano "E" Company of World War II, chronicled in Raul Morin's *Among*

the Valiant: Mexican-Americans in World War II and Korea (Alhambra, Calif.: Borden, 1966).

61. *Personal Justice Denied,* p. 256; for accounts of the Nisei MIS, see Joseph D. Harrington, *Yankee Samurai: The Secret Role of Nisei in America's Pacific Victory* (Detroit, Mich.: Pettigrew, 1979); and Ano, pp. 273–87.

62. Wilson and Hosokawa, pp. 240–41.

63. Harrington, pp. 11–12.

64. Ano, pp. 273–87.

65. Harrington, p. 89; Ano, pp. 277–79.

66. Ano, p. 283.

67. Ibid., p. 287.

68. Kiyoshi Yamamoto interview, Cortez, Calif., February 6, 1982.

69. Ibid.

70. Harrington, p. 87.

71. Kiyoshi Yamamoto interview, Cortez, Calif., February 6, 1982.

72. Ibid.

73. According to educator Robert O'Brien, 4,300 Japanese American students were relocated altogether. Robert O'Brien, *The College Nisei* (Palo Alto, Calif.: Pacific Books, 1949), p. 90.

74. Ibid., p. 135.

75. Mark Kamiya interview, Cortez, Calif., February 8, 1982.

76. O'Brien, p. 74.

77. Mary Noda Kamiya interview, Ballico, Calif., February 13, 1982.

78. Leonard Bloom, "Transitional Adjustments of Japanese-American Families to Relocation," *American Sociological Review* 12 (April 1947): 206.

79. Ibid., p. 208.

80. Leonard Bloom and Ruth Riemer, *Removal and Return: The Socio-Economic Effects of the War on Japanese Americans* (Berkeley: University of California Press, 1949), p. 36.

81. Wilson and Hosokawa, p. 218.

82. Miye Kato Baba interview, Cortez, Calif., July 18, 1982.

83. Ibid.

84. Mary Noda Kamiya interview, Ballico, Calif., February 13, 1982.

85. Florice Morimoto Kuwahara interview, Cortez, Calif., January 25, 1982.

86. Ernest Yoshida interview, Cortez, Calif., January 24, 1982.

87. Wilson and Hosokawa, p. 219.

88. George Yuge interview, Cortez, Calif., February 8, 1982.

89. Ernest Yoshida interview, Cortez, Calif., January 24, 1982.

90. George Yuge interview, Cortez, Calif., February 8, 1982.

91. Wilson and Hosokawa, p. 220.

92. Kitano, p. 75.

93. I have examined the wartime experiences of Nisei women — particularly those who left the camps to seek work and education — in greater detail in an article, "Japanese American Women during World War II," *Frontiers* 8, no. 1 (1984): 6–14.

Making Connections

The questions that precede each selection are intended to help students deal with a particular piece of writing. But all the selections here are in dialogue with one another around one larger problem. That problem is how we can best understand the internment of Japanese Americans during World War II. As the selections show, there are many possibilities for addressing that problem. They may be mutually exclusive. Or they may complement one another. It is certainly the case that each of these selections makes much more sense if read as part of a discussion rather than standing alone. The questions that follow should aid students to realize that the discussion is not finished and that everyone is free to join in.

1. Valerie Matsumoto ends her book by declaring, "Perhaps scholars should be reminded that we, no less than those we study, are actors in history, making choices that affect the lives of others." Do you agree? How would you compare the choices made by these five authors and the impact they can have on the lives of Americans?
2. How might the research agendas and interpretations of these five historians reflect their personal backgrounds, the social movements of the 1960s and 1970s, and their relationships with the Japanese American community?
3. How do these selections shed new light on the history of racism, governmental policy, protest, families, and ethnic communities in America?
4. In the 1970s, the focus of historical research shifted from the architects of internment to the internees. How did this shift change people's understanding of internment?
5. These scholars use a variety of sources — Army transcripts of phone conversations, intelligence reports, office memos, court documents, camp records, and oral histories. Evaluate the strengths and weaknesses of the sources used by each author.
6. In 1981, two surviving architects of internment — Karl Bendetsen and John J. McCloy — tried to defend internment by suggesting that

Japanese Americans were "evacuated" for their own safety and protection. How does the research by Roger Daniels cast doubt on this explanation?

7. How did Peter Irons's research help Minoru Yasui, Gordon Hirabayashi, and Fred Korematsu overturn their wartime convictions?
8. After suing the government, internees from Latin America were offered $5,000 in redress. Could you use Michi Weglyn's research to argue that they deserved the same compensation of $20,000 offered to Japanese American internees?
9. Gary Okihiro argues that internment "is not so much a moral lesson to white America as it is a part of the history of Asians in America." How might this perspective have affected his research and interpretations?
10. Valerie Matsumoto was able to take advantage of the oral history sources that became available in the 1980s. How did such sources change the way people understand internment?
11. Matsumoto calls herself both an insider and an outsider in the Cortez community. She considers herself an insider because her family did agricultural work and was interned. She considers herself an outsider because she did not grow up in a Japanese American community. Compare the value of "insider" and "outsider" relationships to someone conducting oral histories. What might be the advantages and disadvantages of both kinds of relationships?
12. The Civil Liberties Act awarding Japanese Americans redress was passed on August 10, 1988. Over ten years, the government paid $1.6 billion to 81,974 eligible claimants. But many who received redress in the early 1990s have since died. Given the dwindling number of former internees, what questions should historians explore before it's too late? What research agendas should they pursue? In other words, what do we still need to learn about the history of internment?

Suggestions for Further Reading

This volume is not intended to provide a massive bibliography, but any interested student will want to delve into the subject more deeply. For a selection drawn from a book, the best way to start is to go to that book and place the selection within the author's larger argument. Each selection is reproduced with full annotation, as originally published, to allow interested students to go to the author's original sources, study them, and compare their own readings with what the author has made of the same material.

There is a wealth of material on Japanese American history and internment. Students who would like information on the general history of Asian Americans during this period, as well as an overview of internment, should consult Roger Daniels, *Asian America: Chinese and Japanese in the United States since 1850* (Seattle: University of Washington Press, 1988); Sucheng Chan, *Asian Americans: An Interpretive History* (Boston: Twayne Publishers, 1991); and Ronald Takaki, *Strangers from a Different Shore: A History of Asian Americans* (Boston: Little, Brown, 1989). Brian Niiya, ed., *Japanese American History: An A-to-Z Reference from 1868 to the Present* (Los Angeles: Japanese American National Museum, 1993), provides many entries on internment and other historical experiences and includes Gary Y. Okihiro's essay "The Japanese in America," summarizing all of Japanese American history. Roger Daniels gives a concise review of prewar racism, internment, and redress in *Prisoners without Trial: Japanese Americans in World War II* (New York: Hill and Wang, 1993). Multiple views of Japanese American experiences before, during, and after the war can be found in Roger Daniels, Sandra C. Taylor, and Harry H. L. Kitano, eds., *Japanese Americans: From Relocation to Redress* (Salt Lake City: University of Utah Press, 1986). An overview of the prewar anti-Japanese movement can be found in Roger Daniels, *The Politics of Prejudice: The Anti-Japanese Movement in California and the Struggle for Japanese Exclusion* (Berkeley and Los Angeles: University of California Press, 1962). John Dower, *War without Mercy: Race and Power in the Pacific War* (New York: Pantheon Books, 1986), compares racial stereotyping on both sides of the Pacific during World War II. Social psychologist Harry H. L. Kitano provides an early examination of Japanese American culture and community in *Japanese Americans: The Evolution of a Subculture,* 2nd ed. (Englewood Cliffs, N.J.: Prentice Hall, 1976); Jere Takahashi revises Kitano's analysis and extends his study to the third generation in *Nisei/Sansei: Shifting Japanese American Identities and Politics* (Philadelphia: Temple University Press, 1997).

To understand the causes of the decision to intern Japanese Americans, students should first review the official (and mendacious) rationale presented in U.S. Department of War, *Final Report: Japanese Evacuation from the West Coast, 1942* (Washington, D.C.: Government Printing Office, 1943). Contemporary critiques of this rationale are offered by Carey McWilliams, *Prejudice: Japanese Americans, Symbols of Racial Intolerance* (Boston: Little, Brown, 1944) and *What about Our Japanese Americans?* (New York: Public Affairs Committee, 1944). Eugene Rostow also attacks the decision in two articles, "The Japanese American Cases—A Disaster," *Yale Law Journal* 54 (1945): 489–533, and "Our Worst Wartime Mistake," *Harper's,* 191 (1945): 193–201. Morton Grodzins denounces the West Coast politicians, press, and economic groups that advocated internment in *Americans Betrayed: Politics and the Japanese Evacuation* (Chicago: University of Chicago Press, 1949). Jacobus tenBroek, Edward N. Barnhart, and Floyd M. Matson challenge Grodzins's analysis of the role of West Coast groups and emphasize DeWitt's responsibility in *Prejudice, War, and the Constitution* (Berkeley and Los Angeles: University of California Press, 1954). The authoritative historical account of the decision, excerpted here, is still Roger Daniels, *Concentration Camps, USA: Japanese Americans and World War II* (New York: Holt, Rinehart & Winston, 1971). Daniels revised this account and includes a comparison of policies toward Japanese Canadians in *Concentration Camps, North America: Japanese in the United States and Canada during World War II* (Malabar, Fla.: Krieger Publishing, 1981). Daniels also provides nine volumes of primary sources on policy development in *American Concentration Camps* (New York: Garland, 1989). The book that had the most influence on the Japanese American community's views of the government and internment, excerpted here, is Michi Weglyn, *Years of Infamy: The Untold Story of America's Concentration Camps* (New York: Morrow Quill Paperbacks, a Division of Morrow and Company, 1976). Gordon Hirabayashi's experiences, also described here, can be found in Peter Irons, ed., *The Courage of Their Convictions* (New York: The Free Press, 1988). A more detailed account of the government's misrepresentation of evidence before the Supreme Court in the Hirabayashi, Yasui, and Korematsu cases is presented in Peter Irons, *Justice at War: The Story of the Japanese American Internment Cases* (New York: Oxford University Press, 1983). Peter Irons, ed., *Justice Delayed: The Record of the Japanese American Internment Cases* (Middletown, Conn.: Wesleyan University Press, 1989), provides transcripts of the Hirabayashi, Yasui, and Korematsu trials, with an introduction summarizing the *coram nobis* cases.

Self-serving views of the "positive" aspects of camp life are promoted in War Relocation Authority, *WRA: The Story of Human Conservation* (Washington, D.C.: Government Printing Office, 1946); and Dillon S. Myer, *Uprooted Americans: The Japanese Americans and the War Relocation Authority during World War II* (Tucson: University of Arizona Press, 1971). Histories by the "community analysts" in camp include Alexander H. Leighton, *The Governing of Men: General Principles and Recommendations Based on Experience at a Japanese Relocation Camp* (Princeton: Princeton University Press, 1945); and Edward H. Spicer, Asael T. Hansen, Katherine Luomala, and Marvin K. Opler, *Impounded People: Japanese-Americans in the Relocation Centers* (Tucson: University of Arizona Press, 1969). Orin Starn analyzes the role of these community analysts in "Engineering Internment: Anthropologists and the War Relocation Authority," *American Ethnologist* 13, no. 4 (1986): 700–720. For more revisionist works that emphasize the injustice of the decision and suffering within the camps, see Audrie Girdner and Anne Loftis, *The Great Betrayal: The Evacuation of the Japanese-Americans during World War II* (Toronto: Macmillan, 1969); and Alan R. Bosworth, *America's Concentration Camps* (New York: Norton, 1967). Former internee and activist Raymond Okamura denounces terms such as *evacuation* and *relocation centers* in "The American Concentration Camps: A Cover-Up through Euphemistic Terminology," *Journal of Ethnic Studies* 10, no. 3 (Fall 1982): 95–109. For a searing denunciation of the paternalism of the WRA's director, see Richard Drinnon, *Keeper of Concentration Camps: Dillon S. Myer and American Racism* (Berkeley and Los Angeles: University of California Press, 1987). One of the few recent works to defend the WRA from charges of racism is Page Smith, *Democracy on Trial: The Japanese American Evacuation and Relocation in World War II* (New York: Simon & Schuster, 1995).

Numerous studies focus on individual camps. These works include Sandra C. Taylor, *Jewel of the Desert: Japanese American Internment at Topaz* (Berkeley: University of California Press, 1993); Leonard J Arrington, *The Price of Prejudice: The Japanese-American Relocation Center in Utah during World War II* (Logan: Faculty Association, Utah State University, 1962); Paul Dayton Bailey, *City in the Sun: The Japanese Concentration Camp at Poston, Arizona* (Los Angeles: Westernlore Press, 1971); and Anthony L. Lehman, *Birthright of Barbed Wire: The Santa Anita Assembly Center for the Japanese* (Los Angeles: Westernlore Press, 1970). Jessie A. Garrett and Ronald C. Larson, eds., *Camp and Community: Manzanar and the Owens Valley* (Fullerton: Japanese American Project of the Oral History Program, California State University at Fullerton, 1977), includes interviews with non–Japanese American residents who lived near Manzanar. For an account of Tule Lake from a JERS perspective, see Dorothy Thomas and Richard S. Nishimoto, *The Spoilage: Japanese American Evacuation and Resettlement during World War II* (Berkeley: University of California Press, 1946). Yuji Ichioka, ed., *Views from Within: The Japanese American Evacuation and Resettlement Study* (Los Angeles: Asian American Studies Center, University of California at Los Angeles, 1989), contains reflections and critiques of the JERS research. Lane Ryo Hirabayashi critically analyzes the ethics and politics of ethnographic fieldwork by examining the experiences of Tamie Tsuchiyama, the only professionally trained Japanese American female JERS researcher, in *The Politics of Fieldwork: Research in an American Concentration Camp* (Tucson: University of Arizona Press, 1999). Peter Suzuki denounces the practices of the community analysts and JERS researchers in "Anthropologists in the Wartime Camps for Japanese Americans: A Documentary Study," *Dialectical Anthropology* 6, no. 1 (August 1981): 23–60, and "The University of California Japanese Evacuation and Resettlement Study: A Prolegomenon," *Dialectical Anthropology* 10 (1986): 189–213. For the views of individual JERS researchers, see Charles Kikuchi, *The Kikuchi Diary: Chronicle from an American Concentration Camp, the Tanforan Journals of Charles Kikuchi,* ed. John Modell (Urbana: University of Illinois Press, 1973); Richard S. Nishimoto, *Inside an American Concentration Camp: Japanese American Resistance at Poston, Arizona,* ed. Lane Ryo Hirabayashi (Tucson: University of Arizona Press, 1995); and Rosalie H. Wax, *Doing Fieldwork: Warnings and Advice* (Chicago and London: University of Chicago Press, 1971).

Early accounts of Japanese American responses to internment were written by the Japanese American Citizens League. JACL leader Bill Hosokowa, *Nisei: The Quiet Americans* (New York: William Morrow, 1969), emphasizes the experiences of internees who "proved" their loyalty on the battlefield. Hosokowa's *JACL: In Quest of Justice, History of the Japanese American Citizens League* (New York: William Morrow, 1982) provides an insider's account of the JACL's history. JACL leader Mike Masaoka's memoir, *They Call Me Moses Masaoka: An American Saga* (New York: William Morrow, 1987), also defends JACL cooperation during the war and praises JACL achievements in the postwar period. Yuji Ichioka, "A Study in Dualism: James Yoshinori Sakamoto and the Japanese American Courier, 1928–1942," *Amerasia Journal* 13, no. 2 (1986–1987): 49–81, analyzes the attitudes of an important JACL leader. Bob Kumamoto, "The Search for Spies: American Counterintelligence and the Japanese American Community, 1931–42," *Amerasia Journal* 6, no. 2 (1979): 45–75, reveals evidence of JACL informing on immigrant leaders in the decade before Pearl Harbor. Paul Spickard, "The Nisei Assume Power: The Japanese Citizens League, 1941–1942," *Pacific Historical Review* 52, no. 2 (May 1983): 147–74, notes JACL attempts to replace Issei leaders, promote military service and assimilation, and suppress camp protest during the war. Kevin Allen Leonard shows how the JACL used patriotic images to undermine anti-Japanese legislation after the war in "'Is That What We Fought For?' Japanese Americans and Racism in California: The Impact of World War II," *Western Historical Quarterly* 21, no. 4 (November 1990): 463–82. Accounts of Japanese Americans who served in the armed forces include Joseph D. Harrington, *Yankee Samurai: The Secret Role of Nisei in America's Pacific Victory* (Detroit: Pettigrew Enterprises, 1979); Masayo Duus, *Unlikely Liberators: The Men of the 100th and the 442nd* (Honolulu: University of Hawaii Press, 1987); Thelma Chang, *"I Can Never Forget": Men of the 100th/442nd* (Honolulu: Sigi Productions, 1991); Lyn Crost, *Honor by Fire: Japanese Americans at War in Europe and the Pacific* (Novato, Calif.: Presidio Press, 1994); Chester Tanaka, *Go for Broke: A Pictorial History of the Japanese American 100th Infantry and the 442nd Regimental Combat Team* (Richmond, Calif.: Go for Broke, 1981); Tad Ichinokuchi, ed., *John Aiso and the M.I.S.: Japanese-American Soldiers in the Military Intelligence Service, World War II* (Los Angeles: Military Intelligence Service Club of Southern California, 1988); and Tamotsu Shibutani, *The Derelicts of Company K: A Sociological Study of Demoralization* (Berkeley and Los Angeles: University of California Press, 1978).

In the 1970s, researchers reexamined the history of resistance in the camps. Gary Y. Okihiro's study of Tule Lake under martial law is included in this collection. Other articles by Okihiro include "Japanese Resistance in America's Concentration Camps: A Re-evaluation," *Amerasia Journal* 2, no. 1 (1973): 20–34; and "Religion and Resistance in America's Concentration Camps," *Phylon* 45, no. 3 (September 1984): 220–33. The other seminal work on resistance is Arthur A. Hansen and David A. Hacker, "The Manzanar Riot: An Ethnic Perspective," *Amerasia Journal* 2, no. 2 (Fall 1974): 112–57. Hansen also provides an insightful analysis in "Cultural Politics in the Gila River Relocation Center, 1942–1943," *Arizona and the West* 27 (Winter 1985): 327–62. A firsthand account of Manzanar by the man whose arrest sparked the riot can be found in Sue Kunitomi Embrey, Arthur A. Hansen, and Betty Mitson, eds., *Manzanar Martyr: An Interview with Harry A. Ueno* (Fullerton: Japanese American Project of the Oral History Program, California State University at Fullerton, 1986). For a contrasting view, see Karl G. Yoneda, *Ganbatte! The Sixty-Year Struggle of a Kibei Worker* (Los Angeles: Asian American Studies Center, University of California at Los Angeles, 1983). Draft resistance at Heart Mountain is discussed in great detail in Douglas W. Nelson, *Heart Mountain: The History of an American Concentration Camp* (Madison: State Historical Society of Wisconsin, 1976). Firsthand recollections are provided by draft resister Frank Emi, "Draft Resistance at the Heart Mountain Concentration Camp and the Fair Play Committee," in *Frontiers of Asian American Studies: Writing, Research, and Commentary*, ed. Gail M. Nomura et al.

(Pullman: Washington State University Press, 1989); and James Omura, a journalist who supported draft resistance, "Japanese American Journalism during World War II," in *Frontiers of Asian American Studies: Writing, Research, and Commentary,* ed. Gail M. Nomura et al. (Pullman: Washington State University Press, 1989). Arthur A. Hansen interviewed Omura for "James Matsumoto Omura: An Interview," *Amerasia Journal* 13, no. 2 (1986–1987): 99–113. The experiences of the renunciants are reexamined in Donald E. Collins, *Native American Aliens: Disloyalty and the Renunciation of Citizenship by Japanese Americans during World War II* (Westport, Conn.: Greenwood Press, 1985).

Valerie J. Matsumoto, *Farming the Home Place: A Japanese American Community in California, 1919–1982* (Ithaca, N.Y.: Cornell University Press, 1993), excerpted here, examines the impact of internment on families and gender roles. Other works that look at the experiences of women include Valerie Matsumoto, "Japanese American Women during World War II," *Frontiers* 8, no. 1 (1984): 6–14; Mei Nakano, *Japanese American Women: Three Generations, 1890–1990* (Berkeley, Calif.: Mina Publishing Press, and San Francisco: National Japanese American Historical Society, 1990); Dana Takagi, "Personality and History: Hostile Nisei Women," in *Reflections on Shattered Windows: Promises and Prospects for Asian American Studies,* ed. Gary Y. Okihiro et al. (Pullman: Washington State University Press, 1988); Evelyn Nakano Glenn, *Issei, Nisei, War Bride: Three Generations of Japanese American Women in Domestic Service* (Philadelphia: Temple University Press, 1986); and Sylvia Junko Yanagisako, *Transforming the Past: Tradition and Kinship among Japanese Americans* (Stanford, Calif.: Stanford University Press, 1985). For more information on family life, consult John Modell, "The Japanese American Family," *Pacific Historical Review* 37 (1968): 78–79; and Leonard Bloom and John I. Kitsuse, *The Managed Casualty: The Japanese-American Family in World War II,* Culture and Society, vol. 6 (Berkeley: University of California Press, 1956). The best study of educational policies within the camps is Thomas James, *Exile Within: The Schooling of Japanese Americans, 1942–1945* (Cambridge: Harvard University Press, 1987). Information on the experiences of college students can be found in Gary Y. Okihiro, *Storied Lives: Japanese American Students and World War II* (Seattle: University of Washington Press, 1999).

Although there are many studies of the WRA camps, literature on the Department of Justice camps is sparse. Michi Weglyn, *Years of Infamy,* excerpted here, provides an early exposé of the plight of Japanese Latin Americans. For more information on the internment of Peruvians, see C. Harvey Gardiner, *Pawns in a Triangle of Hate: The Peruvian Japanese and the United States* (Seattle: University of Washington Press, 1981). The experiences of Japanese, Italian, and German "alien" internees are discussed in John Christgau, *"Enemies": World War II Alien Internment* (Ames: Iowa State University Press,

1985). More information on Italian American internees can be found in Stephen Fox, *The Unknown Internment: An Oral History of the Relocation of Italian Americans during World War II* (Boston: G. K. Hall, 1990). The voices of Hawaiian internees are prominent in Gary Y. Okihiro, *Cane Fires: The Anti-Japanese Movement in Hawaii, 1865–1945* (Philadelphia: Temple University Press, 1991).

Researchers have only started to explore the history of Japanese Americans in Japan during the war. Most of these works focus on the life of Iva Toguri, who was convicted of treason as "Tokyo Rose" during the war and then pardoned in the 1970s. See Masayo Umezawa Duus, *Tokyo Rose: Orphan of the Pacific* (New York: Kodansha International, 1979); Stanley I. Kutler, "Forging a Legend: The Treason of 'Tokyo Rose,'" *Wisconsin Law Review* 6 (1980): 1341–82; David A. Ward, "The Unending War of Iva Ikuko Toguri D'Aquino: The Trial and Conviction of 'Tokyo Rose,'" *Amerasia Journal* 1, no. 2 (1971): 26–35; Raymond Okamura, "Iva Ikuko Toguri: Victim of an American Fantasy," in *Counterpoint: Perspectives on Asian America,* ed. Emma Gee (Los Angeles: Asian American Studies Center, University of California at Los Angeles, 1976); and Clifford I. Uyeda, "The Pardoning of 'Tokyo Rose': A Report on the Restoration of American Citizenship to Iva Ikuko Toguri," *Amerasia Journal* 5, no. 2 (1978): 69–72. John Stephan, *Hawaii under the Rising Sun: Japan's Plans for Conquest after Pearl Harbor* (Honolulu: University of Hawaii Press, 1984), profiles several Issei who spent World War II in Japan. Firsthand accounts by Nisei who lived in Japan during the war can be found in Mary Tomita, *Dear Miye: Letters Home from Japan, 1939–1946,* ed. Robert G. Lee (Stanford, Calif.: Stanford University Press, 1995); and Jim Yoshida and Bill Hosokowa, *The Two Worlds of Jim Yoshida* (New York: William Morrow, 1972). The life of a Nisei who died while serving against his will in the Japanese army is described in Floyd C. Watkins, "Even His Name Will Die: The Last Days of Paul Nobuo Tatsuguchi," *Journal of Ethnic Studies* 3, no. 4 (Winter 1976): 37–48. Yuji Ichioka examines a Nisei who willingly served in the Japanese army in "The Meaning of Loyalty: The Case of Kazumaro Buddy Uno," *Amerasia Journal* 23, no. 3 (Winter 1997–1998): 45–71. Brian Masaru Hayashi, *"For the Sake of Our Japanese Brethren": Assimilation, Nationalism, and Protestantism among the Japanese of Los Angeles, 1895–1942* (Stanford, Calif.: Stanford University Press, 1995), discusses two Japanese American Protestants who served in the Japanese military during World War II and documents Issei nationalist support for Japan during the war.

Dorothy Thomas, *The Salvage: Japanese American Evacuation and Resettlement during World War II* (Berkeley: University of California Press, 1952), still provides a useful starting point for the study of internees' views of leaving the camps and resettling in the Midwest. The study's bias against individuals affiliated with ethnic groups can be corrected by examining Stephen S.

Fujita and David J. O'Brien, *Japanese American Ethnicity: The Persistence of Community* (Seattle: University of Washington Press, 1991). Other useful studies of resettlement include Leonard Bloom and Ruth Riemer, *Removal and Return: The Socio-Economic Effects of the War on Japanese Americans,* Culture and Society, vol. 4 (Berkeley: University of California Press, 1949); Mitziko Sawada, "After the Camps: Seabrook Farms, New Jersey, and the Resettlement of Japanese Americans, 1944–47," *Amerasia Journal* 13, no. 2 (1986–1987): 117–36; and two articles by Sandra C. Taylor, "Japanese Americans and Keetley Farms: Utah's Relocation Colony," *Utah Historical Quarterly* 54, no. 4 (Fall 1986): 328–44, and "Leaving the Concentration Camps: Japanese American Resettlement in Utah and the Intermountain West," *Pacific Historical Review* 60, no. 2 (May 1991): 169–94. Memories of the resettlement experience are recounted in Brian Niiya et al., eds., *Nanka Nikkei Voices: Resettlement Years, 1945–1955* (Los Angeles: Japanese American Historical Society of Southern California, 1999); Tetsuden Kashima addresses internees' suppression of memories of the war in "Japanese American Internees Return, 1945 to 1955: Readjustment and Social Amnesia," *Phylon* 41, no. 2 (Summer 1980): 107–15. Donna K. Nagata explores internees' unconscious transmission of trauma to their children in *Legacy of Injustice: Exploring the Cross-Generational Impact of the Japanese American Internment* (New York and London: Plenum Press, 1993). Don Nakanishi analyzes the resurrection of these suppressed memories of internment in "Seeking Convergence in Race Relations Research: Japanese-Americans and the Resurrection of Internment," in *Eliminating Racism,* ed. Phyllis A. Katz and Dalmas A. Taylor (New York and London: Plenum Press, 1988), and "Surviving Democracy's Mistake: Japanese Americans and the Enduring of Executive Order 9066," *Amerasia Journal* 19, no. 1 (1993): 37–60. Arthur A. Hansen notes the impact of redress on attitudes about oral history in "Oral History and the Japanese American Evacuation," *Journal of American History* 82, no. 2 (September 1995): 625–39.

A growing number of works examine the history of the redress movement. Edited transcripts of Japanese American testimony during the 1981 Commission on Wartime Relocation and Internment of Civilians hearings are included in "Testimonies to the Commission on Wartime Relocation and Internment of Civilians," *Amerasia Journal* 8, no. 2 (Fall/Winter 1981): 55–105. The commission's historical report, which concludes that the decision to intern Japanese Americans was the result of "race prejudice, war hysteria, and a failure of political leadership," was published as *Personal Justice Denied: Report of the Commission on Wartime Relocation and Internment of Civilians* (Washington, D.C.: Government Printing Office, 1982). William Minoru Hohri, *Repairing America: An Account of the Movement for Japanese-American Redress* (Pullman: Washington State University Press, 1984), recounts the struggle of the National Council for Japanese American Redress to sue the government. Yasuko Takezawa, *Breaking the Silence: Redress and Japanese American Ethnicity* (Ithaca, N.Y.: Cornell University Press, 1995), documents the history of the redress movement in Seattle. Leslie Hatamiya, *Righting a Wrong: Japanese Americans and the Passage of the Civil Liberties Act of 1988* (Stanford, Calif.: Stanford University Press, 1993), examines the battle for legislative redress. Lillian Baker, a former hat pin collector and columnist, denounces the revisionist scholarship and the movement for redress in *Concentration Camp Conspiracy: A Second Pearl Harbor* (Lawndale, Calif.: Americans for Historical Accuracy Publications, 1981).

Early firsthand accounts by internees include the drawings and captions in Mine Okubo, *Citizen 13660* (New York: Columbia University Press, 1946), and Monica Sone, *Nisei Daughter* (Seattle: University of Washington Press, 1953). The list of firsthand accounts mushroomed during the 1970s to include Yoshiko Uchida, *Journey to Topaz: A Story of the Japanese American Evacuation* (New York: Charles Scribner's Sons, 1971); Jeanne Wakatsuki Houston and James D. Houston, *Farewell to Manzanar: A True Story of Japanese-American Experience during and after World War II Internment* (Boston: Houghton Mifflin, 1973); Jack Matsuoka, *Camp II, Block 211: Daily Life in an Internment Camp* (San Francisco: Japan Publications, 1974); Takeo Kaneshiro, comp., *Internees: War Relocation Center Memoirs and Diaries* (New York: Vantage Press, 1976); James Oda, *Heroic Struggles of Japanese Americans: Partisan Fighters from America's Concentration Camps* (KNI, 1981); Kiyo Hirano, *Enemy Alien*, trans. George Hirano and Yuri Kageyama (San Francisco: Japantown Art and Media Workshop, 1984); Robert S. Yasui, *Yasui Family of Hood River, Oregon*, ed. Holly Yasui (N.p.: Holly Yasui, 1987); Mary Tsukamoto and Elizabeth Pinkerton, *We the People: A Story of Internment in America* (Elk Grove, Calif.: Laguna Publishers, 1988); Reverend Yoshiaki Fukuda, *My Six Years of Internment: An Issei's Struggle for Justice* (San Francisco: Konko Church, 1990; translation of *Yokuryu Seikatsu Rokunen*, Okayama, Japan: Tamashima Kappansho, 1957); and Yamato Ichihashi, *Morning Glory, Evening Shadow: Yamato Ichihashi and His Internment Writings, 1942–1945*, ed. Gordon H. Chang (Stanford, Calif.: Stanford University Press, 1997).

More researchers began collecting oral histories in the 1970s. Arthur A. Hansen and Betty E. Mitson, eds., *Voices Long Silent: An Oral Inquiry into the Japanese-American Evacuation* (Fullerton: Japanese American Project of the Oral History Program, California State University at Fullerton, 1974), is a pioneering collection of interviews. Arthur A. Hansen also edited a five-part, six-volume collection of oral histories of internees, administrators, analysts, resisters, guards, and townspeople titled *Japanese American World War II Evacuation Oral History Project* (Westport, Conn.: Meckler, 1991; Munich: K. G. Saur, 1993–1995). Oral histories of Japanese American immigrants can be found in Kazuo Ito, *Issei: A History of Japanese Immigrants in North America,* trans. Shinichiro Nakamura and Jean S. Gerard (Seattle: Executive Committee for the Publication of Issei, 1973); and Eileen Sunada Sarasohn, ed., *The Issei: Portrait of a Pioneer* (Palo Alto, Calif.: Pacific Books, 1983). John Tateishi, *And Justice for All: An Oral History of the Japanese American Detention Camps* (New York: Random House, 1984), contains diverse views and experiences of internment. Anthropologist Akemi Kikumura explores the experiences of her mother and father in *Through Harsh Winters: The Life of a Japanese Immigrant Woman* (Novato, Calif.: Chandler & Sharp Publishers, 1981) and *Promises Kept: The Life of an Issei Man* (Novato, Calif.: Chandler & Sharp Publishers, 1991). Finally, for photographs of camp life, see Ansel E. Adams, *Born Free and Equal: Photographs of the Loyal Japanese-Americans at Manzanar Relocation Center* (New York: U.S. Camera, 1944); and Ansel E. Adams and Toyo Miyatake, *Two Views of Manzanar: An Exhibition of Photographs* (Los Angeles: Frederick S. Wright Art Gallery, University of California at Los Angeles, 1978). For photographs and an essay on the remains of the ten WRA camps, see *Whispered Silences: Japanese Americans and World War II,* photographs by Joan Myers, essay by Gary Y. Okihiro (Seattle: University of Washington Press, 1996).

Acknowledgments, continued from p. ii.

Truman's eighth Presidential Distinguished Unit Citation to the 100/442nd. Photograph from the archives of the National Japanese American Historical Society, 1684 Post Street, San Francisco, CA 94115, used with permission.

ROGER DANIELS, "The Decision for Mass Evacuation," from *Concentration Camps USA: Japanese Americans and World War II* by Roger Daniels (New York: Holt, Rinehart & Winston, 1971), 42–73. Reprinted by permission of Roger Daniels.

PETER IRONS, "*Gordon Hirabayashi v. United States:* 'A Jap's a Jap,'" from *The Courage of Their Convictions* by Peter Irons (New York: The Free Press, 1988), 39–49. Reprinted by permission of The Free Press, a Division of Simon and Schuster, Inc.

VALERIE J. MATSUMOTO, "Amache," from *Farming the Home Place: A Japanese American Community in California, 1919–1982.* Copyright © 1993 by Cornell University. Used by permission of Cornell University Press.

GARY Y. OKIHIRO, "Tule Lake under Martial Law: A Study in Japanese Resistance," from *Journal of Ethnic Studies* 5, no. 3 (Fall 1977): 71–85. Reprinted by permission of the author.

MICHI WEGLYN, "Hostages," from *Years of Infamy: The Untold Story of America's Concentration Camps* by Michi Weglyn (New York: Morrow Quill Paperbacks, a Division of William Morrow and Company, Inc., 1976), 54–66 and 285–89. Reprinted by permission of California State Polytechnic University, Pomona.